MORTAL THINGS

A NOVEL

Publisher's Cataloging-In-Publication Data
Bachus, Ned
    Mortal Things

ISBN: 978-1-7349563-7-5

Printed in the United States of America

First Edition

Editor/Publisher: Joy E. Stocke
Developmental Editor/Copyeditor: Raquel B. Pidal
Design and Composition: Tim Ogline / Ogline Design

Published by Tree of Life Books
PO Box 81
557 Rosemont-Ringoes Rd
Sergeantsville, New Jersey 08557

www.treeoflifetreeofjoy.com

MORTAL THINGS

A NOVEL

NED BACHUS

Tree
of Life
Books

To Stephan and Anna

Sunt lacrimae rerum et mentem mortalia tangunt.

Mortal things touch the mind and there are tears
for such things.

–Virgil, *The Aeneid*, 1.462
Translation by Gregory Eirich

*When my griefs sing to me
from the bright throats of thrushes
I sing back.*

–Linda Pastan,
"Old Woman," *The Five Stages of Grief*

PROLOGUE

The apartment looked like nothing happened. A hard run along the Wissahickon might offer the best possibility of doing something with the seething mixture of fear, disgust, and anger that had gripped her since she double-locked the door, but Sarah Goins would not leave the apartment to run or to do anything. Tomorrow would be soon enough. The son of a bitch was not coming back.

With a fresh damp cloth, she wiped off the living room baseboard then stretched her sore back and neck. She dusted the two library biographies about Mary Cassatt and the book of baby names, then returned them to the shiny coffee table. Using the corner of an old pajama top, she gave the TV screen a soft wipe, amazed, as always, at how quickly dust gathered. If he hadn't turned and bolted, she would have killed him, somehow. She was sure she would have found the strength. Like one of those mothers lifting a car to save a pinned child.

Here, in the corner of the city she chose because it offered refuge from so much, she suddenly felt like a prisoner. The irony roiled her. In the sixties, *Time* or *Newsweek* had proclaimed her adopted neighborhood a model of racial integration. Neighbors of all faiths or no faith rolled out the same welcome mat to all. Lawyers and doctors lived on the same blocks with laborers. *Brigadoon*.

She was doing what she'd always warned her students against, painting with too broad a stroke. Nothing was that simple and clear cut.

"Brigafuckingdoon," she muttered, her first words since the attack. *This is not Disney World. I'm in Philly.*

Mount Airy was part of Philadelphia, but furtive, edgy, hurt-you Philly was part of Mount Airy too. Despite the recycling drives, peace marches, and natural birth classes, it sprouted right here in her crunchy zip code.

Three hours after being attacked in her own apartment, she was spinning out lines of analysis. How had he gotten inside the building? Post-traumatic multitasking? Perhaps pregnancy hormones at last were announcing their arrival like bugle-blowing cavalry troops.

Blocks away in the shops along Germantown Avenue, barbers and hairdressers and their customers were consorting about the usual matters. Professors and students at the Lutheran seminary were scheming ways to reach the unreachable. Just across the avenue's Belgian blocks and trolley tracks, Wawa patrons were buying copies of the *Daily News* in search of answers and cups of coffee for consolation. Bartenders and afternoon drinkers down the avenue had settled nothing but now were identifying fundamental questions.

I do not think too much or think on too many channels, no matter what Mike or some of my students think.

Vacuum, Sarah.

Standing in the middle of her living room, in the middle of her neighborhood, in the middle of her pregnancy, *in medias mess*, Sarah Goins surveyed her work. The room was ready for the Hoover. She checked the time. If the neighbors hadn't responded to the ruckus three hours ago, a little vacuuming shouldn't bother them.

A sudden pain bent her over, stopping her short of the closet door. Crying out, she held her middle. When the spasm passed, she realized that it had lasted less than a minute, as had yesterday morning's crippling surprise, that one so brief that she'd let herself believe she'd imagined it.

She recalled a colleague who'd experienced nightmarish cramping throughout her pregnancy. *These first two cramps have passed quickly.*

Sarah walked past the closet where she kept the vacuum cleaner, pausing at the coffee table to pick up a notepad and pen. She touched her belly, pleased that she finally felt something down there, not just a bit more girth but a presence.

Tuesday Morning, she wrote, then underlined the two words. *Doctor*, she added. *Vac bedroom. Finish living room.* Looking up from her list, she stared vacantly at the wall. A truck's rumbling down the street pulled her back to her task. *Bathroom*, she wrote. A couple of bills had to be paid. The two library books must be nearly due. She would prioritize the list later. Something else? She couldn't make out the scrawled reminder on the calendar by the window. The picture for May was her favorite so far, a spring morning in Tuscany, an ancient villa's peach stucco exterior glimmering in perfect early sunlight. She remembered penciling in the time for her ultrasound.

Standing up, a sudden gripping cramp bent her over. She dropped the pen onto the table and shuffled to the bedroom, collapsing on top of the bed cover. Pain rippled through her, ebbed then overwhelmed her again. She curled up on her side and worked the pillow until it cradled her head the way she wanted. When the cramps finally passed, she rolled over, glancing at the clock. *Five minutes?* She was conscious of breathing fast, panting as if she were in the middle of a run. Three hours ago, she'd screamed and fought back. *Can I do anything, feel anything but fear?* She willed herself up from the bed and stumbled to the bathroom, feeling another cramp as she switched on the bathroom light.

Shuddering, she reached the toilet and pulled down her sweatpants and underwear. As she landed on the seat, she saw the bright patch of red on the pad.

1

FRIDAY, JANUARY 20, 1989

Mike Flannagan was pushing it, tires screeching, as he cut corners on the river drive. *Drive it like you stole it.* One of Sarah's community college students had taught her the expression and she'd shared it with him over pizza from Golden Crust one night, but he wasn't about to say that or anything else. He hadn't been that late, but he swore he could hear a sizzle steaming from the top of her head. He should have been able to settle on a brand of saké in fewer than fifteen minutes. Then identifying bok choy in its uncooked state at the food co-op had set him back another five minutes. Even so, ten minutes of silence in the car was unlike Sarah. Maybe she'd had to deal with a horrible student today. By the time they were halfway to Center City, he'd acknowledged that after seeing her for nearly two years, it was right that he finally meet some of her work friends from the college.

"Finally!" she echoed him.

No, he assured her, he hadn't said it to further antagonize her. She'd used the word every time she'd spoken about this outing. He'd never suggested they do something with her friends. No, he had nothing against her coworkers—*colleagues*—that he'd never met.

"You don't need a passport to go to a dinner party in Center City," she sighed.

"I know." Gripping the steering wheel even harder, he thought back to the odd feeling he'd had scanning the aisles of the state liquor store and the co-op, reluctant to ask for help, not sure if he even had the words to ask the right question—exactly what he imagined he'd feel if he were in a foreign country. And now the good people of Sarah's work life were waiting to meet him.

No doubt they would be welcoming, as if he were a visiting foreigner. He would listen to them intently and smile when the situation called for it, give them a fair chance.

The apartment building was just off the art museum circle.

Mike pulled his Reliant into a parking space in front of the high-rise building and turned off the ignition.

"Come on," she snapped, flinging the passenger side door open.

Mike grabbed the bags on the back seat and hustled toward the building. He'd found a clean L.L. Bean plaid shirt that went with his dark green corduroys, so he'd look respectable enough. He'd intended to brush off his Dexters, a step up from the work boots he'd left by his bed, but the afternoon had gotten out of control, compressing his prep time. At the curb, he paused to give them a quick wipe with his hand. Sarah, her leather boots clean and bright, opened the glass door and strode into the vestibule.

"I won't embarrass you," Mike said, catching up at the elevator. She glowered at him then poked the already lit button for the fourteenth floor. He immediately regretted his comment. *Stupid.* As much as he'd dreaded this encounter, the last thing she should think was that he wanted to derail this little coming-out party. Riding the elevator, he watched her inspect the bouquet of flowers he was holding then study the closed elevator doors. *The Goldmans,* he remembered, suddenly feeling a layer of stress peel off. *Sharon? Yes.* The flowers he clutched gave off no real scent. He wished they did. A cheerful array of colors for the winter, the florist had assured him. He watched Sarah take in every detail and could tell from her softened expression that she liked them. Even in a winter coat, she was the picture of a fit and attractive young woman. Her curly black hair framed her small oval face to just below her ears, making her look cute but not pixie-like. Somehow, her spending little time fussing and fretting over her physical appearance made her shine even more.

"Look," he said. When her eyes locked onto his, he went on. "I'm saying this because it's true. You look wonderful. Really. And you're the kind of person that deserves a better evening than you've had so far."

She stepped closer, their bags of food and saké bumping, and leaned her forehead against his chest. "Did you say that because you remembered it from the movie?" she said, still tucked against him.

"No," he replied, ransacking his memory.

When they reached their floor, she glided onto the thickly carpeted hallway, the swish of her skirt and muted laughter from behind the door to his left the only sounds.

From an opened door at the end of the corridor, a woman in jeans and a designer top appeared. She and Sarah hugged. "Mike, I'm Sharon," the woman lilted. She pecked him on the cheek. She was in her early fifties, with a touch of gray in her blonde hair and fullness to her torso, but she seemed like someone who liked the way she looked. While she took their coats and hung them in the wall closet, Mike eyed the ornate stenciling at the tops of the walls and the African mask across from them. *Don't break anything, Flannagan.*

Sarah apologized for being late. "Nonsense," Sharon said. "Leona and Tom just arrived."

"Here," Mike said, extending the bouquet. He felt just a bit like he was playacting. *Did money and the lives they'd lived make this all seem natural to them?*

"Lovely," Sharon gushed. She took the flowers. "These will dress up the table nicely. And I see you've got *bags*," she said, her eyes twinkling.

Where had he seen that smile before? Then he remembered. On a Christmas special he had watched for five minutes, one of Santa's helpers had flashed the same smile just before Mike hit the remote.

"Bok choy," she cooed, peeking into one of the bags. "If Sarah hasn't told you, our monthly adventures are work parties as much as they are dinner outings. Follow me."

The hallway walls were covered with original artwork that Mike was sure had to be Sharon's. "You and I," she said to Mike in a confidential tone, "are all that's keeping this from being a faculty convention."

"Oh," he said. *We?*

"I'm an attorney," she said, winking, "and I've heard *all* the jokes."

"And they're all true," said a mustached man with gold wire-rimmed glasses who appeared at the entrance to the kitchen, wearing a blue apron that had something in French written on it. After wiping his hand on the apron, he extended it to Mike. "I'm Larry Goldman. A pleasure."

Mike shook his hand. Larry and Sarah hugged.

"I teach with Sarah," Larry said. "I am *not* an attorney."

Mike wondered whatever happened to lawyers.

"Suit up, brother," Larry said, nodding toward a Sabatier knife and a clean white apron on the counter. "We're on a Pacific Rim run. Last time, we did Thai." The professor leaned in conspiratorially. "Coconut milk versus soy sauce," he whispered, "beyond that, I can't tell the difference." He winked at Mike, as if they were old cronies. *Another winker.* No wonder they'd found each other.

Mike gave him the bag with the two bottles of saké, suddenly realizing that though he'd gotten the right corner of the world, he'd missed the mark.

"Great," Larry said, lingering over the label of one of the bottles. "I'll set these aside."

Sarah, already decked out in an apron that advertised a cookbook from the *New York Times*, smiled at him. She was practicing what she preached, living in the moment. Across the kitchen island from another couple, she washed the bok choy while he sliced florets from broccoli stalks. More introductions. Leona Henderson-Hennessey and Tom Hennessey. "You're the Mike," Leona said, smiling.

Mike gave her a cheerful salute with the knife then returned to his trimming. *Were they watching him? Was that why he was working at such a plodding pace, as if he'd never handled a kitchen knife before?*

"My main job is to keep everybody's glass filled," Larry said to Mike and Sarah. "What can I get for you?"

"White wine would be great," Sarah said. Leona was drinking what looked like soda and Tom had a whiskey.

"Mike, we've got Grolsch and a few of those micros if you'd like a beer."

"I'll take the first cold beer you come to," Mike said, his voice cracking. Had his voice cracked even once since he was a teenager? "Thanks." Glancing across the table, he saw that the others' chunks of vegetables were about the same size as the ones he'd cut.

"Perfect," Sarah said, looking at his work.

"It's a central coast Chard, Sarah," Larry said, handing her a glass. "Hope you like it." He gave Mike an opened bottle of Stoudt's Golden Lager. It was soon obvious that these people had all heard about him, the nice former student of Sarah's office partner whom Sarah had finally worked up the nerve to ask out. Sarah loved to bring up the story.

"How did you grade us?" Larry said.

"About the same as Ms. Devereaux graded me," he said.

They all laughed. "Very coy," Leona purred. "I'm guessing that means you did pretty well in Florence's 101?"

"Don't worry," he said, "I'm not about to run any of you out of a job."

They asked him more questions about his experience at the college and seemed genuinely interested, but when the conversation turned to cats, he felt his chest tightening. Leona and Tom didn't have children; they had cats. Were all college professors cat people? He failed the cat test. He didn't hate cats, but they were so different from dogs. "Wiscasset has some sort of flu," Leona said. "The vet doesn't seem to know what to do." She shook her head.

"The poor guy *knows* what's in store for him when our car pulls up to the vet's office," Tom said. "He just knows."

"I make Tom take him," Leona said. Looking up from the odd-looking mushrooms on her cutting board, she brushed the hair from her eyes. "I'm not proud to admit that, but it's true."

"I don't particularly enjoy it," Tom said with a pained expression. He was going on about a trip to the vet, but he might have been talking about watching the nurses do heel sticks on his premature newborn in the NICU. What good would it do to tell this guy to get a grip? He was as likely to tell him about losing Laurie and little Michael. Mike took a pull on the beer. He might not need a passport to enter a Center City high-rise apartment, but was there a guidebook? But now that the conversation had turned his thoughts to the two people he loved more than anything in the world, he wasn't sure he cared.

Standing at the stove below two large woks hanging from an iron rack, Larry lined up bowls of chicken pieces, shrimp, and scallops next to him. Mike watched him place metal rings on the two front burners, set the two woks on them, then turn on the gas under each unit. *Did those rings have a name? Do you buy them in Chinatown?* He held his tongue. The worst moment in his English class had been when Ms. Devereaux made him read aloud part of his essay. She'd wanted others to hear a good introduction. Now he took a deep breath and tried to focus on what people were saying, but instead he pictured himself rushing through the ER entrance in upstate New York, remembered knowing what the young doctor was about to tell him just from the look on his face.

The conversation took the inevitable leap to comparing cats and dogs. To weigh in with his opinion on this issue would pretty much end Sarah's long-anticipated night right there, so he felt profound relief when Larry tossed the chicken and minced garlic into an oiled wok and the loud sizzle pulled everyone's attention back to the business at hand.

Seated for dinner beside Sarah and across from the Hyphen-Hennesseys, Mike sipped alternately from his glass of water and his beer, nursing both beverages. When Sharon brought in a pair of steaming platters, even Mike joined in the oohing and aahing. Larry opened another bottle of some California wine, and Mike did not bother to remind anyone that there were two bottles of saké in the refrigerator.

"Knives and forks?" Sharon asked. He glanced to see if she was looking at him. No doubt she was too polite for that. He picked up his chopsticks with one movement of his right hand and clapped them three times like a maestro tapping his baton. He recalled Friday night takeouts up in New Paltz when he thought he would never get the hang of chopsticks, Laurie laughing at his fumbling, little Michael in the high chair, laughing because his parents were hysterical.

Sharon ladled the softest-looking rice he'd ever seen onto his plate and topped it with a bit of the seafood combination. He wanted to praise her for the rice, but it was hardly the star of the meal.

On the serving plate, the food looked like something he'd expect in a fine restaurant. Portions on the other plates had been laid out like pieces of artwork, with lots of border, not overflowing like the memorable dinners of his childhood, nearly all of which had been at the homes of his Italian friends. The table looked like a photograph from one of Sarah's food magazines or from the calendar of photos of Italy he'd given her for Christmas.

Lifting his glass, Tom offered a toast to the great people of China. After a round of self-congratulations, they quieted, occasionally commenting on the quality of the shrimp or scallops. Halfway through his plate, he noticed that he was far ahead of the others. Clicking his chopsticks together, he looked at Sarah.

"Great," he said to her.

"Isn't it?" she said.

He breathed out slowly. *Do I do everything at a different pace than the rest of them?* Fast or slow, he was out of step, on his way to failing another test: his plate would be empty in a few more bites. He put down his sticks and sipped again from his water. Sarah had never set out to test him, but his scarfing marked him as an outsider as surely as his ponderous knife work had done in the kitchen.

They'd all seen the PBS special on sharks last week and loved it. "Missed it," he said. Larry took the opportunity to refill everyone's wine glass and brought Mike another Stoudt's without asking him.

"Thanks," he said, picking up his sticks again.

"So, Tom," Sharon said, "speaking of sharks, what's it like running this division-wide committee for the vice president?"

Mike heard Tom's words, understood what he was talking about if not the exact points he was trying to make, but after five minutes he let the thread slip, the way he imagined he would tune out someone speaking a foreign language he'd studied but not mastered. Other voices joined in. Revivification. Anti-vivificationists. They all laughed again. Systems. Linguistics.

When the others finished eating, Leona asked Sarah about her background in linguistics. Yes, she told Leona, she did work for Billibow when she was in graduate school. She explained that she had done all sorts of gofer work for him while she was a grad student. Mike couldn't see Sarah being anybody's gofer.

"Strange bird, wasn't he?" Leona asked.

Sarah rolled her eyes. "A man at the end of a very different era. He had this system for teaching, and he expected absolutely everyone to follow it." They were all glued to her, sort of smiling, the way a comedian's audience looked when they were anticipating the next punch line. Mike grasped that somebody named Richards, whom they'd all heard about before, was this guy's rival, and that Sarah was caught in the middle of this college professor spat. She rolled through the story like it was a performance she'd rehearsed and waited all her life to do. He imagined this was the way she acted at work.

"Billibow decided that I should be the one to observe all the faculty and report back to him," Sarah said. "Me, fresh out of graduate school, checking on people who had been grading me the year before. Of course, I protested. 'Ms. Goins,' he said to me, 'you are low man on the totem pole.'"

Mike laughed with the others, though it seemed barely humorous.

"Richards suggested lunch at the Faculty Club," Sarah said. "We had drinks then ordered. More drinks. Finally, I screwed up my courage.

"'Dr. Billibow is a good friend of yours,' I said. 'But he's a little upset that you're not teaching the method.' I swallowed. 'But I know that you can,' I said. 'Because any idiot can,' he cut in."

Everyone laughed. Sarah glowed. She almost looked like another person.

"I looked him straight in the eye. 'Tell me a time, Dr. Richards, when you will teach the method,' I said, 'and I will take copious notes, otherwise the consequences to both of us will be a little dire.'"

She paused for effect. "'Have another drink, Ms. Goins.'"

"Oh God," Sharon howled. They were convulsed in laughter. Seeing Sarah so triumphant made Mike smile. Larry hiccupped, spritzing wine out of his mouth. Mike had known room-rocking laughter with Laurie and their Michael, and before that with work pals. It was what you did on a Friday night—cut loose with your own people. Right about now, the roofers and plumbers down at Gilhooley's were hooting it up. He pictured his brother Brendan pulling another six-pack out of the refrigerator, Delores taking the kids to Dalessandro's for cheesesteaks. These people were just blowing off a little steam their own way.

"When the deed was done," Sarah said. "I told Billibow, 'You wouldn't believe the transformation in Dr. Richards.'"

Laughter filled the room again. Sarah's eyes sparkled. Her beaming face flushed, like a kid who'd been out sledding all afternoon. Mike wondered how many other stories like that she had in her. He had seen her glowing before, full of herself, happy, but he had never seen her like this. He wished she could taste that more often. For Laurie, that natural joy was an almost daily experience, and he and little Michael always seemed to be involved. *No more.*

"The field attracts very strange types," Sarah said. She put her hand on Mike's, smiled at him, then looked across the table. "Poor Mike," she said, shaking her head. "We've convinced him that professors are a bunch of loonies."

"Nothing he's heard tonight," Larry said, "would make him think otherwise."

They laughed.

Mike smiled again, picked up his napkin, and wiped his mouth.

"You've all seen those special train displays around the holidays?" Sarah said, catching her breath. "Right?"

She was looking at him, a wry smile on her face.

"Train clubs," Tom said. "Enormous displays."

"That's Mike's basement," Sarah said.

Mike reddened. Kind-hearted Sarah would not let him feel left out. He wished he could think of a way to make her stop.

"Just a hobby," Mike stammered.

"Nonsense," Sharon said.

"The wiring alone," Sarah said. "Houses, roads. Sheets of plywood for the platform base with a layer of foamboard neatly screwed in on top. He's painted the walls around the layout to blend in. It's an inviting little world."

"There are books," Mike cut in. "And you just make your mistakes." It was sweet of her to do this, but enough was enough.

"I had American Flyers when I was a kid," Larry mused.

"Pity," Tom chirped. "Lionels were the real deal."

"The three rails make them look like toys."

"Toys?"

"Children!" Leona barked.

They all laughed.

"It's not just a Christmas thing for him," Sarah said. "He works on it all year 'round."

Is no one else pained by her campaign to make something of me to these people? Such a move was not in Laurie's repertoire. Never would have been. *Stop it.*

"Like those guys in the Mummers Parade," Larry said. "Everyday people. They work on their costumes, their drills and music, all year.

Tough to put so much into your hobby after laboring forty or fifty hours a week doing some kind of hard work. I respect that kind of devotion. I bet you're a real artist, Mike."

"Keeps me off the streets," Mike said. *Please.*

"You wouldn't believe your eyes," Sarah said.

There was talk about dessert in the den, sweet news to his weary ears. Sharon announced that her guests were to relax. She was going to take care of the mess before dessert. "It's my neurosis," she said.

Mike offered to help clear the dishes. He knew the last thing they expected from him was an offer to do what the boys in the neighborhood would call women's work. He stacked plates and carried them to the kitchen sink.

Sharon put the plates, platters, and silverware into the dishwasher, and Mike ended up standing over a soapy sink with everything else. After cleaning out the rice pot with a scouring pad, he turned his attention to the wok they used for the chicken dish.

"Whoa!" Tom cried. "You never clean out a wok like an old stewpot. It ruins the flavoring." He looked like he had just discovered his cat in the wok. "Hold back on the elbow grease, Mike."

Mike felt like he had just caught a glimpse of a cop car's flashing lights in his rearview mirror. He remembered hearing third grade's Sister Angelina Mary calling his full name and lifting him up by his cheeks, punctuating each syllable she screamed at him with a pull on the left cheek then the right. You didn't smack *her*, he told himself. Let it go.

"A gentle touch works well with these babies," Tom said.

"Got it," Mike said. Somehow, they all knew how to cook and clean like Chinese people. He let Tom take over at the sink and started drying. He heard Sarah's voice amidst the others in the dining room.

"I watch the commercials every year," Leona insisted. "I even watch the game, but I couldn't tell you the first thing about the 49ers or which team's got the best quarterback."

If he were sitting among them, they'd all turn to him now. Time to glean authentic salt of the earth wisdom from the visitor. He gently and slowly dried the woks, and Tom hung them on the rack above the stove. When Mike glanced at his watch, he realized that it only seemed later than it was. He dried his hands on a fresh towel, fished a tumbler out of the cupboard, and got himself a glass of ice water. Tom poured himself some scotch. They were the first people into the den.

"Sarah tells me you work as a groundskeeper at the Lutheran seminary in Mount Airy," Tom said.

"Almost five years now." After Mike set his drink on the coffee table, he slumped into the couch. Tom sat opposite him in the easy chair.

"And you'd been a carpenter."

"This works out better for me now."

"Do you see yourself in this position for a while, or is it a good stepping stone to another spot?"

Stepping stone? "It suits me."

Tom inspected his drink.

Mike stretched his legs under the coffee table. How much longer would the hiring interview continue? He'd stumble if he tried to explain to Sarah why he'd rather spend time with just about anybody but this guy. The poor man can't help it, Laurie would say. He missed her gentle steering every day, and being trapped in a room with Tom was needlessly reopening that wound.

Tom walked over to the window and looked out at Center City. "What a view," he sighed.

"Right," Mike said.

"I admire people who are willing to get their hands dirty," Tom said, still gazing out the window. "You must get hit with all of it—snow removal, floods, downed trees," he said, shaking his head. "Got to be ready for any kind of mess."

Mike stared at the back of Tom's head and breathed out slowly. He thought of the mess this guy would make if he jumped out the window from this high up then felt his late wife's disapproving eyes on him. *I didn't mean that I'd throw him out, Laurie.*

"Any kind of disaster," Tom said. "Right?"

"Right," Mike said. He looked at the reflection of the lights on the window behind Tom. That nighttime view of the city. Their house in upstate New York had looked out on the Christmas lights of the older couple across the road. The rest of the year, it was black night, nothingness, but he remembered letting his eyes adjust to the country black sky, finally making out the form of the old house. How could a man long for such a plain sight? Then his eyes flinched under sharp hospital lights. He pictured the forms of his wife and child each under a white sheet then Michael's stony, swollen little face when the doctor raised the sheet, so he could identify him. Not a trace of blood.

"Guess you can get used to anything," Tom said.

"You can try," Mike said, willing a different image before him. *The framed photograph of Michael laughing with Robert the puppy.* Mike forced himself to conjure up Robert's hindquarters in mid-wiggle, the open-mouthed delight on Michael's face, the little house in the background.

Tom turned back to Mike, sniffed his scotch, then took a slow drink. "Heard you did a bang-up job in Florence Devereaux's English 101 course."

Mike shrugged. Taking the course had been his boss's idea. When Delores, his sister-in-law, heard about it, she told him it was long due, that he wouldn't regret it. Then the secretaries at work prodded him until he registered. To the carpenter's surprise, the precision of academic writing felt familiar and welcoming, but not enough for him to take another course.

"Of course, you did that while holding down a full-time job. Still got an A." He walked to the couch and sat beside Mike.

That this stranger knew so much about him was creepy enough, but now he had perched beside him like an old aunt. *The man can't help it.*

"Some killer courses kept my GPA a tad humbler than I'd have liked." He laughed and slapped Mike's knee.

"Jesus," Mike muttered, pulling back in his seat. He strained to listen to the voices down the hall but heard nothing to suggest that relief was on the way.

"It happens," Tom said, finishing his drink, "to all of us."

"All of us," Mike repeated. *Stay.* For Sarah.

Tom sat back and stared across the room. "It's like," he said, "when I was doing my graduate work at Yale. Have you ever had to take a course in stat, Mike? Statistics?"

"No."

"Required course, Mike. For me, it was a regular bloodbath."

Mike heard Sarah's laugh in the kitchen. So near yet so far. Fontella Bass's oldie leaped into his consciousness: "Rescue Me."

"Now, I got into the program on the strength of my liberal arts coursework—not my math and science. Kingsley Wells, who at one point was up for secretary of health, education, and welfare, was the dean back then. He knew my background. I'd sworn up and down to him that I could handle statistics. We all had to take it."

Mike sipped the last of the water in his glass and swirled it around in his mouth. Listening beats talking, he assured himself.

"Three days into the term, Mike, I'm hopelessly lost. I knock on the man's door. Of course, Wells was expecting me."

Mike felt himself blink. He swallowed. *Of fucking course.*

"The long and short of it was that he bought my argument that a course like comparative religion would be at least as relevant to someone working with ESL folks—foreign students. So, through the grace of God, or at least Kingsley Wells, I was spared statistics."

"A bloodbath," Mike said.

"Well!" Tom said, slapping his knees with a flourish.

Mike startled.

"Refill," Tom declared, now standing. "You?"

Mike shook his head. "Had enough."

Tom stepped away with his not-quite-empty glass in hand. He paused at the entranceway, as if pondering something, then spun around. "Did you see the Sixers game the other night?"

"I heard they won for a change," Mike said.

"Unbelievable finish. If they played like that every night, they might have a chance this year."

Sarah and the others entered with coffee and dessert. "We're not interrupting anything, are we?" Sarah asked.

"We were just talking about the Sixers," Tom said. He made a sweeping bow before Sharon. "By your leave, madam. I'm off to find the Laphroaig." He stepped between Larry and Sharon and minced out of the room.

Sarah placed a dish of small pastries and a bowl of fruit on the coffee table then sat beside Mike. He sank back into the cushions and felt her nestling against his side. When she put her hand on top of his, he let it rest there. He breathed out for what felt like the first time in ten minutes. The differences between him and these people didn't matter. He didn't have to join their tribe. It was Sarah.

Laurie would have put her hand on his too. Closing his eyes, her presence felt more vivid than since the day of the crash. His heart rose, but the buoyant rush in his chest suddenly turned into weight that pinned him down. He could not budge it. *I am not bawling like a baby. How?* He opened his mouth, breathed out then in. He was at the Goldmans'. A woman's warm hand rested on his. It was Sarah.

Sharon brought in cups, napkins, and small plates. Standing at the window, Leona pronounced the view of the Philadelphia Museum of Art and the Benjamin Franklin Parkway practically breathtaking. Tittering something in French, she sat on a cushion on the floor. Tom returned with a half-filled glass, found a big cushion, and slumped beside his wife.

Larry pointed to his music collection. "Tom, you listen to jazz all the time. Something different tonight. You guys up for some world music?" Stacks of CDs and tapes cluttered the shelves above the stereo system. "Celtic?"

Sarah tapped Mike's hand. "Help us out here," she said.

"Clancy Brothers?" he ventured.

"Not since college," Larry said. He started reciting a list, mostly Gaelic-sounding. Mike had struck out on the Clancy Brothers, apparently not their kind of Irish music.

"I know we've got an old Planxty CD. How about that?" Sharon asked.

"Sure," Mike said. "Put him on."

"It's a group, Mike," Leona said.

"Actually," Larry said. "It's a term I've heard in titles. It's not a particular kind of dance tune, like a slip jig or a schottische. More like a self-reference to the kind of music they play."

"Oh," Mike said. "Sure."

Sarah squeezed Mike's hand.

Larry pulled a disc out of a case, inserted it in the player, and pressed play. "Speaking of dirges," he said, "did anyone catch any of the inauguration today?"

"Please," Leona groaned. "Not while we're eating."

They all laughed.

"Welcome to the Bush years," Sharon said, raising her coffee cup. "May they number four, at most."

"I don't know how much better we'd have been with Dukakis," Tom grumbled.

When Mike looked up from his dessert plate, he saw that they were all looking at him. "I didn't vote," he said. "Tell you the truth, I don't trust any of these guys."

"Fair enough," Larry said. "I swear … Dukakis would have won if he hadn't stumbled on that question about what he'd do if somebody raped and murdered his wife."

There was murmuring agreement. Mike nodded, not mentioning that he wouldn't have voted for anybody who was indecisive about what to do with his wife's rapist-murderer. He knew these people were smart, but still.

"A real shame," Leona said. "A more nuanced answer would have made a difference."

"That's true," Larry said. He looked like he was straining to think of such a perfect response.

"You mean," Mike said, "he should have at least *sounded* like he wanted to kill the guy who raped and murdered his wife?"

Sarah shot him a look.

"Would have played differently in certain quarters," Tom said.

The others nodded solemnly.

"You've got to be realistic," Tom went on. "There are a lot of knuckle-dragging Neanderthals out there, and they vote."

Mike snorted twice like an ape, as surprised by his action as the rest of them.

Sarah blanched, as if he'd suddenly farted and belched at the same time. He felt himself redden, but then Tom laughed and the others joined in.

Larry snorted. "Beautiful!" he exclaimed. "Brilliant." He snorted again, and they all laughed. Sarah forced a smile.

"Maybe we would have won the election," Sharon said, "if we insisted on the use of opposable thumbs as a requirement for voting."

They roared. Even Sarah joined in.

"If you can't do this," Leona said, tapping her thumbs against her index fingers, "get the hell out of the voting booth."

Larry laughed so loudly that Mike thought he might fall off his chair.

Mike said nothing as he drove through the late-night downtown traffic. He stopped for the light at the far side of the art museum circle. The gold-plated statue of Joan of Arc on her horse gleamed under the streetlights. She looked like she was ready to cross the road, climb up the embankment, and storm the museum. He thought of what Ms. Devereaux had said to his class. You couldn't count on reaching agreement with people, but you could expect them to be clear in what they said.

"Radio?" Sarah said, reaching for the on button.

Mike shook his head. She sat back. He glanced at her, wondering if the sparkle was still in her eyes, but it was too dark to tell. He could use *love* to describe his feelings for her, but only in his head, because they were so different from what he still felt for Laurie. Admiration and respect, for sure. Gratitude. He concentrated on the road ahead of them. For the moment, she was willing to be quiet, but soon she would want to talk about the food, the view from the apartment, her friends' recipes, and cats. He had listened, smiled, kept all inappropriate thoughts to himself, except for the snorting bit. Other than being late, he had not slighted her, as far as he could tell. He was proud of her, even when she embarrassed him. She wanted her friends to like him. It came from love. He got that.

When the light turned green, he rounded the art museum. They made it past Boathouse Row without a word. The car wound past the statue gardens along the riverbank. The last time he had walked through there, he had been struck by the state of disrepair. In the dark, he could imagine only scurrying rats, underage beer drinkers, muggers lurking in the bushes. The road snaked around the bend in the river. Just before the railroad bridge and the reviewing stand for regattas, he glimpsed the outline of one of the three music-playing little angels perched atop thin pillars on the riverbank. He remembered that they were the first or last of the statues east of the regatta course, depending on which direction you were coming from. Blinking, he shielded his eyes from an oncoming car's high beams. He passed the finish line, wound down past the Temple boathouse and the turnoff for Hunting Park Avenue.

Sarah reached over and rested her hand on his thigh. He felt her hand's warmth and knew how much she had hoped this evening would bring them closer together. She had been right: things did look different under other kinds of light. When she'd told her story at dinner, he'd seen her shine like never before. But now, in the car, heading back to their separate homes, he did not foresee anything from her involvement with him that could elicit that kind of response. She'd tried so hard to make him feel like he belonged, that he was loved. In that company, he saw her beauty, grace, and decency. He also saw how she stuck out from the others. *I admire and respect you.* He owed her honesty.

Sarah believed they had something. He might as well fault her for breathing. But he would be at fault if he led her on. Admiration and respect didn't add up to love.

When he turned onto Wissahickon, Sarah cleared her throat. "We never got to that saké you brought," she said. "I hope you don't feel bad about that."

"That's nothing." When the dinner party was breaking up, one of them joked about Russian dinners that turned into entire weekends, guests who wouldn't leave. For his money, Mike couldn't have imagined anything longer than their Chinese-themed soirée, but now this ride felt like it might never end.

"It's awkward when you don't know the people and they all know each other. But we never do anything with anyone else. I'm glad you got to meet some of my friends. And they got to meet you."

Seeing the green traffic light at Wayne, Mike sped up, hoping to make it through, but it turned. "Shit," he muttered, the car screeching to a stop.

"Listen," Sarah said. "Maybe we shouldn't have gone there tonight. Just stopped and talked."

Oh God.

"You know?" she said.

Mike cracked the window a bit and felt the cold air on his face. The car rattled over the trolley tracks and Belgian blocks of Germantown Avenue past the seminary and the beer distributor. Turning onto Sarah's street, he pulled into a space in front of her apartment building. He left the car running.

"You felt all right tonight, didn't you?" Sarah asked.

He steeled himself against laughing or cursing. "I failed the test," he said.

"It wasn't a test." She bristled.

"I don't mean that you were testing me," he said. "It's not you."

"They tested you?"

Maybe they'd tested *her*, but those words would not come out. He shook his head. "I admire you more than I ever have," he said, their eyes locked onto each other's.

"Yes?"

"I do," he said, the words hanging in the air as she sighed wearily and turned away. He was sure he'd said the worst thing possible. "You deserve a lot better."

"Meaning?"

"I'm not a prize, for one thing," he said. "You deserve people around you that appreciate you for all that you are."

Her head spun back again, fury on her face. "That's it? My friends don't appreciate me?"

He shook his head desperately. Did she think he meant no, they didn't appreciate her? Or no, he was stuck for the right word?

Her eyes were pleading for him to go on, her open palms extended as if impatiently waiting to be handed something. "It's okay," she said, "tell me."

He'd landed in a minefield, one where she seemed to have complete knowledge of where the explosives were planted, allowing her to dart about while he froze in place. Did she realize how much he didn't know, or that he didn't even want to know about most things? He got that she valued being part of that world, of those people's lives. He, too, liked it when she made him laugh and think. *Colleagues.* People only showed a slice of themselves at a party but still. Did she think she belonged with them? "We all like you, Sarah," he said. "We'd be idiots not to."

"And?"

"You deserve better than all of us."

"You keep grouping yourself with my friends," she said, chafing. "Painful enough that you apparently found them so wanting, but where exactly are you in all this?"

He felt the breath rush out of his burning chest. He turned from her to the steering wheel then gripped it, looking at the darkened old Chevy parked in front of them. "Just don't want to hurt you."

"By doing what?"

I wish I loved you. He let out a long slow breath. *The way you love me.* Dropping his hands from the steering wheel, he started patting his knees. *Give her clarity.*

"Flannagan, I can't compete with a dead wife and child. I'm sorry."

"Jesus!" he snapped. "Maybe we should back off a little bit."

"Mi-chael," she groaned. "Shit!"

"I don't want to make things worse."

"And that'll help?"

"I won't be disappointing you as much. I just mean like maybe one fewer get-together a week."

"Instead of two?" she said. She'd never sounded more sarcastic.

"Sometimes it's more."

"Sure, Mike. So, less is more? For growing the relationship?"

"Maybe just not this Tuesday, okay?"

"And obviously not tonight," she said, turning to reach for the door handle. She exited, slammed the car door shut, and tromped up the sidewalk to her apartment building steps.

2

FRIDAY, JANUARY 20

When the entrance door closed behind her, Mike drove off.

He rolled his window almost all the way down, jerked the car around, and headed for the avenue. A blast of icy wind slapped his face but he kept the window down. *Fuck me*. He'd earned the pain. After dodging icebergs all night, he'd just crashed into land. He'd also come up short in the courage department. Couples were supposed to be bonded to one another by mutual love, but theirs wasn't the same love. He felt disgusted with himself. Sarah didn't deserve to be hurt. She would be better off rid of him, but he hadn't done that. When push came to shove, he even backed down from declaring a break in the relationship. And now, he'd ruined her night.

He drove past the Wawa convenience store, braking for the red light at Mount Airy Avenue. The co-op on the corner where he had tracked down bok choy sat dark. Across the street, the state store where he had decided on two bottles of the most expensive brand of saké also was shuttered. Ahead, lights still blinked at the pizza place.

A figure in an overcoat, hat, and scarf clumped toward the intersection. As the person neared the corner, he saw that it was a woman holding a cat. Once he had known people on every block of this neighborhood. Sometime between his childhood here and his return from upstate New York, cat-holding midnight strollers had moved in, but he could not pinpoint when they and their antique shops had replaced the Lewis Brothers' hardware store, Neulander's bakery, and the Sunray drugstore of his youth. No matter—the two-block commercial stretch was a place he used more for dog walks than shopping now.

A gust of wind unwrapped the woman's scarf. Taking one hand off her precious cargo, she tossed the loose end of her scarf back around her neck and turned smartly onto Mount Airy Avenue. Maybe if he lived in the moment, as Sarah preached, he could follow through on what mattered.

Up Germantown, the only other lights still on were the neon beer signs in Gilhooley's window. He'd bought a six-pack there during the World Series. Walking Robert during Christmas week, he had run into Tommy Coyle out front. He used the dog as an excuse when his fourth-grade classmate had tried to talk him into a quick beer. As the light turned green, someone pulled out of a parking space in front of the bar. Fuck it. Mike steered the car into the spot.

Inside, he waded into the crowd of drinkers, mostly loud-talking guys. Some might be current versions of old classmates. Above the din, the jukebox blared a song he had heard the young secretaries play in the administration building.

A voice from across the smoky room called his name.

Tommy Coyle. Mike squeezed his way toward him. Above the bar, silent hockey players skated across the television screen on the sports recap.

"Where's the big German dog?" Tommy shouted, pumping Mike's hand.

"Home."

Tommy drained his glass of beer. "In his bunker?"

"Probably getting anxious by now," Mike said. He counted the hours he'd been away. Robert, too, would be adding Mike's name to his shit list.

Tommy slapped a twenty on the bar. "Jackie!" he called, and the bartender came to their end of the bar. "Hit me again, and the same for Flannagan."

Mike reached for his wallet, but Tommy stopped him.

The men clustered beside them were arguing about the upcoming Super Bowl.

Mike felt a finger in his side. "I'm giving that blowhard the Bengals and a touchdown," Tommy rasped into his ear.

Mike nodded. His eyes burned from the cigarette smoke.

Tommy reached up to the bar, spun around, and handed him a shot and a mug. Sarah would take two whiffs of a place like this and be gone.

"To you, Mr. Flannagan."

Mike clinked his shot glass against Tommy's. They poured down the whiskeys.

"Whew," Mike said. They plunked the shot glasses down onto the bar. He raised his mug. "To Officer Coyle," he said.

"Not for a long time," Tommy said. "That was two jobs ago."

"Right." Tommy had left the police department under dubious circumstances while Mike was up in New Paltz.

When Tommy lit a Pall Mall, Mike asked him for one. Inhaling, he let the smoke fill him then blew it out slowly. It had been a long time since his last cigarette, but already the smoke in the room bothered him less.

"I parlayed all that time I spent on the beat in South Philly into a job with a beer distributor down on Two Street," Tommy said. He took a long pull on his draft, emptying the glass.

Mike downed his beer. "I got next," he said.

"No way, José," Tommy chirped. He flicked the ash from his cigarette into the dented tin ashtray on the bar. Catching the bartender's eye, he made a series of gestures then turned back to Mike.

"I owe you," Mike said.

The barman brought them two more Yuenglings then planted shots in front of two guys at the other end of the bar. Tommy leaned in closer. "Got an easy fifty coming in Sunday night from that painter." He lit another cigarette. "What happened to you New Year's? I thought you were going to march with us."

"You could say I pussied out," Mike said. "I was with somebody."

"Best parade ever," Tommy said, beaming. "And that's not counting the post-prom party on Two Street."

Mike wondered if the guy would have looked and sounded any more ecstatic describing the birth of his firstborn.

"Like the old days," Tommy said, giving a thumbs-up.

"Your sign language skills have gone through the roof," Mike said. On New Year's Day, he and Sarah had rented some movie. "Help me out here, Flannagan," she said when she came across the television coverage of the parade.

"Nuts," he said, watching a group of men in satin and sequins stagger past the crowd at City Hall. Even though his neighborhood was miles away from Mummers' turf, somebody at the bar had gotten a bunch of them involved around the time Mike became legal. Many of the regulars at Gil's would stagger up Broad Street New Year's morning dressed as clowns. They'd plan some sort of skit and do it every block or two, but by the time they got to the judging stand at City Hall nobody could remember it.

TV cameras never followed the Mummers from Broad to what Mike thought of as Narrow Street, block after block on South Philly's row house–lined Second Street, home ground for clubhouses of string bands and comic division clubs. Once finished with the official competition, these whiskered, ponytailed clowns and saxophone and banjo-wielding paraders marched again, banging out their encore shoulder to shoulder, squeezed into the middle of the wee street to avoid the rivers of crushed beer cans that filled the gutters to their right and left.

"Really, Mike?" dumbfounded Sarah said.

"Really."

Tommy took a drink of beer, holding his forefinger up to Mike: a stop sign to any shift in conversation. "You know what kind of weather it was," Tommy said, as if spending the day outside in the elements had burned the day's conditions into every Philadelphian's memory. "It's snowing. It's raining. It's fucking snowing again. They stuck the string bands and the Fancy Brigades on buses and drove them to Walnut Street, so they'd look nice at City Hall." Tommy's eyes were wild. "Still got their sequins and feathers totally soaked," he said, smirking. "Comics don't give a shit. Know what I mean? We're the clown guys. Feather guys worry about that shit. Pussies."

"Figured you guys would survive," Mike said. He was in the middle of another test, another failure. Had he ever told Laurie about the Mummers? He thought not. Too many other things to talk about.

"It was a beaut, Mike. Some broad clocks Hogan on Broad Street. He passes out on the trolley and rides to the loop in Chestnut Hill and halfway back downtown."

Mike took a drink. On those long-ago nights on Second Street he'd been ready to leave before anyone else. An old fart before his time. His New Paltz life would have bored Tommy and the guys. Working all hours, changing diapers, driving to jobs in an ice storm then learning that he'd been hired by the biggest asshole in the county to redo a kitchen that didn't need it. He longed to sit across the table from Laurie and moan about assholes.

"Next morning, we find Delaney in here," his old classmate tittered. "Fell asleep New Year's Eve, got locked in." He shook his head. "Imagine being that stupid?"

It was one o'clock. *Enough failing for one day.*

"The old lady was out with the girls, so I was the babysitter until she got back."

"A nightcap," Mike said.

"Yeah," Tommy said. "Different crowd than after work. You don't know most of these guys."

Mike shook his head.

"From the neighborhood, but most of them live outside the city now. You know, all the stuff that drives people out. Filth, city wage tax." He leaned closer. "Niggers," he muttered.

Mike winced.

"What, what?" Tommy huffed.

"You grew up next door to the Andersons, for Christ's sake."

"They're good people," Tommy said. "I'm talking about *niggers.*"

Mike tapped his thumbs on his index fingers several times. "Can you do this?" he said.

Tommy did it with both hands, a puzzled look on his face.

"Unbelievable," Mike said. "I gotta get out of here."

"You're a walking conscience," Tommy said. "Next time, I'll spring for Jameson's. Atone for my sins."

"I'm bringing the whole Anderson family," Mike said, rising from his stool.

"Fuck you."

Mike ground his cigarette out in the ashtray. "My dog's gotta go," he said. He turned and headed for the door.

"Probably dreaming of fire hydrants right about now," Tommy called out.

"See ya," Mike said, without turning around.

Out on the sidewalk, the air felt colder than before he'd gone inside. He pulled his jacket zipper all the way up and climbed into the cold car. Smoke, whiskey, and Tommy Coyle. He was in no hurry to revisit any of them. *Robert*. The poor dog's bladder might have exploded by now.

Fumbling with his keys on the doorstep, he heard the familiar sound of the German shepherd spinning in small circles in the foyer, his paws clicking feverishly on the tile floor. The drumroll lasted until Mike bent over Robert, receiving his wet greeting. The house was dark, except for the kitchen and foyer. "I'm sorry," Mike said, starting toward the kitchen. The answering machine's light blinked. "Great," he muttered. Robert nudged his food bowl with his nose. "All right, a snack. But I'm going to take you out first."

Robert charged to the hallway closet's open door, where his leash hung. Mike cringed. The *out* word. "Real quick," Mike said, pausing at the answering machine. Robert sat beside the door, studying the leash. Mike heard his sister-in-law's voice.

"It's me. Give a yell, will you?"

The machine clicked.

"Mike, it's Delores again. I don't want to be a pain in the ass. But call."

Perfect. After resetting the machine, he hustled to the closet and hooked the leash onto the dog's collar. They quick-stepped to the front door.

Mike got him to the curb before the dog started peeing. When Robert was done, he pulled Mike toward the woods at the end of the row. The last house in the row still had porch Christmas lights turned on. The wind blew enough to make Mike wish he'd put on another layer. The colder the weather, the younger Robert acted. When they reached the bit of woods and clearing that separated Mike's row from the supermarket atop the hill, Mike let the excited dog loose. Robert sped to a pile of old Christmas trees at the far end of the clearing. Mike watched him sniff the base of one of the trees then raise his leg on it. Somehow, he'd reserved enough pee to do his marking. Robert ran off into the dark.

Two messages from Delores in one night. The kids probably wanted to come over and watch him run the trains. Had he detected an undertone of desperation in her voice? *Fucking Brendan.*

All evening he'd held back. But now, if that Tom somehow walked out of the darkness, Mike would run him down. If some other dog suddenly attacked Robert, he'd kick it to the ground. When Robert jogged back to Mike, he clipped his leash onto his collar and they trudged off together.

Back home, he dropped a couple of dog biscuits into Robert's food bowl, topped off his plastic water bowl from the kitchen faucet, and poured himself a glass of water. His hands were shaking. If the phone rang, he would let it ring.

Robert inhaled the biscuits and started lapping up his water. "We eat like sharks, buddy," Mike told him. He swirled the glass of water under his nose and slowly breathed in the smell of fluorination. "A great year, Robert." He cackled. "Central coast maybe?"

He shut his eyes but all he could see was two graves, side by side. It was not Sarah's fault. It was the harsh light she shone on his life. What had he not fucked up? He steadied his hand, took a long swallow, then slammed his glass down on the counter.

He crossed the room, opened the basement door. He flipped the light switch and tramped down the wooden steps, Robert trailing.

The train platform looked the way he left it when his nephew and niece had come over to run the Pennsylvania Railroad passenger train and the long Reading coal train. Other nights, he'd lost himself in building and operating the trains, but now the whole world he'd created sickened him. A half-built caboose kit lay beside the power pack. Box cars and coal cars he had built from kits sat alone on sidings.

When he switched on the power pack, lights in the little buildings flickered on. Standing beside the ancient upholstered chair that the kids kneeled in to watch the trains at eye level, he turned the control until the chugging of the approaching Pennsy locomotive covered the buzzing hum of the power pack. He watched it roll past the hospital, schoolhouse, laundromat, and movie theater at the other end of the platform then over the trestle bridge he'd modeled after the one he'd seen in the Hudson Valley. A miniature rustic world come to life. Everything but a cemetery.

Face frozen, with his mouth barely forming an O, he drew in air, blew it out with a whistle, pulled it in, whooshed it out. He watched the black locomotive and the maroon coaches, a Pullman and the observation car, pass by the lake and the mountain in the middle of the layout. The train approached the village on his side, again masking the power pack's hum. It rolled by, blocking his view of the passengers, the workers, and the baggage on the other side of the train. Then the train was gone, headed for the trestle and the town across the way. Passengers stood on the station platform.

Like a bodybuilder preparing to lift far more than he'd ever raised above him, he sucked in air, blew it out. The little train chugged into sight on his side of the mountain. One of the figures on the platform had fallen. He noticed that it had not been completely painted. He'd bought it and a collection of other "citizens" in New Paltz for when his little boy could help him set up a layout.

The train stormed past the station, surprising him. But quickly it was gone again. His hands had not stopped shaking. *The train has left the station.* Before he'd felt empty, weak. This drive was different. He needed something in his hands.

He turned and walked toward his tools at the rear of the basement. Ignoring the neatly pegged hammers and screwdrivers on the wallboard, he rooted through the old plastic trash container filled with yard tools from New Paltz until he found a dusty ax handle. He pulled it out, wiped it clean, and rushed back toward his layout. With the train on the other side of the platform, the power pack's buzz sounded louder than before, even as the train neared the village on his side of the layout. Noise groaned out of his diaphragm, blending with the power pack's sound into a steady drone.

He swung the ax handle like a baseball bat, blasting his vintage locomotive across the platform, where it landed against the base of a papier-mâché mountain. The rest of the train derailed, crashing into the station and the schoolhouse. *That droning noise.* He swung again, smashing the school building into pieces. His next follow-through cleared the rest of the buildings from his end of the platform. Robert paced beside him, barking. Groaning and swinging, Mike moved to the side of the layout.

One automobile remained on the village street. *The bastard's?* He pictured it swerving across the center line straight toward Laurie and Michael, felt her car lurch to the right as she wrenched her car's steering wheel, heard the screech of tires, then the sudden cacophony of crushed metal, glass, and plastic. Silence. Then a car door creaking open. The bastard's door.

Mike whaled at the car, sending it caroming off the back wall. The mangled metal car landed on the layout not far from where it had sat. Like a striker at a carnival ring-the-bell game, he raised the ax handle then slammed it straight down, mashing the metal car into the platform's surface. Stepping to where the village gave way to a mountainside lake, he chopped down again, opening a gash in the mountain. *Hit*, he told himself, but his body was already doing what he told it. He watched himself hit the platform again, swinging left-handed then right-handed until half of his layout was covered with chunks of papier-mâché.

He saw the dog, cowering at the base of the stairs. He'd never scared Robert before, but it was too late to worry about him now. Another test failed. Moving to the freight yard, Mike swung, sending half a dozen freight cars scattering on the other side of the layout. He watched himself yank the power pack's cord out of the electrical outlet, stopping the damn buzzing. Had he just stopped moaning too? Robert was still barking. Panting, Mike dropped the ax handle beside the platform, turned, and slumped into the old stuffed chair. He was no longer watching himself or hearing that droning sound, just shaking.

3

MONDAY, JANUARY 23

As much as Sarah loved the woman, Florence Devereaux could trash an office in about a day of teaching. On weekdays, Sarah was there to make sure that things didn't get out of hand in the little office they had shared for the past five years, but Florence accepting a Saturday morning class this semester had been a terrible mistake, at least from Sarah's perspective. Already she had learned to associate Monday mornings with unpleasant surprises.

Discovering the remains of her office partner's Saturday lunch, apparently overlooked by the weekend housekeeping staff, Sarah dumped the wastebasket liner into a large receptacle safely down the hall, then returned to the office to turn her attention to the bookshelves on three of its walls. After moving the items from the top of the bookcase by the door to her freshly sanitized desk top, she sprayed the bookcase top with cleanser and gave it a good wipe. Using a different cloth splashed with a bit of disinfectant, she gently wiped the framed photographs of Virginia Woolf and Kate Chopin then returned them to their places of honor. Again using her desk as her workstation, she made three piles of the books from the highest shelf then cleaned each one's covers, spine, and page edges. *Dusting and sweeping clear out the mind.* So she'd assured her mother, who once called her a "wipe-scallion," goofing with high school student Sarah's favorite word, rapscallion. *Practical aerobics.* Except that now she was thinking about her parents again, which would only usher into her brain the architect of Friday night's fiasco, Mike Flannagan.

In short order, she again was shuffling books back and forth between the bookcase and her desk, panting a little, which convinced her that furious engagement with the day had indeed been her strategy for managing the weekend's accumulated anger, sadness, and frustration. Admiring the first cleaned bookcase, she stretched her back and leg muscles and gave the office a quick reassessment. The other shelves could wait.

Knowing her office mate would not show up until about an hour before her Monday class, Sarah furtively ran a wet wipe across the top of Florence's desk, careful not to touch any of the knickknacks from the single woman's solo trips taken over the thirty-five summers of her teaching career. She gave the wastebasket a good spray of her favorite aerosol and blasted the air above both desks, but the cramped little space still gave off a strong hint of cooked onions.

Florence's messiness was in direct opposition to former colleague Russell Grimmet—who also was a neatnik and who had briefly been Sarah's husband. "Long enough for you to share a cup of coffee," was how Florence summed it up once. After six months of dating, they'd married without fanfare at City Hall during spring break, telling family and friends afterward. A year later when she showed him an announcement for a position in Georgia, he promptly applied, as if he'd been waiting for his cue. She'd been more in love with the idea of a match of souls than with Russell. They'd been as accommodating with one another in getting divorced as they'd been in getting married. She'd described the whole mess to Florence as "a bland sojourn from single life's ebb and flow between desperate mistakes and hope-destroying loneliness." She'd been embarrassed but relieved to let him go.

Mike Flannagan again appeared front and center in her con-sciousness, roiling her gut—the same hungover feeling that had greeted her each morning since Friday night. She swirled around and set her sights on the next bookcase. "Fuck," she muttered, grab-bing a large armful of books and dropping them onto her desk where they sprawled, unlike her previous precise stacks. "Shit!" When she finished that shelf, she closed the door, lit the pine forest candle she'd bought in Chestnut Hill, and went over the notes for her next class.

"Do they still love you?" Florence asked, breezing into the office an hour later.

Sarah looked up from her roll book. *They?*

"Didn't your parents come down from New York?"

"Oh God," Sarah said. "Of course they love me."

"You just seemed so nervous on Friday," Florence said, clearing space on her desk for her book satchel and a white paper bag containing what Sarah was sure were fresh buttery croissants from La Belle Hélène.

"It was a pretty full weekend," Sarah offered. She watched Florence sip her coffee. Sarah already had downed her morning cup, but the coffee's aroma was tantalizing.

"One of zeeze, mademoiselle?" Florence sang, offering her a croissant.

"Death by butter," Sarah said, breaking the pastry into two pieces and taking the smaller one. "The perfect suicide."

"That bad?"

She told Florence that her father's cancer wasn't back but that he would be undergoing another round of chemo anyway. George and Esther assured their daughter that everything was going to be fine. "He looks great," Sarah said. "Seems strong. Positive."

Florence nodded.

Sarah told her about Saturday's visit to the art museum, dinner at the London, shopping with her mother. Explained how convincing her father had been about the state of his health. Told her everything about her parents' visit except the fact that she'd hoped to talk Mike into coming over to meet her parents, a hope that had been dashed after dinner.

Florence sat at her small desk and began slowly transferring papers from her briefcase to the top of her desk.

"I know I should feel good about that," Sarah said. "But they've known this for weeks and didn't tell me until Saturday."

"Ouch," Florence said, closing the file folder and setting it on top of several others. She looked up from her papers and gave Sarah a sympathetic look.

"My brother got to know."

"Mmm."

"His old classmate is the oncologist," Sarah said. "I still should have been told."

"And you let them know this?"

"In no uncertain terms," Sarah said. She filled her in on the details of the visit, concentrating on the low moments.

"No wonder you snatched up that croissant, Ms. Brown Rice," Florence said.

"And Mike and I are not in a good place."

"Your beau?" She seemed genuinely surprised.

And then Sarah was off, giving Florence the ugly details.

"Poor guy," Florence said. "Must have felt like there were a thousand professors in the room. One academic at a time is probably all that most normal people should have to handle."

Sarah laughed. Was this her first light moment since Friday night?

"But what about him and you?" Florence said, savoring a bite of croissant.

"Seems like he wants less and I want more. It might be awful of me to hate him for that, but that's how I've felt since Friday."

"*Awful* would be seeing the one you love close the door on you."

"Which might be around the corner," Sarah said, welling up, then cursing Mike, mad at her own vulnerability. "Son of a bitch!"

"The one you love?"

"He's still an SOB."

"Whom you're anxious to clobber. Fighting *for* him might be a different rhetorical approach."

"Of course," Sarah said. "The bastard." She raised her eyes to the skies. "When I catch myself crying, I hate myself."

Florence nodded, and Sarah sat with her thoughts. Florence had been going over Mike's essay draft with him in this office. His earnest brown eyes had gotten Sarah's attention, as had his deference to his teacher, but she was used to seeing working-class students respond to Florence's demanding but respectful approach. The assignment had to do with two contrasting views of human nature, not a topic that struck her as particularly exciting. They'd all read a book about it by Thomas Sowell. While reading Mike's draft to herself, Florence had burst into laughter. "Where did you see these bumper stickers?" she demanded, beaming at Mike.

"Near the naval air station in Willow Grove," he said. "The other one in Mount Airy."

Sarah looked up from her papers. Laughing again, Florence immediately caught her eye. "Sarah, which of these two bumper stickers do you believe my wonderful student Mike Flannagan saw in your neighborhood?"

Sarah felt his eyes on her but fixed hers on her senior colleague.

"US Navy Seals: For When It Absolutely Positively Must Be Destroyed Overnight."

"Oh," Sarah said, wincing.

"May All Beings Be Free From Suffering."

"Ha!" Sarah winced again. She and Mike both reddened.

"I don't mean anything bad," he offered. "Wherever you live."

Sarah laughed. "Well, you probably guessed correctly that I live in Mount Airy."

"Me too, though it's changed a lot since I grew up."

She'd hit the library on the way home that day to pick up a copy of *A Conflict of Visions*. "That book," she'd told Florence the next morning, "is very challenging."

"If I were your age, I'd like him too," Florence said.

"Who, Sowell?"

Florence tittered conspiratorially. "His face is the map of Ireland," she sighed. "Craggy in all the right ways."

"Indeed. I confess, I watched him walk out of the office. There's nothing wrong with the way he looks from behind."

"Absolutely nothing," Florence agreed.

When he'd entered the office a week later, Florence called out in her classroom voice, "The man from Mount Airy," causing Mike and Sarah to blush. Sarah bemoaned the neighborhood's lack of restaurants, to which Mike merely nodded. But when he left, she caught up to him down the hall and suggested they drive over to Roxborough for coffee and a pastry at a little Italian café on Ridge Avenue, where they spent an hour inventing outrageous lives for the people around them.

A week after coffee, they walked the carriage road along the Wissahickon Creek, imagining entire conversations among the squirrels, dogs, ducks, and horses they passed. Afterwards, she brought him to an upscale bar on Main Street in Manayunk—"Never been here, but sure," he told her, opening the door. She had a glass of pinot grigio and he sipped at a pint of Yuengling lager. As they neared the end of their drinks, she told him that her cheek muscles hurt from smiling. "Mine too," he said, looking amazed.

"So, next time?" she said.

"Something less painful."

Sarah roared.

She jolted out of her reverie to check her watch. "My class!" she exclaimed, causing Florence to drop the book she'd been holding. Sarah jumped out of her seat and gathered her materials. On her way across campus, she chided herself for spending so much time and energy focused on Mike. What kind of fool agonized over a man after learning that cancer treatments were yet again a family topic? She pictured her father, lagging behind at the art museum on Saturday to gaze at Manet's *Le Bon Bock*. The nonsmoking teetotaler, with his freshly shaved face and balding head, stood before the painting's bearded man with pipe in mouth and beer in hand. Such an unlikely pair. She should have guessed that something was going on with him.

Other patients might speak of going for treatments. He talked about "going after the bad guys." She wondered if he was all that confident on the inside. And Mom had adopted his terminology.

She recalled the three of them in cavernous 30th Street Station, waiting for the New York train to be called. People crisscrossed the concourse. Standing beneath the towering bronze statue of an angel, wings aloft, lifting a fallen soldier, she had tried to remind her parents that she could get to New York at a moment's notice, but her father was lecturing on the statue.

"Always gets me," her father said, shaking his head. "Forty feet tall if it's an inch."

"Less than three hours, Dad," she said. "Door to door." An

announcement echoed off the high walls. She thought she made out "Washington" at the end.

"So sleek and dark," her father said, still craning his neck. "There's a sheen to it."

"Almost black," her mother said.

"Mom!" Sarah blurted. "Call every night. Remember!"

"I guess you wouldn't notice it," her father said, "if you came through here every day."

"Please."

Now, Sarah held the door to her classroom open, letting one of her students in ahead of her. Bob Lusk from the psych department had already left the room. Several of his students passed by her. A male voice she did not recognize cut over the bustle and chatter of the class change. Another voice barked an obscenity.

Suddenly, the room filled with the noises of scuffling near the chalkboard and startled cries and gasps from farther back in the room. Letting go of the door, Sarah entered the classroom. Students were shoving and punching each other by the chalkboard. Amidst the blur, she saw a young man grab a classmate by the throat and slam him against the chalkboard, toppling the podium. Someone bolted from the classroom, almost knocking her down. It seemed like everyone in the room who was not fighting was screaming. A guy with a slick black pompadour right out of the fifties grabbed a student who'd pinned someone against the board.

"Stop it!" Sarah screamed. She grabbed the pompadour guy by the back of his collar and jerked him away from the kid he'd just smashed against the blackboard, who then straightened himself out and reared back to hit his combatant. She shot out her left hand, grabbing the second student's neck before he could swing and pushing both further apart. They froze in her grip, but the others kept fighting.

"Stop it *now!*" she yelled, but students kept hitting each other, one pair slamming against the venetian blinds, rolling onto the floor.

"Bitch!" the student on her left hissed, pulling against her grip.

"Get your fucking hands off me!" the one on her right yelled, then spit in her face.

With all her strength, she pulled down on the collar of the guy on her left. "Sit *down!*" She flung the pompadour kid back toward the crowd of students at the door, her back suddenly spasming. He sprawled against a desk, falling to the floor.

"Don't move!" she shouted at him, wiping the spit from her face. She threw herself between the next pair, her legs immediately becoming entangled with theirs. The next punch brought the three of them to the floor in a heap, but the pair kept swinging. People were screaming. Someone grabbed her from behind by the collar and jerked her up to her feet, then suddenly let her go. She turned. The guy with the pompadour was now trading blows with his earlier opponent. Someone plowed into her back, again bringing her to the floor. "*Stop!*" she pleaded. Then people were pulling the two fighters apart. Holding onto a desk, she pulled herself back up, panting. An older student and a teacher separated the other pair.

The room filled with noisy people who did not belong in the class. A teacher she didn't know sat her in a chair and asked if she was all right. She nodded and tried to catch her breath as people continued to mill around. Eventually, two security guards arrived and began questioning everyone. Her class was sent home. Drained and breathing heavily through her mouth, she sat shaking her head. She looked at the guys who had been fighting. She'd never seen any of them before. What on Earth had caused this mess? None of this made any sense. Her back and shoulder hurt. She'd never been in a fight in her life. How had she managed to intervene? And why?

A half hour later, she sat crying in the waiting area outside Dean Lamarr's office until she was called in. She felt faint but tried her best to stay focused on her hands in her lap. After recounting the story to him, she returned to the waiting area, where she wrote a report on the incident. She flushed and felt her heart race when three of the brawlers were escorted past her into the dean's office. In her report she had singled out the middle one, along with the nightmare out of the fifties, as the prime troublemakers. Warring gangs?

The dean would see her again in an hour. Heading for her office, she passed the guy with the pompadour as he was being taken into the office of the assistant dean. When they made eye contact, he smiled sweetly at her, sending a jolt up her spine. She turned away and kept walking. When she turned back, he was looking right in her direction, smiling that smile. She felt more frightened than at any point during the fight or at any other moment in her life. She reached her office and closed the door. By this time, Florence would be off to her class then gone for the day. Sarah lowered the lights and put her head down on her desk.

When she met with Dr. Lamarr again, he informed her that four students were being suspended, for at least the semester. She sank back in her seat and felt that her heart was finally beating at its normal rate.

"You don't need medical attention?"

She shook her head.

"Sure you're all right?"

"I'm going to be okay," she said. She'd only ever heard about one such fight in the history of the college. "I love this place. This doesn't happen here."

The dean gave her a quick smile then looked down at papers on his desk she took to be reports on the incident. "Sarah," he said, looking up over his reading glasses. "We all make mistakes. Fortunately, you should survive this one."

Her face reddened and burned. "Mistake?" she said. "I'm lucky I'm not in the hospital."

He nodded gravely. "You know how bad I feel for you," he said. "To have gone through that, to be in such danger. But by your own account you did some things that, while well-intended, were way out of line with what is expected of a faculty member. You know you do not have the right to assault students."

She gasped.

"I realize that you were in a very bad situation, but you did not show the best judgment. Physically grabbing students, pushing them."

"I was separating them," she said, struggling to keep her voice even. "Keeping them from doing further harm to one another."

"Becoming part of the incident?" he asked, his voice arch.

"Part of it?" she said.

"Sarah, you will not be disciplined for this. Nothing will be put in your file."

She felt her eyes widen further. Her mouth remained open, as if she'd stopped mid-word. Her hands balled into reddened fists. Would he read something into *that*? She opened her hands and stretched her fingers open then relaxed them.

"I don't think a student would be likely to win a case against the college or against you," he said. "And I don't think it's very likely that they'll go that route."

"Did I do anything that you wouldn't have done, Dr. Lamarr?" she asked in her calmest voice.

"We have guidelines, Ms. Goins," he said, frowning. "My God, you served on the conflict resolution committee last semester. Nowhere do *your* guidelines suggest that a faculty member should ever grab a student, yank one down to the floor, throw one across the room."

Had witnesses used that language? She stopped herself from asking. "Has anyone complained about what I did?"

He looked down at the forms arrayed on his desk, picked up several sheets and tapped them against his desk, rotated them and tapped again, then set them back on his desk in a neat pile. "The reports all say the same thing," he said, looking up at her. "Not much question about your actions in this incident. Maybe you thought you were somehow defusing the situation by getting physically involved. As I said, I do not expect that this matter will go any further. And I know that a bright person like yourself learns from her mistakes."

Keep your expression fixed. Breathe in normally, breathe out. Again. "Is there anything else?"

"Well, no," he said.

Sarah went straight to Leona Henderson-Hennessey's office. Leona had heard about the incident, but Sarah sat in the overstuffed chair in the corner of the little office and blurted out the details. She found herself breathing more easily by the time she'd finished her retelling.

"A nightmare," Leona finally said, shaking her head.

Slumping back into the cushy old chair, Sarah felt some of the stress pass with each exhale, and she realized how tight all her muscles had gotten, even those that hadn't been banged, bumped, or punched. She let her eyes close and exhaled slowly, feeling calmer than when she had walked in the door.

"You poor dear," Leona said. "Thankfully, they're going to put those students out. And I very much doubt that they will come after you."

"I should hope not," Sarah said, opening her eyes.

"I mean, the college or the students," Leona said. "You were under unbelievable stress. I don't know what I would have done in the same situation. I think there's a good chance this whole thing will blow over. Litigation is not the first thing our students think about. And Lamarr's not going to want the ugliness of going after you."

"I just reacted, Leona. I've never done anything like that in my life." She had followed her nose, that's all, but this was like nothing else. Had the weekend's pain and frustration tilted her toward this in some way? Ridiculous. Would she have acted this way last week, or tomorrow?

"I think you're going to be lucky in all this," Leona said. "You'll dodge this bullet. As you said, you just overreacted."

Sarah's brow creased. "I didn't say that." She studied Leona's face. Her colleague was looking away, as if in deep thought.

"And I suspect we'll all think differently about how we intervene in things like that, heaven forbid something like that should happen again."

"Lamarr is an ass," Sarah said. "I'd always given him the benefit of the doubt."

Leona nodded, but avoided Sarah's eyes.

Right? Her friend's nod felt like woefully weak support. *And?* "I wish I had been five minutes late for class," Sarah said. "But I didn't think. I just tried to do something. To keep anyone else from getting hurt." Her face felt hot enough to sear scallops. She touched her stomach. She thought she might throw up.

"Sarah?" Leona said.

Sarah realized that her eyes were squeezed shut. She opened them. Leona was frowning. "Slow down, dear."

Sarah shook her head.

"Your brow is all knotted."

Sarah looked at Leona, whose forehead was also creased with concern as she peered into Sarah's eyes. She remembered her first department meeting when the only members of the department she knew were those who had served on her hiring committee, before Leona had introduced herself and offered to share course syllabi with her young colleague. Watching this woman dissect and discredit a colleague's proposal, Sarah had felt awe and admiration mixed with a touch of fear at the prospect of this commanding woman ever being an adversary.

"You picked the right place," Leona said, flashing a more familiar smile.

How could she see it this way? Sarah gripped the thick arms of the chair and rose to her feet. "I need to go," she said, casting about to see if she had brought any papers with her.

Leona hugged her and kissed her cheek. "I'm glad you came."

"I need to keep moving," Sarah said.

That evening, Sarah wrote *B* on the last page of an essay and dropped it face down on the short pile of graded papers. She counted the unmarked ones. Fifteen more. Somewhere in the next essay, flashes of men yelling and punching each other, desks falling over, and she in the middle of it all yanked her away from Latanya Wilson's defense of Antigone's actions.

Why had she become warrior woman? *Had* she become warrior woman? If she'd arrived a couple of minutes later, the fighters might have carried their battle out into the hallway, where someone else might have intervened. She pictured herself opening the door at the end of the hallway, glimpsing the distant fracas, and keeping a safe distance while others pulled the creeps apart. God forbid she'd actually been late for class, it might have all been over and done before she even entered the building.

She looked at her watch. Nine fifteen. She'd already leaned on

Florence today, and she wasn't even sure she had the woman's home telephone number. Leona had hardly said anything to make her feel like she ought to call her. In thirty minutes her parents would go to bed. Way too late to give them even a sanitized version. Was this one of Mike's late nights? He'd nixed Tuesday's late-afternoon hike near Valley Green. She'd penciled in "video & pizza" under Saturday on her Italian calendar. Now that date felt as distant as Italy.

She picked up her empty water glass and marched to the kitchen. Standing by the table, she looked from her pocketbook beside the kitchen telephone to the car keys on the counter. He might not answer if she telephoned. She could not remember the last time she had to run to someone, not through the unfortunateness with Russell Grimmet, not through countless hiring committee squabbles, tenant–landlord hassles, star-crossed relationships.

She marched back to her desk and began rereading the essay she'd been grading. The introductory paragraph still made sense. She approved of her mark-up of the run-on and the subject-verb agreement error in the second paragraph, then flipped to the second page. Clean. Like Sarah's record. Consistent, like Sarah's independence. During the eight years she'd spent in Philadelphia, she had gone it alone. She told herself that she ought to be able to take a difficult day on top of a difficult weekend without dumping what was terrorizing her onto someone else. *Sarah can do it*. With a wry smile, Mike had always been able to stem her grandiosity before it reached the level of embarrassment, and he could do it without hurting her. Why was she telling herself she didn't need help on one of the worst nights of her life?

Sarah realized that she'd been on the same paragraph for fifteen minutes. She refilled her glass, returned to the desk in her living room, and flipped back to page one, beginning a third read-through of Latanya's essay.

4

MONDAY, JANUARY 23

Clutching his Wawa bag, Domenic Gallo limped the last ten yards to the traffic light where Allens Lane dead-ended at Germantown Avenue and turned right, his body stiff and sore. When he'd left the church hall bingo game in West Philly an hour ago, three guys had beaten him for the twelve dollars in his wallet. Hunched over, the seventy-five-year-old had trudged three blocks to the El station, where, using the SEPTA token hidden in his left shoe, he began his journey back to Northwest Philadelphia, making his way up and down dank, dark stairways to the El, the Broad Street subway, and finally the 23 trolley. The bench on the other side of the avenue looked so near and welcoming and he had the green light, but it might turn yellow before he reached the middle of the intersection. Better to wait for a full green. Speed was never an old man's strong suit, but now it took all of his strength to move more than a few feet at a time. Because it hurt to turn his neck in any direction, he kept his head straight and put most of his weight on his left leg, but his right knee still throbbed. Eyes locked on the light across the street, he concentrated on the prospect of stepping over the icy rails and Belgian blocks in this dim light, climbing the three stone steps up to the sidewalk, reaching that bench in front of the Lutheran seminary wall.

When the light went green again, he flat-footed into the street, making sure one foot landed securely before starting the next step. He reached the other side just as his light was turning red again. He realized that he hadn't even considered that some late-night driver flying to the end of Allens Lane might try to hang a right onto the avenue. Thank you, God, he thought, his first good luck of the night. He pulled himself up the first step then stopped. When he caught his breath, he took the last two steps, made his way to the bench, then plopped down.

"Can I help you?"

Startled, Domenic turned toward the man's voice, bristling. There was nothing solicitous in the sound of the voice. "No," Domenic grunted. He clutched his plastic Wawa bag. "On my way home," he said, pointing down the avenue.

"Plenty of time before last call at Gilhooley's," the man said, now towering over him at the edge of the bench.

"Have one for me," Domenic said, glancing at the scowling face above him. Mid-thirties, forties? With a woolen Navy cap pulled down over his forehead and ears and a bulky winter coat, it was hard to tell.

"The way you waddled across the street," the man said, "I'd say you've seen the inside of that place before."

"Never have. Anybody ever tell you that you're a great judge of people?"

He gave Domenic a look.

"Didn't think so," Dominic said.

"You can't stay here all night."

With the load off his feet, Dominic's knee pain calmed down a bit. Now the aching in his gut, neck, cheek, and jaw vied for center stage. "*Madonna*," he muttered.

"If you were trying to get to the bar, you were on the right side of the street to start with."

"Who put you on the welcoming committee?"

"Come on, now."

"Close your eyes, and I'll be gone from your bench," Domenic said. "This *is* your bench?"

"I work for the seminary," the man said. "Grounds department. We've had some vandalism lately."

"Sonny, I can tell you all about late-night crime. You're working awful late. Don't they ever give you time off?"

"I think it's time for you to move."

"I will," Domenic said. "About two shakes, I'll be out of here." He opened his bag, pulled out a pack of gauze bandages, medical tape, and a bottle of Betadine, and placed them on the bench beside him. "Thank God for Wawa, huh?" he said, rolling up his right pants leg.

"Jesus," the man muttered.

The cut on Domenic's knee was still bleeding. Sitting on the subway, he had applied the handful of tissues he carried in his pocket and that had mostly stopped the bleeding.

"How'd you do that?" the man asked.

"Three *citrullos* jumped me coming out of my Monday night bingo game, cleaned out my wallet," Domenic said, taking some gauze from its wrapper and dabbing at the wound.

"There's no bingo around here."

"Transfiguration," Domenic said, "over in West Philly." He winced as he tried to clean the area. Blood had dried around his knee, and the lighting afforded by the streetlamp was not much help.

"What were you doing all the way over there?"

"Besides losing my walking-around money and getting my butt kicked? Not much."

"If they took all your money, how'd you buy those supplies?" the man said.

"I didn't say they took all my money," Domenic said. "They emptied my *wallet*—and my pockets. I keep a ten in my right shoe."

The man sat wearily beside Domenic. "You didn't think about going to a hospital?"

Domenic made a face as he balled the gauze pad and the wrapper, stuffed them into the Wawa bag, then twisted off the top of the Betadine container.

"You need stitches," the man said. "I can drive you to Chestnut Hill, unless you're opposed to *all* hospitals."

"Now you're catching on."

The man put his hand on the Betadine container. "You shouldn't be doing this out here."

"Four hundred and two homicides in our fair city last year," Domenic said. "My guess is that number's going up this year."

"It will if you keep going out alone at night. All over the city, at that."

"Sometimes it don't matter where you are. It just finds you." Domenic watched him pull the knitted cap off and wipe sweat from his forehead, all without taking his eyes off Domenic. The guy obviously had been chugging along with his work and probably was on his way home. A look of deep exhaustion replaced his scowl.

"Just where are you headed?" the man said, putting his cap back on loosely.

"I live upstairs from Al's Barbershop," Domenic said. "Across the street from that bar you keep talking about."

The man squinted in the direction of Gilhooley's.

"Farther than I can walk without fixing this thing up," Domenic said.

"It's got to get cleaned better than that. And you ought to do something about your cheek. And your forehead."

"Most of that'll come off in the shower," Domenic said. "I'm not going to the hospital. *Capisce?*"

"You need a crutch or a cane."

"Got one handy?"

The man replaced everything in Domenic's bag. "Come on," he said, rising, the bag in his hand. Domenic gingerly rolled down his pants leg and struggled to his feet.

"I'm Mike Flannagan," the man said, hunching over and slipping his left arm around the back of Domenic's waist.

Domenic stretched his right arm around the tall man's lowered shoulder and took a step down the sidewalk toward his apartment. He slogged ahead with his other foot, and his new dance partner matched his halting pace. After a few steps, they picked up speed. When they reached the corner, Domenic realized that even with the temperature around the freezing point, he, too, was sweating now. By the time they reached the downstairs door, he was panting. He pulled out his key and got it into the keyhole on the first try. "I'll be good from here," he said, turning to Mike.

"You said you lived upstairs. Let's get you all the way up there."

Domenic opened the front door and flipped on the stairway light switch. Leading with his left foot, he started up, one stair at a time. He advanced, creaking up the first few steps, sighing and cursing. He heard the door close behind him.

"I guess you don't have any neighbors you're worried about disturbing?" Mike said.

"They're—"

"I know. Already disturbed."

Domenic stopped to take a break. "If I had any, they'd be disturbed," he puffed. "This is the only apartment in the building, and you may have noticed it's not hair cutting time."

"And the buildings next to us?"

"Businesses." He took a deep breath. "Here we go," he said, starting up again.

He clumped and banged his way to the top stair where he planted himself in front of the apartment door. When he pulled out his key ring again, it fell onto the stair below him. Mike, his face still holding that wearied look, picked up the keys and handed them to him. Domenic unlocked the door, switched on the light, then stepped into the dining room of the apartment. "*Madonna*, I'm sweating like a Sicilian." He shrugged off his overcoat, dropping it to the floor. Mike picked it up. "I got a closet here," Domenic said, handing him his gloves. He nodded toward the closet on the other side of the room. "In there would be great."

Mike slipped the gloves into the pockets, put the coat into the closet, then closed the door.

Domenic leaned his weight against the dining room wall. "I'll be fine," he said.

"If you don't get that thing cleaned out, you're going to have real problems," Mike said, setting Domenic's bag on the table. He pulled out a chair from the small dining room table and motioned for Domenic to sit down.

Domenic settled in the chair, wincing. "It's late. You go home."

Mike tucked his cap into a coat pocket then took off his coat and draped it behind one of the chairs. The guy's hair was a mess. Why did people with anything more than a crew cut think they could get away with pulling those knit caps on and off all day? *Buy a comb, for God's sake.*

"Bathroom?" Mike asked.

Domenic directed him down the hall. He carefully rolled up his pants leg. Mike returned with a towel and two wet facecloths.

Domenic looked at the ceiling while Mike cleaned his face then washed the gash in his knee. "When's the last time you got a tetanus shot?" Mike asked, patting the wound dry with the towel.

"Couple of years ago, Doctor Finnegan."

"*Flannagan*, with two n's. Call me Mike."

Domenic flinched when Mike doused him with Betadine.

"I found these in your medicine chest," Mike said, holding up two butterfly bandages.

"Layer of dust on them, I bet. Probably from the last tenant."

When the bandaging was done, Domenic rolled down his pants leg. After a quick check, Mike pronounced Domenic's forehead and cheek okay.

"Tell you the truth," Domenic said, "it's more my jaw." He moved it sideways, grimacing.

Mike disappeared into the kitchen, returning in a couple of minutes with a glass of water, a plastic bag filled with ice cubes, and a fresh dish towel. He set the glass on the table then handed the bag and towel to Domenic.

Domenic wrapped the ice bag in the dish towel then held it against the side of his face. "When this swelling goes down a bit, I'll be back to my normal talkative self."

"Right."

Domenic watched his grim-faced benefactor head back to the bathroom.

He returned in a minute with three pills in his hand. "I found some ibuprofen," Mike said, giving Domenic the pills. "You need to eat something with this, a sandwich, anything."

Domenic tossed back the pills with a drink of water. "Crackers okay?"

The man nodded.

"You're not a doctor or a nurse?"

"I lived with someone who knew more than me."

"I'm familiar with the concept," Domenic said. He adjusted his ice pack.

"You look like you ran into the entire Marine Corps out there."

"Didn't think kids could punch that hard," Domenic said. "Pushed me down some stairs after they cleaned out my wallet."

"They took your Medicare card?"

"Didn't mess with that."

"That lets you ride for free. You know that."

"It's a handout," Domenic scoffed. "The ten I keep in my other shoe," he said, pulling off the right shoe. "That's social security."

Mike shook his head. "Somebody who knows more than me ought to look at that cut in the morning." He reached for his coat.

"Not so fast, Mr. Dog-Walker," Domenic said.

Mike glared at him.

"I didn't recognize you at first," Domenic said, slowly rising from the chair. He pointed to his front room that overlooked the avenue. "You walk that German shepherd down the avenue." Forgetting about his knee, he took a step toward Mike, but the pain stopped him. "*Madonna,*" he whispered in a high pitch, leaning against the wall, and the sound of the word that his Angela used to say made him think about his dead wife. Mah-Doughn. *Thank God she doesn't have to witness this evening's spectacle.*

"You shouldn't be on your feet," Mike said, giving Domenic a severe look.

"You thought I was drunk or crazy *before*. Now you're wondering what's with this crazy old *paesano* sitting up here looking down on you and Rin Tin Tin." Domenic could not tell if the guy was going to hit him or bolt, but there was something animal-like in his eyes.

"You're not going to insult me now, are you?" Domenic said. "You get me home. Help me climb Mount Everest and patch me up. You must accept my thanks, Flannery."

"Mike," he said. "And you're welcome."

He pointed his finger at Mike. "Not so fast, sonny. You didn't *get* my thanks yet. I'm Domenic Gallo. The coat can wait, for God's sake." He nodded toward the front room. "Go have a seat."

"Mr. Gallo, it's after one."

"It's Domenic, remember?" He pointed at Mike, with the index and little finger out. "You don't want me to have to put the maloiks on you, do you? *Malocchio.* It's a terrible thing."

"No," Mike said. Looking worn out, he returned his coat to the chair.

"I'll bring the bottle and glasses," Domenic said. "And I got some saltines to go with my pills."

"Tell me where they are. You got all you can handle, getting down the hallway."

Letting more of his weight slump against the wall, Domenic sighed. An hour earlier, he would have given the guy hell. "*Grazie,*" Domenic breathed. "The cabinet under the sink," Domenic said, pointing toward the kitchen. "There's a bottle of port behind the cleansers and the plastic bucket. And the crackers are in the top right cupboard."

When Mike left the room, Domenic fetched two cordial glasses from the hutch.

"Gallo port," Mike said, returning to the dining room with the bottle in his right hand and a plate with crackers in the other. "I should have known."

"They don't know me, and I don't know them," Domenic said. "But I drink their port." With the bottle tucked under his arm, Mike reached for the two small glasses and helped Domenic hobble into the living room. "The light switch is on your left." Domenic said. When they reached the end of the hallway, Mike nudged the light switch on with his elbow and set the bottle, the glasses, and the plate of crackers on the little end table that sat between a small couch and the frayed but clean high-backed chair at the window. Domenic slumped into his chair and rested his feet on the little ottoman his wife had bought for some long-ago Christmas. It didn't go with the chair he had now, but he was not about to throw the thing out.

Mike bent down and looked out the window. "Your spot," he said.

Domenic settled. He figured the throbbing in the knee would subside if he kept it still for a while.

"Give me a minute," Mike said, leaving the room.

Domenic heard him in the kitchen, opening one of the ice trays. He leaned forward, reached for the bottle, and filled the two glasses. He picked up three saltines and ate them, surprised that he had any appetite.

Mike returned with a large ice pack and placed it on Domenic's knee. Grabbing his glass, he sat on the couch beside Domenic's chair.

"*Cent'anni,*" Domenic said, raising his glass.

Mike clinked his against Domenic's. "Here's to bumps and bruises," he said. "And better luck at bingo."

"Tell you the truth, kiddo, you look like you had a bad Monday after a bad weekend. But if you can get a cranky old man home, you can stay long enough to turn that friggin' frown upside down."

"Ha." Mike sighed, a wan smile creasing his face for a moment. "I was surprised you let me come inside."

"It's usually me that gets on the wrong side of people just looking at them," Domenic said, lifting his glass again. He watched his Samaritan sip his wine then lean back on the couch. Angela would have replaced the burnt-out light bulb in the overhead fixture long ago, he thought. The dimness of one weak bulb did not bother him, but he made a mental note to replace the bad bulb one of these days. He took a sip then watched Mike survey the television, the faded print of a lake with trees behind it, his chair and ottoman. Domenic rolled the sweet wine around in his mouth, savoring the tingly sensation before swallowing. Setting the glass down, he brought the small ice pack to his jaw again.

"Nice here," Mike said, resting his drink on the table. Domenic watched him turn around and take in the line of unlit votive candles atop Angela's old nightstand, centered against the wall beneath two pictures. He examined the photograph and locked onto Angela's eyes.

"My Angela," Domenic called out. "God rest her soul. She died ten years ago, and that's about how long I been here."

"I'm sorry," Mike said, looking at the woman in the photograph.

"You don't know sorry." Domenic sighed.

Mike swiveled his head around and glowered at Domenic, making the old man feel like he'd seen a curtain flash open for just a second. "I mean people in general," Domenic said.

"Right," he said, his eyes boring into Domenic's.

"I'm just saying." Domenic thought he saw that animal look again for a moment.

Mike looked back at the photograph. "Kids?"

"No." Domenic glanced at the picture of his wife. "Almost."

They reached for their wine glasses at the same time.

"Almost is tough," Mike said. The wildness in his eyes was gone, replaced by that deep veil of weariness. He turned to the other frame on the same wall.

"Go ahead," Domenic said. "Take a look."

Mike rose and walked behind the couch to the framed collage of ticket stubs and yellowed newspaper clippings that shared the wall with the photograph of Angela Gallo. "World Series," he said, craning his neck to make out the items in the patchwork of keepsakes. "Must be worth something."

"Nah," Domenic said. He ate another cracker as Mike leaned closer to the frame.

"Never got used."

"Turn on the light," Domenic said, gesturing to the floor lamp, but Mike did not move his eyes from the collage.

"Sixty-four," Mike said, nodding. He turned on the lamp and stepped back, bumping into the table, unmooring several candles. "Whoops," he said, turning back to Domenic.

"Never seen candles before?"

"Nine?" Mike noted, realigning the blue votive candleholders. "Nineteen sixty-four," he said. "I get it. I mean, I grew up here. I was fourteen."

"Almost a year after Kennedy was killed. Watching the Phillies lose the way they did."

"Like part of the same curse," Mike said.

"People would think you're crazy, saying that, anywhere else in the country." Mike's face had brightened. For the first time, it felt like they were speaking the same language. Domenic watched him work his way around the newspaper and Phillies Yearbook clippings, ticket stubs and baseball cards.

"Johnny Callison's ninth inning home run in the All-Star Game," Mike said, nodding at the display. "Jim Bunning's no-hitter. I remember that."

"Father's Day," Domenic said.

"You picked a hell of a year to memorialize." Mike walked back to the couch.

Domenic refilled their glasses then took a sip from his.

"Even when they looked like a lock that summer," Mike said, "my brother never had any faith. When they started losing, he cursed them to death. 'Never won it, and they never will. F-ing Phillies.' I must have heard him say that a thousand times that year." Mike picked up his glass and returned to the Phillies memorabilia. "You got everything in this collage but a picture of Gene Mauch."

"It's in there."

"Damn," Mike said, his finger on a corner of the collage. "They were fated."

"September 21, 1964," Domenic intoned. "Twelve games left and the Phils are six and a half games up. Two out in the sixth. Scoreless game. The Reds' best hitter is up at bat and you're at third base. Would you steal home?"

Turning toward Domenic, Mike shook his head. He returned to the couch and bit off a piece of cracker.

"You're the Red on third," Domenic said. "Understand, your team is still in the race, but you're way behind, and you're at the ballpark of the team that's been pulling away for a month now."

Mike sipped his drink and studied Domenic.

"You're a rookie," Domenic said, narrowing his eyes. "With a veteran heavy hitter at bat."

"Robinson?"

"Frank Robinson," Domenic said, nodding. "You do not have a steal sign from your third base coach, and your manager will rip the uniform off your worthless body if you try to steal home and get tagged out. What do you do?"

Mike shook his head, frowning. Dominic couldn't tell if he remembered how bad that year was or if he was humoring him.

"The Phillies don't expect you to run home any more than the

Trojans expected soldiers and death to come out of that damned wooden horse. You wait until Mahaffey's at the top of his wind-up. Sure, you've been inching down the line, but now you're gone. Bam. Mahaffey notices a blur on the third base line, and instead of concentrating on Robinson, now he's thinking about you. The ball sails away from the catcher, and you score. There it is. One-zip."

Domenic topped off the other glass. "It doesn't make any baseball sense. No kind of sense. Makes about as much sense as cancer. But it's all over on that play."

"You said it was the sixth inning."

"Doesn't matter. It's over. Not just this game. You know what happened next."

Mike nodded.

"Eleven games left," Domenic sighed. "And they lose the next nine. The whole baseball world sees it happening to them. A fourteen-year-old kid like you sees it happening. But nobody can stop it once it starts."

"The guy who stole home?"

"Chico Ruiz."

"Sort of rings a bell."

"If he doesn't steal home, everything's different. They maybe win that one. They certainly win *something* during those two weeks. They win the pennant. Everything's different. But that's yesterday's sin."

Mike seemed to consider Domenic's statement for a moment then cast his eyes around the room again. Domenic watched him drink his wine. The building vibrated as a trolley lumbered up the avenue toward Chestnut Hill.

"Good place to watch the games," Mike said, nodding toward the TV directly across the room from him.

"I don't," Domenic said. "Anyway, the tube busted months ago. So there it sits. I don't miss it."

"I couldn't tell you who's on the team now," Mike said. "Not a fan."

"Fan?" Domenic said, making a face. "It's a cheap word."

Mike took another sip of wine. "Are those ticket stubs up there yours?"

"Got that stuff later, at yard sales, junk stores. Dead fans."

Domenic became aware of an ambulance siren approaching from the south. Just as he figured it must be at Mount Pleasant Avenue, the sound leveled off and began to fade away. *Why am I talking about 1964 with this guy?* He glanced at his left wrist, not yet used to the fact that the guys who mugged him had taken his watch. He knew it was well after one in the morning. "You got a job, and so do I. We better get our beauty sleep, although it don't seem to be doing much good in my case."

"I'll take these things back to the kitchen," Mike said. After downing the last of his wine, he reached for Domenic's empty glass and the bottle.

"Listen," Domenic said. "This is no more than a drink of wine, a way to get ready for sleep. I'm going to give you a haircut. Hear?"

"Haircut?"

Domenic grimaced. "You need one, and it's what I do."

"You're still working?"

"I work at Al's downstairs. Nearly ten years." Domenic pointed to his eye. "I see everybody. Heads I cut and heads I don't cut. You're going to get a haircut on me."

"Okay."

"*Bene.*"

"Do you want me to call and set it up?"

"You must be going downtown for haircuts," Domenic said. "It's a barbershop. You don't need an appointment."

"As a matter of fact, I had a friend who'd been trimming it for me.

That might not happen anymore." Carrying the glasses and bottle, Mike started down the hallway, and Domenic slowly followed him.

When Domenic reached the kitchen, Mike was down on one knee with the cabinet door open, returning the bottle of port. Domenic saw the two glasses in the sink. He had already run some water in them.

"I can lock the door downstairs myself," Mike said, standing up at the sink. "Right?"

"They're both dead bolts," Domenic said, following him to the upstairs door. "I'll get the one up here. Don't worry about double locking the one down there."

"Good night, Domenic." He offered his hand and they shook.

Standing in the open doorway, Domenic watched him tread down the stairs, open the lower door, and wave back.

"Good night, Mike." Domenic closed the door and threw the double bolt on his lock. He hobbled back into the living room and found the box of matches in the top drawer of the nightstand. Yesterday he'd begun again, so two tonight. He bent over and lit the two candles on the far left. Back in his chair, he rested his feet on the ottoman. He looked up at Angela's face. The slight flickering of the candles made her expression change so that she almost looked like she was talking. "*Basta*," he said. Enough. "Sleep," he said, closing his eyes.

5

MONDAY, JANUARY 23

Is this still Monday? Tinkering on the seminary's old snow blower after work had made it into a long day, then tending to the old man turned it into a marathon. Mike had wronged the poor dog Friday night, and here, three days later, he was returning late at night. The weight of exhaustion finally registered as he squeezed past the jubilant dog in the warm foyer. He grabbed Robert's leash and clipped it to the eager boy's collar. Peripherally, he took in the two blinks on the answering machine. This was becoming too much of a pattern. The messages could wait. He owed Robert.

"You are the only creature I would do a damn thing for right now."

Shivering again, Mike trudged up the hill behind the dog. He had not opened the basement door since Friday night. Had done little more in the kitchen than make sandwiches. Had gone to his job, but even there he avoided all unnecessary conversations. After Robert pooped at the edge of the overgrown wooded lot, Mike bagged the dog's droppings then let him off the leash. At dinnertime, he had walked him up the avenue almost to the seminary, past Al's Barbershop. Maybe the old guy had been up there, getting ready to take SEPTA all the way to West Philly for his bingo and subsequent beating. Shaking in the cold, he watched Robert lift his leg on a mound of leaves in the shadows of the Acme parking lot lights up on the ridge. From where Mike stood, the mound looked like a person, lying supine on the ground. Rock Templeton's bachelor party, he thought.

That summer. He had driven to the party by himself, passing up Brendan's offer of a lift, knowing that Brendan, as best man and self-proclaimed president of the Maxwell House Club, would be "good to the last drop."

After reviving the passed-out Templeton, Mike had left his brother in the hands of friends who would make sure he did no more horrors to the groom. *Adrift* was the word that stayed with Mike that weekend. He needed to get away, to try something different in a new place. An adventure. Brendan was getting married that summer too. He would wait until then.

But where to go? He scoured maps of surrounding states. Town names in upstate New York evoked benign scary tales he'd read sometime in school. Placing a hundred miles or so between him and everything he knew sounded just about right. He put his finger on the map. New Paltz.

The week after the wedding, he loaded his tools into his Chevelle and drove north.

He couldn't put a name on whatever Sarah and he had shared. It was nothing like what he'd had with Laurie.

Carrying a paperback novel, the ponytailed young woman walked into the New Paltz church basement while Mike was filling out a donation form for the blood drive. Jet-black hair and those blue eyes. Where had he seen her before? After she deposited her completed form on top of his on the stack at the table, she settled into a chair in the waiting area and opened her book. The laundromat. Early one Sunday morning when he'd been doing his wash down the street.

Finally, a stout, gum-chewing nurse called his name then walked him to another card table where she checked his blood pressure and got a tiny sample of blood from his earlobe. Without looking up from the form Mike had filled out, she asked him the same questions he'd just answered and walked him back to the waiting area. A minute later, she returned and summoned the young woman.

Across the hall, a starchy, stern-faced nurse moved among six donors, each lying on a table. Mike scanned the crowd of donors reading around him. He had allowed an hour for this good deed.

The ponytailed young woman returned to the waiting area from her interview with the gum-popping nurse and took a seat two places away.

"Don't worry," she said to Mike. "They don't make you answer the same questions again. Twice is enough."

They laughed, and he felt his face redden. Their gazes held, her blue eyes sparkling. Several nearby readers looked up at them.

"Laurie Harris," she whispered.

"Mike Flannagan."

An hour later, on his back on one of the tables, he heard her voice as she took her place on a table at a right angle to his, and he studied her sneakers, taking in every little nuance. When the needle was extracted from his arm, an elderly volunteer escorted him to the snack area. A few minutes later, the same volunteer brought Laurie over and sat with her while she drank. After the volunteer left, the nurse who'd taken their blood marched past. Mike leaned toward Laurie. "I think she's more into blood than people."

When they stopped laughing, they continued to hold aloft their bandaged arms and smiled, neither of them looking away.

"Some people are more cut out for this kind of work than others," she said.

He offered her an opened box of sugar donuts from the snack tray.

"You could walk in here tomorrow," she said, looking right into his eyes, "and do a better job than that one."

He smiled. He had experienced brief moments when he and a woman had clicked on the same wavelength, when nonverbal communication spoke volumes more than words, but it had never happened instantaneously. He did not worry about this connection lasting. It just existed, like the color blue or the pretty, smiling woman sitting beside him.

They ended up at the Yankee Lady, sitting on the deck out back, nursing iced teas so they wouldn't have to leave. He never felt disconnected from her after that day. With one exception, each of them was always willing to do what the other wanted. Their only tension came from external sources.

Freezing wind now smacked Mike's uncovered face, bringing him back from his musing. This one ended the way it always did, the sweetness flooded out of his psyche by the sudden realization he'd come to and that the only real thing was his being alone. Standing several feet inside the woodsy area where Robert, his New Paltz dog, had disappeared, he clapped his gloved hand against his thigh. Suddenly, he heard the jingly sound of Robert's tags off in the distance. The dog trotted up to him, breathing out clouds in the bitter cold, wagging his tail. Laurie's puppy. "Thank you, Robert."

Naming both him and the baby had been Laurie's doing. The baby came at thirty-four weeks, a wee five-pounder destined to stay in the hospital for two weeks. After all Laurie had been through with the pregnancy-induced hypertension and the rushed delivery, Mike told her she could name him anything she wanted. To his surprise, she said, "It has to be Michael." Then with Mike doing carpentry work all around New Paltz and Laurie home with the baby, they decided that they wanted a big dog for security. She picked the quiet but alert one out of the litter. "He looks like a Robert," she said.

A gust of wind smacked his face. "Jesus," he muttered, cursing the cold and his missing her. He clipped the leash onto Robert's collar, then they headed for the house at a quick clip.

Inside, he secured the door. He returned the leash to its place and checked the answering machine. Two calls. He listened to Brendan ask him to call when he got home from work. *Tuesday morning will be soon enough.*

The second message played. "Mike, Brendan again. It's nine o'clock Monday night. Just call when you get in. I'll be up."

Mike smirked at the thought that Brendan would give anybody a green light to disturb his family around midnight. But it was hours past that now. Not even Brendan would encourage a call at this time. Mike switched off the kitchen light. Robert had already curled into his bed beside the living room couch. Mike walked over and patted him. Laurie had banned the dog from the bed, but half the time Robert followed him up to the queen-size bed. Tonight, the dog gave no inclination that he was capable of moving an inch. "Same here," he said to Robert.

The telephone's ring jolted Mike awake.

"It's me," his brother said. "Delores is in the hospital. Roxborough. Saturday, she was playing with the kids in the yard and had some kind of seizure. We called 911."

"Slow down," Mike said. It hurt to turn on the juices again, but he felt himself coming to.

"They don't know what's going on. She's in critical condition. Not conscious, not yet."

"What happened?"

"She started convulsing by the sandbox," Brendan blurted out. "They had to strap her down in the ER. They don't know what the fuck it is."

"She's been out since the seizure?"

"She said a few words to the paramedics in the rescue wagon. Nothing since. They gave her something to stop the convulsions, but she still doesn't respond. They're clueless."

Mike paced as far into the dining room as the phone cord allowed then pivoted back toward the kitchen. "Never had any kind of seizure before?"

"No."

"How are the kids?"

"Her sister Lucy's been helping. She and her kids are here again. In case I got to run to the hospital. Man, this is fucked up."

Mike had seen his brother in an agitated state when their parents died, but this was different. Brendan sounded like another person.

"They want me to believe she's going to make it," Brendan said. "She's stabilized some. She's not thrashing around like Saturday."

"Jesus, Brendan." Mike had paced back into the dining room.

"It's been fucked up. Her vital signs are better. They weren't saying shit to me Saturday." Brendan let out a loud breath.

"What can I do?" Mike said.

"I don't know. Lucy's been great, but I might need a hand with the kids."

Mike heard something from the front of the house, then Robert stirred. Mike stopped pacing.

"I didn't go to work today," Brendan said. "I may try to put in a few hours tomorrow."

He heard the noise again. Robert barked twice and ran to the foyer. "Hold on a sec, Brendan. I got to check the porch." He put the telephone down and hustled to the front. Flicking on the porch light, he saw Sarah through the front window. She looked like hell. The dog sniffed the front door while Mike fumbled at the dead bolt lock. Robert wagged his tail. "Fuck," Mike muttered.

6

MONDAY, JANUARY 23

Sarah had assumed that words would come to her if Mike opened the front door. When he did, she looked down at the welcome mat and at Robert, whose tail wagged slowly back and forth.

"Come in," Mike said. Taking her by the arm, he led her to the living room couch. When she sat down, he held his hand up to his ear like a phone. "Hold on," he said, heading toward the kitchen.

A call? At this hour? *How little I know this man.*

Robert pushed his head next to her knee. Patting him, she saw contentment in his big brown eyes. When Sarah stopped, he waited to see if she was really done before settling on the floor beside her. Back in the kitchen, Mike was talking on the phone. Only a word here and there came through, but he sounded like he was trying to reassure someone.

Leaning forward, she wrapped her arms around her knees. She closed her eyes, swayed forward, back. Mike's voice rose for a moment, then there was quiet, then more muted talking. When she'd been seeing Russell, she never would have thought to approach him like this. Even during the year of their marriage—two disappointing semesters of her life—she'd never found herself wanting to lean on him. Arriving like this, so soon after Friday, couldn't be what Mike had in mind for a new normal, but there was no one else. Was she willing him to still be the person she trusted? Breathing in through her nose and out through her mouth, she rocked slowly back and forth, trying to block out the talking. She counted slowly to five with each breath, matching her breathing to her motion. She tried to think of nothing other than her breathing but saw the bastard with the bad haircut, the dean, her so-called friend. She focused again on nothingness, until that frightening face hove into view. *Back to nothingness.* She rocked forward. Bastard.

"Sarah."

Opening her eyes, she swiped at her tears with the back of her hand. She had no idea how long she'd been crying.

Mike stood in front of the couch. "Not a real good time," he said.

"It's ridiculously late."

"No," he said. "Not that."

"I know. I wanted to give you time to yourself."

"No. Go ahead." He slouched on the other end of the couch. The living room equivalent of the classroom back row, she thought.

"Something happened at school today," she began, trusting that words would come to her the way they did when she taught a familiar text. "A brawl. I tried to break up a fight among students."

Mike leaned back on the couch and sighed. "Jesus," he mumbled. His eyes were heavy.

"I shouldn't be doing this," she said.

"Go on."

He looked like he meant it. She recounted the entire incident and her encounters with the dean and the friend, whom she did not name, realizing at the story's end that she had not been looking at him. She cleared her throat, looked back at Mike. He and Robert both had their eyes fixed on her, but Mike looked like she had woken him from a sound sleep. "It was like a battlefield," she said. "I guess I shouldn't have done that. Was I wrong?"

"Breaking up a fight?"

"Grabbing people. Throwing them around."

"How are you the bad guy?" he said, sighing.

"I've never done anything violent in my life."

"You stopped the violence," he said. "A lot of people would have done nothing."

"But I *threw* that guy."

"Worried you're going to kick everybody's ass now that you've started?" He gave her a wan smile.

"I guess the whole thing scares me."

"Could you use a glass of water?" Mike asked.

She nodded.

When Mike went to the kitchen, she patted the dog again. He and Mike were so alike. Mike's more communicative brother, she'd called him. She loved the dog's steadiness and the sincerity in his brown eyes. Mike without the baggage.

Mike reappeared with a tumbler of water.

"Thanks," she said. She took a long drink, placed the glass on the coffee table, and sank back on the couch. "I'm afraid to go back in there."

Mike sat beside her.

"In the parking garage, I saw one of those guys. Why was he there if he wasn't looking for me?"

"Sure it was the guy?"

"Yes," she said. "I'd seen him with Security in the hallway after the incident. How many guys do you see with a pompadour haircut out of the fifties? He saw where I parked, what kind of car I drive."

"But they know about this at the college."

She shook her head. She was sure she was going to lose it but felt herself getting on top of the tears. "This whole day," she said, "except for when I just jumped into it all, I've been clueless and scared. I can usually manage. Now, I really am afraid to go in again." Why was she opening up to him like this? "I don't know what to say."

"This is a first," he mumbled. His eyes were locked on hers.

"I had to get this off my chest," she said.

"You're telling Security tomorrow," he said. "Is there a number you can call now?"

"Tomorrow morning." She pulled a tissue out of her jeans pocket and blew her nose. "You didn't need this," she said, "but you let me talk." When she finished her water, she stood up and walked to the kitchen. After putting the glass in the sink, she returned. Mike was leaning forward on the couch, his head buried in his hands. The dog's head rested on his foot. Mike looked up. His forehead was wrinkled, his mouth turned down in a frown, making the sharp lines of his face seem even stronger. Had he just dropped off to sleep while she'd been gone?

"I didn't even ask how you are," she said, sitting in the middle of the couch. "I know I look like something the cat dragged in, but it's late for you too."

"You mean it's my turn?"

He wasn't being sarcastic. He sounded dazed. "You're upset about something bad," she said, "on the phone."

He leaned back on the sofa, letting out a long groan that could have meant "Not really" or "I'm too tired to explain" or "I'm already asleep." He scratched his head, looking off with a pained expression. "They have my brother's wife in the hospital," he drawled. "Seizures out of nowhere. Nobody knows much." He sighed and looked at her with his "That's all I got" expression.

"Horrible," she said. "You just learned about it?" From the little he'd said, she knew that his brother's name was Brendan and that he and his wife had two children, but he'd never suggested that she meet them.

He nodded.

"I'm so sorry you all have to go through this," she said.

"Appreciate it." He looked at his watch and winced. Turning to her, he said, "Sarah," looking like he was ready to make another effort to stay awake. "You need to sleep if you have to teach in the morning." He pulled himself up from the couch.

You're projecting. She held her tongue. Spare him playing the professor, even though three nights ago he wasn't so kind. She stood up and faced him. "Teaching I can handle," she said. She found her keys in her pocket and played with them.

"I know."

His careworn expression changed to a look of high alert. "I'll pick you up and drive you in," he said curtly. "Walk you to your office. I don't have to go in early tomorrow."

She shook her head. "I'll do what I have to do."

"No," he said slowly, as if he was working out something in his exhausted head.

"Thank you so much, Mike. I promise I will tell you the instant you can be of help. You have no idea how much I appreciate it. Especially tonight."

His distraught face reminded her of a child struggling to find the words to explain himself. "Please let me drive you in," he said.

You silly dope. She stopped herself from saying it. Saying one more word of any sort seemed wrong and unnecessary. *Just live in this moment of trust and closeness, tantalizingly familiar yet never a regular part of our relationship.* She stepped forward and pressed herself against him, resting her head against his chest. His arms wrapped around her and they hugged. Robert stretched out on the floor, groaning. "Thank you," she said.

Mike squeezed her. She felt the back of his neck and pulled herself closer. His hands dropped to the back of her waist. She turned her face toward his and they kissed.

He stopped for a moment then bent down to her mouth again.

Sarah pulled back. "I don't want you to go in with me tomorrow," she said. "But can I stay tonight?"

"Here we go," he said, sighing loudly. It struck her as the funniest thing she'd heard from him.

Neither giggling nor kissing had seemed remotely possible when she'd driven here. She kept her eyes closed but his voice said he was smiling too.

We. They'd practically broken up, but in one sentence he'd made her feel like they were together in something, although she couldn't say what. "I don't have to stay," she said. His fingers combed through her hair. She held his head in front of her and planted little kisses all over his face. She felt his arms around her waist, his legs against hers. She stopped kissing and met his gaze. "This is not why I came," she said.

He shook his head. "Not why I opened the door."

When she closed her eyes, he kissed her. His fingers kneaded the muscles of her shoulders, and she felt her whole body loosen. He gently raked his fingers down her back. He kissed her on her neck, her cheeks, then on her mouth again, her mouth opening to his, and she held herself tightly to him. Losing her balance, she felt him lean back, pulling away. He pulled his arms from her and stood back. Holding up one finger in front of her, he turned and walked to the foyer, switched off the porch light, and went to the rear of the house. The kitchen went dark. Then the dining room. Robert slumped beside the couch, forming a black and tan oval. When Mike switched off the living room lights, she started up the stairs and he followed.

They shed their clothes, entering Mike's bedroom, then she did an about-face. In the bathroom, she found her diaphragm in its case on the top shelf of his medicine chest. When she returned, he was sitting up, under the covers. He switched off the table lamp.

Shivering, she climbed under the covers and clung to Mike. She kissed him, and he returned her kisses, his hands moving down her sides. She wrapped her legs around his, and they rolled over to his side of the bed. After she had kissed him all over his face and neck, she felt him ease her over onto her back. Traveling the length and breadth of his body, she no longer felt the room's chill. She interrupted their wordless rolling and clutching to tell him that she wanted to be on top. They rocked together, on and on, and when she finally fell off to her side, panting from exhaustion, she heard his winded breaths matching hers.

She felt him against her side. He let out a long breath and rested his hand on her thigh. She lay there, listening to their breathing become easier and slower. When she lay her hand on his leg, he squeezed her thigh.

Crawling over him, she found his alarm clock. The ambient light proved enough for her to set the alarm. Rolling back, she kissed his cheek. In five minutes, she knew from his breathing that he was asleep. She did not get up to go to the bathroom or to brush her teeth but lay there beside his warm body. Wide awake now, her eyes roved across the room, just able to make out the lines of his tall dresser, the shorter one with the mirror on top, the straight chair by the window. He sighed in his sleep and rolled over onto his side.

The way he had been waiting for her in bed when she came in from the bathroom made her think of the night during Christmas week when they brought in the VCR from the living room and watched rented movies in bed. She wanted each of them to select an all-time favorite film that would be new to the other person, but he could think of nothing she had not seen and insisted she do the selecting. He would take care of the food. They had taken off in their cars, going in different directions. Propped up in bed that night, they ate Dalessandro's cheesesteaks and half of a cream-iced chocolate cake from the Night Kitchen in Chestnut Hill, watching *A Night at the Opera* and *Casablanca*. She loved hearing him laugh at Harpo, and when *Casablanca* ended and he had not said anything since the opening credits, she had asked him what he thought.

"Can't believe I never saw it," he said.

"You liked it?"

"Of course," he said. "Even if I don't quite get how those letters of transit worked."

He laughed when she recreated scenes from the movie, doing her best Bogart and Peter Lorre impersonations. She talked about how each minor character added something, about how perfect the music was, about the fact that it was both a great movie and a fine film.

"I'm sorry," she said. "I'm lecturing."

He laughed. "It's worth lecturing about."

She had put the leftovers in the refrigerator and come back to the bedroom, finding Mike sitting up like that, looking like he was ready for another double feature. They had lain in bed, looking at the photographs in her coffee table book of Italy. "You can't find colors like that," she declared, "except in Tuscany."

"Beautiful."

"I could live there just for the colors."

"I thought it was just for the food," he said. "Or was it the hills? Or the people?"

"Am I gushing?" she said.

He scrunched up his face.

"Not the best word," she said. "Rhapsodizing?"

"Not my field," he said.

She'd left her book on the floor beside his bed. Two weeks later, when she noticed it in the same place, she asked if he wanted to keep it any longer. She took his shrug as indication that it was time to bring the book back to her apartment. He'd let down his guard that night too, but now she was too tired to sort out that or anything else.

She looked at the clock and winced when she saw how late it was. She closed her eyes and rolled over. Six-thirty would arrive sooner than she wanted it to. She listened to Mike's breathing, matched it, felt herself drifting off.

7

TUESDAY, JANUARY 24

Lying in bed beside Sarah's sleeping form, Mike stared at the corner of the room where the light from the street lamps came in through the blinds. He raised himself up on his elbow enough to peer over Sarah at the clock: three-thirty. He fell back onto his pillow and looked at the ceiling. Sarah moaned, whimpered in her sleep, and that was no wonder. A true friend would have gotten her to her apartment. *I am not as good as you think I am.*

When her leg twitched and bumped his, he moved away. The conversation in the living room was a blur, more dreamlike to him than real. Then they had sex? He knew he wasn't making that up. She was the only person he'd gone out with since returning from New Paltz, and that was because she had approached him. He'd heard from enough people that he should consider dating, and there she was. He'd gone for coffee with no expectations, but before he knew it, she'd gotten him to both slow down his humdrum activities and to feel excited. Asking him once if he was happy with the sex had taken him aback. "As far as that's concerned, I feel like I hit the lottery," he blurted out, as surprised by his own frankness as he'd been by her directness. "Everything else vanishes," he told her. "I can't see myself doing that with anyone else." If it were only about sex, he'd do whatever he needed to do to hold onto Sarah. But weren't they too old for it to be mostly about rolling and tumbling?

Sarah moved in her sleep, turning toward him, her head and shoulder coming to rest on his upper arm. He felt pressure rising from his stomach, turned his head to the side, and opened his mouth. The low growl that rumbled out brought with it a sour taste of wine.

Was what she felt for Mike along the lines of Laurie's love for him? His feelings for Sarah were not what he felt for Laurie, so could he even call it love? He mouthed "Laurie." Sarah had been right when she said that she couldn't compete with a dead wife and child. She was always right. She deserved better. Now they were in bed together. So much for slowing things down a bit. What the hell was she going to think when she woke up? Probably that they needed to do more talking. Didn't they need to do some sorting first?

Mike slipped out of bed and dressed in the dark. In the bathroom, he brushed his teeth quietly, avoiding the face in the mirror. He was a bastard for bringing her to bed. Now he was a coward, making a getaway. Robert stirred when Mike tiptoed downstairs, raising his head and yawning. "Back to sleep," Mike whispered. He put on his winter coat and woolen cap and closed the front door quietly behind him.

At the all-night gas station off Lincoln Drive, he filled the tank. Wide awake with nowhere to go, he took dark comfort from at least having a full tank of gas. Inside the building, he paid for the gas and bought orange juice and a soft pretzel. Back in the car, he stopped at the lot's edge, letting the engine run. He gazed into the darkness, his eyes adjusting enough to make out a few trees in the park across the road. Biting into the pretzel, he immediately realized it was a day old, then washed down the stale taste with juice and tossed the pretzel onto the seat beside him.

This shame was better than the dread that had weighed him down in bed as he looked at Sarah sleeping, but he felt like he was bolting from an unfinished task. He hoped she would let him take whatever next step they should take, but not now. Putting the car in drive, he eased around the park and turned back onto Lincoln Drive. *Faster.* At the river end of the drive, he crossed the Schuylkill and turned onto the expressway, the taillights of a tractor trailer the only thing he could see ahead of him.

He took it up to seventy and looked in the rearview mirror. Empty lanes on the Schuylkill Expressway: a night full of rare occurrences. When he thought he heard a clicking sound from the engine, he glanced at the instrument panel. No warning lights. Listening hard again, he heard nothing. "Not nothing," Laurie, the auto mechanic's daughter, would say; "just not what you were expecting." Even when he tried to think about Sarah, there was Laurie. She heard differently than he did. Growing up beside her father's garage, she knew engines. Mike quickly recognized her skill, but what impressed him was how she went out of her way to avoid trampling his ego. "You got to respect cars," she told him, with a twinkle in her eyes. "They're bigger than you." His little family, he realized, was the only thing he considered like that—bigger than he was. And she was the reason it existed.

A car and a delivery truck whooshed by on the expressway's westbound side. He felt as if he were halfway across the country on some desolate stretch of highway. The pressure in his gut returned. He popped a handful of Tums into his mouth and chewed.

When he reached Center City, he circled City Hall and drove back up the Ben Franklin Parkway past the apartment house where Sarah's friends lived. *Hello, dahlings.* They'd not shown him anything to make him think they deserved to be her friends either. At the end of the parkway, he rounded the art museum and drove to the topmost parking area near the long steps Rocky had run up in the movie and thought: what a perfect place to watch the sun come up. One July evening here, he and Sarah had looked east at City Hall tower's statue of William Penn. Crossing to the other side of the museum, high above the storm-muddied Schuylkill, the dilapidated Waterworks, and the gingerbread houses of Boathouse Row, they faced west and watched the sky turn sunset colors. Monet colors, she had called them.

At all other hours, the city's noises blared and blurred, but now he heard individual vehicles in the distance. The streetlamps in the parking area and on the parkway below him cast dim pools of light in the gloom. Squinting into the rearview mirror, he saw no movement. But he could not be sure. Anyone out here at this time was up to no good. In the country around New Paltz, he and Laurie were more likely to run into a bear than a mugger. Perhaps that had changed since his return to Philadelphia. He turned the car around and eased it onto Kelly Drive, retracing Friday night's drive home. The black sky across the river was turning purple. When he reached Lincoln Drive, he took a last glance to the east and saw pinks and blues in the distance.

Back in the neighborhood, he drove onto his block. At the bottom of the street, a man he didn't know walked downhill, perhaps headed toward the train station. Sarah's Tercel remained parked across the street from his house. Did Robert recognize the sound of his car slowly making its way up the hill? Did Sarah? He felt his face redden. He'd snuck past her twice in the same night. *Fuck me.*

Then he was on the avenue. No house lights interrupted the line of dark buildings, including the apartment above the barbershop. Bins overflowing with empty bottles sat on Gilhooley's curb. He drove past the Wawa, its lot nearly filled with pickup trucks and cars: people of the early morning, getting their coffee and newspaper. He turned onto Sarah's street. One, two, three apartments showed lights. Soon her neighbors would be dressing and pulling together lunches for the day. They would stream off to the train station or into their cars.

When he approached Holy Cross, site of his baptism, first Communion, and confession, he swore he heard the clicking noise again. Pulling over across from the church, he put the car in park but again heard nothing out of order. He glared at the tall stone building. He and his brother had been confirmed there two years apart. He'd watched pallbearers lift his father's casket up those stone steps. Then his mother's. He'd been there for the funeral of a guy from high school who'd been killed in Vietnam.

Stained glass, cold stone walls, and hard wooden pews. He remembered the spooky Gothic beauty inside, perpetually dim lighting adding to the stone interior's austerity. As an altar boy, he and the other server had marched up the aisle behind the priest and stepped up to the altar. Standing under the nave, he had noticed the flickering sanctuary light high above the altar: God's "Open" sign, according to the nuns. *Nave.* The word was too close to *naïve.* He couldn't have been the first person to see the joke.

Laurie never doubted, though. So her college chaplain from Canisius came down to Syracuse to do the wedding. Everybody but Mike received Communion. Her family and friends filled the place.

Laurie seemed at ease in churches. As he had promised, Mike accompanied her and little Michael to Mass every week. Her parish in New Paltz looked nothing like Holy Cross, but he was anxious to leave as soon as he entered the place. He looked hard at the tall red wooden doors across the street. As an altar boy, he had known the church's every dark corner. He thought about the imposing line of statues that looked down on those in attendance. The apostles. Strong men, the nuns had called them. *The vestments room.* He could have used the help of a strong man when Father Malloy reached under the back of his shorts. By eighth grade, he hadn't yet filled out, but he used his strength to pull away from the priest and run out those doors, never speaking about it to anyone.

A monster holding such a position made no sense at the time. His brother and half of the baseball team had gone for weekends down the shore with the coach, a Father Ross. The man had tutored the weak ones in math, helped some of them get into college, eventually presided at all of their weddings. No other priest Mike had known before or after had been like Malloy. Mike quit the altar boys that day, told his parents he was too old for all that.

Arriving home from school one day, he found his mother passed out beside a bottle of whiskey in the basement. Kennedy was killed around that time. He never was positive about the sequence of those events, but that year he stopped believing people simply because they had said something.

"*Father,*" he muttered, turning away from the huge doors. The engine was still running. Nothing on the dashboard suggested anything wrong, but he realized that he hadn't heard anymore of the funny noises from the engine. He turned the engine off. When news about abuse in the Church started coming out, he never checked to see if Malloy's name came up. He cursed Malloy for that day and for all the days he spent avoiding being alone with him. He hoped the evil man was dead. After a minute, he started the car again.

He pulled out of the parking spot and headed to Devon Street, where he and Brendan had grown up. He inched the car toward their old home, laid out like his row house on Sedgwick but even smaller. Old paint flaked off the empty porch's flooring, railings, and posts. His father had always kept the two iron chairs on the porch through the winter. Brendan and Delores probably had no room or use for them when Mom died. Whoever owned the place now still had their Christmas lights on. Keeping lights this far into the year would not have bothered his father, but leaving them on all night would have struck him as wasteful. Mike and Brendan always had the job of putting up and taking down the porch Christmas lights. It was one of their few joint projects that did not end in chaos and a sore jaw for Mike. Brendan loved Christmas and lights even more than he loved beating on Mike, despite their mother's erratic efforts to preserve the peace.

When Laurie suggested making Brendan their son's godfather, Mike went along with the idea. It made his mother happier than he'd ever seen her. The next winter, he invited Brendan up and they went ice fishing on a nearby lake. Bundled up in lawn chairs, they smoked cigars, drank Genny Cream Ale, and watched skywriting jets silently crisscross the blue sky. The adventurous move to New York state and the distance from his brother seemed to have given their relationship the normalcy and warmth they'd never had.

That next summer, Mike had found himself more patient with his work, his family, and the neighbors, a description of himself that no one, himself included, would offer now. Things that used to bother him didn't make a big difference, a change that he chalked up to Laurie. She got him to start doing little things for the old people across the road. Since she was still nursing little Michael and couldn't donate blood, she made sure he thought about doing it himself. Every time shit came along, the woman knew what to do about it and when.

When Mike returned to his own block, Sarah's car was gone. Off to face her demons. This time, he felt no momentary relief, only that hot flush reddening his face again. He'd said nothing about Malloy to anyone. The monster's name probably was on one of those lists. Sarah was in danger. He would not remain paralyzed this time.

He let Robert stretch his legs, walking him down neighboring streets on which they rarely ventured so he would be free of neighborly chitchat. Back on the block, he saw Mrs. Lamont sweeping her porch next door. When he let Robert off his leash, the dog ran up the steps ahead of him. The older Black woman had lived on the block since the sixties. As Mike climbed the steps, she bent over to pat Robert. She was wearing a black satin jacket advertising a long-closed downtown rock club where her youngest son had worked as a bouncer.

"Go ahead and tell me, like everybody else does," she said as Mike reached her. "It's too cold to be out sweeping. Right?"

The ruffling curtain in her living room window caught Mike's eye, then it went still: Mr. Lamont. The old woman leaned on her broom, smiling at Mike.

Robert sat beside her, looking up at Mike from the other side of the railing that divided the two porches. They looked to Mike as if they were waiting for him to say something. Finally, Robert barked. "At least I keep regular hours," Mrs. Lamont said, raising her eyebrows. "Still eating Tums for breakfast?"

Mike nodded.

"Not even here to know about all the comings and goings," she said, glancing out to where Sarah's car had been parked.

He felt embarrassed again and hoped it wasn't obvious.

She pulled the zipper on her jacket all the way up. "Hard to stay healthy with so many things going on," she said, turning with her broom. Robert joined Mike on his porch. "All hours of the day and night," she sighed. She pushed her broom across a clean section of her porch, facing away from Mike.

"We all have to watch our health," Mike said. "Say hi to Mr. Lamont." He opened the door and let the dog trot in ahead of him.

It was high time to get his own broom and clean up the mess in the basement, but he couldn't face the idea. He began straightening out the back shed instead. By the time he made it into the kitchen, he realized that Sarah already would be on campus by now. Fuck. How had he not put this together while he was driving around? He'd be ready by the time she went back to the parking garage to head home.

At eleven, the telephone rang. He turned off the vacuum cleaner and headed to the phone in the kitchen. "Yes."

"Yo," his brother said. "She moved her eyes, following a nurse across the room."

Delores.

"That's got to be good, huh?"

"Yeah," Mike said. "What happened?"

"I didn't see it, but Lucy was sure she saw her eyes move."

"Once?" *Get to the point.*

"Yeah, but Lucy's not imagining things."

"What room is she in?"

"Two seventeen-B. The bad news is they found some plastic in her vomit. Sunday, that was. I forgot to mention it last night."

"Plastic?" Mike reached for the notepad on the table and scribbled the room number.

"They've been asking a lot of questions about drug use."

"Delores?"

"I went ballistic. Some shit about maybe cocaine. Doctor's fucking talking about my wife, man!" Brendan let out a dark laugh. "That's when I just about dropped him. Of course they didn't find any coke in her system. They did find traces of pot. Now that surprised me."

The shoe was on the other foot, Mike thought. What she didn't know about her husband could fill a book.

"Get this," Brendan said. "Plastic is what they find when someone is body packing cocaine. The guy looks at me like Delores was transporting the shit across zip code lines into Manayunk."

"They must have run all kinds of tests on her," Mike said, tracing the letters of her name below the room number.

"Pumped her stomach and did some kind of filtering."

"And?"

"Nothing besides this drug bullshit. I didn't know she smoked weed, Mike. What the fuck?" Brendan cleared his throat. He excused himself to get something to drink. "I swear," he said, returning. "I haven't seen her smoke that shit in years."

Mike heard him swallow. He hoped it was water. It was early, even for Brendan.

"Probably just a freak thing, Brendan. They don't think smoking a joint caused this?"

"Nah," Brendan said. "But I don't trust those bastards. I want her out of that place."

"Want me to be there when you talk with them again?"

"*I'll* talk to them."

"Your call," Mike said. He heard him drinking again.

Brendan told him that he had to get going. He would keep Mike posted. He hung up. Mike put away his cleaning supplies. From what he could tell, his brother hadn't gone all Brendan on anyone yet. That was about the only good news.

"Fuck," he growled. He felt the way he did whenever he was coming down with a cold or flu, sore all over with a low-grade headache. He showered, shaved, and changed into his work clothes. Downstairs, he filled a bowl with cereal and milk and ate half of it. Walking past the refrigerator, his eyes settled on the class schedule that Sarah had given him at the beginning of the semester. Tuesday was an early day for her. He poured the rest of the cereal down the drain, rinsed out the bowl, and left the spoon and bowl in the sink.

At work, he found the snowblower where he'd left it. The beast was fixable, but he lacked the patience to attack that job. His now full-blown headache, straight out of his younger, hard-drinking days, forced his every thought and movement to a crawl. He schlepped his toolbox to the old dorm's back door. He'd replaced dozens of lock fixtures in the seminary, but the lock parts on the door refused to line up right, and the screws proved slippery in his weary hands. The ten-minute job took an hour.

At noon, he told Mr. Lutz he'd run some errands on lunch but would return in time to see that enough chairs were moved into the auditorium for that evening's talk.

After picking up a tuna hoagie and a Pepsi at Fiesta, he drove by St. Brigid's. Kids in school uniforms swarmed all over the concrete schoolyard. Boys were playing touch football at the end of the play area. Clusters of girls in animated conversation dotted the perimeter. Neither group paid any attention to the other. He scanned the little crowds but could not pick out his niece or nephew.

Mike pulled over and parked outside the chain link fence. From inside the car, he heard the loud laughter and shouting of the football players. His head throbbed, so he cracked the window. The cold air stirred him, but he felt the headache more keenly. In the glove compartment he found a container of ibuprofen and washed down two tablets with Pepsi. He spotted Robbie running for a pass. He got open and waved his arms wildly, but the quarterback threw to another kid who dropped the ball. Robbie went back to the huddle. Mike scanned the clusters of girls and finally saw Jessie standing by the door, talking with another girl. Seeing them busy relieved him. *They're not thinking about their mom.*

He checked his watch and drove off. He drove through the college's parking garage until he found Sarah's car on the fourth level and backed into a spot at the top end of the level where he could see

her when she returned for her car but she wouldn't see him. Her last
class ended in fifteen minutes. He ate his hoagie while he waited and
scanned the garage, looking to his right and his left.

Ten minutes after Sarah's class ended, she walked up the ramp
toward her Tercel with her satchel in one hand and her car keys in the
other. She approached the car slowly, taking a sweeping turn around
the front to get to the driver's side door. She opened the door, closed
it behind her, screeched out of the parking space and down the ramp.
Level four, Mike reminded himself. After ten minutes, he drove out.

On the way back to work, he stopped at the hospital and rode
the elevator to the second floor. Name signs for two patients marked
nearly every room in the hallway, but he found only one posted outside Room 217. Flannagan. He stepped inside, taking in the IV lines,
monitor hookups, and respirator. Delores looked almost two-dimen-
sional, lying so still beneath the bedsheet. *Gravity*. Her hair, too, had
settled and lay in still strands upon the small pillow. Her face, while
immediately recognizable, struck him as false, imitative, alien. *You
don't fucking deserve this*. She lay there like a fallen limb on the forest
floor. Her breathing sounded like that of a sick person, a patient, not
Delores. They'd help her. She hadn't died, but that familiar hopeless-
ness numbed and halted him. He knew he should talk to her; he had
learned that in circumstances like this, one should assume that the
patient could hear. Talking could do her no harm. But he could only
stand mute before Delores Flannagan's flattened, wired body.

Driving home from the evening program, Mike focused on every
minute detail of operating the car, the way he remembered driving
after smoking weed in his twenties. He knew he'd put off sleep too
long. Sooner or later, you had to pay the piper. A little after eleven, he
eased the car into the open spot closest to his house, four doors down.

Using what felt like the last reservoir of his strength, he climbed the steps to his porch. Robert greeted him in the foyer and he winced, realizing that his endless day was not quite over.

Robert showed as much eagerness returning from his favorite watering spot as he had in getting there. "Yes, my friend," Mike said, taking off the leash so Robert could run up the steps to the porch. "I'll find something in the cupboard."

After dropping two biscuits in Robert's bowl, he staggered upstairs. A night without calls or visitors? He set the alarm, even though he had comp time in the morning for having worked the evening lecture. Still in his work clothes, he dropped onto his bed.

Wednesday morning, Mike's alarm got him up an hour and a half before Sarah's research paper class. This time he found a street with free parking three blocks from the campus garage. He climbed up the stairway to the fifth level and walked down the ramp to where she'd parked the day before. *But you might be smart enough to park on a different level. Please be that smart.* He walked to the 17th Street end of the level where she would enter and where the building's open sections afforded a view of the one-way traffic below. A pickup truck had parked in the end spot at the level's unlit southeast corner, where he had found a perfect hunter's blind. *Fuck.* He could not call and tell her that if she indeed had a stalker, parking in the same place just made the guy's work easier. She'd never let him do this if she knew. Still, he liked that about her. *Focus. Do not think about her. Think about her danger.*

Twenty minutes later, Sarah pulled into the building. He kept his eyes trained on the pavement below. Seeing her there would mean that she had parked on a lower level. What were the chances that the guy was in the garage and near enough to do something to her down there? How would he know to be there? Then he saw the Tercel reach his level. She pulled into the same parking spot she'd used Tuesday. *Fuck.* Mike watched her exit the car and quickstep to the stairway. He followed at a distance. When she reached the street across from her office, he turned and headed to where he'd parked.

Stopped at a red light on the way home, he looked at himself in the rearview mirror. His hair was all over the place. He did not look like someone who should be trusted with much of anything.

He drove up to the avenue. The only open parking space on the block was in front of Gilhooley's on the other side of the avenue, so he cut left and nosed into it. Jogging across the trolley tracks, he headed toward the striped pole of the last surviving barbershop of the business district. In his childhood, five or six had dotted the two-block strip. He had gone to each of them over the years but had never developed any loyalty to a particular one. He recalled the light, fresh feeling of a new haircut when he was a kid.

A small hand-lettered sign hung in the window of the shop. *Closed Wednesdays.* "Great," he said and turned around. He figured he'd have fallen asleep in the barber's chair anyway. Might as well just take on that snowblower.

8

WEDNESDAY, JANUARY 25

Domenic lifted the blind and peeked out at the darkened avenue. He had seen Mike, without his dog, around noon, crossing from the other side and headed right for Al's. Now the block was empty of pedestrian traffic, the businesses closed and unlit, except for the bar. "*Stonato,*" Domenic said shaking his head. This Mike had a few things to learn. He would be back.

Domenic let the blind fall and turned around, his eyes settling on the large photograph of Angela. She would have appreciated what Mike had done for him. *Would you trust him? You trusted me.*

She had loudly proclaimed that he'd brought home the perfect cheese or pasta as easily as she'd let him know when he could head straight back to 9th Street for the correct item. Natural and automatic. Unavoidable. Like Domenic recalling Angela's ways. He put on his old cardigan and stepped closer to the baseball collage.

Where was the picture that went with the fourth loss? Domenic inched his finger across the glass past the article about the third loss to the Reds, Vada Pinson's two home runs inspired by the Philadelphia newspaper piece in which a Phillie wife was quoted saying that "we ought to have this thing wrapped up by Thursday." The sin of counting your chickens, he thought, yesterday's sin. His finger crept further across the collage. *Fools.*

"Here," he said, tapping the glass. He turned back to the candles on the coffee table. Starting at the left, he lit the first four candles with one match, blowing it out just as it started to burn him. He blew on his finger and straightened the line of nine candles. He switched off the lamp and took two steps back. The spot on the board where he had found the article was bathed in soft blue light. Though positioned too far from the collage to read in the dim light, he knew it by heart.

"Even your best pitcher can't stop the streak. Five-three, Braves. The six and a half game lead is now down to three." He bowed his head. "Fourth of the nine sins. The sin of trying too hard. Think you're so smart!" He took a deep breath, letting his eyes travel across the length and breadth of the display.

He hobbled over to his chair, exhausted. With the addition of the fourth candle tonight, the baseball collage had come alive from this vantage. Angela's image, still muted, had begun to take shape with the increased light. He did not need all nine candles to know the features of her face, but he looked forward to the ninth night when her image would be as well-lit as the collection of baseball scars. As angry as the candle-lighting made him, each additional candle let him better glimpse his Angela. What had made him think he could talk with her tonight? The Phils hadn't deserved to win that year, and he didn't deserve to talk with her without taking in the worst of it all. He was trying too hard, expecting too much.

After twenty minutes, he blew out the candles and went to bed.

When Domenic limped into the barbershop, Al stopped returning magazines to the rack near the door and pointed to the wall clock in the waiting area of the shop. "Can't tell time anymore?"

"I'm here to give you a hand. Fine me for earliness."

"Lucky me," Al said, closing the door behind Domenic. Al

straightened out the waiting area, a mismatched collection of old kitchen chairs lining the wall opposite the business end of the shop.

"Going to be a big day," Domenic said. "Christmas haircuts only go so far. Everybody's overdue."

"An hour early," Al said, handing Domenic the morning *Philadelphia Inquirer*. "Here," he said, barely pronouncing the h. "Go to work." Forty years in the US had barely taken the edge off Al's French-Canadian accent.

Seated in his barber's chair, Domenic clutched his newspaper and watched Al organize the tools of his trade, lining up scissors and clippers, disinfecting combs. Al dusted his hand-carved statue of Saint Anne and returned it to the end of the counter. Domenic scanned the front-page article about the serial killer executed in Florida on Tuesday night. He flipped through the metropolitan section and the sports. Only the article about Michael Jordan held his eye. "Good for him," he said, setting down the newspaper.

"Who?" Al said, still fussing at his section of the counter.

"Anybody who can score ten thousand points deserves an article in the paper."

"Jordan," Al said.

"Although I don't recall any press coverage when you or I did our ten thousandth haircut."

"That's because we get paid the big bucks," Al said. "Don't need publicity."

Domenic walked to the small back room, pleased that he was limping less than the day before. He poured water into the coffee machine, found a packet of coffee and a filter, and set the machine. When he returned to his area, Al was washing the big mirror that ran the length of the wall. Domenic rooted around in his cabinet area until he found a spray container of cleanser and a clean rag. Per their arrangement, Dominic could hang out all day, working with the handful of customers that he and Al agreed would keep him active but never overworked. Most days, he returned from the coffee to his barber chair to work the crossword puzzle, but today he cleared his counter and cleaned the entire area before returning his scissors, talc, comb disinfectant container, and towels to their proper places.

"Some bug bit you, eh?" Al asked, a puzzled look on his face.

"Tis the season," Domenic said.

Al made a face and curled up in his barber chair with the weekly neighborhood newspaper. "A regular employee." The door opened, and in walked Clement and Nick, both in their eighties.

"Ah, the shut-ins," Al said, looking up over his paper.

"Respect your elders," Nick said, pointing a finger at Al. "It's Frick and Frack, white and Black," he sang, taking the seat at the far end of the waiting area.

Offering Al and Domenic a little salute, Clement walked to the chair at the front window, a straight line of empty seats separating him from his friend. He repositioned the green plastic chair to his liking.

"You don't have that many years on me," Al said.

"Expecting a big day, I see," Clement said, nodding toward Domenic, who stood in the entrance to the back room pulling on his blue barber's smock.

"I don't know what to expect from that one," Al said.

"Smells like somebody's making coffee this morning," Nick said.

"Twenty-five cents," Domenic said. "Fifty for pensioners."

"What's that old guy from the Lutheran Home say?" Clement asked. "*Pshaw?*" He and Nick laughed from their bookend spots.

"The *old* guy?" Al said, rolling his eyes.

At quarter after nine, the man who did maintenance work at Sedgwick playground walked in. "Good morning," he chimed.

"Hey," Clement offered.

"Morning," Nick said.

Al rose, dusted off his chair, and stood back as the man took the seat. Domenic sat in his chair, swiveling it so he could watch Al work on his customer. Domenic did not know the man's name. He knew that Al did. A good barber got to know every customer's name, one way or the other. Al might be ten years his junior, but Domenic knew him to be the real thing. The customer asked Al how his son the priest was doing. Al and Ginette had heard from him a week before. Gerry was teaching at a seminary in Princeton. Having a son like that could make a father unbearable, always tooting the kid's horn, but Al wasn't like that. It was, Domenic told himself, one of the reasons the French Canadian had never really seen the ugly side of Domenic, reserved for offenders with "an addytude."

By noon, Al had done ten cuts, and after a vigorous debate, the boys had concluded that not one of the Philadelphia professional sports teams would win a championship again within their lifetimes. "Or within my great-grandson's lifetime," Clement said.

At twelve thirty, Al was finishing a man in a suit Domenic had seen only once or twice before. Domenic went to the back to use the bathroom. When he returned, he saw Mike Flannagan stepping inside and starting for the seats.

"*Buon giorno*," Domenic called to him, gesturing him to come to his chair. He watched Mike glance at Nick and Clement. "My twelve-thirty appointment," Domenic said.

"A live one, eh?" Al said.

"Mike Flannagan," Domenic said.

"Thought you looked familiar," Al said.

"It's been a long time," Mike said.

"Ay-ah," Al said.

Mike stopped short of the chair. "Aren't they ahead of me?"

"If we got haircuts every time we came in here," Nick said, "we'd be bald as a cue ball." They all laughed, and Mike sat in Domenic's chair.

"Probably twenty years since my last visit," Mike said.

Domenic pulled a piece of tissue paper from the dispenser. He wrapped it around Mike's neck.

"I cut your father's hair," Al said. "And yours and your brother's. If you can remember that far back."

"I probably put you through hell," Mike said.

"Your brother did," Al said. "Just kidding."

Domenic snapped a fresh barber cloth then fastened it around Mike's neck, adjusting the tissue above it so they fit snugly together. "Maybe you're used to that fancy stuff," he said. "Here, you got your choice: short, medium, or long. Don't say nothing, you get medium."

"Medium well," Mike said. "I don't want to take a chance on medium rare."

Nick laughed. "That's good. You better get it right, Domenic, or he'll send it back." He threw his head back and laughed again.

"*Citrullos*," Domenic muttered, studying the unruly back of Mike's reddish-brown hair. "Neighborhood kid, huh?" Clement said as Domenic tidied up one side of Mike's hair.

"Devon Street," Mike said.

"Holy Cross boys, you and your brother, right?" Nick asked.

"Eight years of grade school."

"That was an easy one," Clement said.

"Yeah," Domenic said, pausing to stand back and check his progress.

"Didn't have to guess that one," Nick said. "Still live in the neighborhood?"

"Sedgwick Street. Down from the Acme."

"The Acme side of the avenue, not the playground side?" Nick said.

"Yeah," Mike said. Domenic combed out the back of Mike's hair. He stole a glance at the boys. Clement was watching Nick, waiting for him to pounce like a cat on a mouse. Mike had a quizzical look on his face.

"So, you're close to being in St. Madeleine's, but up to the end of that block, you're still in Holy Cross," Nick said triumphantly.

"I guess," Mike said.

"Oh, that was easy," Clement laughed. "It's in the neighborhood." The others chorused an affirmative grunt.

"It's a Catholic world," Clement said. "I mean, for Nick here."

Mike made a face, not looking as if he were following Clement's point.

"Me?" Clement said. "I was raised in the Baptist church, come over to the Romans. So, I'm a Baptist Catholic. Right, Nick?"

"I don't know *what* you are, mister," Nick said.

Everybody in the shop except Mike laughed.

"And he knows what parish you live in," Al said. "Even if you don't." They all laughed again.

"I'm just a regular Catholic," Nick said, pointing to the two barbers. "I don't know about religion, not like them two."

"Don't start with me, you," Al said. "My son's the priest in the family."

Domenic was ready to clean up Mike's sideburns. He picked up his scissors from the counter.

"Don't be all shy in front of somebody you know," Nick said.

"You talking to me, old man?" Domenic said, stopping to glare at Nick, whose offenses always summoned Domenic's ire, but his snarls at the *cafone* and the barbershop crew were swipes at litter-mates.

"You know what we call him?" Nick asked Mike. "The Baltimore Catechism."

"Never been to Baltimore," Domenic said.

"Yeah, but he might as well be from Vatican City," Clement said. "As much of that stuff as he knows."

Domenic leaned closer to Mike. "I'm not going crazy with your parting or your sideburns," he said in a low voice. "Understand? No surprises."

"We got a whole collection of baseball caps, fellow," Nick said to Mike. "Might not have come in here wearing one, but you'll want one when he's done with you."

Clement slapped his leg. "Don't get stopped by the po-lice," he shouted to Mike. "'Cause you won't look like your driver's picture for a while."

Guffawing, the two old men raised their hands to give each other long-distance high fives.

"*Mon Dieu, Seigneur,*" Al mumbled, shaking his head.

"*Et cum spiritu tuo,*" Nick replied.

Clement shook his head. "Easy for you to say."

Domenic stepped over to the shaving cream machine on the counter while Al rang up his customer and said goodbye. He pressed the button with his left hand until his right hand was full of the warm, foamy soap.

"Break time," Al said. He brushed off the chair and sat down.

Domenic turned from the counter to Mike. His Samaritan's eyes were closed. He soaped up around the back of Mike's ears and his sideburns.

"As good a job as you're doing," Al said, "maybe I'll have you do the next three, four customers."

"Only my regulars," Domenic barked. He ran his straight razor back and forth across his strop.

"No wonder I do so much work around here," Al said with mock anger.

Domenic put down the strop. He studied his blade.

"You must be special, mister," Clement said to Mike. "Usually, any rusty old blade'll do."

Mike startled. Domenic patted his shoulder. "That's just that old man talk."

"Domenic must be the richest barber in the world for the number of haircuts he don't do," Nick said.

"Independently wealthy," Clement said.

"Just independent," Domenic corrected. He shaved a clean edge on both of Mike's sideburns then wiped the blade with the flair of a matador.

"Ooh, he's still got it!" Nick exclaimed.

"Mmm-mm," Clement agreed.

"This ain't no show," Domenic said, leaning to get a good angle on the area around Mike's left ear.

"But we sure got an audience," Al said from the other chair.

"*Cafones*," Domenic mumbled. "And that's giving you more credit than you deserve."

"Don't let him get started with his Italian," Nick said.

"You know what the murder rate was in Philadelphia last year?" Domenic said, brandishing his straight razor.

"There you go," Clement said, turning to Nick. "Religion and numbers. The man wrote the book."

"The Baltimore Catechism!"

They laughed. With four clean strokes, Domenic was done with the area around one ear. He moved to the other ear, repeated his economical work, and wiped off the shaving cream residue. "There," he said softly.

Pausing at the back of Mike's head, he used his scissors on a couple of spots that bothered him. Mike had opened his eyes and was watching him in the large mirror. When Domenic held up the hand mirror, Mike checked the work, nodding. Domenic moved the mirror to show another angle.

"It's good," Mike said. "A real haircut."

Domenic unhooked the barber cloth, flapped it, then put it away. When he took off the tissue around Mike's neck, he went over the shaved area with his talc brush, admiring his work. "Okay."

Mike stood and reached for his wallet, but Domenic put a hand out as if he were stopping traffic. "This one's on me," he said, patting Mike on the back. "This is the guy who patched me up when I hurt my leg the other night."

There was a chorus of recognition from the others.

"You're moving around better than the last time I saw you," Mike said. "Nice meeting you all," he said to the crowd.

"Looks like you survived," Nick said.

They all laughed.

"I thought the Marx Brothers were all dead," Mike said. "Now I know how that fat woman must have felt."

"Margaret Dumont!" Clement exclaimed, clapping his hands.

Mike nodded to Al. "I'll tell Brendan I saw you, Mr. Pellerin," Mike said.

"Give him my best," Al said.

Mike shook Domenic's hand.

"An improvement," Domenic said, eyeing his work. "Rome wasn't built in a day."

"How many days *did* it take?" Nick asked.

"Oh, shut up."

Mike opened the door, turned, and nodded back to the four of them. "Just don't break into one of those musical numbers."

They all hooted at him.

"See you," Domenic called out.

When Mike had walked out of view, Domenic began sweeping the hair cuttings around his chair.

"So, he saved you?" Clement said.

"Not exactly."

"Well," Nick said. "He sure has the magic touch."

"What do you mean?" Domenic said. He swept the cuttings into the dustpan and dumped them into the tall wastebasket at the back wall.

"Most people, you yell at. He got you to clam up. A near miracle."

"Damn if he didn't," Clement piped up.

"You don't know nothing," Domenic said.

Al stepped behind Domenic. "You're proud of your hero, aren't you?" he said softly.

Domenic scrunched up his face. "*He* could feel proud for what he did, I guess, not me. But I do like the cut I gave the guy."

"Our Domenic," Al said.

"That's what *I'm* talking about," Clement said.

"Razor murders accounted for less than one percent of all the homicides in the United States last year," Domenic said.

The three men groaned loudly.

"Now, three in a barbershop at one time," Domenic went on, "could completely change the average for this year."

Domenic left the shop an hour before closing, so he could do his food shopping at the Acme and get home while he still had

energy to cook. Coming back, he took the hill up to Mount Pleasant
Avenue without aggravating his leg. He passed the post office, crossed
Germantown, and waited, panting, for the light to change on Mount
Pleasant. Even though he had picked up only necessities, the weight
of the two bags made him realize he had overdone it. Leaning against
the pole, he wheezed and let the traffic light go without moving. He
could not recall feeling frightened when those punks mugged him,
probably too busy trying to kick their butts. Now, frozen with fear on
the corner, he told himself that this might be it. He let the traffic light
go through a whole cycle.

When it turned green again, he made his way across the street.
The rest of the way is downhill. He'd had a big day, had cut Mike's hair,
cleaned the guy right up. He'd make it home, just not push it. At his
door, he paused and cocked his ear toward the shop but heard only
the sound of his own wheezing. He took his time climbing the stairs,
put the cold things away, then slumped into his chair by the window.
Angela had to adapt to the cancer and the treatments in short order.
As he'd aged since then, his limitations arrived like new neighbors on
the block, one here, another one there, adding up over time. He ought
to be able to find the damn patience to handle life at a slower speed.

He let the passing traffic on the avenue carry his thoughts. Within
half an hour, he felt comfortable again and went into the kitchen to
put away the canned items in the cupboard one by one, eliminating
possibilities for the night's dinner with each placement of a can or jar
onto a shelf. The can of beef barley soup wasn't talking to him. Neither
was the chicken noodle.

Finally, he opened a can of tuna into a bowl on the kitchen table.
He rough-chopped a stalk of celery and a small onion then dumped
them into the bowl. He pulled a clove off a head of garlic, smacked it
with the flat of his knife, and cracked off the peel. He finely chopped

it, scraped into the bowl with the blade, then added a dollop of mayonnaise. Spooning a bit of mustard into the concoction—Angela's touch—he stirred until the color looked like hers. He tossed in a pinch of salt and pepper before tasting it. "*Perfetto*," he pronounced. But the exhilaration vanished as automatically as he'd reached for the mustard.

Letting the salad sit, he examined the living room collage until he located the story about the West Coast scout for the Phillies, who had bought two suits in September in anticipation of the World Series. That sin of counting chickens again. *Don't go doing that with your new buddy.* Domenic lit five candles and told himself to return to the kitchen. The candles would wait.

He poured himself a glass of Chianti, broke off half of an Amoroso's roll, and said grace. He had missed Tuesday bingo at St. Matthew's and Wednesday at St. Leo's. He figured he would be able to manage the two blocks to Holy Cross for the five o'clock Saturday evening Mass. At least the muggers had timed their attack so he wouldn't miss Mass this week. Until now, each day's gains had rallied his spirits. Still, a bingo outing could not be far off. A return to the scene of the crime in West Philly? The doorbell rang, startling him.

After hobbling down the stairs, he cracked the door. Mike Flannagan, a package tucked under one arm and a toolbox the size of a Buick in the other hand, stood on the sidewalk.

"Can I come in?"

Domenic opened the door so Mike could pass by. "Speaking of chickens," he mumbled.

"What?"

"Never mind," Domenic called up to him.

"I'll be out of here in an hour," Mike said. "I should have called, but I don't have your number."

Domenic trailed him up the stairs. Panting, he stopped halfway up. Mike paused on the top step. "You were here three nights ago," Domenic said. "I saw you this afternoon. Does this mean we're dating?"

"Not quite."

When Domenic reached the second floor, Mike was standing by the dining room table, his toolbox in his hand.

"I don't need any new tools," Domenic said, irritation boiling up. "And the chef's done for the day."

"I'm not here for dinner."

"Funny," Domenic said. "I am."

"Don't let me disturb your dinner. I just want to do something in your front room."

"Something?"

"Think of it as working off a haircut."

He nodded then wondered what he was doing. *Why am I giving him a green light?* Angela liked to say, "This is happening for a reason," but he wasn't sure her explanation applied.

"Go eat," Mike said. He carried his gear into the living room.

Domenic shuffled into the kitchen. Picking at his tuna salad, he heard the snap of a tape measure then the whir of a drill. The tuna salad, closer to room temperature now, tasted right. He still could not tell what Mike might be doing in there, but it appeared that he'd turned on every light in the apartment. Dominic heard furniture being moved, the sound of the tape measure again. He bit off a piece of the roll and chewed it slowly. He told himself that this all would turn out okay. A jangly noise suggested Mike rummaging through his toolbox. Domenic spooned a bit more of the tuna salad onto his plate. By this time, he should have straightened out the kitchen and finished the *Daily News* crossword. What next?

"You ought to be icing that knee," Mike called. "I saw you limping."

Domenic washed the dishes and gathered the trash. Remembering that he had bought half of a pound cake, he held his hand over his eyes and stepped into the hallway. "Last call for dessert," he boomed. "I'm coming in there with dessert in five minutes. *Capisce?*"

"Ten minutes. Did you ice yet?"

"Holy Mother of God."

Something else clanged into the toolbox. Domenic returned to the kitchen and cut two large slices from the pound cake, topping each piece with a spoonful of applesauce. He placed the plates and paper napkins on the stainless steel serving tray Angela had bought at Gimbels the year they were married. The sweetness of all those after-dinner coffees in their old living room never banished the sadness he felt touching the tray again but made it doable.

Shaking the kettle, he felt enough water in it for two cups. He turned on the burner then pulled a bag of peas from the freezer. Sitting in his chair, he lifted the sore leg onto the seat of the other chair then planted the frosty bag on his knee. He opened his prayer book. *Finding lost things? St. Anthony is your guy. Close enough.* He read the prayer to St. Anthony in the hope that Al, owner of the building, would find Mike's renovations a good idea. When the kettle whistled, he dropped tea bags into two mugs. He finished his prayers while the tea steeped. "*Basta,*" he murmured after three minutes. He picked up the tray and started down the hall.

"All set," Mike called.

"Luck of the Irish," Domenic said, entering the living room. Mike sat at the end of the couch beside Domenic's chair, an expectant look on his face. Domenic stopped inside the doorway. "*Madonna.*" Spotlights from the ceiling now lit the two pictures on the wall. A third new spotlight pointed toward the front corner of the living room, giving the whole space a softer yet clear look. "Never lived in an art gallery," Domenic said, setting the tray on the coffee table.

"Track lighting," Mike said. "Should be good for the pictures."

"It's something all right." In Mike's eyes, this was nothing but a home improvement, a neighborly kindness. Domenic's Samaritan would not become the first person to hear about the candles. "It's great," Domenic said.

Mike breathed out a contented sigh. His mouth curled at the edges, giving a hint of what a full smile might look like. His eyes settled on Domenic's old lamp. Turned off and in the corner, it looked like it was ready for the trash. What was next? A bathroom reno?

"Can you use the lamp somewhere else?" Mike asked.

Domenic shrugged. "Al lets me put stuff in a corner of the basement. I guess I can stick it down there. Or have a yard sale. A yard sale with no yard."

"You don't mind?"

"Not if I make a buck on it."

"I mean, me changing your room around like this?"

Domenic shook his head. "They turn off, right?"

"You don't like it."

"No, no. It's great for when I want to perform surgery, and I can turn it off when I don't." He handed Mike a plate of cake. He sat in his usual spot with the other plate on his knee. "Could have done that myself if I'd taken the idea."

"I believe you," Mike said. "Not trying to embarrass you."

He'd named the discomfort Domenic hadn't been able to identify. Somehow, that lessened the feeling.

Domenic admired the lighting. "You're pretty good. You learn that from your father?"

"I used to be a carpenter," he said.

"My old neighborhood, everybody did their own electrical, plumbing, whatever."

"South Philly?"

"11th Street."

"And you left."

"Yeah," Domenic said. "If you don't want your tea to taste like tar, you better take that bag out of there."

Mike removed the bag from the mug, setting it on the tray.

"Good," Domenic said.

"What?"

"Most 'mericans squeeze the bag against a spoon and let it drip into the cup, like they're killing a bug."

"Med-a-gahns?"

"*A-mer-icans*," Domenic said, waving his left hand as if he were going to slap him.

"My mother taught us never to do anything but toss the bag."

"They taught you something about tea. So, your family wasn't all bad?"

"No."

The two men ate their desserts. Domenic sipped the last of his tea and set the mug on the table. He admired Mike's work. Clean. The guy had even brought his own trash bag, which now sat at the doorway, tied up and ready to be put outside. "Your place must be real nice," Domenic said.

"Because I was a carpenter?" Mike said, with a little laugh that startled Domenic. "Sometimes nothing works like keeping moving. My tools were gathering dust. I got an impulse." Mike finished his tea and set the mug on the table next to Domenic's.

"Your age, you ought to get the impulse to leave this old man and go out and have some fun."

Mike looked at the candles, the new lights, the pictures on the wall, the lights again.

Is he planning another project? His hands might be still, but his mind was moving like crazy. And not considering Domenic's advice. Domenic rose halfway out of his seat and leaned forward. "Boo!"

Mike flinched. "What the hell?"

Domenic studied his visitor. Even at Domenic's age, a fresh haircut still made him walk around with a lift to his step, but not this guy.

Mike leaned back in his seat, his brow furrowed.

"Why so solemn, for godsakes?" Domenic said. "Somebody put the maloiks on you?"

"I got women on my mind," Mike said. "But it's not what you think."

A trolley's passing rocked the windows. Domenic looked at the five flickering candles. Under Mike's lighting, the candles no longer altered the look of Angela or the collage. But he could switch off the new lights when it was time. He just wasn't sure how he felt about the candles now. He'd worry that later.

"You heard about my brother today," Mike said.

"The one who gave Al a hard time?"

"Gave everybody a hard time. We've had our ups and downs. But his wife and kids are great."

"You're an uncle."

"They're nine and seven. We go to movies, the zoo. And I'm close enough to his wife that I know things about my brother. Delores had a seizure. He just moved her to a different hospital. Some kind of encephalitis. Memory problems. It's complicated."

"You and her?" he said.

"Well, no," Mike said, with a pained expression that did not entirely convince Domenic. "There is no past if you don't remember it. Right?"

How do you not remember the past?

"If Delores doesn't remember bad things from the past," Mike said, "she gets a clean slate."

Did anyone ever get a clean slate? "How's it clean if she's still in such a bad marriage?"

"He's playing the good husband." Mike rubbed his hands back and forth across his knees. "If she doesn't remember anything bad, it's like it never happened, right? And nobody has to feel like shit about anything."

"Is that supposed to be persuasive?" Domenic said. "Not that I'm exactly following this, mind you. I thought maybe you had girlfriend problems." He watched Mike's expression change from concern to disdain.

"I know somebody." Mike let out a long breath. "But I don't know what I'd call it."

"It?"

"Her and me," he stammered. "The relationship. She's a teacher. We've had our moments, but I don't know. She'd be a lot better off with a real boyfriend. But that whole issue has moved to the back burner. I can't get Delores and the kids off my mind."

Domenic nodded. Mike's eyes were locked on his now.

"The other day, she knew who I was ten, eleven years ago," Mike said. "When my brother went down the hall to talk with the nurse, Delores heard his voice and said, 'That's my brother-in-law.' I told her that *I* was Mike. She shook her head. 'I know Mike Flannagan.'

"I looked her in the eyes. 'At least a year before you and Brendan got married, when you started coming over the house,' I told her, 'we met.'

"'Arthur Flannagan,' she said.

"'Yes,' I said. 'That was our dad.' I went and got Brendan. He reintroduces me to her, and here we go again. She was like a gracious host with a strange house guest."

"Strange for her," Domenic said. "Poor woman."

"She's in for lots of surprises. Marrying Brendan, having kids."

"Her life."

"The doctors suggested tape recording family members and playing the tapes for her with the person not there. I taped mine the other night. They're going to try that."

"Terrible." The talk about this Delores ushered Domenic's own pain into sharp relief. He wanted to say more but he was no longer thinking about this woman or about Mike.

"We'll see," Mike said.

My Angela. But he could not say her name. It was not right. "I'll pray for her," he said.

Mike nodded.

He offered Mike more tea and dessert. Mike declined the offer.

"So those are the two women?" Domenic asked.

"The college teacher," Mike said, nodding. "You might as well pray for her too." He gathered the mugs and dishes and put them on the tray. "It's late, Domenic. Tomorrow's an early start."

"You don't start the same time every day up at the seminary?"

"A lot to do," Mike said. "I have to be sharp." Picking up the tray, he started for the kitchen but paused for a last look at his handiwork. "Want me to light the rest of the candles?"

"No, that's good," Domenic said, pulling himself up to a standing position. He followed Mike into the kitchen.

Mike pointed at the pattern on the dishes he'd put into the sink. "Somehow these flowers don't seem like you exactly."

"Angela got them at Snellenburg's. You were in short pants. Maybe your parents were in short pants. I kept about half of the set when I left the old neighborhood."

"Still have people there?"

Domenic shook his head. "I'm here. What you see is what I got." He rinsed off the dishes and dried his hands. "What do I need more than this for?"

When Mike left, Domenic returned to the living room. *Don't worry, Angela. I'll still be counting sheep tonight, not chickens.* He turned off the new lighting, but instead of sitting across from the pictures, he blew out the five candles and went to bed.

9

THURSDAY, JANUARY 26

After her parents' call, Sarah made herself watch *Jeopardy!* while eating her Greek salad. She was sure her father would have called out the same wrong answer about New Jersey beach towns that she did. It felt almost like they all still were talking on the phone. Dad's paraphrase of the oncologist's update was that "the bad guys are on the run." Mom sounded less hyper but equally confident.

An hour later, sitting at the kitchen table, she checked to see if any ungraded essays remained in the four file folders for her courses and recalled that uncomfortable moment when her parents laughed and told her for the second time in the conversation that everything was "comfortably under control." Had that flash of awkwardness been disappointment that they didn't need her help? It lasted only a second, but still.

Enough embarrassing moments for one week. Bustling was driving her through this week that was like no other and hadn't quite ended yet. She'd bustled her way to record levels of cleanliness in both her office and the apartment. Of course her satchel contained no ungraded student work. Housecleaning and paper-grading might have done the trick had the week's madness consisted only of Monday's brawl.

Her late-night appearance at Mike's had felt surprisingly right until she woke Tuesday morning to find herself alone in his bed. Lying there, something kept her from calling out his name. That sinking feeling plummeted with the sound of Robert clopping his way up the stairs. The dog stood in the open doorway, tail wagging, his eyes bright with expectancy. "Fuck," she sighed. No sign of Mike on the second floor or the first. Silence from the basement.

She had just enough time to walk the poor guy then feed him—if Mike had already fed him, Robert didn't object—and still get to campus ahead of class. She dashed home to change and grab her satchel then sped down Kelly Drive.

Wednesday's morning class—its first meeting since Monday's brawl had preemptively sent them all home—greeted her with cheers and applause. She blushed, feeling like she'd just returned from Hollywood as a ten-time *Jeopardy!* champion.

Then Larry Goldman popped by her office, which he rarely did, asked how she was doing, then quickly confided in her that while the entire department felt deeply for her, she needed to know that the incident had provided quarrelling factions with fresh bones of contention. "Some of the union fringe will want you to challenge whatever the dean says," he cautioned.

Checking her mail cubby, she found a memo from the dean, informing her that she should report to his office at noon. Why was she suddenly feeling as if she were the suspended student?

"We don't believe we are likely to see anything damaging be put into your personnel file, Sarah," he said. *The regal "we," the use of the conditional, and the passive voice.* She panicked but kept her facial expression neutral.

"Right," she said, nodding. She'd let him do the heavy lifting, and he did, spieling on about seriousness, the importance of mutual respect, and the strides both faculty and administration had taken in facing challenges during the three years since he'd come to the college. "Your own committee established guidelines for situations like this, though the faculty senate has not yet okayed the process of developing the workshop for teachers involved in conflicts like this one."

Like the conflict between students that I broke up? "Right."

"You hardly can be forced to undergo a program that your own people have yet to finalize." He chuckled.

"But I could do something that would fulfill the spirit or intention of the yet-to-be created program." *My cultural reeducation begins.*

"Exactly," he gushed. "You and, say, one of the counselors—someone of your choosing—could meet over a series of weeks. Talk about your incident, possible implications or repercussions of faculty responses, such as yours. Maybe put together a joint program for Professional Development Week next August."

To demonstrate proper atonement. And to set up a precedence without (yet) giving the union something to throw back at the administration. "Interesting."

"Leona Henderson-Hennessey could become director of all the collaborative teaching programs at the College very soon, and if that eventuates as I think it may, she'd be the ideal person to oversee that whole counseling educational program that you and the counselor would be doing."

"Didn't realize she was interested in that role."

"You're comfortable with Leona, aren't you?"

"Of course."

"What I said about Leona and that position," he said, "stays between these four walls, of course."

She nodded. *Might Larry, too, be headed for some coveted slot?* If Sarah were on the rise, shouldn't she find an angle for herself in all this? Perhaps they'd already skulled that out. Fuck them if they had. Fuck them if they hadn't.

"Take a proactive role, Sarah. Reach out to someone you trust in the Department of Counseling. I'm sure it will get green-lighted by both departments."

So you don't have to order me to do it. "Really creative idea, Dr. Lamarr."

When she told the story to Florence, who'd been a union rep before Sarah joined the faculty, Florence laughed. "They can barely keep up with necessary battles. You're not letting the side down by failing to provoke an unnecessary fight. But tell me about Mike."

"Funny you should ask," Sarah told her. "I've decided that I love the bastard."

"Fair enough."

"Just don't know yet what I'm going to do about it."

Walking to her car in the garage Wednesday, her newly gained comfort vanished when she swore someone was watching her. She didn't stick around to see if she'd been correct but cautioned herself that it had been more a sensation than an observation. Irrational fears just below the surface, when she'd thought they actually moved away—why not, in this nightmare week?

Thursday's classes went well. No fresh nonsense from the dean. On her trips from and back to the parking garage, she'd not gotten that strange feeling that she was being watched, but the panic had returned nonetheless, pumping urgency into her running legs. Through it all, her anger at Mike lingered, though her drive to call him eclipsed it.

Every time she'd returned to her apartment since Tuesday morning, she'd held her breath as she opened the door and turned to the living room answering machine, finally breathing out but hardly encouraged when she saw no light blinking. Tuesday, after her walk in Valley Green, her heart caught when she found it blinking. Two messages. The first voice was Jim Earlham's, urging her to come to next week's department meeting and vote for his proposal to add one member to the executive committee. When the other message turned out to be Becky Childress, urging her to vote against the proposal, she sank into the couch.

Through the last three days, she'd shuffled through approaches she might take if Mike called, along with her options should she be the caller, and what message, if any, she might leave on his machine— all without deciding anything except the one suggestion she would make—unless the conversation crashed in flames before she found an opening. Their as yet uncanceled plan for Saturday called for pizza and a video at his place. Offering to change the venue to her apartment would enable him to feel free to leave whenever he felt the need. He'd have to see that as preferable.

Another check through the folders? No. When was she ever caught up on grading? Right now. "Grading's got to be the hardest and worst thing about your job," Mike told her once. She thought she ought to kiss him on the spot but didn't want to be ridiculous.

Once that memory arrived, her waiting had ended. She rose and picked up the wall phone. *Don't sit down. Stay on your toes.*

"Hello," Mike said.

"You're alive," she replied matter-of-factly.

"Yeah," Mike said. He sighed.

She thought she heard the sound of a chair being moved. *He wants to settle in for a real conversation?* Shifting her weight from left to right, she took in the view of the street, another useful focus.

"I didn't help you at all," he went on. "Monday or Tuesday."

Wait. Let him do this. His chair squeaked again. This couldn't be easy for him.

"And I should have called you to apologize before you called me."

"I can't say I haven't been angry. And hurt."

"You don't deserve this," Mike said.

"But you listened to me Monday night, even though you were dead on your feet—and so worried about your sister-in-law. And how the hell are you?"

"I'm fine," he said. "Aside from hating me, you're okay? Nothing's happened with that guy?"

"No," she said. "He's out of the picture."

"You haven't seen him," Mike said.

"I bought some pepper spray."

"Good."

"He's not allowed on campus for the semester. Probably won't be back at all. The rest of them are all gone."

"Thought about carpooling?"

"I'm careful, Mike," she said. *Except with you.* "This had been a long week." *Three days ago, we made love.* She realized she'd moved as close to the window as the curled phone cord allowed, stopped and breathed out.

"I didn't want to make things worse," he said. "Should have called. I wasn't thinking. And my sister-in-law. No excuse, but it's a mess."

"I'm sorry."

"She's lost a lot of memory," he said. "They're still guessing what the hell caused her seizure."

From the little she knew about the couple, she already felt sympathy for the woman. "Very scary," she said.

"I've been at the hospital, keeping Brendan from taking out the whole medical staff. I'm hardly talking to anyone besides my brother. And this old guy I met on the avenue."

"Old guy?"

"Domenic Gallo," he said. "Lives near the co-op. He cut my hair."

"Cut your hair?"

"He's a barber. I helped him get home when he got beat up

last week. He gave me a haircut for patching him up. It's kind of snowballed from that."

"Slow down."

"No criticism of your haircuts, Sarah."

"This sounds weird, Mike."

"It's fine. He lives above the barbershop on the avenue. Works downstairs."

"Mike, what's going on?"

"Like you said, it's been a long week," he said.

"I'm not following this." *Mike and some old man?* She was back standing at the phone, staring at the wall fixture, as if Mike might suddenly appear there.

"Everything's going a hundred miles an hour. Too much." She could not recall hearing this tone from him before. *Confused apprehensiveness? Dread?*

You sound anything but fine? This must be hell for all of you? Mike, you're all over the place? I want to help you. Nothing came out. *Damn.* She squeezed her eyes shut, gritting her teeth.

"I don't know why I got into all that," he said. "You *are* being careful?"

"Of course." Saying anything about her fight-or-flight moments in the garage would hardly help him—or her. She wanted him to feel like he could talk about his sister-in-law, his brother, and—God forbid—about himself. Maybe when they were in the same room.

"Good," he said.

"About Saturday," she said. "Why don't we watch the movie here? Doesn't have to be a long night. Pizza. Maybe a box of Entenmann's. I mean, if Saturday's still good." She was pacing again.

"Yeah," he said. "You pick up a movie, whatever you want. I'll get a large sausage and mushroom."

"Is seven good?"

"Seven's fine. I'll try not to be a jerk." He hung up.

She had marched back to near the window. Sighing, she brought the phone back and hung it up.

Lying on her bed, she let out several deep breaths that turned into groans, as if she were grunting through a weight-lifting session. Could have been worse, she reassured herself. He'd agreed to her suggestion. Why did she feel she needed a strategic study group to help her frame a sentence to the man? Her mind spun. But her materials for tomorrow's classes were safely tucked into her satchel. She'd already moved Friday's planned dinner of frozen leftovers to the fridge. She could eat off the floor in any room in the apartment. No need to bustle through another task tonight. Somehow, she would get to sleep.

10

FRIDAY, JANUARY 27

Parking up the ramp from Sarah's usual space and across from it gave Mike a good view of her car. Because she took the elevator to the level just below and then walked the short distance up to her car, she had no reason to look higher than where her car sat. Opening the mint-looking copy of *Best American Short Stories 1984* he'd bought for Ms. Devereaux's class, he scanned the rest of his level. In five minutes, a bald West Indian librarian who'd helped him with a research paper would climb into the pickup truck parked two spaces from Sarah's car and head home. Sarah always moved quickly to and from her parked car, but that, after all, could be her normal pace at work. He wanted something good and safe for Sarah, which brought Laurie right into his consciousness. *No. Read.*

He settled on a James Salter story, not one assigned for the course. After reading the first paragraph, he checked the line of cars on each side of the level and tried to picture what this Salter might look like. His story had been selected as one of the best in the country, so Mike figured he was experienced, probably older. Writing wasn't like roofing work; if the guy didn't lose his faculties, he probably could work into his eighties or nineties. But some people lose it far sooner than that. He read a line from "Foreign Shores" and realized that he'd read the sentence twice. He went back a paragraph. "Are your parents still married?"

He blinked then focused on the last word he had read. But he was back in their home in New Paltz.

"It's not enough that we do things for them," Laurie said, smiling, neither smug nor sanctimonious. "It's because he's not well that we ought to talk with the man."

Thereafter, when Mike crossed the road to cut their lawn, he began to accept Monica's offers to linger for a glass of iced tea. Sometimes Roger wandered in to look for cookies or for their son who lived in Rochester. After a few months, Mike developed a sense of Roger's limits and managed to have little conversations within those limits.

One morning in late spring, he teased Roger about the azaleas at the back of their yard. "I'm going to trim those suckers 'til they look like the hedges down at the post office," he said with a straight face.

"Suckers?"

He brought Roger to the kitchen window and pointed to the four large azalea bushes out back. "Make 'em perfect rectangles."

Roger stared intently out the window.

"Sure, we'd lose half the flowers, but neat, neat, neat," Mike said, waiting for Roger to catch on to his effort at humor.

"Not rectangles." Roger shuffled to the kitchen sink and poured himself a glass of water.

Mike crossed the room and patted the old man on the shoulder. "Might not get around to that, though."

All that week, he'd found himself thinking about Roger and about azaleas. Kidding that way had been thoughtless, unkind. He once had seen azaleas trimmed. When he was a kid, a retired military man lived on his paper route. The man owned a large stone single, a corner house, and he posted little "Curb Your Dog" signs on both streets. Once, while delivering the *Evening Bulletin*, Mike noticed that the man's hedges were abloom with bright flowers. Within a few weeks, the hedges had reverted to their normal green. Years later, driving past the house, he noticed them again and realized that instead of regular hedges, the man had cultivated tight rows of azaleas. If limiting nature's finest gift in Philadelphia—where they seemed to grow and multiply with a mind of their own—was foolish, then to do so here in New Paltz, where they were comparatively rare, had to be a crime.

While renovating a customer's kitchen in town, he grasped the wrongness of his joke. He chalked his realization up to Laurie. The next Saturday morning, he and Laurie and little Michael brought over freshly baked chocolate chip cookies. While Laurie and Monica chatted in the kitchen and little Michael played with the toys that Monica kept just for him, Mike walked Roger around the property, pointing out little landscaping touches he had made. When they got to the back of the yard, the old man stopped in his tracks and pointed to the azalea bushes.

"I got a man," Roger confided, "who's supposed to trim them." He shook his head. "Used to cut those damn things back for me, but now I don't know what's the matter with him." He continued past the azaleas. "Annoying."

By the time they returned home, Michael was ready for lunch. Later, during Michael's nap, Laurie mentioned that Monica had been having a difficult time. "She was pretty weepy this morning."

Her frown reminded Mike of Roger.

"She's found a few notes around the house. Stuff he must have written before."

Mike nodded.

"He's much worse," Laurie went on. "Last week she found a note in her sewing basket, addressed to her. Another one was under the couch cushions. He writes about how he thinks he's losing his memory."

Laurie dropped her eyes, and Mike was sure she was about to start crying, but she continued. "She told me what he wrote in one of them. He said, 'I'm so damned scared. I feel like I'm dying bit by bit, a little every day.' Then he listed where certain things belonged, when things were supposed to be done, like the trash goes out on Tuesday. What if one of us had to go through that?"

"No," he said, trying to imagine constantly shifting between confusion and fear.

Laurie walked across the room, leaned against his chest, and sobbed. He held her, patted her back. He was going to ask if she thought the old man was still writing the notes, but he decided he knew the answer. Standing there in the middle of the day holding his sobbing wife made him think of the soap operas that women in the homes in which he worked sometimes watched. They made him sick. They were not real. They were not sad, not like this. He pulled Laurie closer to him. Relief that they did not face such horror eased his sadness. He felt Laurie's hot tears on his neck and knew she was thinking only of Roger and Monica. A lesser person, it was his undeserved luck to have a life with her. His consolation vanished, replaced by shame for harboring such a thought, but his guilt passed as quickly as it had come, like a dark cloud scudding across the sky on a windy day, leaving behind the steady, endless blue.

Two weeks later, Laurie wanted Mike to go out food shopping with her and little Michael after dinner, but Mike was hell-bent on re-caning one of the two old rocking chairs they'd picked up at a tag sale over the weekend.

"Last chance," she called down to the basement. "The train's leaving."

"I just got started," he whined.

"I'll let you drive Michael's shopping cart." He heard her still standing at the top of the stairs. "I was hoping you'd come with us."

He kept working. Why was he acting as if this were a game of chicken? He dropped his hands from the chair, amazed at how thick he could be. "Be right there," he called.

She was talking to Michael about what he would wear. "No," she yelled down. "You're having too much fun."

"I could get both of these done by the weekend," he said, blushing at his exaggeration.

"Want I-C-E C-R-E-A-M?"

"Y-E-S."

He pulled a strip of cane up over the frame at the rear of the chair, then set his sights on the open expanse of the chair back. Beside him, Robert sighed in his sleep. At this error-free pace, he might actually finish this part by bedtime.

He heard her walking to the back door. She was talking to Michael in a soothing voice, the voice that always worked with him.

By the time he heard the door close and the car start up, he was convinced he would have time to rub both chairs with linseed oil before turning in. He instantly became lost in the rhythm of working the cane across the back of the chair. When he'd bought them, a few dried-out strips of cane were all that remained of their backs, and the seats were open space. Mike was creating something where there had been nothing. He concentrated on each move as if his life depended on it, but it was the most relaxing thing he had done all day.

The sight and sound of Sarah's car door opening jarred him back. He watched her clamber into her Tercel and toss her satchel onto the passenger seat. He'd been looking straight at her car. *How did she make it down the ramp before I realized she was there?* Grabbing the steering wheel, he leaned forward as she pulled out of her space and drove down the ramp. *Safe.* He sank back in his seat and looked at his watch. Five minutes earlier than usual. He was glad he'd arrived plenty early.

The book had fallen off his lap. He picked it up and put it beside him. His own memory had chased the book's story from his mind. Seeing that Sarah was all right was one thing, but it hadn't done anything to remove the chill that lingered from his memory. Throwing himself into an activity would flush that, he reminded himself, but he felt no inclination to move. *It will pass. And the rest of it too.* He looked down at the cover of the book on the seat beside him. He'd lost interest in it, but he'd bring it next time.

The sound of footsteps pulled his eyes up. A young man in a dark jacket and jeans, his dark hair in a full-blown pompadour, walked slowly up the ramp past where Sarah had been parked, glancing from the vehicles on one side of the garage level to the other side then spinning around and heading back down.

Again, Mike leaned forward, peering through his windshield until the guy was out of sight. Mike quietly got out of his car and slipped down the ramp. Nothing. Checking between the cars on both sides, he walked down the whole parking level without seeing Mr. Pompadour. The guy had upped his pace, and Mike had waited too long to follow.

Back in his car, Mike made a note of the day and time. If he'd acted more quickly, he might have been able to confront him and put an end to this whole thing, though he had no idea what he would have said or done to the bastard. He'd been right to be there, but still. Was this guy smart enough to tail her to her apartment? Pompadour would be back, maybe Monday. This was the best place to stop the scumbag. Now the anger that had energized him suddenly felt like more than he could carry. His eyes fell to the book again. No help there. He sank back in the driver's seat and tried to think about the jobs waiting for him at the seminary, about the basement mess—anything but his rage at Sarah's predator. He was shaking.

New Paltz. He'd failed there, but he would act this time. Whatever his relationship with Sarah was, he would not let this predator hurt her. *Laurie.* The ache over having failed her and Michael roiled his gut. He squeezed his eyes shut, but he was in the New Paltz basement again. Once the quiet sound of Laurie's car pulling out of the driveway ended, all thought of his wife and baby faded away like dry leaves in a rearview mirror. Not a worry in the world. He wound another strip of cane where he wanted it.

When the hospital called an hour later to tell him that Laurie and little Michael had been in a serious car accident and that he should get there right away, he was sure from the sound of the woman's voice that they were dead.

Rushing to the hospital in his work van, he decided that he was wrong. They were seriously injured but would pull through. He remembered the interstate crash he came upon the previous summer, how sure he was that no one could walk out of that overturned camper, but an old man and a little girl did. He remembered Laurie's advice to him during childbirth, when she continued to remind him at each stage that they need only concern themselves with the particulars of that stage by saying, "It's too early to worry about that." He nearly tipped the work van over when he turned into the ER parking area and screeched it to a stop. It might not even require a miracle. Doctors, he thought.

Parked, he broke into a run and charged up to the intake receptionist in the ER. "My wife and son," he blurted. "A car accident."

Expressionless, she told him to sit in the chair in front of the counter.

"Please," he said. "Tell me."

"The doctor will be right with you." She picked up the phone and called for a Doctor Shiffer.

To his left, he saw a waiting room full of people, all staring at an overhead television blasting a commercial for Toyota. The hallway doors separating the waiting area and the treatment area slid open, and a man in scrubs, about his age, called, "Mr. Flannagan?" and gestured for him to join him.

Mike hustled to the door and followed the doctor into an examining room. It was empty, the stretcher covered with a fresh paper sheet. The doctor pulled the hallway curtain shut behind them. His forehead was creased. "Mr. Flannagan, your wife's vehicle was involved in a collision with another vehicle about seven o'clock."

"Tell me," Mike said.

"Rescue personnel were on the scene in under ten minutes. The vehicle rolled over, but they got her out within minutes. Your wife sustained multiple injuries and severe head trauma. The rescue people did everything they could possibly do."

Mike dropped onto the chair beside the stretcher.

"They were brought here by seven forty," the doctor said. "I am so sorry. She was pronounced dead here, but it appears that she was dead on impact."

"My God," Mike moaned. "No."

"Mr. Flannagan, she may never have known what happened." He sat on the chair beside Mike.

"Michael?"

"Your son was in his car seat, but he suffered multiple head and chest injuries. The rescue people started treating him immediately at the scene. They worked on him all the time they were in the rescue—"

"Tell me!"

"He was pronounced dead at the hospital."

Mike stared at the doctor. The man was talking. Mike caught a word here and there, when his mind was not picturing and hearing Laurie and Michael at the moment of impact. He replied to a question then to another question then was unaware of what he answered. *Let it have been so fast that they knew nothing, felt nothing.*

He was walked to a chilly room where he looked at their bodies and nodded twice when he was asked: Is this your wife? Is this your child? He had the sense that he was watching himself walking into the room with these strangers, peering at the bodies of Laurie and Michael, that this was something he would tell Laurie about later, the way he let her recount her story about Roger and Monica. They were not Laurie and Michael now, just damaged likenesses, statues laid out before him. Rigid and horizontal, like a sculptor's project on a worktable, they resembled two real people but were only abstractions of them. He saw himself telling Laurie about it.

When they left the room, the doctor asked him if he wanted a prescription for something to help him sleep, but he refused it. He was sure that characters in soap operas released torrents of tears when they learned that their families had been crushed to death in a high-speed car accident. He was grateful that events were moving in slow motion. It gave him the time he needed to move through these scenes, like being allowed to ride a roller coaster that moved at a speed that did not frighten.

Against the recommendations of the doctor and nurses, he said he would drive himself home. As he left, he realized he had not even inquired about whoever was in the other car. He should feel some concern for the other driver. Another family might be going through their own hell, but he felt no such concern, and this realization made him feel less connected to Laurie. Without her influence, he already was less like the man who had lived with her and little Michael.

Driving back to their little home, he avoided the place of the accident. That would wait until the morning. At home, he fed Robert but did not eat anything himself. He walked from room to room and looked at their things. The telephone rang. It could be Laurie's parents, whom he'd called from the hospital. The ringing filled the room. It could be the undertaker, or a mother calling to ask what time she and her little girl should come by for Friday's playgroup. "No," he said. The ringing finally stopped. Robert, still more puppy than adult, bounded over and licked his hand. Mike sat on the carpet and slumped back against the wall, and the dog stood beside him, wagged his tail, and lapped his tongue against the tears running down Mike's face. The sound of his keening reverberated throughout the house most of the night. He awoke at dawn with a stiff back and a headache.

In the morning, he told the funeral director that, yes, there would be one funeral, not two. He would try to get through this once. One of everything: one wake, one service, one burial. Laurie's parents and brother had come down from Syracuse. His brother was there.

Laurie's friends from work came to the wake. Stylish teachers. They reminded him of characters in soap operas. He felt himself start to shake. He recognized the parents of one of the kids in Michael's playgroup. Inhaling deeply, he steadied himself by the stand where people were signing their names in a book he would be given.

When the two caskets rolled past him in the church, one big and oak, the other miniature and white, he thought about The Three Bears. The flowers sent by her family, friends, and coworkers were arrayed across the front of the church. He sat in the first pew beside his in-laws but could not speak with them. Had he heard the name of the priest who presided at the Mass? He, too, Mike decided, looked like he should be in a soap opera. The hymns, each in turn, made everyone around him cry. At the end, Laurie's brother read the eulogy that he and his parents had written. Mike listened to him extol Laurie's qualities and sometimes mention his name. He told himself that he was lucky to have had this man in his life for a while.

At the cemetery, he thought that the choking fragrance of the flowers would make him sick, but a breeze came up, and the feeling passed. "Give them away," he said when he was asked which ones he would like to take home. He told Brendan that his own little family needed him and sent him off.

Playgroup mothers brought over turkey and ham. Monica came from across the street with a pot of stew. The priest arrived unannounced. "Don't make any big decisions for a long time," he told Mike. He was a kind man, but Mike kept seeing him in a tuxedo at a TV awards show. When Mike tried to give Michael's toys to one of the playgroup moms, she refused, telling him the same thing the priest had said. A cop whose bathroom he'd redone the previous winter stopped by. The driver of the other car was an honor roll teenager. This Jerry Wells had lost control of his father's Mercury, trying to avoid hitting a jaywalking pedestrian. Mike had blocked out his in-laws' heated talk about lawsuits and criminal charges— part of the funeral day's blur. The teenager's father was a prominent lawyer. The kid was taking it pretty hard. Something was happening legally, but the cop wasn't sure what. Mike did not know what he would do, but he knew that he must keep moving. He put the house up for sale.

Sorting through all of the kitchen things on a spring afternoon that was hotter than most summer days, he found Monica's stewpot and set it aside. The next day, he crossed the street to their house. Monica opened the kitchen door without saying a word. She gestured toward the rocking chair. He pulled up short of the chair. "Jesus," he grumbled. "The stewpot's still sitting by my door."

"Sit," she said, turning on the kettle.

He thanked her for the food and for the Mass card as he settled in the rocking chair.

"Oh," she sighed. She turned from the stove and brought her hand to her breast. "You probably want iced tea. Don't you?"

"No," he said. "Hot tea's good."

Roger entered from the hallway without a word. He walked to the kitchen, peered out the window, and shuffled back out of the room.

"This won't take but a minute, Mike," Monica said from the stove, facing away from him.

Her shoulders shook a little, and he knew that she would not turn to look at him until the tears were gone.

"Excuse me," he said. He rocked forward and got out of the chair. Monica nodded without turning around.

Roger sat in the living room, and Mike passed him as he walked to the front of the house. Soon the roses out by the steps would be budding. The lawn could use cutting, and he figured he was good for one last mow. His own lawn needed it too. A young couple was lined up to come over and take a look at the place the next evening. After cutting his own lawn and this one, he'd wheel the mower over to the side of the garage where he had gathered furniture, kitchenware, and toys for the yard sale. He should talk with Laurie's family about the toys and the clothes, but this would be easier.

He went outside and walked around Roger and Monica's house then headed for the property line in the back. The azaleas looked more greenish than anything else, with shiny new leaf growth show-ing through the remaining flowers. Most of the flowers had turned brown and fallen to the ground at the base of each bush, but a few clusters remained on the branches. He touched a spray of pink blos-soms, bent over, and sniffed. They gave off no real scent. He heard the sound of the kid's car slamming into Laurie's car, sending it careening off the road. He had pictured the crash every day since the accident, pulled his hand back from the hot metal, recoiled from the stink of gasoline. He saw the kid who drove his family off the road, sitting in his living room, nursing his injuries. Mike was screaming in his head, not caring if anyone heard it. The back door opened. The kettle was screeching. Panting, he hurried back to the kitchen.

While they drank their tea, he told Monica about his plans to return to Philadelphia. She offered to help. He had felt smothered by such offers from other people, but he knew that she was not in a position to do much, so her offer touched him. He wondered if she had found any more notes from Roger and hoped that she had not. He thanked her for the tea and walked into the living room.

He sat beside Roger on the couch. "Place looks good, Roger," he said.

"Yessir."

On the television, a woman talked about how white her wash was. He squeezed the old man's shoulder then rose from the couch. Monica had been watching from the doorway. He walked over and they held each other as the television droned on behind them. When Laurie popped into his mind, he closed his eyes and told himself to think about Monica, Roger, azaleas.

11

SATURDAY, JANUARY 28

Seven videos, none of which screamed *yes* to her. She'd been in the video store for a good half hour. Who hunted for a Saturday night movie with pages of notes? Captioned foreign-language films would be a disaster; likewise any obvious date movie. Nothing historical. She couldn't abide a stupid comedy. She had *some* standards. It should be nothing either of them had seen before. She discreetly pulled her tiny notebook out of her jeans pocket, extracted the nub of a pencil from its wire spiral, then scratched a line through all but two titles.

Any film that two people as smart and different as Florence and her brother raved about merited consideration. *The Princess Bride.* "As entertaining as the book," Florence had insisted, "and perfect casting." She pictured Mike studying the box in her living room, puzzlement all over his face. Two of the title's three words might be enough to put him off. She'd preview it some other time. She stashed the notebook in her pocket, pulled the ticket for *The Big Easy* off its display box, then headed to the checkout.

Stopping at the Night Kitchen on the way home, Sarah strode resolutely past the chocolate cakes and tortes—too fraught with memory, too romantic—to more neutral baked goods, settling on oatmeal raisin cookies. A sealable bag would keep their aromatic presence a secret once she'd stashed them up high in the cupboard—yet accessible should events warrant a call-up of reserves. Driving the few blocks to her home, her self-satisfied smile vanished when she remembered Friday's call from Tom Hennessey. After a cursory question about her emotional status, he told her that he and Leona and the Goldmans were all feeling impossibly behind on home matters and had decided to put their monthly dinner get-togethers on hiatus. Not forever, of course. "Have you felt as swamped as we do this semester?" he asked, then sighed.

"No worries," she told him, allowing herself the smirk she'd have suppressed if they'd been face to face. When she'd hung up, she swelled with an odd combination of relief and hurt. *Chalk it up, kiddo.*

At home, she left the video on the coffee table, where Mike might or might not notice it. Every appliance and surface in the kitchen glistened. She called her parents, mentioning that she had a date that evening with the guy she'd been seeing now and then. "Yes," she said, "the Mike whose last name you still haven't heard. It's Flannagan but with two Ns in the middle. Don't say you don't know anything about my friend. We're just watching a movie." It was quarter to six. All she had to do tomorrow was read the paper and take a walk in Valley Green.

Did her tiny revelation to her parents account for the buoyancy she felt now? The sour taste from her conversation with Tom felt like an ancient and irrelevant wrong. She and Mike would like the movie. The pizza was their favorite. A six-pack of Yuengling lager sat in the coldest part of her refrigerator.

In the living room, she gave the audio system's power button a friendly poke. She couldn't remember when she'd last used the phonograph, but following an impulse she turned it on. In seconds, acoustic guitars and the powerful baritone of folk singer Stan Rogers filled the room.

When she heard the rat-a-tat, rat-a-tat on the door, she looked at the clock. Six on the nose. Even though he had the key, he always gave his little drumroll before opening the inside door.

"Michael!" she called as he stepped in. Balancing a paper bag that must contain something sweet atop two large pizza boxes, he made for the kitchen to unload his cargo on the table. Turning to her, he half-smiled, and they hugged briefly beside the table.

"Somebody got *styled*," she said, admiring his hair. "Looks like I'm out of a job." One worth losing, from the look of him.

"Got myself an Italian barber, the real article."

"I'd hold onto him." The aroma from the steaming pizza boxes instantly stole her concentration. "How did you not eat one of these on the way over," she said, breathing in the hearty bouquet of scents.

"More than we need," he said, now pressing his palms down on the steamy box on top. "Not cold enough out there to wear gloves, but cold enough."

"I beg to differ," she cheeped. "I wore mine this afternoon. What are we going to do with all this pizza?"

"Maybe Sunday dinner for some of us, Monday lunch for others?"

She laughed. "Not a problem."

From the brown bag, he produced a smaller brown paper bag and a bottle of rosé, something she'd never seen him drink. "Brownies from the farmer's market," he said. "Didn't eat much today."

"Looks like you will tonight," she said.

Standing beside his haul on the table, he nodded, a weary expression on his face.

"Busy day?" she asked.

"They've all been," he said, forcing a smile.

"You need a beer," she pronounced. "And claim your spot in the living room. We can nosh while we watch."

"What's tonight's feature?" He was still warming his hands on the pizza box.

"We don't even have to watch it if you don't want," she said. "*The Big Easy.*"

"Heard it's good," he said, looking a tad more chipper. "Good soundtrack too."

"Great."

"This is Stan Rogers," he said, pointing toward the living room.

She nodded, reaching into the refrigerator and pulling out two beers.

"The wine's chilled, if you want."

When she turned to hand him his opened beer bottle, he was looking off. "Really lucky I got to see him perform."

Somehow he'd revealed that tidbit in the early days, a surprise that fueled her growing interest in him, especially since nothing suggested that he had been trying to impress her. His lack of guile continued to draw her to him. Odd that he combined such honest transparency with stealth-like privacy. Guileless would hardly describe her own sensibility tonight. If he couldn't see that they belonged together, perhaps she could help him out. "I wish I'd known about him before he died," she said, heading to the living room. "I'll put the album on from the start. It's the concert one."

Again the rousing ballad about a wounded knight rang out in the living room. When Mike sat at the end of the couch, she took the stuffed chair beside him. They would drink their beers—her first in months—and listen together. Deal with later when it arrived. They had set this course without any suggestions or questions. No "processing," as they liked to say in department meetings.

"Man!" Mike said, nodding at the end of a verse. Stan Rogers hadn't written this song, but like so many of his own, "The Witch of the Westmorland" made you want to charge off on your steed or at least roar the words of the refrain. The lyrics of the tale floated over Sarah, and the rising and falling guitar chords carried her along. *Just listen. No analysis. No commentary. He's already made his comment. Enjoy that.*

The second song was Mike's favorite, "Barrett's Privateers." Desperate call and response. A chorus right out of the most urgent sea shanty, yet mournful. Had Mike shocked her by singing along with the refrain, she'd have belted it out with him. She sipped her lager and nodded to the beat like Mike.

"Damn," he said, when the song ended to the hoots and hollers of the live audience. He was shaking his head, a severe look on his face. *Great song? Such a story? That poor bastard?*

She almost said, "Yes!"

The next song, a slow ballad, seemed to have less hold on him. A verse in, he turned to her. "How did your week finish?"

"All right." Aside from the slap in the face she'd taken from the friends she'd been so anxious for him to meet. And she'd grown so accustomed to scurrying to and from the parking space in the garage that she'd decided actual runs in the park might be a good idea. *My parents know your last name now.* "My classes went well," she said, "and I'm all caught up on grading!"

"For the moment," he said, with a twinkle in his eye.

"I am starved," she announced. "We could eat in the kitchen then watch the movie, or just bring pizza out here and start the flick." *Why had she used a term she hated?*

"Either way, as long as food is involved," Mike said.

She rose and stood beside the couch. "What if we start with a slice or two while watching the first twenty minutes then hit pause, see if we want to keep going, and maybe take a break for dessert?"

"I can get it set up while you bring in the food," Mike said, rising. He was on his way to turn off the stereo when the next song, "The Mary Ellen Carter," came on.

"Wait!" Sarah called. "Oh my God. I have to hear it."

"I can get the video ready."

"No, do you mind listening too?"

"Okay," he said, and returned to his spot on the couch.

Back in the chair, she leaned back and closed her eyes. They listened silently. "Thank you," she said when it was over. She let out a long breath and nodded toward the video machine that he'd been ready to start up.

"Good song," he said. He opened the video box and extracted the video cassette.

"You know about the guy who kept singing this song when his ship sank in a storm and he thought he'd drown? Waves taking him under again and again."

"Now that you mention it," Mike said, nodding, "I'd forgotten."

"I can't imagine," Sarah said, but that was exactly what she was doing. Gasping for air between immersions into the freezing waters, reminding herself that she must find her way back up again.

Mike turned off the stereo, hit power on the video machine and the TV, then inserted the cassette.

"I'll get the pizza," she said, standing up. Rushing to gather napkins and plates helped focus her. She filled a glass of ice water for herself then placed two slices on each plate.

When she carried her first load into the living room, Mike's eyes were closed. She set the plates and napkins on the coffee table then padded back to the kitchen for her water.

She poured the rest of her beer into the sink. Pizza and a movie, she thought. Simple. She drank down her water then refilled it. Carrying it in, she found him sighing gently in his sleep.

When she sat beside him and took a bite, Mike stirred. "Shit," he said.

"You need sleep more than pizza."

"No, no," he said, pulling himself up. He smiled at the slices on his plate. "Great," he said. "It's all cued up."

"Let's enjoy this a bit before we multitask."

Looking relieved, he picked up a piece and took a bite. "Mmm."

"Take out one of these two toppings," Sarah said, "it's totally different. I couldn't say why."

"You're right," he said. "Like cheese on a cheesesteak."

She laughed. "Demon cheese," she sneered. "Direct to your arteries, but so good." She was still working on her first piece when Mike finished his. How had he done that?

"Not ready to distract myself yet, if you don't mind," he said, reaching for another piece.

"I'm with you," she chirped.

"And I'm multitasking already. Eating a mushroom pizza and a sausage pizza. Doesn't that count as two?"

He was giddy. Was he drunk, high? Or so knackered from working crazy hours that he'd gotten downright silly? "You are sleeping at night, aren't you?" she said.

"Yeah," he said. He took a bite. "Just putting in longer hours than I'm used to."

"Doesn't that worry you? It worries me."

He frowned. "It worries me if I *don't* put in the hours."

"Is your sister-in-law any better?"

He shook his head. "Hard to say. I mean, it's hard for the doctors to say."

"Awful," she said.

"Some things just take time and patience. That's enough to tire out anybody."

"You're right."

"Things I need to do, have to do." Finishing his second piece, he shook his head. "A three-piece night," he said, rising. "At least."

"I'll stop the barrage on my waistline," she said. "But I'm saving room for brownies."

When he returned and sat again, he landed with an engineer's precision, neither closer to nor further from Sarah. "I know you're working hard, Sarah, and being careful at the college. That's important. People can be dangerous. Have you heard anything more from the authorities?"

"The dean seems to think I'm Jesse James or something."

"Ridiculous," he said. Using his hands as guns, he fired them both in the air like a cowboy. "But nothing new about that punk?"

"No," she said. The last thing she wanted was for him to start worrying, but this sounded a lot like worry. "It's all going to pass."

"Yes," he said. "You're going to be fine. I'm sure you always keep your eyes and ears open, right?"

"Of course," she said.

"These are just days when everything seems to be going at warp speed. For both of us. No wonder we're tired, hungry, whatever. That expression: running around like a chicken with its head cut off. That's me these days, and maybe you too."

Warp speed exactly described the way he was talking, not taking a breath between sentences. "What else is going on, Mike?"

"Like I said, all the usual stuff, lots of it. New tasks, unexpected. Adds up. The old guy who cut my hair at the shop on the avenue? Domenic Gallo. Robert and I ran into him again today walking past the shop."

"Whoa," Sarah said.

"Robert took to him immediately, like old friends. Some people have that. He laughed when I told him he might be one of those guys who has that special channel with dogs."

How to say something about this manic flash without anger-
ing him? But the thing with this Domenic seemed to be positive.
"We don't have to watch the movie, Mike. We can just be here
like this."

"No, no, no," he said. "Let's give it a look. Okay?"

"Sure," she said.

He moved into action with the electronics. In seconds, she'd
dimmed the lighting and they were zooming over southern Louisiana wetlands with Cajun music zipping them along.

They both liked the movie, though the romance scenes felt to
her like they'd never end. The two stars seemed to be a couple at
the end. "Fucking corruption," Mike said, when the credits wound
down. "Didn't see that coming, the cop," he said, shaking his head.
"Good story, though."

After brownies at the kitchen table, Mike said he had an early
start at the seminary, not a whole day, but still.

"Not a problem," she said, packing up the beer and all but one
slice of the pizza for Mike.

"Thanks for all this," he said, "I mean, getting together here and
all. And not being insulted that I couldn't see you earlier this week."

"Who says I'm not insulted?" she drawled.

"You know," he said, reddening.

"It's okay," she said, handing him his takeaways.

"Looking pretty slammed this whole week," he said, "but we
could go for a walk Sunday if it's nice?"

"I'll put it in pencil on my calendar. Two on Sunday, okay?"

He hugged her then gave her a kiss on the forehead. "'Night," he
said, then turned and left.

She watched through the window as he got into his car, but he
did not look up or tap his horn when he pulled out. It had not been

a bad night, but she almost wished they'd fought, if it would have moved things.

Sunday's walk in Valley Green did nothing to improve her spirits. Nothing she found in the *Sunday Times* or the *Inquirer* made her crack a smile, but that was hardly unusual.

Her Monday classes went as planned, but the unsettled feeling persisted. Sometimes a few students would follow Sarah to her office, but hardly anyone ever showed up during the second half of the day's final office hour. When Natalie from the last class finished going over her draft with her, Sarah began tidying up the office.

She lined up her handouts for the next day's classes, unable to see anything in Saturday's "date" that had moved the relationship forward. Mike's nervousness and the business with the old man was just strange. She pulled out the yellow pages from her desk drawer. There was only one possibility on the avenue in the neighborhood, Al's Barbershop. So, it was not his shop. She called the number and listened to the ring, feeling the way she had when she was in high school and called a boy for the first time.

"Barbershop," a man's voice said.

"May I speak with Domenic?"

"For you," the voice said. Al? She imagined him giving the old man a look, maybe teasing him about getting a call from a woman.

"This is Domenic."

"I'm sorry," she stammered. "You don't know me. My name is Sarah Goins. I know a little about you through Mike Flannagan. I hope I'm not scaring you."

"You're confusing me."

"Sorry. I would like to talk with you, if you don't mind. Maybe we could meet?"

"Meet?"

She thought she heard laughter in the background. "I'm not a kook," she said. She explained that she was a teacher at the community college where Mike had taken a course and that they were friends. "I'm worried about him."

"I don't know," he said. There was a long pause. "I'm afraid you got the wrong guy." Then he hung up.

"Maybe I shouldn't own a telephone," she muttered, as she put the phone down.

12

MONDAY, JANUARY 30

After the shop had closed and he'd had a quick bite to eat, Domenic took the trolley to Chelten Avenue where he caught the bus that brought him to the Shrine of Our Lady of the Miraculous Medal, Angela's "little cathedral." He arrived in time for the six o'clock devotion, the seventh such service of the day. He sat in a pew a third of the way back from the altar.

Long ago, at Angela's request, they had made one novena here after the other, completing one every nine weeks then beginning another one. Three years of novenas and trying to conceive a child. He leaned back in his pew, feeling greatly fatigued. It was, after all, the end of a long day. Domenic did not sing along with the opening hymn but closed his eyes and listened to the voices around him. He did not need the little prayer booklet sitting at the end of the pew any more than he needed an instruction guide for trimming a man's hair.

Reciting the prayer along with the congregation, Domenic, as always, tried to think about the words as he said them. Suddenly, the prayer paused, letting congregants silently ask for Mary's intercession on their behalf—the moment when he and Angela had begged that they might have just one child. Today Domenic silently said: *Thank you for my Angela.*

The prayer resumed, and after a short sermon, the congregation sang another hymn. During these activities and through the benediction of the Blessed Sacrament, Domenic did his best to keep his mind on Mary, on Jesus, and on his Angela, but his thoughts kept drifting, as they did every week, this time focusing on the puzzle that was Mike Flannagan. A week ago, he'd never met the guy, but now it seemed he couldn't make it down his apartment stairs without running into him, or someone who knew him.

Mike's brother and his hospitalized wife. The woman so worried about Mike that she'd called the shop—he'd written down her name, but it wasn't coming to him now. Domenic wondered what Mike's people might be like. They all needed prayers. All around the church, voices sang and prayed aloud, but Domenic remained preoccupied by this new sadness that invaded him whenever he thought about Mike. He did not want this new yet familiar complication in his life, but here it was. Mike Flannagan's sadness reminded him of his own and probably could fill a book, but Domenic already had sensed that he would learn no more about his new acquaintance except what he might ferret out of a fleeting look during an unguarded moment.

When the service concluded, Domenic descended to the small grotto shrine on the church's lower level then dropped a quarter into a slot that electronically triggered the lighting of one of the hundreds of candles in blue holders around the statue of Mary. *For Mike.* He settled his creaky knees onto one of the padded kneelers facing the statue and candles. Soon, a family of three took their places in the row in front of his. He heard someone moving onto the row behind him. *Kneelers.* They came, knelt for two minutes, for twenty minutes, then slipped away without a word. For them, too, he thought, there's reason to pray just a bit more before returning to the challenges and burdens that had propelled them out of their homes and into a car or onto East Germantown-bound buses on a winter Monday.

He closed his eyes. The woman in front of him softly said

something in Spanish to the little boy beside her. Twice today, he'd heard the sound of a young woman's voice. When was the last time? He'd hung up on the college teacher who'd called. It all happened so fast. Still confused him. Had some part of him wanted to run away? *The glance.* He felt Angela's eyes on him: *Oh, Domenic.* Never lasting for even a full second before the sides of her mouth curved and her eyes again said, *My Domenic.* Did she know that he'd have withered if she held that look?

He recited to himself the Act of Contrition then repeated it, fearing that he might have truly felt only some of the familiar phrases the first time through. The Lord would forgive him. But had he pushed Angela too far by not at least listening to the young stranger? She'd done him no wrong. He needed to learn from Angela's glance.

He'd hugged Angela close every time that glance had dissolved, neither of them needing to say a word. Disappointing no one else in the world could hurt him that much, but he'd welcome the pain if it meant feeling her clutch her arms around his neck and pull herself tightly to him one more time. *Why, God?* Around him, others prayed for rescues, cures, reprieves. God would answer all of them, one way or another. He knew not to ask to find her kneeling beside him when he opened his eyes, but he imagined turning and finding her there every time he closed his eyes in a church.

13

TUESDAY, JANUARY 31

Walking through the parking garage, Sarah was not able to rid herself of the image of the man who had scared her the day of the fight. When the garage elevator door closed, leaving her alone inside, she felt her entire body relax. She stopped at the bagel truck outside her building for coffee. Teaching her poetry class brought both a rush and a relief. The students talked as if the material, some of her favorite texts, mattered to them. She sprang down the Mint Building steps, pausing only to treat herself to a yogurt and a bag of hard pretzels from the machines at the end of her floor en route to her Tuesday office hour.

She had spread out the *Inquirer* food section on her desk and held a pretzel in one hand and a spoonful of yogurt in the other when she heard feet shuffling at her doorway. She twisted around and saw an old man peeking at her around the corner.

"Miss Goins?" The man stepped into the open doorway, an overcoat slung over one arm. "I'm looking for Sarah Goins, the teacher?" he said.

His accent: Italian? South Philly? His craggy face bore some resemblance to the guy with the pompadour, but she couldn't be sure.

"And if I am?" she said.

Her pepper spray sat inside a pocket of her coat, which hung on the back of the office door.

"I'm not trying to be funny," he said.

"I don't think you're funny at all." She slid the drawer open and put her hand on the scissors.

"Somehow," he said, "I think you are."

"What's it to you?"

"What's it to *you*?" he said. "You called me."

"You're the barber!" she gasped. She closed the drawer. He looked at her as if she were foaming at the mouth, and she felt her face turning crimson. "Domenic?"

He shook his head. "I don't know what I'm doing here."

She took a deep breath. "No, please. Sit down."

Warily, he took the chair closer to the door and laid his coat across his lap.

Sarah realized she was shaking. "Your voice sounded different," she said. "I'm sorry." He looked much older than her parents, but she couldn't tell by how much. His hair was mostly gray, cut short but not quite military short. He wore a baggy pair of gray slacks and a white button-up shirt that needed ironing.

"Never talked to a college professor," he said drumming his fingers on his overcoat.

"You're a friend of Mike?" she said.

"He's my go-to guy whenever I get mugged," he said. "Nah, he helped me one night. That's all. You probably know him a lot better than me."

Sarah blushed again. "I don't know. Maybe I know him too well."

The old man seemed to consider that for a moment. "Who is it exactly that you're worried about?"

"Whoa," she said, bristling. She breathed out slowly. "All right, it hasn't gone as well for him and me as I wanted it to. And I didn't exactly help him when he probably needed it." She told him about her classroom brawl and the consequences.

He listened to her story the way she'd hoped the dean would and the way she'd expected Leona would.

"Mike knows about this?" he said, when she finished.

She nodded. There was a definite edge to this old man, but she no longer feared he might say or do something dangerous. "I knew something was wrong, but he wouldn't go into it. He tried to listen, like you."

"Doesn't sound like such a bad guy."

"Things have gone badly in his life. I do worry about him."

"Is anything going well for him?"

She shrugged. "I guess I'm not the one to ask."

"Probably that dog of his gets the inside story," Domenic said.

"Tell you the truth, I think I was a little jealous of you," Sarah admitted. "There's a list of things he won't go into with me."

"We talked about sports and indoor lighting," Domenic said. He looked away from her, scanning the walls. "I don't know that we should be talking like this." He shook his head again. "And I'm afraid I can't be much assistance to either you or him." The old man rose to his feet.

"Thanks for coming, Domenic," she said.

"Thanks for not stabbing me," he said, glancing at the drawer.

Sarah's face reddened again. Three times in one conversation. Nobody had ever done that to her before. The old man turned and was out the doorway.

Driving out of the college garage that afternoon, Sarah reached for her sunglasses against the bright slanting sun. Several hours of daylight remained, so she drove straight to Valley Green Inn and parked the car. She walked up Forbidden Drive, the dirt and gravel stretch alongside the Wissahickon closed to motor vehicles, except the occasional police car. Sarah passed a troop of joggers wearing shorts and T-shirts and cheerily plying their way down the broad path. Last day of January. Philly weather fuckery, she called it. Next week might bring both a blizzard and a heat wave. The swath of woods bordering the Wissy drew crowds of walkers, runners, bikers, and horseback riders from Roxborough on one side of the creek and Chestnut Hill, Mount Airy, and Germantown on the other side. For Sarah, it had been one of the main attractions of this part of the city, enticing her to walk or jog on the trails and bridle paths at least once a week.

Mike had agreed to go for a walk here on Sunday, a rare return to his childhood turf. Two weeks earlier she had attended a Wild Wissahickon meeting tasked with finding humane alternatives to hunting the deer that overpopulated the park, a conclave that Mike never would have made it through. He did not even like the broadness of the much-used Forbidden Drive. When he did bring Robert down here, they spent their time on the small trails that snaked their way up and down the heavily wooded ravines on either side of the creek. Sarah hiked past the first dam toward Chestnut Hill trying to picture Domenic and Mike having a conversation. Oh, to be a fly on the wall for that get-together. She decided that she liked this Domenic and that he might be more helpful than he thought.

14

SUNDAY, FEBRUARY 5

Three walks would be enough for Robert. Mike double-locked the front door behind the two of them, set Robert loose, then hung his knit cap and winter coat back in the hall closet. The temperature wasn't going to be quite as low as yesterday but close enough. Two more times out into the damn cold.

Sarah had no idea how much time he spent outside. The garage building might as well be a hilltop in the blustery north woods. When Mike wasn't on his twice-a-day missions to her campus, his regular and make-up hours at the seminary included enough outdoor jobs to make him feel that heated buildings were mostly for breaks. After last week's weather tease, he felt ready for real spring, with blooming flowers other than the defiant crocuses that held their purple noses high above two or three inches of Philadelphia snow. She would understand that he didn't want to take a stroll in freezing weather. He just couldn't think of an alternative, a counteroffer.

Their planned walk was only a few hours off. When he'd finished cereal and coffee, he stood up and reached for the wall phone.

"I'm sorry, Sarah," he said, leaning against the refrigerator door and hoping for inspiration. "Not a day when I want to be outside more than I have to be. I know it's different for people who don't spend much time out there."

He thought he heard her breathing out. "I had been looking forward to it," she said.

"Shit."

"I mean, you would have to wear gloves," she said. "And a winter hat, maybe something more formidable than that flimsy woolen thing you wear. Plus a really thick coat. Some people wear a sweater underneath their coat too. Layering can make such a difference."

"I'm a total wuss."

She laughed but it sounded forced.

"I'm not the best company these days," he said. "This special project's got me coming and going. If I fall asleep on you again, it's not you."

"So nothing today?"

Did her voice catch?

When he didn't respond, she asked, "Is your sister-in-law any better, Mike?"

"Delores," he sighed. "The memory thing's still a mystery. And how she could come down with equine encephalitis is beyond me, but that's what they're thinking now. Medically, they seem to think it's under control."

"Well, that's a start."

"More people I'm not seeing as much as I should," he said. He paced toward the natural light of the kitchen window. Stopped by the cord as he neared the sink, he stared blankly out the window across the six-foot breezeway between the adjacent row houses.

"You're needed."

"Never been the best at stepping up."

"Mike, you're trying—even if you are a wuss."

"For the people I'm trying to help," he said, "it can't feel like I'm doing a bang-up job."

Movement startled him. His neighbor was cleaning the inside of her kitchen window. Holding a container of Windex, she smiled and waved at him across the short distance between their windows. He nodded and managed a smile.

"How are they treating you at work, Sarah?"

"Not a topic we can cover in less than a weekend conference," she said.

"Fuck," he said. *Hey, you missed a spot, Lanie. By the way, got any profound words I should offer the woman I keep hurting?*

"Good news: the college leadership believes I am trainable. I'll leave it at that."

"Not right."

"As you know—better than I seem to—not all people should be trusted. Your instincts are good, Mike. More topics for that weekend conference I hope we can arrange."

"Ever the professor," he said. "Your brain thinks in college terms."

"Is that a problem?"

"I didn't mean that, no." *But it was cute.* But saying that might send the wrong message. At least now. It was all about timing, always. "Wait, you know how you get hit with all those papers and exams at the end of the semester?" he said. "That's what this feels like. I wish I wasn't slammed. I'm working hard, trying to do the right thing."

"I believe you, Mike."

He crossed the room to the wall calendar and peeked at February, but the blankness under each number suggested no activities they might do together.

"Look," she said, her voice brightening. "I know we just watched a movie—well, a week ago—but I saw one you might like. Don't go by the title. *The Princess Bride.*"

"Great movie," he said.

"What?"

"Saw it with Brendan's family, back around Christmas."

"It's my turn to say *shit*," she said.

"In-con-*ceiv*-able," he said, mimicking Wallace Shawn's voice.

"You bastard."

They both laughed.

February, or *Febbraio* on this calendar she'd given him, offered the fewest possible dates of the year. Groundhog Day, Mardi Gras—please, no. Valentine's Day—steer clear, Flannagan, talk about sending the wrong message. Presidents' Day. Nothing. "How long do your grading binges go on?" he said.

"Why?"

"I think mine might own me for another week or so."

"Call me when you've turned in your grades," she said.

"I promise."

"I'll still hate you."

"I know. Everybody hates the authority figure."

"Don't I know it," she said.

Pompadour could drop the whole thing, start volunteering in a soup kitchen, or move across the country. How would Mike know? Or he might show up tomorrow. No matter, Mike would keep watch as long as he needed to. "This may clear up faster than I expect," he said. "I'll call as soon as possible."

"Stay warm, Michael. You big sissy."

"You stay safe," he said. "Bye."

When she'd said goodbye and hung up, he dropped back into his chair. *Sissy* and *wuss* were far too kind. This could have been a time when he said something that might point them toward an end, but that hadn't felt right either. Whether or not they were a real couple, he was her friend.

Robert strolled in from the living room, looked at Mike, then headed back. "I'm disappointing you too, buddy?" Robert turned at the sound of his human's voice, giving him a look that Mike swore was a smirk. "Right back at ya," he called. He leaned back in his kitchen chair and sighed. "We're a couple too," he said. "Aren't we? *That's* love. He and Sarah were something, had something. Did it matter what he or she called it? They'd just made each other laugh, even though it wasn't a happy moment. A kind of love? *Why can't that be enough?*

When it was time for Robert's afternoon walk, Mike took him up the avenue to Domenic's block. Walking on the sidewalk across the street gave him a better view of the apartment's windows. No sign of activity. When he reached the edge of the seminary, he jiggled Robert's leash, and they turned back. A gust of wind caught him in the face, stopped him for a second. Cold, but hardly so brutal that he should have nixed the walk with Sarah. He'd wronged her again.

Across from the barbershop building, he let Robert sniff the edge of the sidewalk and a parking meter. The dog lingered, as if finally allowed to do the work he was meant to do. Domenic's canine reach again? Were the old man to appear in the window above the shop and wave him over, Mike would head right over, dog and all. He knew it, though he couldn't explain it if his life depended on it.

Sarah had called him passive-aggressive once, teasingly. "Oh, Mike," she'd snickered, and given his cheek a peck. Sarcasm? Irony? He didn't ask, just laughed along. She'd have a term for whatever he was doing now.

He pulled Robert ahead, relieved that he and Sarah at least had avoided having a big fight, and disappointed that he hadn't seen Domenic.

15

THURSDAY, FEBRUARY 9

After her call with Mike, the walk in Valley Green by herself had proved a mixed blessing. She locked her car in the lot beside Wissahickon Creek, sniffed the air, then wrenched down the zipper of her jacket, as if her gesture might have some impact on Mike. Her frustrations with him were a distraction, she told herself. *Enjoy the damn trees.*

Still gritting her teeth, she'd hit the trail at a quick pace then realized after a half mile that she was practically jogging. The exhilaration reminded her of former levels of fitness. The path, dappled with shadows and brightly sunlit patches, beckoned her on. Above her, calling birds flitted from one side of the creek to the other. This was a soundtrack she could live with. *Even pain and anger bring unexpected rewards.* Next time she'd stretch out beforehand then do a proper run for the first time in months.

She sent her eyes across the gurgling creek and the pair of shivering ducks on the far rocky shoreline, the high wall of trees behind—so much to take in, yet apparently not enough to banish occasional intrusions by Mike's sullen and silent face in her purposeful walk. Her creekside ruminations followed upstream. Had those awkward gaps in their conversations increased in frequency, or did they just hurt more now? *Fuck.* She turned abruptly and started back. The ducks, the iced-over edges of the far side of the creek, and the bare trees that she'd just passed all looked different with her headed in the other direction. Despite her efforts, the relationship might just be running out of gas. Sobering, this new possibility—or was she merely grasping what had been there for a while? She turned her head slightly to her right, shifting her view from the creek to the unpeopled trail ahead of her, the woods that bordered it on the right. A car running out of gas, she thought, hardly required the same drastic measures as did discovering that its engine needed replacement. Suddenly, building a relationship with Mike felt within reach again. *If I can trust my analogy.*

Later at home, reorganizing and tidying the shelves in her medicine cabinet, she realized that again she was mentally inventorying the by-products of therapeutic cleaning. Energy expended begat fresh energy and ideas of where to use it. Scurrying around a cleaned apartment left her nearly as rejuvenated as a hot bath. A cleared desktop invited her to set right in on grading, not waste a minute.

Two phone calls to her parents that week and one to her brother, Jeffrey, had yielded no causes for alarm, but it crossed her mind that concern for her father was playing itself out in her constitution. Sunday night she felt miserable, not sure whether she was experiencing the beginnings of a cold or her period that was due on Monday. But her period might not be coming just yet, and a third skipped period in a year's time would not be a first for her crazy system.

A baby? A whirlwind of emotions pulled her up then down, then the same thing again. She took a thousand milligrams of vitamin C and went to bed early. In the morning, she took another heavy dose of vitamin C and reminded herself that she should go for the decaf. Monday's classes went fine, but she still felt run down. Her symptoms had abated. The missing period and the dodged cold felt like a warning, and she vowed to be more healthful, to pay more attention to her needs. She would follow her instincts. With her history, there was no reason to give any time to the possibility that her birth control had somehow suddenly gone kaput. After a false positive on a home pregnancy test five years ago, she wasn't about to go that route again. If she missed another one, sure. But if that day came, she wouldn't need a calendar note to tell her. She'd be on the phone to her doctor.

She studied the mostly empty blocks on February's calendar page. The shortest month. She pulled the page up to sneak a look at March. Spring break. Then the usual meetings. Soon, she'd be expected to line up sessions with a counselor to work out her atonement. She let the page fall back. February again. All those things could wait. Fuel, she thought.

Driving down the avenue after Thursday's classes, she noticed the barbershop, four doors away from the food co-op. She had to have noticed it before, but she could not remember even looking in the window. Not a thing needed cleaning at home. No fresh papers had arrived in the day's classes. She parked the car across from Gilhooley's Tavern, another unexplored site that held no allure. She had not figured out how Domenic was going to help with her Mike situation, but she knew she needed to get to know the man better. The barbershop was his domain, so she would approach him there. She had survived rather than starred in the improvisational acting class she'd taken as an undergraduate, but she would walk into the shop with faith that the right words would come out of her mouth.

At four-thirty she turned the door handle and stepped inside Al's Barbershop. At the chair closest to the window, a barber she took to be Al was cutting a teenager's hair. Domenic, also wearing a light blue smock, was seated in the other barber chair. An elderly Black man sat at one end of the line of chairs, and an equally ancient white man sat at the opposite corner, like bookends. She had expected it to be an all-white enclave, and the Black man's presence pleased her and made her feel less the intruder in this all-male world. The barber paused in his cutting and smiled in her direction.

"Well, well, well," Domenic said from his seat. "Of all the gin joints in all the world."

She felt her face redden.

Domenic walked over and offered his hand, half-smiling at her.

She shook his hand. "I owe you for helping me the other day."

The others looked at her and Domenic as if this were a routine they were getting used to. "I hope you don't mind if I visit."

"Here?" Domenic said.

"Believe it or not, I've got a little experience at cutting hair," she said, wondering where that had come from.

"I should have guessed," he said.

"And I used to do my girlfriends' nails in high school," she said.

Al stopped clipping the young man's hair and looked her up and down. The teenager, his mouth agape, was looking at her in the mirror. The elderly man nearest her stifled a laugh. She looked around the room. Two barber chairs. Near the man at the other end of the room sat a chair that looked like a coin-operated horse seat. Nearby, a sink with hot and cold water taps hooked high above the bowl dominated the middle of the room. "I'm pretty good with shampoos, Mister Al." She flashed upon the moment in improv class when she'd tried to say something funny about the teacher's toupee.

The kid in the barber chair looked frightened. The barber stared at her the way she had stared at the freshman who said to her, "What do you mean, poems don't have to rhyme?"

"Not Mister Al," he said. "I'm Al. This is a barbershop. We don't do shampoos."

He wasn't rude, just informative, but Sarah felt like she'd crashed a party and been found out. "I understand."

"Sarah," Domenic said, cupping her elbow with his hand and steering her around the room. "You've met Al. Meet Clement over here, and the lovely and talented Nick."

She smiled at the two men.

"Do you guys want a shampoo?" Al asked Clement and Nick.

"You run the water in that faucet," Nick said, "ten dollars says something orange comes out."

"If you're lucky," Clement added.

"Honey, you don't have to prove that you can work here to walk in the door," Al said to her.

"But this is foreign territory," she said.

"What, no visa?" Al said.

"I'm genuinely curious," she said to Al. "And if you'd let me write about it, you could help other women learn about a part of life they probably don't know about." There, she thought. She hadn't had the idea until she said it. "Just like you don't know about places women go to get their hair done." *Was it such a stretch?*

The bookends gave each other a look.

"When's the last time you saw an article about barbers?" she asked.

"That's the point," Clement said.

"People already know," Nick said, "or they don't care."

"So, what am *I* doing here?" Sarah said.

"Stick around five minutes," Domenic said. "You'll know all you want to know about barbering."

"Domenic's your man," Al said. "Been doing this longer than me."

"Yeah," Nick said. "Tell her what it was like trimming General Grant's beard."

They all laughed, including Sarah. She had no idea where this mad stunt was headed, but she felt the best she had in weeks.

Domenic was flapping his thumbs against his fingers, miming little chattering mouths. "*Chiacchierones!*"

"New vocabulary," Clement said.

"What's this 'cackle' bit?" Nick said.

"Exactly," Domenic said. "Like a bunch of hens. Or in this case, some cranky old roosters." Nodding toward the row of chairs, he told her to take her coat off.

Sarah sat in a chair midway between Nick and Clement and placed her coat in the empty seat beside her. "I would want quotes from both barbers. And from customers." She wished she'd had a pen and notebook with her. When she looked at the kid getting the haircut, he averted his eyes. As soon as Al finished his work, the teenager paid him quickly and was out the door before Sarah could hit him with a question. The four men roared when the door slammed.

"Well, fortunately it looks like you have a couple of customers who would be more willing than that fellow," Sarah said. The laughter halted, replaced by the stillness of an empty church.

Nick broke the silence by rising from his seat. He headed for Al's chair.

Al looked to the heavens. "A day to remember," he said.

"I figure I'm due," Nick said. "Shave and a haircut."

"Always thought Nick would look smart in a mohawk," Clement said.

"Woman needs quotes from a customer," Nick said. "Ready for you, ma'am." He plopped himself into the chair. Al walked around him, inspecting his bald pate and white back and sides.

"You won't know I'm here," Sarah said.

"If you were a man," Clement said to Sarah, "that old coot would still be sitting in his corner."

"This I got to see," Domenic said, taking his place in his barber chair again.

Al draped a clean cloth around Nick.

"And what would you like, sir?" he asked sarcastically. "You're not getting a shave. No one's gotten a shave here in thirty years."

"Take a little off the top," Nick said, pointing to his shiny pate.

Al clicked his scissors six inches above Nick's head. "Check," he said.

"And whatever else needs work," Nick said.

"Didn't barbers used to bleed people?" Clement said. "Al? Give her something good to write about."

Al started clipping the sides of Nick's hair.

"What you *doing*, Domenic?" Clement said.

Sarah turned to see Domenic pointing at Nick with his index finger and his pinky. He did not look happy.

"He's putting the maloiks on you, Nick," Clement said.

"I'm thinking about it," Domenic said. "Sizing him up is all."

"Don't do your Italian voodoo on me," Nick said.

"You'll know it if I put them on you, mister."

"I'm just getting a haircut."

"And making a lot of noise," Domenic said.

Al moved to the back of Nick's head.

"If he doesn't talk, I won't get any quotes," Sarah said. "What are these maloiks?"

Al stopped cutting and squinted theatrically at Sarah. "Evil eye," he said. "Bad things happen if somebody puts them on you."

"Domenic can take them off too," Clement said.

"There will be no sacrilege in my shop," Al said.

Domenic shook his head. "I'm not doing anything."

"It's like a curse?" Sarah said.

"It *is* a curse," Nick said.

"They call it *the gift*," Clement said.

Sarah didn't know which one to look at. "This is an Italian thing?"

"Not every Italian can do this," Nick said. "That's why they call it a gift."

"It's a gift to be able to give a curse?"

"Can be." Nick laughed.

"Just behave yourself," Domenic said. "Stop showing off in front of the woman."

"I'm getting a haircut. That's all." Nick looked to Clement, as if he might help him.

"Don't look at me. I ain't getting a haircut."

"You're next," Sarah said. "Aren't you?"

"I'm just waiting for him," Clement said, pointing to Nick.

"You know, Domenic," Nick said, "the Church don't like people doing that curse stuff anymore. Not my church."

"What do you know?" Clement said. "Place I go is pretty tolerant."

"What church is that?" Sarah asked.

"St. Vincent's," he said. "Catholic church down in Germantown. Run by the Vincentians, same bunch that got Al's son."

She turned to the shop's owner.

He frowned at Clement. "My son's a Vincentian priest," he said. "Nobody's *got* him."

"So you're Catholic," Sarah said.

Al nodded.

"And what church are you from?" she asked Nick.

"Holy Cross."

"And that would be?"

"Catholic," he said. "Regular Catholic."

"Oh," Sarah said, wondering if she was about to learn about warring Catholic factions.

"And don't go getting the idea that any Catholic should do that kind of stuff," Al said, looking at Domenic. "You know the rules here."

"I'm not saying anything," Domenic said, looking to the ceiling and making a gesture with his open hands that Sarah thought she had seen the Pope do on TV.

"It's got to be reserved for people who need it," Nick said. "Then I can accept it."

"Like murderers?" Sarah said.

"No," they chorused.

"That's evil," Clement said. "That's stone cold evil, and God deals with that stuff."

"Oh," Sarah said, bemused but curious.

"Certain personal wrongs," Nick said. "Wouldn't you say?" he asked Domenic.

Domenic looked like he was heading for a boil. Nick waved his hand at him in disgust.

"He knows, but he's not saying," Clement said. "Numbers and religious rules. He's got 'em. Right up in that head."

She had lived among Catholics and ex-Catholics in New York but had never had close friends who were Catholic. Half of her ancestors had been Jewish. Now half of her Jewish friends didn't believe in God. She'd had periods of curiosity but didn't know what she believed in anymore. The extent of Mike Flannagan's expressed views to her on the religion of his youth were the words, "Real crap."

"Maloiks," Nick said pensively. Al was carefully shaving around the back of his ears. "You'd put 'em on people who were *stunad*, as Domenic would say."

"Stupid," Clement said, mimicking Domenic's gesture from earlier.

"*Stonato*," Domenic enunciated.

"But *stunad* with an *attitude*," Nick said. "Like those people who would rather shoot you than do something about the deer in the woods?"

The men murmured their agreement.

"Want to curb the population in some half-baked way that even a kid can see don't make sense instead of just getting rid of some of the critters. Giving food to the hungry."

"They've destroyed almost every garden within a mile of the park," Al said.

"Gardens?" Domenic said. "Try finding something alive in the park. They eat everything."

"They want the deer to practice birth control," Nick said with a chuckle.

The others howled.

Sarah swallowed. "You'd put the maloiks on them?"

"Yeah," they roared back at her.

"You're not one of them bunny-huggers?" Nick asked her.

"I wouldn't call myself that."

"I mean, you come in here, talking about shampooing people and writing stories, but you don't strike me as someone who'd go and march around the park with a little protest sign like it's Vietnam or something," Clement said.

Al wiped off the last of the shaving cream around Nick's ear. She struggled to think what she might have written down if she'd brought a pen and pad with her.

Nick rose from the barber chair. He stepped closer to the big mirror. "Mmm," he said. "Sharp. I must admit, Al."

He returned to his former seat. He had not paid for his haircut. Clement made no move toward the open barber chair.

"Nothing much worth writing about in here, Miss," Nick said, looking very comfortable in his perch.

"She's a professor, for your information," Domenic piped up.

"Professor," Nick clucked. "You don't have anything to worry about. Domenic's not going to put the maloiks on you. He's sweet on you."

Domenic readied his fingers and slowly aimed them at Nick.

Nick made a cross with his index fingers.

"You can't ward me away."

Sarah had not improvised any great scheme involving Domenic and Mike. She was leaving with no actual quotes or points to make in any article, but she rose from her place with a smile on her face. "I think the article might not be about barbering per se. Not sure what I've learned, but I see that I need a notebook, if not a camera or tape recorder."

"Come back any time," Al said.

They all smiled at her. "But forget the shampoo idea," Al said. Domenic disappeared into the back room.

Coat in arm, Sarah walked to the door and turned to say goodbye. Domenic, now wearing a regular button-up shirt, walked briskly across the room to Sarah.

"Just one thing," the freshly coiffed Nick said. "Birth control for deer would involve the use of contraceptive devices. Right?"

"In some form," she said.

"Given the dexterity of deer, wouldn't this require some human involvement?"

"Oh, shut up!" Domenic squawked. They hooted. Domenic announced that he was done for the day. She and the old man stepped out of the barbershop to a hail of catcalls. "Don't let those fools get to you," he said to her, pausing on the sidewalk out front.

"They're great."

"I'm honored that you came here."

"My car is right up the street," Sarah said.

"No such thing as a sane thought or a private conversation in there," he said. "It's in the license. I know they won't let me live this one down, but why don't you stop up and visit my place for a few minutes."

"Now?" she said, glancing inside the barbershop.

"Yeah. Unless you have to be somewhere else." He led her to a door just past the end of the shop.

"No, I have a meeting for an outdoor group, but that's not until seven."

He pulled his key from a pocket and opened the door. He ushered her upstairs and showed her to his front room. She sat on the end of the little couch beside a chair she assumed was Domenic's and pictured Mike sitting where she was.

"Tea?" Domenic asked. "Or I can make coffee?"

"A glass of water would be great," she said, placing her coat beside her.

"Water coming up." He padded down the hall. The television looked like something her grandparents got rid of when she was a child. The woman in the framed picture had to be his wife. Later she would make sure she got a good look. She could not make out the jumble in the other frame. A line of little candles guarded the front of the small table beneath the pictures.

Domenic returned with two glasses of water on ice and handed one to Sarah. He sat in the stuffed chair beside the couch.

"Two people up here this month," he said. "Al and his wife, Ginette, maybe, but that's normally it."

She took a sip. The room was tidy in a way that the barbershop had not prepared her for. Lace curtains hung on the window. Doilies topped the end table and the top of Domenic's chair. "Rescue them from one of those churches?" she said, pointing to the candles.

"Go on," he said. "You got to take what you hear downstairs with a grain of salt."

"I never knew so much about Catholics."

"Don't go by them. Nick's an encyclopedia about what doesn't matter. Clement too. Salt and Pepper, Al and I call them. They got rooms down the street, one's across from Holy Cross, the other's down the block."

"Nick's church?"

He nodded. "Clement hangs out with the helper crowd down in Germantown. Soup kitchens, stuff like that. Drags Nick down there to help out once in a blue moon."

"Where do you go? I assume you're Catholic too."

"Five o'clock Mass Saturdays at Holy Cross."

"Five o'clock?"

"In the evening," he said. "It's about the only change they came up with that I don't mind."

"No Sunday?"

"Mondays sometimes," he said. "At another place."

"Mondays?" she said.

"Extra credit," Domenic said, winking.

"Where does a Baptist or a Jew or a Hare Krishna get a haircut around here?"

"Downstairs," he said. "But when *they* die, they go to hell."

They both laughed.

"You believe everything I say," he grumbled, but she noticed a glow in his eye. They drank at the same time then set the glasses down on the coffee table in front of them.

"You've been living up here as long as you've been hanging out down there?"

"The museum? Maybe you noticed: Al collects old men. Years ago, he added me to his collection—down at the shrine, place I go Mondays." Domenic pointed to the portrait on the wall. "When Angela got sick with the cancer, we went there every Monday. Al's always praying over something, even though he don't let on about it. Probably why his boy became a Vincentian. Anyway, one day I was waiting while Angela made her weekly confession. She had some kind of imagination. Came up with something to tell that priest without lying every time. So, I was sitting in a pew, minding my own business, when this guy sat down next to me. Al. When the fellow sitting in front of us got up and left, I leaned over and said, 'Shabbiest looking haircut I've ever seen.'

"He laughed. He said, 'Pretty shabby, I gotta say.' I'd just told him I was a barber when Angela came out, forgiven for all of her horrible sins, and that was that. Never saw him again until after Angela had passed away, and I'd started going down to the shrine there by myself. Then he reappeared. After I told him about Angela, he told me I could move in here and help him out a bit. Ten years ago. Believe that?"

"So much for a quiet life," she said. "You end up talking with almost every male in the neighborhood."

"Nah," he said. "People tend to go to a barber that looks like them. Al would cut anybody's hair, but I guess most of the Black men in the neighborhood go where they see a Black guy cutting hair."

She nodded. "Cultural thing."

"If you're going to do justice to somebody's hair, you got to know about its texture, needs, and so on. Most white barbers don't bother to learn. Kind of proud that Clement lets me cut his. Anyway, most of the new people in the neighborhood wouldn't think of getting a haircut at a place like this. They get *styled* downtown. Or they got a friend who cuts hair and gives shampoos."

"Very funny."

"Oh, I'm a regular ball of laughs," he said, wistfully.

Sarah followed his eyes to the picture of his wife. "Cancer's a horrible thing," she said. She reached over and patted his hand. "It's very sad."

"That's what your Mike said."

My Mike. Something knotted in her chest. For the first time in their chat, she felt tongue-tied.

"The thing going on with his sister-in-law really gets to him," Domenic went on. "Equine something."

"Encephalitis."

"They can't figure it out for sure. Her memory may never come back. That seems to really get Mike." Domenic sipped his drink then jiggled the ice in the bottom of the glass. "I guess he wouldn't mind you knowing this," he said. "He's seen his share of sadness."

She suddenly realized that Mike had opened up more to this eccentric old man than he had to her in all the time they had been together. "You're right," she said. "I mean, that whole thing with his wife and son."

Domenic looked like he hadn't understood a word she'd said.

"I'm sorry. I thought he must have told you." For a moment she considered whether or not she should reveal this dark part of Mike's life but decided that Domenic deserved to know. She shared what she knew about the accident and Mike's return to Philadelphia. She felt unsettled by the extent of this man's knowledge about Mike's life, but what she told him now obviously stunned him. The jokester's glee in his eyes had disappeared. "I've known Mike for a while," she said. "Some things don't come up."

Domenic's face slowly changed; his more familiar half-smile reappeared, as if he suddenly had returned from some faraway place inside himself. He nodded. "Like at the barbershop," he said. "You said all the men in the shop talk in front of me, but they never talk about what's really going on inside, like I guess women do with other women."

"Not all women," she said. "It depends."

"Guess it always depends." Domenic's creased forehead indicated that he continued to puzzle out what they'd just said. He hadn't yet moved on.

"You know how to talk with people," she said. "But you're selective with who you'll do it with."

He shrugged.

"I mean, you don't make it hard for a person to open up to you. At least, with me you don't."

He sipped from his water. "I do what I can," he said. He glanced across the room again at the photograph on the other wall. When he turned back, his misty eyes locked onto Sarah's. "I hope everything works out. With all the troubles on your mind."

She knew he wasn't prying, wasn't pushing. As little as she really knew about him, she was sure she'd be back here. "Do you mind having a second stranger come up to your nest?"

"Nest." He chuckled, then got up and walked over to the window. "That's how Mike sees me. The guy who watches from on high." He pushed open the curtain and lifted the shade. "Pretty good spot, huh?"

"Time for me to get back to my work," Sarah said. Standing up, she put her coat on, then leaned over Domenic to get a glimpse out of the window. The sky had turned dark now, and the streetlamps and store lights along the avenue twinkled. "Not bad at all," she said. A trolley rattled past, down the street, and the building trembled slightly. "I didn't feel that when we were downstairs. Can you sleep with that?"

"Some things you never get used to, but sleeping through the trolley racket ain't one of them."

Sarah approached the photograph of his wife. "Her eyes," she said. She turned back to him. "I can feel a real person in there."

He nodded.

Again, the durable man's feisty look had vanished from his face, replaced by a fragile smile. She asked, "Can I do anything for you?"

As soon as she said that, he mumbled something that sounded to her like "reaching," then waved his right hand at her, as if bidding goodbye to a little child.

"I'll let myself out," she said, but turned and went into the kitchen. "Wait," she said, turning around. "Do you have a notepad?"

"Bedroom," he called back. "Stubby little pencil beside it on the bedstand."

In the neat little bedroom, she scribbled down her name and home phone number, said goodbye again, then left.

Downstairs, the inside of the barbershop was dark. She leaned her forehead against the glass. Someone had swept the floor and faced the two barber chairs toward the mirror. All the magazines and newspapers that had dotted the seats on the opposite wall had disappeared. The seats formed a neat line facing the barber chairs and the wall-length mirror on the other side of the room. Add the people and it would feel like a cozy cabin, she thought. *I'll be back here.* Then she smiled and strolled away down the sidewalk.

16

WEDNESDAY, FEBRUARY 15

Domenic found Mike's address in the local telephone book: Sedgwick Street, down the hill from the Acme. Unless Mike was prowling around the seminary grounds, he ought to be home. If not, Domenic would simply wait until he felt up to walking back home. He added the address and telephone number to the short list beside the wall telephone in his kitchen then underlined it, as he had done with Al's home number, the number for the shop, and the one Miss Sarah Goins had left on his little notepad during her whirlwind visit six days ago.

What had prompted her to come to his neck of the woods, he couldn't say. He did not remember what he was thinking when he invited her to see his apartment. At some point during that conversation, he'd known that someday soon he would walk the three or four blocks to Mike's house. *Instinct?* People didn't always have clear logical reasons for what they did.

Dinner time and the temperature had just broken into the fifties. Crazy. But because it might drop more than KYW was predicting, Domenic donned his winter coat and jeff hat. He pulled his gloves, a Christmas gift from Angela, out of the coat pockets and left them on the dining room table. They always made him think of Angela. Though he might convince himself that he had outgrown gifts, he knew for certain that he had outlived the people who once gave him presents. The dark and cold would return soon, but if Mike were not there to give him a ride back, his old coat would get him home in one piece.

He felt steady all the way to the Acme and halfway down the hill to Sedgwick Street. Seeing the terraced lawns and steep front steps of the houses on Mike's block, he stopped. "*Madonna.*" A gust of wind pushed him from the side. Doing anything became more difficult in the cold, especially for an old man. In most people's eyes, he had been an old man for some time, but he knew that ten years ago he had ached far less and tired far later. He paused to locate a house number in the line of row houses. Four more. The houses were set back above terraces of lawn and rock gardens. Breathing heavily, he stopped on the sidewalk at the foot of the cement steps that separated at Mike's and his neighbor's adjacent porches. A lower set of steps, a long landing, more steps. He took the first set slowly, stopped on the landing, and waited for his breathing to slow. Turning around, he brightened, recognizing Mike's car parked across the street. His forehead now beaded with perspiration, he surveyed the entire block from the terrace. Still breathing hard, he dabbed his forehead with his handkerchief.

Halfway up the second set of steps, a dog's loud bark made him flinch. *Robert*, he remembered. The barking intensified with each step. The porch floor vibrated under his feet as he approached the entrance. Domenic pressed the doorbell. The door shook as if someone inside were trying to break through. He stepped back from the entrance step. *Could the barking be any louder if the dog were already on the porch and nose to nose with me?* He heard footsteps and Mike's voice trying to quiet the dog. When the door swung open, he saw a confused-looking Mike standing in the foyer, holding the growling Robert by his collar. "Can you see Billy Penn's hat on top of City Hall from up here?" Domenic said.

Mike pulled the dog back.

"Tell me I'm early for the tour," Domenic said.

"You didn't bring the rest of the crew?" Mike asked, stepping back against the foyer wall to make room for Domenic.

"They can't afford the nickel," Domenic said, ignoring the sarcasm. He stepped through the foyer into the living room. The German shepherd, his ears perked up, sniffed at his legs. He started wagging his tail. "That's a boy," Domenic said, patting the dog's head.

"Good thing I already fed him," Mike said, the scowl on his face replaced by a look of exhaustion. "You didn't get mugged again?"

"Nah," Domenic said. "You look whipped. Bad time?"

Mike looked like he was working out a difficult problem. "Long days," he said, finally. "That's all."

Domenic took in the living room couch, two easy chairs, a framed print of an ocean scene. "Nice place," he said. "I'm not interrupting supper. Am I?"

"You can't interrupt what's not even planned," Mike said.

"Don't let me slow you down." Removing his hat and coat, he laid them on the near end of the couch. His breathing felt nearly normal.

"You really want to see the place?"

"If it doesn't cost extra," Domenic said.

"You must be taking your vitamins."

"Hey, I'm always agreeable." Reaching down, he patted the dog.

"I take it you didn't eat," Mike said, picking up Domenic's coat and hat.

Domenic shook his head.

"I'm not much of a cook," Mike said, hanging Domenic's things in the closet. "You want to order hoagies or something?"

"What would you have done if I hadn't shown up?" Domenic said.

Mike shrugged.

"Show me what you got," Domenic said. He followed Mike into the kitchen, the dog trailing him curiously. A window above the sink, directly opposite the kitchen window of the adjacent house, revealed a dim, narrow, shared breezeway separating the rear sections of the two homes. A hanging light bulb shone through the glass-paned top half of the back door, revealing an attached wooden shed. When Mike opened the door, the draft startled Domenic.

"Good for storing soda and beer in the winter," Mike said. "Steps lead down to the ground, which is level with the basement here in the back. No yard, but we all share a driveway back there."

"You don't park there?" Domenic said.

"More convenient out front," Mike said, leading Domenic back into the kitchen. "The kitchen's not exactly cutting edge." The refrigerator and Mike's table with its two chairs sat against the wall he shared with the downhill neighbor. Three boxes of cereal stood atop the refrigerator. The stove, sink, and a floor-to-ceiling wooden cupboard painted yellow occupied the wall with the window. The dog sniffed his leg and settled under the table. "Reminds me of 11th Street," Domenic said. "Only bigger. Could fit two of those places in this house."

"So, you know about having people right up on you."

"Big families back then. Grandparents, uncles. You might have every living member of your family packed into the same house down there. Here, you and your buddy can spread out." The dog rose and approached him. When he scratched the dog's ears, he sat beside Domenic's feet, watching Mike.

"Robert, you remember Domenic?"

Robert nestled his snout on Domenic's shoe.

"A little of some people goes a long way," Mike said. "Only Robert would put up with me."

"Think it's an accident I live alone?" Domenic said. "But don't worry. I'll leave before I frighten your neighbors."

"We're ten minutes from Dalessandro's," Mike said. "They make a world-class cheesesteak."

"You weren't going to Dalessandro's before I came," Domenic said. "Show me what you got here. I'm not expecting you to be my personal chef. We'll do this together."

"Brace yourself," Mike said, opening the refrigerator door.

Accompanied by the dog, Domenic peered at the insides of the refrigerator. Two cartons of milk and a can of dog food had the top shelf to themselves. A carton of eggs sat on the shelf below. Domenic did not bother to open the crisper drawer at the bottom. The dog turned and walked away. The racks on the refrigerator door offered little encouragement. The butter bin was empty. Gherkins and raspberry jam made the odd couple on the next shelf; below them, two bottles of soda, a beer, and an opened box of baking soda. He glanced back at the two cartons of milk. "Eat a lot of cereal?"

"You're probably one of those old-world cooks."

"I didn't do the cooking," Domenic said, closing the refrigerator door. "When I finally had to, it was hard. Necessity is a hard teacher."

Nothing in the refrigerator or on Mike's face indicated that he had made such an adjustment. "I warned you. Slim pickin's."

"The cupboard?"

"Cans, I got," Mike said. He opened the yellow cupboard's bottom doors.

Domenic knelt down gingerly. From Robert's nook beneath the table, the dog lifted his eyelids then closed them, sighing. Domenic moved cans, jars, and packages to see what lurked behind them. "Cannellini," he said, pulling out a can. "What were you going to do with this?"

"Soup. A while back, I bought some barley. I'll get a soup bone one of these days and make a pot of soup."

"Tubetini," Domenic mumbled, sliding an unopened package beside the beans. "Wouldn't have garlic or onions anywhere?"

Mike produced two onions and a head of garlic from the cabinet below the sink.

"I could survive here for days," Domenic said. "Don't need to be a genius."

"To do what?"

"To make *pasta e fagioli.*"

"Va-zule?"

"Right," he said. "A salad would be nice, but you wouldn't want to eat anything that came out of that icebox. And I don't expect a loaf of Italian bread to fall from the skies." He spotted a wooden cutting board on the counter by Mike's toaster, pulled it out, then centered it on the counter space. "Sharp knife?"

Mike pulled a knife out of the drawer and set it on the cutting board.

"You could throw a stone from here to that Acme," Domenic said.

"I haven't been in a cooking mood lately."

"Chop," Domenic ordered. As Mike went to work on the onions, Domenic explored the top part of the cupboard until he found the right-sized skillet. He held up a bowl from the dry rack on the sink. "Clean?"

Mike nodded.

Domenic placed the bowl beside the cutting board. "When the onion looks like grains of rice, put 'em in here. I'm no expert, but I remember how things are supposed to taste." He picked up the head of garlic. "Prehistoric," he pronounced, frowning. "Trash bag?"

"Below the sink. Beside the bag with the onions and garlic."

Dominic opened the bag and peered inside. "Ooh," he said, wincing. He dumped the onion skins and the dried-up garlic into the trash container, reserving the four firmest cloves.

"Jesus," Mike said, backing away from the counter, his eyes red and wet.

"Don't rub them," Domenic said. He turned on the faucet and let the cold water run. "Get some air."

Cursing, Mike shuffled to the shed at the rear of the kitchen. Using Mike's knife, Domenic finished off the onion and swept it into the bowl. "They say you should stick onions in the freezer. Cut them fifteen minutes later." He opened the cans of tomatoes and beans. "Or wear a pair of goggles."

"All right," Mike said, reappearing at the cutting board. "Outside the city, people call a shed like that a mud room."

"It's a shed," Domenic said.

"Exactly."

Something felt different about the way Mike had responded. Like he hadn't stopped to work out what he was going to say. "Trim off the stems," Domenic said, sensing that he'd just been welcomed as much as this guy could manage. "Cover the garlic with the blade's flat side, pound it with your other hand until it's a mess. Any chance in a million you got olive oil?"

"With the cans and jars—you must have missed it," Mike said, studying the garlic.

"It doesn't feel pain," Domenic said. "Pound it." He dropped to his knees again, wincing at the sharp pinch in his joints. He finally retrieved a tiny bottle of olive oil from the cupboard. "They didn't give this to you on an airplane, did they?" His knees were in full revolt. Once he caught his breath, he clamped onto the cupboard's counter and pulled himself up from the floor.

Mike hovered over the cutting board. "Must have been a free sample," he declared, nodding toward the miniature bottle.

"Lourdes water comes in containers like this," Domenic said, holding it up to the light. *No more up and down.* He turned on the front burner, set the cast iron skillet on the flame, and poured in a tablespoon of oil. "Need that cutting board," he said, stepping to the right when he felt Mike behind him. "Use the knife," he said. "Leave nothing on that board or on the knife." He spun around then rummaged through drawers until he found a wooden spoon. "Going to need water for the pasta," he said, nudging Mike from the skillet. He adjusted the flame and stirred the onion and garlic as Mike produced a stockpot, filled it up to its three-quarter mark, then started it on a rear burner. "Gas fire," Domenic said. "Angela hated electric."

"I never watched Laurie cook."

When the onion turned translucent, Domenic lowered the burner. He felt Mike watching him. "Never want to burn garlic."

"Thought you didn't know anything about cooking," Mike said.

"I said nobody taught me. Add the tomatoes."

Mike poured the contents of the can into the skillet. Using the wooden spoon, Domenic broke up the tomatoes and stirred the mixture together. "What do you got for spices?"

"Oregano?"

"Yes," Domenic said. "Some basil wouldn't hurt."

Mike went to the top part of his cupboard and produced two spice jars. Domenic poured ancient basil into his palm and dropped it into the skillet. "Not too much oregano," he said. "You do it."

He stood back while Mike sprinkled the tomatoes and onions with a bit of oregano. Domenic handed him the wooden spoon and watched from the side as Mike stirred the mixture. "Beans," Domenic said. As he bellied up beside Mike, his new friend handed off the spoon then pivoted from the stove.

They reversed the procedure when Mike returned with the large can of beans.

"Any sugar?" Domenic asked.

"On the table."

Domenic dropped a pinch of sugar into the skillet. "For the acidity."

Mike gingerly stirred the pot's contents and tossed a handful of salt into the pasta water.

"Now you're showing off," Domenic said. He pulled out one of the kitchen chairs then sat at the table. "You're on your own as far as the antipasto."

"You're not serious."

"It may take a little Irish magic," Domenic said, glancing at envelopes addressed to Mike strewn on the table. They looked like bills. Mike's full name through an envelope's window seemed formal, not what he thought he knew about him. "I left some options on the floor in front of the cupboard," Domenic said. "This chair feels awful good." Even at the shop, he rarely stayed on his feet this long. Slumping back, he scanned the rest of the room. A wilderness calendar hung on the wall above the table. Clean, plain, light-blue curtains adorned the side and rear windows. He wondered how many things in Mike's home had come from Sarah and how many had come from his wife. Years ago, deciding which things from the old South Philadelphia row house should make the trip to his new apartment had driven home the realization that nothing of his was purely his. Box after box of what he kept and bag after bag of what he discarded bore Angela's mark, carried stories in which she played the main character, stories that, no matter how hard he tried to condense or skip over them, stretched his solitary packing and cleaning into two weeks of stops and starts. Even now, one such discarded object might suddenly break into his consciousness and, with it, the object's story. Above Mike's stove, a row of dented and scorched pots and pans hung on the ceiling bar. How many of them carried memories of the woman who had handled them?

A half hour later, they sat at the kitchen table eating *pasta e fagioli* accompanied by wheat crackers and an antipasto that Domenic said demonstrated the powers of Mike Flannagan's imagination. "Anchovies, roasted red peppers, olives," Domenic said, admiring Mike's work.

"I never would have bought that stuff," Mike confessed.

"Gifts."

"This is really good," Mike said, sounding surprised something that tasty could come from his cupboard and refrigerator.

"We ate this like once a week. Met her at the 9th Street market one Saturday morning, and that was that. She was a lot younger, but we both loved food. How did you meet your wife?"

He watched Mike's expression change from curiosity to something harder to read. "We lived in the same small town," he said. "You meet people. Nothing much to say, really."

When Domenic finished his second serving, he slid the bowl in front of him and patted his stomach. "*So 'rivat*," he said. Domenic patted his middle again and sighed. "Kind of like, we've arrived, we're there."

"*So 'rivat*," Mike repeated, cleaning his bowl with his spoon. He ate the last mouthful of *pasta e fagioli*. "You knew what needed to be done and just did it."

Domenic nodded.

"Not everybody's good at doing what needs to be done."

"You going to try to make this meal yourself sometime?" Domenic asked.

Mike made an expression that was pure Abruzzi.

"Next time, we might try bread and living basil," Domenic said.

"Deal."

Domenic sat back in his chair. "Now we can relax with cigars while the staff do the dishes," he said.

"I gave them the night off," Mike said, smiling for a moment. He took their bowls and the rest of the antipasto from the table. Beneath the table, Robert groaned, rolled over, and went back to sleep.

Domenic watched Mike rinse out the bowls then put them and the silverware into the dishwasher.

"We'll have to go out if you want dessert," Mike said.

"A real Italian doesn't want some big, fancy dessert. A little bit of fruit, and there you go."

"That's what you like?"

"Whatever's in season," Domenic said.

"Well, you're a real Italian," Mike said, sitting down again.

"Nah."

"You're the most Italian guy I know." He held up his hands, gesturing the way Domenic did.

"*Cafone*," Domenic grunted, mirroring back the same gesture. "I used to be more Italian. It's hard to explain."

"You were pretty Italian tonight."

"To you. We spoke it around the house. Then I married a woman who was born in Abruzzi. We lived in a part of Philly that was crawling with Italians. Now, I don't. I'm not so Italian." Was Domenic now also 'not so married'? He'd never stopped considering himself married, but talking here somehow made him wonder if he'd been fooling himself.

"You're still Italian," Mike insisted.

"Not so much." Domenic looked at the empty pot and skillet in the sink. He always would be Angela's Domenic, even if he could never shed this painful longing. *That's this life, Domenic.*

"So, why did you move?" Mike said.

"Everything there was over." Domenic looked him in the eye. "You know what I mean?"

Mike's face transformed into a mask of sadness. He rose from the table. "I'll clear up a bit here," he said. "Wait in the living room. Or get a head start on the tour."

Domenic refilled his water glass and walked into the little dining room, followed by Robert. An oval table occupied the middle of the room surrounded by four chairs. Against the wall stood a hutch with serving platters displayed on it. The top platter featured a pattern of holly, ivy, and Christmas tree balls.

"This room's *always* ready for Christmas," Mike said, coming up behind him.

Domenic continued into the living room.

"Move the laundry basket off the good chair and have a seat," Mike said. "It's more comfortable than the couch."

Domenic placed the plastic container of clean laundry on the carpet beside the recliner then sat down. He pulled the release on the side of the chair and slid back, watching his feet rise before him. Robert collapsed into his bed.

"I was bringing the laundry upstairs when you got here," Mike said, turning and heading toward the rear of the house. "I got another load downstairs in the dryer."

Robert opened one eye and repositioned in the bed. Domenic brought the recliner back to the upright position. He heard Mike's footsteps on the basement stairs. He reached the top of the stairs as Mike was landing at the bottom. "Some tour guide," he griped.

"No," Mike called up, "it's a disaster down here. I'll be right back." He stood at the base of the stairway, looking up at Domenic.

Where Mike stood, the clear cement floor hardly suggested mess. "They always say, you don't know a house unless you've seen the basement," Domenic said. "I thought I was getting the regular tour."

"You're getting …" Mike said, his suddenly loud voice trailing off. He shrugged and headed to the back of the basement. "Up to you," he called back. "It's not pretty."

Going down the steps, Domenic held the banister and concentrated on his footing. Reaching the last few steps, Domenic made out what had been a model railroad layout behind Mike, but mangled and bent wiring, chunks of plaster, jagged pieces of plastic and wood, and fragments of freight and passenger cars covered the four-foot-high platform and the floor around it. A dust-laden gash interrupted a stretch of mountain scenery.

Hearing Mike open the dryer behind him, he turned around.

Against the rear wall stood the washer, dryer, and laundry sink and a rack of tools. Mike unloaded the dryer, dropping the clean laundry into a plastic basket on the floor.

"You're seeing it at a bad time," Mike said, still fussing with the laundry.

It did not look like something anyone would show off to a child.

"As long as it's up and running next Christmas," Mike said. "For my nephew and niece. I have almost the whole year to change the scenery, fix some things I didn't like."

Clean up the mess. Domenic walked to the edge of the layout. He picked up an overturned cattle car and set it beside a section of track. In the midst of chunks of plaster and curled wire at the back of the display, a railroad station sat intact. *Armageddon Junction?* Apparently

Mike had begun the demolition phase of his project by dropping a bomb. He couldn't have been as calm as he sounded now when he did this. Domenic decided against joking about a tornado taking such a strange path.

When he heard Mike climbing the stairs, he turned and followed. In the living room, the dog looked like he could sleep through anything, but he probably heard plenty when Mike did in his layout. The dog was as likely to explain what had happened downstairs as his master.

The second flight of stairs proved harder to climb. He paused four stairs short of the second floor. Letting Mike go on ahead, he took the final steps one at a time and lingered at the top.

Mike set the laundry in the narrow second-floor hallway and flipped on the lights in the rear and middle bedrooms, the bathroom, and finally the front bedroom.

Boxes covered the top of a small bed and a desk in the rear bedroom. The smaller middle room featured an ironing board and more storage.

"Male chaos," Mike said. "The bathroom's relatively civilized. Last year's project. Cost me almost what I paid for the whole house in New Paltz."

"It's a lot of work, a house," Domenic said. He entered the front room in time to see Mike dump two baskets of laundry onto the queen-sized bed.

"Sometimes, priorities outside the house take over."

Domenic nodded as Mike picked up a clean blanket, folded it, then laid it across the foot of the bed. The rooms all seemed freshly painted, the floors clean. "Really comfortable place," he said, taking in the rest of the room.

"Thanks."

A framed photograph of Mike, a woman, and a little boy stood on the dresser beneath a table lamp. A wedding band had been placed in front of the frame. Domenic kept his eyes on the three happy faces until Mike noticed. "Those trains downstairs," Domenic said. "Are they his?"

"Would have been. I kept them from childhood, added to them." Mike wiped the glass with a tissue. "Laurie and Michael," he said, offering the picture to Domenic. "They died some years ago. Car accident."

Domenic cradled the frame in his hands. "Beautiful family." He had never been good at gauging a child's age. The earnest-looking little guy was in the toddler range, but Domenic thought better of asking. Facing the camera, the trio beamed the same joyous and genuine smile. "Looks like both of you." He'd seen the same smile for a few seconds during dinner.

He handed the picture to Mike, not letting go until Mike's eyes met his. Clement had declared Domenic's standard facial expression as "an inscrutable half-smile," which made the whole barbershop crew roar, to Domenic's surprise, but now he could think of no better way to describe Mike. His young friend returned the photograph to its place. The Phillies might win the World Series three times before Mike would say another word about his dead family. Domenic knew little more than what Sarah had told him. Nothing good would come from pushing Mike. "It's late for an old man," Domenic announced. "Thank you for the soirée."

"I'll run you home."

"I won't refuse," Domenic said, starting out ahead of Mike. Downstairs, he retrieved his coat and hat, while Mike scooted past him into the kitchen.

"*Buona notte*," Domenic said, patting Robert's head.

"I got enough leftovers for both of us," Mike announced from the kitchen.

By the time Domenic had dressed for outside, Mike returned with half of the *pasta e fagioli* in an old potato salad container. Patting the dog one last time, he followed Mike out the front door and down the steps to the car.

Mike's touch with the car was gentle, not rushed. The car eased around the corner and onto the avenue's trolley tracks and Belgian blocks. If Domenic's wife and child had died in a car crash, he might not ever get in a car again. To say something about Mike's way of driving or about the well-cared-for sound of the engine, even though complimentary, might be so wrong right now. How many triggers did this guy dance around every day? How did Sarah manage?

When Mike pulled over into one of the many parking spots near the shop, Domenic opened the door and said, "Sure beats walking."

Mike nodded. "No problem."

Alone upstairs, Domenic thanked God for letting him climb his own stairs without a fuss. Leaving Mike's fancy overhead lighting turned off, he lit all but the ninth candle and told himself that he'd been right to hold back.

With just the table and candles between him and the collage, he let his eyes travel around until they found a picture of Phillies manager Gene Mauch. Domenic had read newspaper stories about him, at the time and since. Mauch knew his players' strengths and weaknesses but somehow left pitcher Bobby Shantz in the game too long. Another loss. The sin of stubbornness.

Standing before the collage, Domenic slid his finger across the glass to a yellowed clipping. "Numb" read the caption over a box score. His finger found another caption: "Lead Gone." The collapse was on.

Domenic sat in his chair and watched the candles flicker. Was

Mike trying to stop his falling, or could he even see it? The floor reverberated with the passage of a trolley coming to a stop at the corner before it lurched noisily ahead toward Chestnut Hill. The soft light from the eight candles danced against the wall like little devils. His eyes finally felt heavy, but he looked up at Angela. "So close," he muttered.

Really? He couldn't help anyone else or himself. And she was as gone tonight as last night or any other night. He blew out two of the candles with one breath. He blew again, but four remained lit. Winded, he wet the tips of his thumb and forefinger with his saliva then pinched out the flames of the remaining four candles.

In the morning, Domenic hobbled into the bathroom. When he flicked on the light switch, the brightness made him scrunch up his eyes. A hangover without the alcohol, he thought. He took a shower and changed into fresh clothes, but by nine o'clock he still had no interest in breakfast. He took this, along with the stiffness in his back, as a sign that he had not been meant to greet Al at opening time. He waited until he heard footsteps in the shop downstairs before calling.

"You don't *have* to call," Al said, when Domenic told him he wouldn't be down for at least a few hours, "but I'm glad you did."

"I'm not that—"

"Yeah?" Al said.

"Bad off."

"Call me in a couple of hours," Al said. "Or I'll send the Mounties up there."

Domenic lay on the top of the bedspread without taking off his shoes. His breathing was even and relaxed, but he feared that soon it might become labored. Maybe it *was* age. A body's quirkiness that came at a certain age. The telephone's ring startled him.

"You all right?" Al said.

Domenic glanced at the clock. It was noon. "*Madonna*," he mumbled. "I fell asleep."

"So, you're good?"

"I'm going to get myself fired."

"You're lucky I'm such a nice guy. How about I run up and say hello?"

Domenic sat up. "You *are* saying hello."

"I don't want to see you down here until three o'clock," Al said. "And only if you're feeling good. Honest, I got nobody here but Frick and Frack."

"I'm alive and kicking up here," Domenic said. He heard hooting in the background. After he convinced Al not to commission any upstairs expeditions, he hung up and clomped into the kitchen, above where they sat, and made as much noise as he could. Pouring cereal into a bowl, he sang "Come Back to Sorrento," bellowing, "La, la, la," when he forgot the words. Pausing between verses, he detected booing coming from the first floor. He would show up on his own sweet timetable, but he sure as sin would do it before anyone came upstairs.

17

THURSDAY, FEBRUARY 16

Mike sipped his lukewarm Wawa coffee. He'd woken up okay, but after driving downtown and consuming half a tuna hoagie, he'd felt the effects of Domenic's dinner visit. On the day's second trip to the college garage, his headache continued. Now feeling cranky as well as tired, he stretched his arms and legs to the degree that the car's interior allowed. How easy it would be to drift off, but he wasn't going to let that happen. In a seed catalogue, he penciled a black check in the margin at the listing for peas then did the same for Swiss chard. Dr. Schmidt ought to like Mike's choices for the seminary garden. The old professor had been accommodating about Mike's need to absent himself at odd hours. Knowing that the man was a dog lover, Mike mentioned that Robert's arthritis needed attention throughout the day. Now Mike was determined to make Schmidt's garden the talk of the staff—and to wait out the creep with the bad haircut.

The visit from the other old man in his life had been a mixed bag. Making dinner hadn't been that much work, but crashing last night he'd felt like he'd been force-marched around the neighborhood. Somehow, he'd let Domenic go downstairs, and the old guy'd had the sense to let it be. Since New Paltz, the only other person who'd had a pull on him was Sarah. He couldn't imagine doing that whole evening with anyone else. Domenic was all right. Still, Mike had been relieved when Domenic was ready to call it a night.

He needed to keep his eyes focused on Sarah's car. He scanned the quiet parking level. Time on task. Motivation. He remembered Ms. Devereaux's advice to the class. You could control how much time you devoted to a task. Motivation was a different animal, kind of like faith, and faith was subject to an ebb and flow for most believers. So it was with Mike's belief that the punk eventually would show up. His first day of stalking the stalker, he had been full of piss and vinegar, to use Mom's expression. Some days, he expected that within minutes the bastard would grab Sarah as she got out of her car. Other days, he felt like a fool, sitting there with a cold cup of coffee. "Routine," Ms. Devereaux preached. "Trust that."

He tossed the catalogue onto the passenger seat then downed the rest of the coffee. An ancient VW Beetle stuttered to rest several places up from Sarah's customary parking place. It occurred to Mike that perhaps he could use his old ID to get long-term parking. Surely Brendan knew somebody who could make his outdated card look legit. The dark-haired Beetle driver lifted the car's trunk then looked to his right and left. Mike sat up straight. The Beetle's hood was painted green; the front quarter panels were blue. Two pieces of metal stuck out where there ought to have been a bumper. The guy stepped away from the car and glanced up and down the ramp then returned and rooted around in the trunk. Sarah was nowhere in sight, so Mike decided to stay put.

Another guy approached the driver. They both looked up and down the ramp then disappeared behind a van. Mike rolled down the driver's side window and listened. Nothing. The second guy hustled back down the ramp, stuffing a plastic bag into his pants pocket. The driver grabbed a backpack, locked his car, then trotted off toward the stairs. To class? To buyers in the cafeteria or on the street? Maybe he was an agent setting up the bigger fish in the food chain.

Perhaps, if Mike stayed there long enough, he might see Russian agents swap prisoners with the CIA. Or the dean score some weed. Sarah would be leaving class about now. If today was the day, Pompadour might also be on the early side. If not today, he'd show up someday. Assholes didn't usually go away without encouragement.

Parked vehicles occupied most spaces on the level. Mike eased back, reminding himself that he might not have been the only witness to a small drug deal. Thinking about one misdeed ushered in thoughts of others. He could not stop the memories. *New Paltz.*

Mike drove his truck through the leafy section of town where Jerry Wells's family lived. After working his way up and down street after street for hours, the part of him that wished he knew the address had won out over the part that felt relief at not having a target in front of him. He headed home knowing Wells would pay.

At home in the yard, he watched Robert relieve himself on the edge of the sandbox he had built, then went inside. He could not eat. He should return the old couple's stewpot, but the effort of accommodating the man's limitations twisted his stomach.

The next morning, his cop friend called. The Wells kid had hanged himself in his basement. It was all over the local paper. At the gas station and the post office, people talked with him but no one mentioned the kid's death. He hated Jerry Wells more now than he had when the bastard was alive. He walked up from the far end of the cemetery and watched the burial from the side of the old Nichols family mausoleum. More people showed up than did for Laurie and little Michael's funeral. He saw people who had been at their funeral.

He waited until dark then left the stewpot on his neighbors' front steps. He spent the night filling a room with the clothes, cooking utensils, and tools he wanted to pack for Philadelphia. Nearly every item reminded him of Laurie and Michael, but he set them aside.

Would his pain lessen at all if he brought all of them? He forced himself ahead, returning enough of them to the house so that what remained would fit into his truck. He put price tags on everything else.

Mike heard the click-click-click of Sarah's shoes at the same time that he saw her. At least she made herself a moving target. Pompadour could be lurking behind a van right now, having just witnessed the business exchange along with Mike. *Not your scene, Pomp?* Mike leaned forward, peering through the windshield, arms and legs tensed, ready to fly down the ramp.

He winced, seeing the same grim, fearful expression on Sarah's face as this morning, and both times yesterday and every other day since he'd begun stalking her stalker. She shot a quick look to her right then to her left, opened the door with the practiced precision of an athlete, and disappeared into the Tercel. When the car had slipped down the ramp and out of sight, he breathed out. Tomorrow he was due to save on the parking fee and find a street spot somewhere in the neighborhood. Those cold, windy days, walking many blocks to the parking garage then crouching in the shadows, had positioned him for a quick and quiet start. If he could spot Pomp before Sarah showed up, she wouldn't ever need to know. He'd be back to January. Maybe he'd be able to fix things.

18

THURSDAY, FEBRUARY 16

Sarah pulled out of the college garage onto 18th Street, instantly feeling relief at being able to focus on something nonthreatening. Brilliant sunshine lit the riverbanks. She turned off the car heater and cracked the window. Pressing the button for the jazz station, she drew in the spring-like air through her nose then whooshed it out her mouth. The upcoming selection by Grant Green was recorded in New York, the announcer said, and McCoy Tyner played piano on the cut. When she had discovered Tyner's music as a college student, she had found his style sophisticated and urbane; for her, his music was quintessential New York, so she had been surprised years later to learn that he was from Philadelphia. Of course, she reminded herself, he had moved to New York.

She raised the volume as she passed the statue garden along the river. Grant Green's guitar seemed the perfect accompaniment to the lone sculler on the river. All her ducks were in a row, as Frank Weldon of the English department liked to put it. "Send out CVs every year," he advised Sarah when she was promoted to assistant professor. "Even if you're happier than a pig in shit. Know what's out there." She had not done it that year or the next, but the Brooklyn College blurb in November's *Chronicle of Higher Education* had caught her eye, prompting her to dash off a CV and cover letter over the Thanksgiving weekend.

The notion of returning to New York City for a similar teaching job was intriguing, but she had forgotten about it amidst the pressure of finals, the holidays, and the rush at the beginning of the January term. After the dinner party, the brawl, and the news about her father's cancer, she had found herself thinking about the job and her chances of getting it. When the call came on Tuesday, she had taken the first available date for an interview.

Marcie Weinstock was all set to cover Monday's classes. She'd bring Marcie some fantastic Beaujolais. A Monday adventure. Not exactly cutting class, but a three-day weekend nonetheless. Her parents would be waiting for her tomorrow evening, before her Brooklyn College meeting with "some people in the same field." Yesterday's and today's classes had gone better than they had all semester. She had thought about the guys in the barbershop as much as she had thought about Mike, which had to be a good sign. She turned onto Germantown Avenue. Barbers weren't like stylists. They were used to people arriving unannounced.

"Bananas?" she heard Nick say as she opened the door to Al's.

"Hello, Missy," Clement cried.

Al nodded to her. Domenic was nowhere in sight. She smiled to mask her disappointment. She closed the door behind her, suddenly remembering Domenic's reference to Al collecting old people. *They don't come here for haircuts.* They must think she was an idiot.

"You're crazy," Nick whined.

Clement turned back to Nick, the smile he had greeted her with replaced by a scowl. "A banana is more dangerous than a grape," Clement said. "Simple as that."

She sat between a teenaged boy and a fortyish man, reminding herself that she was a professor. She was doing research out in the field.

"Everybody talks about bananas," Nick squeaked, nearly apoplectic. "It's what you always see in the cartoons, people slipping on banana peels."

"I'm not even talking about a banana peel," Clement countered. "If you step on a piece of a banana, you're in trouble."

"Listen," Nick said. "Any kind of fruit, when crushed, is going to be wet, so you get your slipperiness. Berries would be an example here. However, your grape is round."

"Oval," Clement corrected.

"Between round and oval."

"Okay."

Sarah realized that she, the guys beside her, and the man getting the haircut were turning from one debater to the other like spectators at a tennis match. Only Al, hunched over his customer's neck and snipping away, seemed oblivious to the debate.

"A squashed grape is wet and round," Nick said. "In the whole wide world of what you might step on, it doesn't get any more slippery than that. I rest my case."

"Nick, how far does a grape spread?"

"A squashed grape? It slides. Makes a mess. You step on it, off you go."

"Right, but a squashed banana, Nick, covers greater surface. It's got greater mass, so when you step on a banana you're stepping on a lot more slippery surface than when you step on a damn grape."

"He's got a point," Al said, pausing with his scissors held in midair.

"He's got a pointed head," Nick retorted.

"You know he's admitting defeat when he starts calling me names," Clement said.

"I'm right about grapes, *and* I'm right about you having a pointed head," Nick shouted.

"*Ad hominem.*" Clement sighed.

Al nodded without taking his eyes off the back of his customer's head.

"What?" Nick said. "What?"

"You're name-calling, *and* you're shouting," Clement said.

Careworn and exasperated, he and the others paused to catch their breath. The bunch of them might have been rivals at a stormy UN General Assembly session, but she couldn't get the smile off her face.

"You know, you always do this, Nick," Al said. "I'm sorry, but he's right."

"Bananas are loners," Nick said. "Your grape, on the other hand, rarely travels alone. Let me roll out a bunch of damn grapes on the floor, then a stupid banana. We'll see which is more dangerous."

Sarah cleared her throat, wondering how she might get their attention. *When do they sweep up all that hair?*

"Point is, grapes have greater range," Nick argued. "Pound for pound, they're more dangerous."

"I didn't say anything about pound for pound," Clement protested.

"So, you agree?" Nick chirped, leaning forward, his eyes ablaze.

"You're clutching at straws."

"Hey, Nick," Al said. "Where do you get your bananas?"

"*Where?*" Nick huffed. "I get them at the damn Acme Market."

"And where do *they* get them?" Al asked.

"I don't know. Costa Rica?"

"No, no, no," Al said, making eye contact with him in the mirror. "If you wanted to get a crate of them in Philadelphia, where would you go?"

"Food Distribution Center."

"Where's that?" Clement said.

"South Philly. Near the stadiums."

Al nodded slowly. "And what parish would that be?" he said, arching his eyebrows.

Sarah glanced at Clement. He was suppressing a smile.

"Stella Maris," Nick grumbled.

They all laughed, even the teenager. *If this were a TV show, I would start watching TV again.* Nick smirked and made a fist at Al. "Morons." Her face hurt from smiling. Could she extend this visit? How impoverished had her life been that she'd never known anyone like these people? She had nowhere else she wanted to be more than here.

Al brought his customer's money to the cash register. The middle-aged man took his place in Al's chair.

Sarah cleared her throat. "Speaking of, slippery as heck out there the other day," she said. They all turned to her. "Between the trolley tracks and the cobblestones, add a little rain, and you could kill yourself," she added.

Their stares stopped her cold. *Is a woman speaking like this not done?*

Al got the kid ready for his haircut. "You here for a haircut?" he said to Sarah.

She shook her head, her heart racing.

"I don't mean to be rude," he said.

"No," she said, "I'm sorry." The rest of them were still watching.

"You're not from here," Al said to her.

"For heaven's sake," Clement said softly. "Give her a break."

"They're Belgian blocks," Al said, apologetically. "Cobblestones are something else altogether."

"*Different,*" Nick added softly, the strain on his face suggesting he was barely able to control his emotions.

She gasped. "Oh," she said. Even the guy in the barber chair looked aggrieved.

"Belgian blocks came over on the ships as ballast," Clement said. "Cobblestones are generally smaller, and some folks believe they were worn down, or cobbled, by nature's abuse."

"We've been over this a hundred times," Nick added.

"No offense, Miss," Al said, finally picking up his electric clipper. "Only a matter of concern in this barbershop."

"It *is* slippery on the blocks, ma'am," Clement said.

"Sarah," she said. *Stupid Sarah. Foreigner.* Were they correct or had she stumbled onto a linguistic community limited to those who visited Al's Barbershop? "I learned something," she added brightly.

"You're probably here to have the bunch of us committed to Byberry," Clement said.

"Not at all," Sarah said. They looked like nothing had happened. Again, they were making her feel like it was okay that she'd come back, that she'd somehow been allowed to enter into the vetting process for ideas that apparently went on inside these four walls. She wondered how long it would take for her to stumble again, but still. "Do you realize how much you have stored in your heads?"

"Useless information," Nick said.

"No," she said, rising from her chair as if she were in class, surprised that her confidence had returned so quickly. "You've been around this neighborhood most of your lives. Haven't you?" She edged closer to the barber chairs.

"Born and raised within five blocks of here," Nick said.

"I live in Glenside, but I've worked in this neighborhood as long as I've been in the area," Al said.

"How about you, Clement?"

"Since the sixties. But I've been coming here since I was a kid. The Sedgwick was one of the few movie theaters Black folks could go to without problems back in the day."

"That's the kind of stuff I mean," Sarah said, standing between the two barber chairs. "People all over the country are doing this sort of thing, talking about their lives, how things used to be. Al, you probably know more about this neighborhood than anybody else."

"Move, dear," Al said. "I don't want you to get bumped by me or by this palooka's feet when I spin him around."

She stepped away from the barber chairs.

Al gestured toward the empty one, but sitting in Domenic's chair somehow seemed too forward. She planted herself in the middle of the line of chairs against the back wall, just as Domenic opened the door.

19

THURSDAY, FEBRUARY 16

"The prodigal," Nick greeted Domenic, as he stepped inside the barbershop.

"Good *mor-ning*," Clement sang.

Like a rose between two thorns, Sarah was sitting halfway between Nick and Clement. He'd expected to see Sarah again but at his place, and he felt his spirits sag just a little.

"Thought you were going to miss all the fun," Al said.

She beamed at him, quickly ending his momentary slump. He slipped into the back room to find his smock. How long had she been there? When he returned, Sarah was standing between the barber chairs, watching Al clip the back of Tommy Coyle's head.

Domenic headed to his counter to check his equipment.

"You can watch me work any time you want, lady," Tommy said, looking at her in the big mirror.

Nick and Clement stirred awkwardly in their seats. Domenic spun around and glared at Tommy, but the jerk's eyes were glued to Sarah.

"What line of work are you in?" Sarah asked.

"Plumber," Tommy said, "but I can handle most anything."

"Don't you start with the lady," Domenic snapped at him. "Sarah, the less you see of this character, the better."

"Don't want help with your history project?" Tommy said.

"I don't think you're old enough," she said.

the church. The temperature had plummeted since he'd left home. Bingo in the church hall began at seven on Thursdays, but he'd arrived early enough to make a visit. He pulled open the heavy wooden door and entered the cavernous, still church. The elevated sanctuary light and the banks of votive candles at the side altar provided the only illumination. Angela once had gone to confession here before a holy day, dragging him to the church on their way to her friend Elsie's. Three years ago, he had set out to find it again, a search that lasted a year. He had remembered the rack of votive candles on the side altar but not the church's name or location. Its spire towered over an enclave on or near Allegheny Avenue, but in old neighborhoods, ethnic Catholic churches often stood within a pierogi's throw of one another. He recalled the name of a small side street that crossed Allegheny near the church. One day at the barbershop, he had barked out the names of the intersecting streets. "St. Adalbert's," Nick crowed. Domenic tracked it down the next Sunday. He had guessed within two blocks of the church.

Soon, a stocky Polish woman would begin setting up chairs and tables in the church hall, but he never felt rushed to leave this church. At home or on the sidewalk, he might summon up Angela's face, her hands, maybe a bit of a story, but in this church, her image was as vivid as a big-screen Hollywood movie. Domenic knelt before the candles, as he had the day he rediscovered the church and the distant night he had come with Angela to go to confession after picking up kielbasa around the corner.

His sins? Some variation of selfishness. "It's always the same," he told his confessor.

"Pride," the old priest sighed. "We always separate ourselves from God, thinking we can get along."

It never felt like pride, but what did Domenic know? *Stonato.* That evening, after making his confession, he'd knelt on the same candle-lit kneeler. Eyes closed, he had silently prayed the three Our Fathers, Hail Marys, and Glory Bes that he had been given for penance. When he felt his wife settle beside him, he opened his eyes, glimpsing Angela, her eyes closed, lips moving. *I don't want to put you second this week.* He repeated the Act of Contrition until she rose from the kneeler. They walked out together. On the sidewalk, her hand found his, and they walked like that to Elsie's home, three blocks away, neither of them saying a word until they reached Elsie's front door.

Until the year she'd lost the last one, his love had bared her soul to him, had made and shared secrets with him. Then he had tried to reach in there. He knew what had happened to her, felt it in his own way, but it wasn't the same. He never stopped reaching. He prayed for her soul, prayed that if she couldn't heal, she would say something, anything. But she'd been stopped from being the person she was. Like this Mike. He prayed for his new friend, and for Sarah, who also was reaching. They all needed it.

In the church hall, Domenic joined several white-haired women who were moving tables. Opening and closing brown metal folding chairs, his breathing felt no more difficult than it had been all those years ago. When they'd set the room, Domenic stood back while the regulars took their places and laid out stuffed animals, trolls, and framed photos of children at their tables. Domenic took a seat in the back row, the only person without some sort of lucky charm. When full, these halls always reminded Domenic of rummage sales. He paid attention for two or three games, keeping score on four cards as the Polish woman's voice droned out of two weathered speakers.

As always, the puzzle of Angela pulled his attention away from the game. The woman continued calling numbers, but she might as well have been speaking in Polish. Number after number, game after game, it must have seemed like he had the worst cards of all. He did not drop off to sleep like the short scrawny woman at St. Leo's whose cigarettes always burned down to the filter in her dented little tin ashtray. His eyes remained open, his brow creased, but at least Angela was with him.

In the cold outside the church after the last game, Domenic buttoned his coat and wished he had worn his hat and scarf. He could not shorten the wait for the bus, but he could get to the bus stop as quickly as possible, so he picked up his pace. He felt warm by the time he reached the first corner. It became hard for him to breathe and walk, as if someone were holding him back. He halted to bend over. "Nearer the end than the beginning" was the expression all four of them in the shop used when the topic of age came up, but now that thought did not bring him a laugh. Was this the time when a familiar pain would mean something different than before?

At least no one was near enough to hear his wheezing. But the wind had died down and the sidewalks were clear of ice and snow. The last time this happened, he'd walked faster, he was sure of that. His gait was slower than that of Uncle Sweet, the hunchback of 11th Street, whose passage from one end of the block to the other took between two and three innings of a ball game. He stopped at the second corner, looked up and down the streets as if he were waiting for a person to come or for a line of cars to pass. Seventh inning stretch, he told himself. He straightened himself up and shuffled across the street. "We're nearly at Elsie's," he whispered.

20

FRIDAY, FEBRUARY 17

Mike left home fifteen minutes earlier than he did on days when he parked inside the garage. He found a spot five blocks from campus. Every time he'd saved himself the parking fee, he'd needed fewer than ten minutes to hustle to his lookout spot. Ensconced in his dark corner nook, he had an unobstructed view down to his left of Sarah's usual parking spot on the other side of the ramp. He leaned against the cold wall and caught his breath. The temperature had dropped well below freezing again, and if it didn't warm up by afternoon, he might park inside on his second trip.

Just as he expected, five minutes before Sarah's usual arrival time, the woman who parked five spaces above Sarah's spot on Mondays, Wednesdays, and Fridays pulled in, turned off the ignition, and exited her old Mazda. Another creature of habit. Mike stifled a yawn then slowly rotated his neck three times to the left then three times to the right, watching the puffs his breaths made in the bracing air.

Quick footsteps coming down the ramp from the level above made him turn to his right. The man with the pompadour was rounding onto Sarah's level. Mike froze as the man slowed his pace, apparently not noticing him. His heart pounding, Mike leaned forward for a better view.

Nearing the Mazda, the guy slipped off to the outer side of the parking level out of Mike's view. If Pompadour knelt behind one of the cars parked there, Sarah would not notice him when she turned into her space on the inner side. If the guy only wanted to talk, he wouldn't be so furtive. Mike heard no more footsteps. Was he even allowed to be back on campus? The other time Mike had seen him had also been a Friday. *He's not here to apologize.*

Mike realized he was panting silently through his mouth, like Robert when he glimpsed a squirrel. Was his body taking over from his brain? Helping it? Sarah would arrive any moment. Sharply alert but not fearful, Mike listened for the Tercel's engine. Her car's noise would mask whatever sound he made creeping down the ramp. He glanced at his watch. *Wait.*

Mike's otherwise perfect blind prevented him from seeing down along the wall where the bastard had to be. If the cars on his side had parked far enough out from the wall, he could slip between them and the wall. If not, he'd hug the ramp side end of the parked cars on his way down.

She was late. Had she finally parked on a lower level? Called in sick? He heard an engine and the sound of tires from below. The noise grew louder. Familiar. It could be someone else's Toyota. He saw Sarah's face through the windshield. "Fuck," he gasped. Inching out, he saw her Tercel slowing down to turn into the empty space. No movement from the other side.

Two vehicles down from his lookout, Mike slipped behind the rear of a van and craned his head out for a look. He pictured himself rushing to the car, the guy staying in his hiding place, confrontation prevented.

But the bastard would just up his game, maybe follow her home, lay in wait for her there.

Wait. Her car will come to a rest. She'll turn off the engine then gather her stuff so she can dart right to the elevator. *Don't scare him off. Catch him just as he goes for her.* Mike slipped one car further down, crouched behind its left side taillights.

Easing her Tercel up the ramp, Sarah scanned her level's parked cars and empty spaces. *All clear.* As she expected, a Honda Civic sat two spaces beyond her usual spot. Ordering her hands to ease their grip on the steering wheel, she breathed in slowly then exhaled even more slowly. *In one minute, I will be out on the sidewalk.* Glancing at her passenger seat, she saw only her satchel. She remembered standing in the kitchen and making a salad then putting it and an apple into her little insulated lunch bag. She pictured it sitting on the kitchen table at home. *Damn.*

Sarah pulled into her spot, one empty space separating her from a Dodge pickup truck. Seeing no unfamiliar vehicles in her rearview mirror, she turned off the ignition. While her right hand pocketed her keys, her left pressed against her jacket pocket just enough to feel the can of pepper spray inside. Again, nothing in the rearview mirror. She grabbed the handle of her satchel, unlocked the door, then stepped out.

Starting toward the ramp exit, she heard footsteps. She about-faced to see the expelled student coming toward her. "No!" she screamed, frozen in place.

"You fucking bitch!" he barked, slowing down as he approached. "You fucking disrespected me."

"No," she gasped, backing against the pickup's passenger door.

He stopped short of her and sneered. She clutched the satchel against her chest with both arms. Her eyes shot left then right. Seeing no one, she locked her eyes onto his, mustering up a glare and baring her teeth.

"Fucker," he muttered. He stepped up to her, the sneer replaced by a scowl. To reach her pepper spray, she'd have to drop her satchel. She pressed back harder against the truck, heart pounding.

"Pay the fucking price!" When he grabbed her by the shoulder and reared back his right arm, she pulled the satchel up in front of her face and squeezed her eyes shut. Sudden loud grunting and scuffling noises made her flinch. An explosion of force drove her back and legs against the lower part of the truck. She landed on the ramp surface with a cry. Opening her eyes, she saw Mike raising the student by the back of his jacket. He'd apparently tackled him to the ground. Sarah screamed.

Holding Sarah's assailant at arm's length, Mike spun him around then slammed his face against the passenger door of the truck as Sarah shimmied toward the truck's rear tire. Still holding him by the back of his collar, Mike mashed his face against the door again then scraped his head down the side of the pickup, leaving a smear of blood from the window to the base of the door.

"Flannagan!" Sarah screamed. Getting to her feet, she hunched over, moaning.

"Fuck," the guy groaned, struggling against Mike's grip from behind him.

"Just hold him," she cried, grabbing Mike's jacket sleeve. "I can get help."

"No!" Mike yelled. Clenching the back of the student's collar, he pinned his forehead against the lower part of the door, immobilizing him with his knee.

"No more." She jerked Mike's sleeve.

"Your ass is *dead*," the guy muttered. "Who do you think you're fucking with?"

"You don't understand!" Mike yelled at Sarah. Letting go of the student, he pushed her away.

Crashing face-first against the side of her car, she slumped to the ramp surface and looked up. She gingerly touched her face, feeling tenderness where bruises would erupt but no blood. Mike pulled the guy's left arm behind his back, stretching it until it made a popping sound.

"Jesus!" Sarah groaned. The student moaned and collapsed against the truck's rear wheel.

"He's unconscious, Mike." Sarah gasped, steadying herself against her car door. "What is *wrong* with you?"

"You're hurt," he said, looking at her cheek and eye. "Oh shit." When he reached toward her face, she stepped back from him. "We can't say a word," he said, panting. "To anyone."

"Michael!" she screamed, as terrified as when the student had grabbed her. "Oh my God." She grabbed her satchel and ran down the ramp to the stairway door without looking back.

Mike looked around but saw no one. When he heard a moan behind him, he slipped away toward the same stairway door Sarah had used. He stopped at the next landing to let his breathing slow enough that he could walk across campus without drawing attention to himself. Pompadour must have fainted from the pain. He hadn't killed him. He felt sick to his stomach about his deed, but somebody had to stop the son of a bitch. Worse, he'd hurt Sarah.

When he reached her office, the door was closed. He knocked. Nothing. He unzipped his jacket, tucked his shirt into his pants, then bent his head close to the door. "Sarah."

"God!" she shrieked. "No."

"Sarah, please."

When she cracked the door, he slipped inside, closing the door behind him. She had retreated to the other side of her desk. The bruise on her left cheek had already swollen, forming a large tender-looking lump beside her eye. "You need ice," he said, reaching the desk.

"Stay there!" Her fists were balled. She turned away, scowling, slumped into her chair, then swiveled so she faced the other wall.

"I'm so sorry you had to go through that."

"*You* did this!" she yelled, pointing to her cheek.

He dropped into the chair she kept for students. "I know," he said, cringing.

"And my back," she snapped. She swung her chair around and glared at him. "You're dangerous."

"You were right about the guy when you came to my house," Mike said. "Then you said you weren't worried, but you were. Because you were right in the first place. He *is* a bad guy."

"I had pepper spray," she said. "Right in my pocket, but I couldn't even breathe."

"No."

"What the fuck did you do to him?"

"Nothing else. I saw he was coming to, so I got out of there."

Her eyes looked everywhere but at him. "I should have told Security, but I ran here."

"They didn't see me either," Mike said. "And *he* didn't see me."

"I thought you were going to kill him."

Mike grimaced. "I might have broken his arm." He groaned. He couldn't imagine he'd ever say such words. Suddenly nauseated, he felt filthy, as if he'd just trudged through a trench soggy with shit and rotting dead animals. Would he have felt like this if he'd mauled the kid who'd killed Laurie and Michael? None of this made sense.

She breathed out slowly. "Who the hell *was* that in there?"

Mike shook his head. "He had to be stopped."

"I meant *you!*"

Her words were like a punch. "Jesus, Sarah." He dropped his head into his hands. "He was going to hurt you." He'd snapped, reacted, despite his efforts to let the guy have a chance to prove him wrong.

"You haven't been waiting there every day?"

He'd never been this angry with her before. He hated the feeling. He dropped his head into his hands. "You came to me for help."

"I didn't ask you to stalk the bastard and maybe kill him."

"He was stalking *you.*"

"You're as dangerous as he is."

"I haven't hit anyone but my brother since fifth grade," he said, looking up. "And that was pure self-defense."

"You think my worries are over now?" she said. "Maybe he didn't see you, but he knows who *I* am and probably knows where I live."

"It's over. He's headed nowhere but the hospital."

"You think what you did will make him forget that he's angry with me? Are you going to start watching out for me again after he's patched up?"

"The last thing he's going to do is go to the police or Security. He'll get the idea that he shouldn't mess with you. Lesson learned. And maybe he won't mess with anybody else now."

"Lesson learned?" she snarled. She stood up and looked straight at him. "You're the one who did this," she said, pointing to her face. "You need to get the fuck out of this office and stay the fuck out of my life. That much I'm sure of."

He got to his feet, panting, as if he'd just sprinted in. He closed the door behind him and rushed down the hallway.

Driving away, he could not rid his mind of the fear then the anger in Sarah's eyes. *She's safe now.* Going back to work was out of the question. He'd call when he got home, tell them he'd be in early Saturday morning. His season of stalking had ended with all involved feeling—if not actually—brutalized.

Sarah had no idea that he'd protected her. Fine. His violence had shocked him just as much. She was right to be angry at him for being so rough with her, but he had to make sure that bastard got the message *and* didn't see him. By the time he reached home, he'd gone from feeling relief that he'd stopped the punk to shame for hurting and scaring Sarah to an uncomfortable combination of the two. Still, he felt no satisfaction or sense of vindication. Though she might never see it, he had not let her down, not like in New Paltz. *But her eyes.* Making his way up the steps to his porch, his stomach roiled and churned, and he thought he might be sick right there.

After patting Robert in the foyer, he went to the kitchen phone. The machine indicated one message. He leaned his forehead against the wall then pressed the play button. A voice, shaking with anger, filled the kitchen.

"Just in case I didn't make myself clear, Mike, whatever 'we' is, well, it's over. Fucking *over*. Understand? I hope so because I don't want to have to see you or speak with you ever again."

Had this worst possible day been worth it? Robert deserved a walk. Later he'd find something to eat. Catch up on jobs at the seminary in the morning, pick up his nephew and niece after that. It didn't matter if he felt this shitty all weekend or all month. He'd done something. He knew this would not be the last time he would have to remind himself of that. Maybe he'd get through the walk without throwing up.

21

SATURDAY, FEBRUARY 18

Pausing in her survey of the essay drafts on her lap, Sarah glanced out the train window and saw the sign on the Trenton bridge in the early morning light. Did Trenton still *make*, as the sign claimed? "Trenton Makes, The World Takes." Sadly, not so true anymore. She shifted her position, but the soreness in her back and leg remained. Icing frequently since the attack had probably limited the swelling around her eye, at least. Despite the soreness, she'd managed to walk without apparent problem and knew that adrenaline would fuel her through her weekend.

Her phone message to Mike replayed in her mind. Another one-time truth? Or was yesterday the end of what she'd merely deluded herself had been a real relationship, one worth fighting for? *Back to the student drafts*. But her eyes lingered on the post-industrial landscape. She cringed as images of Mike and the student with the pompadour returned to her consciousness for an encore performance.

"What better way to spend the day before an extended weekend trip to New York to check on Mom and Dad and take a job interview," she'd deadpanned to Florence yesterday. She had to tell someone. She trusted her office mate to keep both secrets. A month earlier, she might have gone to Leona, but not anymore.

Though Sarah looked forward to some honest exchange with Betsy Rothman, the dean-approved counselor, whom she'd admired since attending one of the veteran counselor's professional development programs, she was not about to inform her about yesterday's incident at her first mandated session next week. Talking about it with Florence had made her pre-trip call to Mom and Dad less stressful. No reason to work them all up, no matter how much Sarah ached to scream bloody murder from a mountaintop.

The imminent job interview at Brooklyn College no longer felt like a brush-up of her interview skills, a values clarification exercise. Yes, she'd made this wonderful connection with Domenic and the barbershop crew, but what else anchored her in Philadelphia? Until yesterday, she'd have answered that plenty about her life in Philly made her want to call it home, but now?

Mike Flannagan is out of the picture. The thought brought instant sadness, anger, and a solid dose of self-hatred. After yesterday's explosion, how might she feel if she made it to the second round of interviews?

Plan the hours. Do the hours. Repeat. Yes, her approach made sense. She and Mom had worked out a long list of Saturday and Sunday activities. She'd see for herself if both parents were indeed thriving, as they'd insisted on the phone. She'd review her pre-interview notes in the privacy of their apartment's guest room on Sunday night before her "visit with faculty from the same field." At this point, these were necessary secrets, part of protecting her parents from worry. Nothing like what dangerous Mike had done.

Ten times a week she'd rushed through the parking garage. Had Mike been lurking in the shadows every time? The thought settled, giving her a sick feeling of having been violated repeatedly. What could have made him think he was doing a good thing? *Try words, Mike.* But it was too late for that.

Every time her anger at him peaked, she felt more deeply hurt by him. Every time her injuries made her wince, she blamed him. She didn't need a counselor or therapist to tell her to think about other things, about situations over which she had some control. Her pain gradually would abate. Less frequent triggers for all that Mike Flannagan anger. Hating him only worsened the pain. Gazing out at passing corporate parks and lots filled with empty eighteen-wheelers, she made herself visualize Mike's face watching the ducks at Valley Green, then Mike breathing in the aromas from a box of pizza. Tuning in to these "channels" lessened her fury, but she knew her mind would stumble across steel-eyed-stranger Mike in the garage.

As her anger ebbed, an alarming awkwardness took its place. *Yearning.* Not the vaguely realistic pre-yesterday imagining and working desperately toward a future with Mike, but longing that embarrassed her. *Woman, no wonder you feel like shit.*

Channels. Distractions. This imperfect approach needed refine-ment. She found herself right back where she'd started. As angry at herself as she was with him.

22

SATURDAY, FEBRUARY 18

On the ridge trail above the Wissahickon, Mike let Robert set the pace. Stopped while Robert closely inspected a clump of deer scat, Mike checked his watch. In twenty minutes, they should turn around so he could arrive at Brendan's house early enough to get the kids to the matinee showing at the Bala. He wanted them to get the full Bala Theatre experience, a movie plus a raffle, games, whatever the Greek-accented manager had up his sleeves for the kids. Spending the afternoon with his nephew and niece should help. It always did.

The same sourness that roiled his gut Friday night greeted him when the alarm shocked him awake to do the last of his comp hours at the seminary. Stretching out on the walk to the nearby woods served Robert's early morning needs but did nothing to help Mike's stomach. Dry toast and black tea stayed down, but the stomach distress continued throughout his short shift. It bothered him more now.

He told himself that his weeks of patient watching had protected Sarah, even if she'd never forgive him. He'd helped her yesterday, but he'd harmed her too. Had he given her a concussion? Was she limping? Wasn't she visiting her parents this weekend? Would she have a black eye? But things would be better for her now. He'd acted, done something. Still, he felt no relief. She wanted no part of him, probably never would. But wasn't that better for everyone?

An hour later, driving to Delores and Brendan's house, his

stomach pain had subsided a bit. He couldn't point to anything he'd done to account for the improvement but hoped this meant that soon he'd feel normal, if only in his stomach. Wasn't this how healing was supposed to work? Maybe for healing that didn't involve the death of a wife and child.

"Uncle Michael," Brendan said, when Mike arrived, ushering him into the living room. Uncharacteristically, his brother stood slightly hunched over. Still thick and muscular, Brendan looked thinner than the last time Mike had seen him, his cheekbones sharper and his ancient broken nose more pronounced, giving him the profile of a boxer who'd started to show his age. Standing by the couch, he looked worn. His wife had been in two hospitals and now lay in a rehab center bed.

"How is she today?" Mike said.

"Hard to see much difference day to day," Brendan sighed. He called upstairs to the kids and told Mike to sit on the couch.

Mike shook off his offer. "I was calling every couple days. But I've been tied up."

"She asked for you," Brendan said.

"Good."

"Good's how you're doing, or good that she asked?"

"Both."

"I'll tell her. She seems to like the new place. How about coffee?"

The thought of coffee sent a shiver up his spine. Again, Mike declined his offer, thought to make some joke about saving himself for soda at the movies, but nothing came to him.

"Can't force you," Brendan said, frowning.

Unlike family members and friends, Mike had never seen any brotherly resemblance, but today he cringed, seeing something in Brendan's eyes and mouth that brought the lifelong comparison to mind. *The day after I beat the shit out of some guy, no less.* Similar covers on different books, he told himself.

"Drop them off at Lucy's when you're done," Brendan said. "She's been unbelievable. Watches them Fridays so I can walk down the corner for a beer after work. She talks to Delores every day. The kids almost live at her place."

His nephew and niece roared down the stairs, jumping on Mike. He had told them on the telephone that this time they were going to see a movie from their father and uncle's childhood, Disney's *One Hundred and One Dalmatians.*

Brendan stuffed a twenty-dollar bill into Mike's hand. "Candy costs a fortune these days."

"Got it covered," Mike said, setting the twenty on the arm of the couch.

"Be good for your uncle," Brendan barked, as Robbie opened the front door. "I got errands," Brendan said to Mike. "Don't forget. Lucy's."

"Got it."

The kids ran down to Mike's car. He lingered at the porch door, surprised by an urge to tell his brother about yesterday, but when he looked back, Brendan was gone.

He found Robbie in the rear seat and Jessie up front when he reached the car.

"Robbie'll get shotgun on the ride back," Jessie announced.

He started the car. Mike's memories of childhood included no bloodless transfers of power between him and Brendan. Another reason to like these kids. When he heard the click of their seat belts, he fastened his.

"Can we have some music?" Robbie asked as Mike pulled into traffic.

When the radio blared on, the kids began chattering. Seated in the back, Robbie was animated in conversation with his little sister. His voice was still a child's, but his strong chin and high cheekbones matched his father's, giving him a harder look than his voice or manner indicated. *You look like a slightly less scary version of your brother.* Mike had heard it before but had never seen that in photographs of himself.

"I know the name of the movie," Jessie said. "It's about dogs. I love dogs. But I don't know where we're going to see it."

"The Bala," Mike said.

"They never call my ticket number," Jessie said.

"Just because I won something last time," Robbie said, "doesn't mean you always lose."

"I wish they didn't call anybody's number," she said.

"Who doesn't like games?" Mike said, sneaking a look over at the mournful redhead.

"I like to go to the movies," Jessie said. "I just don't like to lose." When she tuned to a song her brother knew, Robbie shouted at her to leave it on. She sat back. Mike glanced at Robbie in the rearview mirror. His head was moving to the music.

Mike was doing something right, taking them out like this. He looked like a regular American father, part of a family, but he felt like an actor in a movie about a secretly horrible man. He reminded himself that the stalker had gotten what he deserved, that he had prevented something bad from happening to an innocent person. Taking the kids out on a Saturday afternoon was simply a different way of helping out. Under the best circumstances, taking them out always ended up a mixed experience. His days as a father had ended before his son got anywhere near this stage. Michael had been getting interested in *Sesame Street*, but Laurie felt that he wasn't ready for movies.

Michael was born the year between Robbie and Jessie, and Mike gauged that he would be closer to Robbie's size than Jessie's. They both still seemed to show new growth every time he saw them. Laurie wouldn't have changed much in appearance in this amount of time, but Michael was another story. Without willing it, he began imagining Michael's changing physical capacity and stature, but a weighty sadness came over him. *Stop.* He focused on where they ought to park. The lot just up from the theater? The side street?

A block from the theater, Mike saw that the waiting line stretched almost to the corner. He found a spot down the block from the Bala. "Plenty of room inside," Mike assured them as they hustled. "Not like at malls. This is a big old-fashioned theater."

"From the olden days," Jessie said.

In four words, she had softened his shell, as he knew she would. They entered the theater during the previews. Mike marched the kids past row after row, finally finding three empty seats in the fourth row. End seats, easy to find in the dark.

"So close!" Jessie said, glowing.

"Dad said that you used to crawl under the seats from the back to the front," Robbie exclaimed. "He was jealous."

"The only advantage of being the smaller guy," Mike said.

He excused himself to run back to the snack bar. He might regret it, but he suddenly wanted to eat and drink with the kids more than go easy on his testy gut. The bass-heavy coming attractions boomed into the concession area while he, the only unaccompanied person in line, listened to a whiny customer hem and haw over selections. Four people remained ahead of him when the feature started. The kids should be fine. *But they're alone.*

Nimbly holding onto three bags of popcorn and three birch beers, he tiptoed down the dark aisle, trusting that his eyes would adjust by the time he reached the front of the auditorium. The kids dug into their popcorn before he was seated. He quickly recalled a few of the movie's characters but realized how little he remembered of the story.

An hour into the film, the projector stopped abruptly, as the house lights came up. People scurried noisily back to the refreshment area and restrooms as the manager and two teenaged ushers climbed onto the stage. They set up a card table in the narrow space between the curtain and the stage's edge then toted three large bulging plastic bags to the table.

"Prizes," Robbie announced to Jessie.

Mike pulled out their three ticket stubs.

The manager spoke into a small microphone, but every word came out garbled. When the PA system failed entirely, he dropped the microphone onto the table. Speaking loudly, he asked three birthday children from the audience to join him on stage. With closed eyes, a little girl produced a ticket from a large pretzel can.

"Six, seven, two, four, nine, four," the manager called out in his thick Greek accent.

Jessie slumped back into her seat.

A kid wearing a Little League baseball cap marched up to the stage to claim a set of movie posters. Another child won a vat of popcorn. Then it was a coloring book and a large stuffed bear.

"Now," the Greek man said. "I want every child with an X on their ticket stub to join the birthday children for a game of musical chairs."

Mike turned the tickets over. One had an X marked on it, but he could not remember whose ticket it was. The kids saw the X.

"Whoa!" Robbie said.

About a dozen kids, some bigger than Robbie, scampered up to the front of the theater.

"Jess, you ready?" Mike said.

"Me?"

"Go," Mike said, handing her the ticket.

She chased the others to the stage, as the ushers formed the fifteen chairs into a line with every other chair facing the audience or the curtain.

"She's got to win," Robbie said to Mike.

"Maestro!" the manager called. A scratchy recording of "Zorba the Greek" began playing. The fifteen kids slowly circled the chairs. When the music stopped, they flew for the chairs, eventually each one finding a seat. The manager removed a chair at his end of the line.

"She'll get buried," Robbie whispered to Mike. He'd never seen Robbie look so upset.

' "Maestro!" the manager called again. Jessie stepped gingerly up one side of the line and sprinted around the end. The music stopped. Jessie dropped into a seat. A boy Robbie's age was out.

The game started again. Mike felt his teeth clench as Jessie approached the corner, bunched behind a girl twice her size. "Hurry *up.*" Midway down the line when the music stopped, she fell safely into a seat, smiling. One after another, kids lost and glumly left the stage.

With three seats remaining, Jessie was the smallest survivor and the only girl.

The music restarted. *Is fucking Zorba setting up somebody to win this game?* Mike's face flushed like it had yesterday. Once the punk started toward Sarah, he'd lost all sense of time. His legs moved. His arms were flying, grabbing, and he threw himself at the bastard, slamming him off Sarah, but he'd felt oddly separated from his body, as if for those seconds his body acted on its own while he somehow took it all in. No planning. Had he thought anything? He might have tripped or made a noise. The guy could have overpowered him, pulled out a knife or a gun.

"Come *on*, Jess," Robbie shouted.

Mike gripped the sides of his seat.

The music stopped. The other kids dashed into the three seats. The manager shook Jessie's hand then pulled out another chair.

Walking up the aisle, she averted her eyes. When she reached their row, she flashed a sad smile. Robbie popped up and slapped her a high five. Jessie collapsed onto Mike's lap.

"You were incredible," he said.

She laid her head against his chest, and he leaned back into his seat. She clung to him, her freckled faced buried in his shirt. She needed and trusted him in this hard moment. His heart swelled. *Michael.* The sadness returned, brushing away his second of pride and joy. He patted her back.

A wiry twelve-year-old birthday boy won a battery-operated video game. In no time, the little crew cleared the stage. When the lights went out, the movie picked up in the middle of a line of dialogue. Jessie turned to watch the screen but did not leave Mike's lap. They all were laughing at the action on the screen, but he pictured the rich kid that had killed his family. Mike had been useless then. But not with Sarah's attacker. He felt himself shaking and did not want Jessie to know. "We need more popcorn," he whispered to her.

She nodded gravely.

He jogged past the snack stand. Upstairs, in the empty men's room, he studied his reddened complexion in the mirror and splashed cold water all over his face. Brendan's face had always turned crimson when he fought. Mike might have looked like that yesterday. He tried to will away his anger, save it for people who truly deserved it. If he got another shot at the bastard, he'd break his other arm, but this hot drive embarrassed him. Sarah's words: "Who the hell *was* that in there?" What had he done?

He ran the faucet until the water was ice cold. Cupping his hand, he scooped water into his mouth. He dried his face and hands with paper towels. His reflection now looked more like himself. Sarah's reaction made sense. But he had been right to act.

Inching his way to breaking up the relationship, she'd acted before he did. Another time when he'd failed to act. She'd made it official. And he'd frightened and hurt her. He threw the wet paper towels into the trash bin. Downstairs, he bought two medium popcorns and hustled down the aisle.

Sitting next to the kids, he concentrated on the movie, wanting to be swept away by the antics of the characters, hoping that he could stop thinking about driving that guy's head against the car door.

Drained, he watched as the dogs of England teamed up to trick the evil Cruella de Vil to free one hundred and one Dalmatians. They covered the spotted dogs with soot to trick Cruella. Melting snow wiped off the disguise on some of them. The chase was on. Kids and grown-ups laughed as Cruella's car careened off the road, sending those spotted puppies back to the kind humans. But Mike's teeth were gritted. When the film ended, Mike applauded with the rest of the audience, but he felt like any moment he might be discovered, arrested, and that he deserved it.

They carried their half-empty containers of popcorn back to the car. "So much better than I thought it would be," Robbie said, sounding like a professional critic.

Mike got them drinks for the ride home from a soda machine.

"I'm stuffed," Jessie said, burping. "Whoa!"

In the car, Robbie read from the back of the soda can about a contest. "You can win two hundred badminton sets," he said.

"Oh, that'd be great," Jessie said.

"No," Robbie said. "You don't get all of them. You win one. Other people get one each."

Mike kept the radio turned down low so he could follow their conversation. He was glad that Robbie did not feel compelled to hurt his sister. Mike drove back to Roxborough, reminding himself to drive to Lucy's home, a few blocks from Brendan's. After dinner, the kids would go bowling with their cousins. He did not mention their mother or their father; they deserved a respite from that for a few hours. When he double-parked in front of the house, Lucy was sweeping the little row house porch.

"Next Saturday, you guys," Mike said to the kids. "Breakfast at Bob's Diner then the whole day out, okay?"

They thanked him and leaped out, popcorn bags in hand, and ran up the steps to their aunt. Robbie was not going to terrorize his sister. He could see that. And losing that game was now history for Jessie, just part of an afternoon's activities that were about to be followed by an evening of bowling and pizza. These kids could move on, he told himself.

Brendan was nowhere in sight. Errands, he had said. He might be doing things for the house or for the kids. He might be visiting Delores. Or he might be adding another decadent page to the Book of Brendan.

Mike told himself that it was natural to think about yesterday. In time, it would pass. Soon, a memory of something other than beating that guy in the garage and throwing Sarah against her car would pop into his head when he was driving the car or walking the dog or trying to go to sleep.

23

TUESDAY, FEBRUARY 21

At the garage entrance, Sarah smiled at the security guard and wondered for a second if after all she should have said something to someone. If the dean knew, he'd immediately turn the mess he'd created for her into a deeper level of hell. Steering into the first open parking place on the second level, she reminded herself that the guy, no doubt in some sort of cast since Friday, had been alone. Mike was probably right about him no longer posing a threat. But she scanned the dimly lit area, hardly breathing, as she turned off the engine. She looked closely in her rearview mirror and put one hand on the pepper spray before opening the door. She walked quickly but not so fast that she might trip.

Opening the door to her building, she heard the chatter of two guards at the Security desk and the hum of the escalator. She felt her fear dissipate and told herself that it would not be so hard when she left in the afternoon. Rising on the glass-walled elevator, she looked down at the bustling throng of humanity on the ground floor. So normal and familiar. Her vigilante ex was nowhere in sight. He couldn't possibly have been lurking between parked cars when she pulled into the garage this morning. That particular concern should depart in time too. For very different reasons, Mike and the guy with the pompadour meant trouble; however, in all probability, both were nonfactors now. If Mike was the helpful hero he seemed to think he'd been, why did she continue to feel as violated by him as by the bastard that snuck up on her?

Closing the office door behind her, she banged it against its frame and slung herself down into her desk chair. She threw a pencil at the chair in which he had offered his lousy explanation.

Her perspective on the Brooklyn College position and on how to approach the interview had changed after she'd been with her parents for a few easy hours. New York, after all, had been home. "There are some great places to live in Brooklyn," she told her parents as Saturday's lunch wound down, right after her announcement that Monday's appointment was, in fact, for a job interview.

"Go where you need to go," her father counseled. "Even if it's Timbuktu."

"No one would complain if you ended up closer than two hours away," her mother said.

"And twenty minutes away," her father added, "would be even better."

Her father's medical reports were all good. Mom brought him to his treatments. He had his low moments, but he experienced fewer side effects than expected. Without any mention of boyfriends or attackers, the weekend passed much like previous happy visits.

She'd handled yesterday's interview better than she'd anticipated. She told the three English professors the same thing she'd told her parents and everyone else, that her black eye was from racquetball. Midway through the interview, she realized that she wanted this job badly, yet she did not feel desperate. When the two men and the woman evinced a different pedagogical bent than her own, she articulated her views and explained her practices, surprised at how calmly convincing she sounded. Again and again, she spoke about her students, their challenges, and their determination. The committee told her that they'd be meeting with other candidates over the next few weeks.

On the train ride back to Philadelphia, she'd listened to Nick's barbershop interview. He sounded sure of himself, seasoned and wise. Looking out at a stretch of flat farm fields, she hoped that her interviewers had felt the same about her performance. For the time being, only Florence Devereaux would hear about her personal day in New York.

Once, she had told Florence about a night when she made boeuf bourguignon for Mike. "Thank you," he intoned, his brow creased as if in pain or concentration. "Jesus. You put a hell of a lot into this."

Had she felt more buoyed when she'd learned that she'd been granted tenure? The food prep had been a work of love, leaving her exhilarated by the sense of closeness she felt to him. She could not hold herself back. She loved him, quirks and all. Putting her hand on his at the dinner table, she assured him that it was okay if he wanted to avoid talking about his wife and son, but that she would be happy to listen if he ever needed to do so.

They ate in silence. Finally, she asked him if the beef was okay.

"Fine," he said.

Dessert elicited nothing further from him—either about the food or her comment.

Perhaps for Mike, *fine* represented a succinct tone-perfect response.

By the time they cleaned up the leftovers and finished washing the dishes, she'd lighted on two sobering realizations: people who don't talk about the meal before them might just be a different species, and, more importantly, her reading of the relationship had taken only her into consideration. *Patience, Sarah.*

"Sometimes the man goes dark," she'd told Florence. "As if he can't manage more than a grunt, can't afford to make a sound, like a submarine in one of those old war movies."

"*Run Silent, Run Deep?*" Florence said, eyebrows arched.

She hadn't told Florence about the time shortly after that dinner when she'd suggested that perhaps the living room might be a better place for Mike's family photo than the bedroom dresser. There'd been nothing silent about his reaction that night. So much for wondering if he might ever keep his old wedding band in his dresser drawer. And so much for her being patient.

After her last class and final conference of the day, she slumped back into her office chair and let out a long sigh. Her aches and pains had lessened since the morning. Florence had left. She would speak to her some other time. The students, her colleagues, the teaching. All of it had seemed normal, comfortable. The college had become her place, her life, but she could leave it. She pulled open the top drawer of her file cabinet. Several years had passed since she'd last purged these files. She stuffed her wastebasket in ten minutes with old student papers, memos, and outdated departmental guidelines, then carried it to the large receptacle at the end of the hallway. Back in her office, she started refilling the wastebasket. In an hour, her once-jammed file drawers swung open at the touch of a finger. The bookshelves were neat and spotless. It was dark outside, later than she usually left on a Tuesday, but she'd gotten something done.

Sarah strode to the garage, unzipping her spring jacket halfway. Taking in the fresh air felt good after perspiring through her clothes. She jogged up the garage stairway to the next level, which she found half-filled. After a quick glance around, she strode down the ramp, clutching her car keys in one hand and the pepper spray in the other. She stuck the key into the driver side door and turned it. Easier every time, she promised herself.

Driving back to the neighborhood, she told herself that Mike's violence had provided her with valuable clarity regarding both him and the relationship. But it wasn't just about that. He was dangerous, to himself and to others. She didn't know who the hell Mike Flannagan was. A Toyota a half-block ahead pulled over and parked in front of the dark barbershop, leaving long spaces in front and behind. The driver got out and headed for the pizza shop. Across the street, the neon Budweiser sign in the window of Gilhooley's twitched on and off. Chipped green paint hung off the door. She pushed down her turn signal and jerked the car into the parking lane, pulling to a halt inches from the fender of the Toyota. Feeling her oats, her mother would call it.

Mike had mentioned the bar once or twice, making clear that it was not on the list of spots they ought to consider visiting after a movie—good enough of a reason to pay her first visit to Gilhooley's Friendly Tavern. Crossing the avenue, she told herself that if she found horror on the other side of the door, she could order a six-pack and go home with enough beer for the rest of the year. It was another part of the old neighborhood that, like Nick and Clement, she ought to know more about, even if she was on her way out.

Letting the door swing shut behind her, she counted eight people, in two clusters of four, seated on the long end of the L-shaped bar. The two booths at the front were empty. Four customers glanced at her as she paused by the jukebox. She walked to the short end of the bar then sat on the stool at the corner by the wall. It was warm inside, and the cigarette smoke made the room feel very close. She pulled her jacket zipper all the way down without taking it off and leaned against the wall.

A man behind the bar wearing a black Harley-Davidson T-shirt strolled to her side of the bar and stood in front of her. "What'll it be?"

The row of taps on the other side of the bar offered no compelling choices. Mike had usually kept Yuengling in his refrigerator. "Rolling Rock," she said.

The bartender took two steps on the duckboard, produced an eight-ounce glass from under the bar, brought it up under the tap, and started filling it. The jukebox boomed some bass-heavy, plaintive pop song. Everyone but the bartender had a cigarette in hand. He set the beer in front of her then reached under the bar, pulling out a plastic container the size of something one might use to serve ketchup or cocktail sauce. He plopped the empty little tub upside down beside her beer. "Want to run a tab?"

She picked up the plastic container and looked at it.

"Two-for-one night," he said, wiping the counter.

She put a ten-dollar bill on the bar. The bartender scooped it up, returning in a few seconds with wet bills and loose change. He returned to the other end of the bar, picking up a lit cigarette from a glass ashtray under the bar. She fiddled with her plastic cup. Mixed in with ashtrays, bottles, and glasses, little cups like hers dotted the top of the bar in front of the other customers.

"Bull," a woman at the other end called over the music. The bartender sauntered over, scooped up her empty cup, stashing it somewhere under the bar, then filled her empty glass with Rolling Rock. *These people know every inch of the place and every soul who walks in.* One group was talking loudly about the Phillies. Amidst them, she recognized the crude young guy from the barbershop.

"They suck," a companion pronounced. "End of story."

"End of season," haircut man said.

She watched Bull work his way up and down the line of drinkers, filling beers, taking money, and making change, all without exchanging a word about anything but sports. He emptied all the ashtrays and interjected a little something into every conversation as he made his way back down to her end. When he reached Sarah, he placed another little plastic cup in front of her.

"On Tommy," he said. "Says he knows you."

Haircut man was smiling at her and holding up his mug as if he were making a toast. "Tell him thanks," she said to the bartender. She lifted her glass in the air and nodded to Tommy, offering only the trace of a smile. He stood up and headed in her direction. The other conversations continued, but she sensed that his actions were not lost on the crowd.

He stopped at the stool beside her. His smile looked glued on. "I forget your name," he said, leaning on the back of the stool.

"Sarah," she said, sure that neither she nor anyone else at the barbershop had spoken her name on Thursday.

"Tommy Coyle," he said.

She nodded. "I don't think we were actually introduced."

"What goes with the Sarah?"

"Goins," she said. She spelled it for him and immediately pictured him sitting in yesterday's underwear, alone in some hovel, looking her number up in the phone book.

Tommy's smile had turned into something closer to a smirk. "Like I'm *goin'* to have a good time," he said.

She swallowed the last of her beer. The instant her empty glass touched the bar, Bull snatched it and one of the plastic cups.

"*Goin'* with anybody tonight?" Tommy asked, his broadening smile suggesting that he had surprised himself with his own wit.

"You know, I really *am*," she said. "But I certainly appreciate the drink."

"Well, all right," he said, giving her a wink. "Good to see you again." He pirouetted, smile intact, and walked back to his place. His fellow patrons remained locked in conversation, but they had to be taking in his failed courtship dance. He had not sat down or asked to sit down on the empty stool beside her, enabling him to retreat gracefully. Clearly this was not his first dance or his first rejection.

She finished the second beer more quickly than the first. The second little cup sat beside her glass. Tommy's treat. Assuming that it would be bad form to leave the cup, she said nothing when Bull swept her glass away.

Did the old guys from Al's ever come in here? Perhaps the crowd at this time of day did not offer a fair indication, but she would have felt more comfortable to see a Black, brown, or Asian patron. When she had raved to Mike about the neighborhood being such a model of integration, he'd told her about the day he had been in traffic, sandwiched between the H bus and a school bus from a Quaker school in Germantown. At every corner, he'd wait behind the SEPTA bus while the Black public school kids got off. In his rearview mirror, he watched the doors of the yellow school bus open, unloading several white kids from the private school. Mostly, she had to agree, they just shared zip codes. She wondered where the Black folks went for a beer.

Mike was either at home or at the seminary. He had little in common with this lot. She was hard-pressed to find a social grouping to which he belonged. He was headed in a bad direction. She drank her third beer, more than she had consumed since she and Mike split a pizza at a suburban bar in December. She left a tip and headed for the door without making eye contact with Tommy Coyle.

Wednesday morning's headache stayed with her through her classes and the drive home, but Sarah woke up Thursday with the best attitude she'd had since before Mike's appearance at the parking garage. All day, she thought about her questions for Nick and

Clement. When she entered the barbershop, she found Domenic missing again.

"Under the weather," Al explained, gesturing toward the ceiling. "In his cell." Al was working on his one customer, a thirtyish man in a suit. Nick and Clement greeted Sarah like long-lost friends. She waved off their concern about her black eye. "Racquetball," she said. An hour later, she finished her interview with Nick.

"I felt nervous," he confided. "Like I was in school."

"You did great."

She pressed record and asked Clement her first question. Clear and soft-spoken, he took his time before responding to her questions. After an hour, she told him she would wrap up with him the following week.

When she put her tape recorder away, she was alone with Al and the two men. "I've got something to tell you," she told them.

"Not letting anybody in at ten of five anyway," Al said. He flipped over the Open/Closed sign on the door. Rubbing his hands together, he walked to his chair and turned it to face Sarah, who stood in the middle of the room. The other two men leaned in from their corner spots.

"You know about Mount Airy Day in May?"

They nodded.

"Stages for music, all kinds of food all along the avenue," Sarah said.

"I don't care for crowds," Al said. "Ginette and I usually stay home."

"I'm done with it in a half hour," Nick said.

She turned to Clement. "More of a young person's thing," he said.

"You might want to come this time," Sarah said. She'd begun pacing across the length of the room, as if she were in her classroom. "Different speakers are going to talk about the neighborhood."

"Speeches?" Nick said, making a face.

"Wait," Sarah said, stopping mid-step for dramatic effect. "When I told Mark Thompson about the oral histories we're doing, he was interested. They need somebody to talk about what it was like in the thirties."

"That's their territory," Al said, nodding to the others.

"They want a balance of people by race and age and gender."

"Of course!" Nick exclaimed. "They'll get at least one of every creature that got off Noah's ark!"

"They need a white male who can talk about the thirties," she said, taking a step closer to Nick.

"A white male?" Nick gasped.

"Don't have a heart attack," Clement said.

"I won't," Nick said. "Because I ain't speechifying in front of those eggheads."

Sarah couldn't imagine reneging on her promise to produce a speaker. "The crowd for any one activity won't be all that large," she said, taking another step.

Nick frowned. "Those people don't want to listen to some guy who got educated on the streets."

"We could medicate him," Al said.

"I might not say what they want to hear," Nick said.

"When have you ever let that slow you down?" Clement said.

"You're already signed up," Sarah said, now standing beside him.

Nick's expression turned sour.

"You could bag out of it," she said, turning toward the others but not moving from Nick's side. "Those people who make all that fuss about shooting deer in the park would understand that you couldn't stand up in front of them, you know, knees shaking, tongue-tied."

"That wispy little guy with the Coke-bottle glasses who marches around with protest signs," Clement said. "He'd be there?"

"Probably front row," Al said.

"I could tell him what the neighborhood was like before the likes of him moved in," Nick said. "Tell me I'm allowed to talk about the deer? There are more of those critters in this state now than when the white man came here."

"Are you saying that *some* good came of that?" Clement asked.

Al laughed. "You've got your man," he said to Sarah.

"It's not meant to be a speech on the deer problem," Sarah clarified.

"We'll see," Nick said.

"So, I don't have to disgrace you by having those bunny huggers scratch your name off the list?" Sarah said.

"We may all live to regret this," Nick said.

Al shook his head. "Sometimes he does hit the nail on the head."

"Just be yourself," Sarah said, patting Nick on the shoulder.

"Careful, Doctor Frankenstein," Clement said.

"Ten minutes on stage," she said. "Clement, you're okay with this?"

He nodded.

"I mean, he grew up in this neighborhood. You and Al didn't."

"Wouldn't miss seeing this for anything in the world," Clement said, chuckling and looking at Nick.

Sarah stayed with Al while he straightened up the shop, watching the two old men walk down the sidewalk. They were still talking when they turned at the traffic light. "I'm going to look in on Domenic," she told Al when he was done with the lock.

"I went up earlier," he said. "He says he's coming down tomorrow morning." Al selected a key from his key ring. "I can unlock his downstairs door. Save him coming down."

"Great," Sarah said. "I'll make sure he knows it's me. I mean, after all this talk about heart attacks."

She took a few steps up the stairwell before announcing herself. The door at the top opened as she reached it. They both flinched.

"Didn't mean to scare you," she said, laughing.

"Likewise," Domenic said, tucking his flannel shirt into his old trousers.

She followed him into his front room where he took his seat by the window. She sat on the couch beside his chair.

"What brings you to the penthouse?" Domenic said.

"Al said you weren't having such a good day."

"Al ought to mind his own business," Domenic said. "I'm just a little slow. I'm not exactly a spring chicken, you know."

She nodded. He looked a bit pale to her but not bad.

"Sometimes I cut down on the number of trips I make up and down the stairs. That's all, but it's been a long time since anybody thought to check on me. Thank you."

"My pleasure."

"You're the one looks like she had a bad day," he said, frowning.

She shook her head. She watched him stand to move the curtain at his window and look up the avenue.

"What's on your mind?" he said, turning back to her. "Wait. Let me guess. Michael Francis Flannagan?"

She reddened. "It's not what you probably think," she said. He returned to his seat and gave her a consoling smile. She poured out the details of Mike's actions in the parking garage on Friday, encouraged by Domenic's pained and caring expression. When she finished reporting about the argument in her office, he turned toward the window in silence, sadness covering his face. Feeling nearly as exhausted as the day it had happened, she remained beside him, watching him.

"He doesn't get it," she said. "Doesn't see that he's dangerous to himself and to others."

Domenic shook his head, still looking off. "You're not worried about this numbskull that tried to attack you?"

"Probably out of the picture," she said. "Do you see how much Mike scared me? He went *off.*"

He nodded, still not looking at her. "And hurt you," he said.

"The scaring part is worse."

"Mike was stalking the stalker?" he said.

Is this all registering to him? Is he holding back? Could anyone see the danger in Mike as clearly as I do? She began retelling the incident, trying to paint a more vivid picture of the injured man. "I don't trust anything about Mike," she said. "But I'm afraid for him."

"I'll probably regret this," he said, finally turning back to her. "But maybe we should pay him a visit, the two of us."

"You think?"

"They got him working late this week," Domenic reported, then added that Frick and Frack had run into him on one of his dog walks. They hadn't found him too cheery. "Why don't you go home and do whatever you got to do on a Thursday evening. Pick me up around nine-thirty."

"I don't believe you're saying this."

"Make it ten."

"Both of us?"

"Unless I get a better offer."

At home, she graded a short stack of essays and dragged three baskets of dirty clothes down to the laundry room, calling the trips back and forth between her apartment and the basement her week's exercise. At nine-fifty, she put on her coat, hat, and gloves then went out to her car. Domenic was waiting outside his door. She drove them up the hill toward Mount Pleasant Avenue. She had no idea what she would say to Mike or what might come out of Domenic's mouth.

Neither of them said a word to each other. She turned slowly onto Mike's dimly lit street, feeling like she was driving to a gangland rendezvous, yet this move didn't strike her as crazy.

"I don't see his car," she said, easing into a parking spot across the street and well up the block from Mike's house and where he usually parked. She cut the lights but did not turn off the ignition. She looked at the clock on the dashboard.

"Let's wait where it's warm for five minutes," he said. "I like our chances of being allowed in if we're already on the porch."

"Taking the high ground?" she said. "Are you sure you haven't done this sort of thing before?" She craned her neck to get a look up at the porch.

"Did you know that Mike is worried about his sister-in-law?"

"Never met her," Sarah said. "Apparently she's got plenty to deal with."

"Surprised the hell out of me when he helped me home. Didn't expect that."

"No, he's full of surprises." Last Friday, she'd recognized that she needed it to be over between Mike and her. Every morning since then, she'd woken up to the same wallop of hurt and anger but had moved through the day taking strength from the clarity she'd earned. Yes, she wanted *them* to be over, but her anger would subside. She didn't want more bad things to come to him.

Three minutes passed. The butterflies in her chest were killing her. "I don't want to wait anymore," she said. "Let's not make this anymore of a caper than we have to."

"Okay, Dick Tracy," he said, pushing open his door.

She turned off the ignition, got out of the car, then walked across the street beside the hobbling old man.

"Going to take my time," he said at the bottom of the steps. He glanced up at the porch. "Go ahead."

When she reached the landing, she turned to wait for Domenic and found him frozen in place halfway up the steps, his hand in the air. He bore the expression of a surprised third-grader, caught by his clairvoyant teacher's deft spin from the blackboard as his spitball hurtled across the room. Domenic dropped his hand to the iron railing, muttering something in Italian.

"His dog always makes a ruckus when I show up," she whispered.

"Robert?" Domenic's face crinkled into an impish grin. "I just communicated with him," he said, winking. "He won't bother us."

Sarah adjusted her speed so that she stayed just ahead of Domenic. Mike's porch light was on. The house to the right sat in darkness; the upstairs lights were on in the house to the left. When she reached the porch stairs, she thought she heard the dog stirring in the foyer. She looked back at Domenic.

"You're not going fast," he whispered. "I'm going slow."

Smiling, she gently planted herself in one of the two metal porch chairs as Domenic stepped onto the porch. She heard Robert moving around in the foyer. Still, not a peep from the big boy. Domenic looked out of breath.

"*So 'rivat*," he murmured, slumping into the other seat.

A pair of headlights came into view at the top of the hill, but she saw that it was a Chevy. A cat yowled across the street. Voices on the television next door chattered away. Otherwise, the neighborhood was quiet. Domenic began humming as Sarah looked up and down the other side of the street. Only two houses had lights on. She finally recognized the tune that Domenic was humming. "'Don't Worry, Be Happy'?" she whispered.

"It's all they play on the radio," he whispered back, then continued humming.

This might be a disaster in the making, but sitting beside Domenic felt as natural as anything she'd done all semester. They made a formidable team. She tucked her shivering gloved hands under the arms of her coat, watching the little clouds her breath made.

24

THURSDAY, FEBRUARY 23

"That sounds like his car," Sarah said. As the noise grew louder, Domenic saw the car's headlights. He stopped humming. Mike pulled into a space down the block large enough for two cars.

Domenic pulled his glove back so he could see the face of his watch: a little after eleven. Meetings? What could they have him doing up at the seminary? He shuddered at the thought of what it might do to Sarah if Mike emerged from the car with another woman, but from what he'd learned about Mike, that was not likely.

Mike shut the door and stepped onto the sidewalk. Another man got out of the other side of the car. When they reached the steps, Mike raised his eyes, squinting slightly in their direction. His companion carried a case of beer. When Mike stopped halfway up the steps, Domenic saw the scowl on his face. He continued slowly, the other slightly taller, broader man following.

"You two *know* each other?" Mike snapped. His companion stopped beside him and studied them.

"I know it's late," Sarah said.

"Why is *either* of you here?"

Domenic squirmed in his seat. He hadn't opened his mouth but felt like his uninvited appearance already had said too much. Maybe Sarah could defuse Mike.

"Can we have a minute?" she said.

Nodding grimly toward the door, Mike climbed the steps to the porch as Sarah and Domenic rose.

Robert let out a bark then a low growl.

"Freezing," Mike muttered, holding the door open for the others. In the vestibule, Robert cowered behind Mike when he saw Domenic. "I'll walk you in a few minutes," Mike said to the dog. "Soon as the company leaves." He closed the door. "This is my brother, Brendan." The man, toting a case of Yuengling lager, stood beside him at the edge of the living room. "Sarah Goins and Domenic Gallo," Mike said.

Brendan lit up. "Hey, glad to finally meet you all," he said. "Just dropping this off. We were out doing some things." He set the case of beer on the living room rug then reached over and shook hands with both of them, far more benign in demeanor than what Domenic had expected. Brendan's stature was imposing, but he must know how to put on a good front.

"What's going on?" Mike said. His brother clumped toward the kitchen toting the beer.

Standing beside Domenic, Sarah leaned toward Mike. "You could have killed that guy," she quavered. "We're afraid for you, Mike."

"*We?*" He was glaring at Domenic.

"Do you mind if we all slow down?" Domenic asked, sitting down on the couch. Mike looked shocked. "We're all just worried about each other."

"Yeah?" Mike said, smirking. "How about this—I don't want to see you again!"

Now Sarah, too, gave Domenic a raw look. He was striking out with both of them. "Come here, boy," he said. The dog crouched, took a step back, his tail between his legs. Domenic opened his arms toward the dog. "It's okay, boy." The dog trotted right over to Domenic, who patted him and scratched behind his ears. Robert's tail started to wag. He settled by Domenic's feet.

"I trusted you," Mike said to Domenic.

"And I trusted *you*, Mike," Sarah said, stepping closer to Mike. She looked like she was about to blow.

Mike's look stopped her in place. "No, you didn't. You parked in the same damn spot every day."

"I was terrified!" She spun around, eyes squeezed shut, and took a few deep breaths. "You're the one who needs to be careful," she pleaded, turning back to Mike.

"Apparently," Mike said with an ugly laugh.

"Sarah," Domenic pleaded. "He saved you from being beaten. Mike, you scared the hell out of her. Can't you both see that?"

The two of them stood above him shooting him the same hostile look. "*Madonna*," he moaned, throwing his hands up in the air. Brendan was opening and closing doors in the kitchen.

Mike turned to Sarah. "Nothing else happened, right?"

She shook her head. "I'm scared, Mike. For you."

"Mike," Domenic said.

"Talking about me behind my back," Mike said to him.

"I know what it looks like."

"Here to share another one of your recipes? Do a little bonding?"

Reeling inside, Domenic looked down at Robert and patted him. The dog snuggled up against his leg. "I didn't get any indigestion the other night," he said. "Did you?"

"Maybe you should go home and light another candle."

Domenic closed his eyes. *Stonato.* He gritted his teeth.

"We shouldn't have come over like this," Sarah said, wringing her hands. "I should have called. And I should have come by myself."

"Which one of you geniuses thought of this?" Mike asked.

"Blame me," Sarah said.

When he looked up at her, she fixed Domenic with a nasty look and nodded toward the door. It was over, a complete failure. He'd ruined it. He pulled himself up from the couch.

"I won't bother you," Sarah said to Mike.

"Correct," he said.

She flinched then turned away, her eyes narrowing.

Brendan padded into the living room, stopping well away from the three of them. "I need to get home to the kids," he said softly. His face showed concern. Was this guy a slick monster or had Mike painted him all wrong?

"You're not interrupting anything," Mike told him.

Brendan turned to Domenic and Sarah. "Not the best time for the Flannagans," he offered. "I'll walk you to your car," he said.

"Good night, everybody," Mike chirped with mock cheerfulness.

"Call you tomorrow," Brendan said, stepping outside with them.

Domenic heard the door close and the double lock turn. Brendan took his elbow, and the three of them walked in step all the way down to the sidewalk. "I'm parked just below Mike's car," he said.

"We're just up there," Sarah said.

He helped Domenic up to the car, Sarah scooting past them, keys in hand. She opened the passenger side door then stepped back to let Domenic climb inside.

"Sometimes nobody wins," Brendan said, then walked Sarah to the other side of the car.

"Very sorry about your wife," she said, opening her door. "I hope she's doing better."

He nodded. "Looking up," he said, but he didn't look convincing.

"I hope she gets home soon."

"Thanks." Brendan patted her on the back then turned away.

Domenic had barely fastened his seat belt when the car's sudden left-right movement snapped everything above his hips toward Sarah then back as she accelerated out of her parking place. At the avenue's green light, he had time to brace himself before she jerked the steering wheel hard to the left. The tires squealed then hit the rumbly surface of Belgian blocks and trolley tracks, making every part of him shimmy until she jerked to a stop at the red light at the top of the hill. "That," she said, turning to him as an H bus lumbered across the intersection, "was largely my own stupid fault. I never go into a classroom unprepared." She squeezed her eyes shut again, cursed herself foully, then reopened them and glared at him. "But what were *you* thinking? 'Maybe we should pay him a visit.' Oh my God! That's not a reason or a plan. Do you live in a land of magic and miracles?"

She didn't mean it, but he felt kicked to the curb. Alone. The car started down past the darkened old commercial strip, everything closed except for the bar. The bar window's faded neon beer sign flickered, cut out, then returned. He could imagine the intermittent buzzing death rattle it must be making, but the car wheels on the avenue's surface masked everything else. When she pulled over in front of his building, the motor still running, he looked at her to see if she had anything else to say. Hands gripped on the steering wheel, she turned to him, her mouth pursed. *Say it: "What are you waiting for, old man?"* He patted her knee twice, then let himself out.

25

SUNDAY, MARCH 12

Mike startled awake. Five in the morning. He had been dreaming about New Paltz, grocery shopping with Michael and another child, a little girl he assumed was his daughter. Laurie wasn't there. Leaving the kids in the shopping cart, he ran to the produce section in search of bok choy. The bin was empty. He rushed back, but only the cart was there. A woman who looked like Laurie walked past him. "Laurie!" he cried out. "You're crazy," the woman said, scurrying away. He ran up and down each aisle, looking for the kids. In the produce aisle, he found the bok choy bin overflowing.

Mike remained in bed, trying to sleep. At six o'clock, he dressed, then clipped Robert's leash onto his collar. Soon, Carpenter's Woods would be crawling with dogs and their walkers, like every Sunday, so Mike's early rising meant Robert could have a bit of a run without either of them having to deal with crowds. They walked west on streets populated by the people who had replaced the neighbors of Mike's youth. People like Sarah. Two weeks and counting since the Allied Invasion and he'd managed to avoid thinking of them for hours at a time. Each time they'd barged into his consciousness, he flamed into disgust and rage. He'd become the king of concentration, of engagement, in whatever he was doing.

Three blocks away, Mike and Robert came upon a man about Mike's age and build, wearing a faded Cornell sweatshirt and a long

scarf. Seeing Robert, the man's golden retriever became excited, its rear end shimmying from side to side.

"Robert, heel," Mike said curtly. Robert's ears pinned back as he fell into line, walking close to Mike's legs. At the end of the sheepishly grinning man's taut leash, the retriever flailed and flailed, slobber flying from its mouth. "Good boy," Mike said as he and Robert approached them. Without looking down, he knew that, despite the mayhem, Robert's eyes would be locked onto each movement of Mike's left leg.

"Come on, Wotan," the man said to his dog. "We're going to be late for your class."

Wotan? Probably Sarah's department head. *Fucking Wotan?* He was glad he didn't have to spend five minutes with the pair of them. Wait, he was being unfair. The dog had not chosen his name or his owner. Several blocks later, the sidewalk yielded to a trailhead at the edge of the woods. When they reached a meadow, silent except for birdsong, Mike let Robert off the leash. He leaned against a maple, watching the dog meander and sniff.

He'd reported to work three hours earlier than usual for two weeks, Saturdays and Sundays included, the perfect arrangement for keeping his brain focused on safe tasks and out of trouble. But here he was out in the woods on the first morning when he could have slept in. Calls to Delores and outings with the kids had filled up whatever free hours remained after doing the extra work at the seminary. She was always glad to hear from him, even on her bad days. He called hoping to be of assistance, but her unassuming resistance to gloom sometimes ended up raising his own sluggish spirits. Friday, she had reminded him of the directions to the rehab center. "Brendan makes it in fifteen minutes, but I know you're up to your eyeballs in work." His brother had been civil to him, had not provided Mike with fresh reasons to be angry. However temporary this grace period might be, Mike gladly accepted it.

Domenic and Sarah were another story, but he told himself to trust time. Eventually they mostly would slip off his radar screen. How many times had he told himself that their departure did not constitute loss? Someday, they would have no hold on him.

When he and Robert returned home, Mike fed him. It was nine o'clock, but Mike still was not hungry. By this hour, places like hospitals and rehab centers were in full swing. He could call Delores, maybe put in a load of wash, or he could drive downtown and see her. He picked up his keys and his coat.

The rehab center was just off the Benjamin Franklin Parkway. Home to museums, apartment buildings, and the cathedral, this part of Center City offered a sense of grand open space. Brendan learned about the facility around the time Delores had been moved from the first hospital. Mike had never heard of the place. After parking in the high-rise garage behind the building, he walked to the main entrance. So far, nothing he saw suggested a Brendan screw-up.

Sunlight and classical music poured out the open door to Delores's room. Standing at the doorway, Mike knocked on the doorframe. Sitting in bed, she looked up and smiled. Pieces of a jigsaw puzzle, mostly unconnected, lay sprawled across the top of a card table beside the bed.

"Mike," she said, brightly. She sounded better than she had on the telephone, almost chipper, as if she were sitting in a resort hotel and he had come to announce cocktail hour. She pressed a lever that stopped the tape player sitting in her lap.

When he bent over and kissed the top of her head, she hugged him.

"Here you go," she said, making room for him on the side of the bed.

He sat on the bedcover near her feet. "I'm a terrible visitor," he said. "No planning. Got the impulse, and here I am. You deserve flowers or candy, but I brought nothing. I'm sorry."

"Don't make me hit you. They might throw me out into the street. I'm just glad to see you."

"I knew I visited the right person," he said. He glanced at the puzzle box: "Autumn in the North Country." The pieces she had fitted together to form the puzzle's perimeter never would have suggested to him the red covered bridge, the maples with their dazzling yellow leaves, or the luminous blue sky, all reflecting off the serene river.

"Looks like you're already being punished," he said, nodding at the jumble of puzzle parts.

She laughed.

He frowned, shaking his head at the disarray on the table. "I wouldn't know where to begin."

"Anyone can do the edges." She picked up a random piece. "Try this one."

He accepted the piece, studying it from several angles. "No yellow or red," he said, inching it across the top of the puzzle. "It's not leaves or part of the bridge." He cocked his eyes at her and shrugged, setting the piece on the table. "End of the road for me."

Taking the piece, she moved it to the open space inside the border and began to guide it on a slow counterclockwise tour. Abruptly, her hand stopped. A moment later, she slid the piece to the right, fitting it into the top border. "It's not hard," she said. "Just slow."

When she picked up another piece, Mike watched her eyes work their way around the border.

She dropped the piece back onto the pile. "Plenty of time to fool around with this," she said, giving him a sly smile.

"Any more news bulletins from the past?"

"A drib here, a drab there," she said. "Mostly little stuff, but it does add up." She nodded at the tabletop's chaos, smiling.

She took a puzzle piece and nudged it around the table idly. "I remember when I first met you," she said. "I'm great on ancient history. You moved to New Paltz." With her index finger she slid the piece in lazy little circles. "When your mother was dying, she read your letters to me," Delores said, gazing out the window. She picked up the piece and rubbed it with her thumb and forefinger like a worry stone. "I hardly knew you, so it didn't seem to matter. She'd say, 'I can read that boy like a book.'" Delores turned back to him. "'That boy loves his Laurie,' she'd say."

He nodded.

"'Got himself a little family up there.'"

He studied the faraway look in her eyes.

"'Better hold on tight to them,' she'd say. Like if you didn't, you were done for."

"Everybody does that," he said.

"'That's all he's got,' she said."

He'd only cried about his mother once, on the day he heard she'd died, but suddenly he was sure he was about to lose it. *You never meant to, but you made me feel so small.* A noise startled him, but when he looked around, no one was near the doorway. When he turned back, her eyes were waiting for his.

"My mother never had much confidence in me," he said, pacing himself to get each word out without crumpling before her.

"When Laurie and the baby died," Delores said, her voice slow and gentle, as if she were coaxing a jumper off a bridge, "I thought of your mother." She dropped the puzzle piece and rested her hand on the table.

"They were my life."

She nodded. "Your mom knew Brendan was a different species from you," she said. "As bad as he was, she didn't worry about him like that."

You knew this? Delores might have been describing the taste of the meat loaf at lunch by the tone of her voice.

"But your mother would have been proud of the uncle you've become. Look at what you've done for us."

"Bullshit." He thought of the times he'd helped Delores with an odd job here and there at her place and how she'd sometimes let slip her frustrations with her husband—the arguments, the yelling, his drinking. "I know it's not always easy dealing with my brother."

"Cro-Magnon Man? He hasn't missed a day of seeing me since the seizures."

Mike stared at the collection of puzzle pieces on the table.

"At least, as far as I can tell," she said, with a laugh.

He wondered what it was like for her to have crystal clear views of some things but also enormous gaps in her memory. "This is not what I expected when I walked in here."

The edges of her mouth bent into a wry smile. "Everyone's starting to sound like me."

"Jesus."

"I know who my kids are," she said. "And Brendan. And my sister. I didn't have that at first. Now I do. There's no rhyme or reason to what comes back and what doesn't."

He nodded. "The kids are great," he said, standing up.

"Thanks," she said. "We both appreciate what you do for them."

"This is impossible," he said. "What you do."

"It gets less impossible every day." Her memory of her own life was about as full and clear as the outline of the puzzle on the table. Some of what she did remember had to be enough to stop most people in their tracks, yet she seemed like she would know what to do about anything.

"I did something," he said. And he was off, telling her how he'd stalked his former girlfriend and finally jumped the guy who tried to assault her.

"It had to be you, doing all that?" she said, when he finished.

How could the woman who was married to the original take-the-bull-by-the-horns guy think like this?

"Trying to prove Mom right?" she said.

"He needed to be stopped. I couldn't think of any other way."

"At least you didn't kill him," she said. "Brendan probably would be on death row now. Or maybe somebody he hired would be. Brendan's not exactly stupid."

"No," he said. In how many ways might he have underestimated his brother?

"What do you got left?" she said, pointing to his head. "Who's in there?"

He shook his head.

When she looked out the window again, his eyes followed what she was looking at. A bird, maybe one of those falcons who loved the tall buildings downtown, soared past the building across the way. He turned and kissed her cheek, walked to the door, then turned around. Her eyes were smiling as she waved to him. She looked like she was ready to resume her slow struggle with the puzzle.

26

MONDAY, MARCH 13

Both Thursdays that Sarah had called the barbershop to tell Al she would not be coming in to do the oral histories, she'd been ready to hang up if Domenic answered. Her anger at him had quickly dropped from high infuriation to moderate annoyance, but she still wasn't ready to reach out to him. Was she a jerk for being angry at him because he'd been as foolish as she?

Spending most of her spring break with her parents at their apartment helped her see things more clearly and brought the unplanned bonus of giving her a sense of what living in New York might feel like at this point in her life. Not bad at all, she decided. She returned to Philadelphia ready to get back to her weekly sessions at the barbershop and, more importantly, to put things right between her and Domenic. She wasn't going to wait until Thursday.

As Sarah approached the door to Al's, she surveyed the situation inside. Al was trimming the hair of an overweight blond man about Mike's age. Clement and Nick, the only other people there, occupied their usual corner spots. Now that she'd cancelled two weeks in a row after making such a fuss about Mount Airy Day, they might have written her off as a flake. She hesitated but opened the door.

She nodded in rapid succession to Al and the old guys then headed toward Nick.

"You know about Domenic?" he said to her.

She froze midway to Nick. The other men exchanged looks.

"In the hospital for two days now," Clement said. "Heart failure."

"No!" she said. *What is wrong with me?* "His heart?"

Al stopped cutting the large guy's hair. "I got him up to the hospital the other night. None of us knew."

"Neither did he," Nick added.

"They did all sorts of tests up there," Al said. "Respiratory problems too." He went back to snipping his customer's hair. "A whole mess of fluid in his lungs. X-rays showed it—or something like X-rays. They'll keep him until that goes down."

She still stood where she'd stopped, her mouth agape. She'd been an idiot to wait this long, to think she didn't owe him an apology for berating him.

"He wasn't good the last few weeks," Clement said. "Nick saw him huffing and puffing on the sidewalk."

Those two Thursdays, she'd told them nothing, really, just said she couldn't come. Had not thought she owed Domenic anything. Had not been there to see for herself. She'd cultivated a connection then disappeared. Had she been a self-serving fraud? Somehow, they were treating her with respect and decency.

"Ginette and I are going up tonight," Al said. "I'll tell him you asked for him."

"Chestnut Hill?"

Al stopped trimming again. "Two-twelve B," he said, looking at Sarah. "You want the telephone number?"

"No," she said, striding to the door. She opened it, turned back to Al and his two friends, but could think of nothing to say. She rushed to the car.

27

MONDAY, MARCH 13

Domenic did not want to hear another word about his room-mate's gall bladder, his grandchildren, or the model railroad that extended from one floor of the guy's split-level home to the other. Domenic's stony silence had failed to get the message across, and now he was thinking about buzzing for the nurse to get her to draw the curtain all the way around his bed. But he fully expected that the jolly, bald SEPTA bus driver would merely raise his voice if the curtain were drawn. That, he decided, would be the opposite of an improvement.

"Tell me, Mr. Gallo," the man said. "Do you have any hobbies? Avocational interests, as my son, the clarinet-playing mailman, would say?" He laughed heartily.

"Breathing," Domenic grunted. Across the room sat the respiratory machinery he had been constantly tethered to when he was admitted to the hospital. "Breathing is my new hobby. I think about it all the time. Pulmonary, cardiology. They're all fighting over me."

After a long silence, the man said, "I mean something like coins or hunting."

"All right, how about patience? You know, not giving in to powerful, violent impulses?"

The roommate rustled his sheets and sighed heavily enough to fill the room, but Domenic did not turn toward him. Had he finally discovered the magical secret of shutting him up?

"Well," the SEPTA driver said, drawing out the word into two long syllables. "I don't know."

Domenic glanced at the TV remote control on the bedside stand. If the mute function worked on people, the thing would be worth millions.

"People who just do their jobs tend to be very boring," the man said. "No offense. Of course, you know what my interest is. My other woman, so to speak." He chuckled.

Domenic could picture the guy, still wearing that ridiculous engineer's cap that one of his three cackling grandchildren had placed on his head at the end of last night's visiting hours. "Stamp collecting?" Domenic said, yawning. He felt a nap coming on and prayed that he could block out the talk about steam engines and gandy dancers.

"Best hobby of them all," the SEPTA man plowed on. "Just don't call them toy trains. Not to a model railroader. They're scale models. *Scale.*"

At least the other model railroader he'd known hadn't tried to convert him to trains. That disaster in his basement, destroyed like probably everything else in his life. Domenic closed his eyes. "Gonna stick with your hobby, are you?" he mumbled.

"Silly question."

"Thinking of bagging mine," Domenic said. *Catching some rest on the damned subway might be easier than this.*

"For my money, you can't beat HO," the guy said. "Scale of champions. My scale since I gave my old Lionels to the Salvation—"

The sudden silence startled Domenic from a half-sleep.

"Mr. Gallo," the SEPTA man said, "you got a visitor."

When Domenic turned his head, he saw Sarah standing in the

doorway, trying to catch her breath, a look of desperation on her face, as if he she'd run up a subway platform as the train was pulling out and he were the engineer looking back.

"The boys at the shop told me," she said. "Ten minutes ago." She stepped toward the bed.

Domenic shut his eyes, but all he could see was her face that night when he'd gotten out of her car. Along with the pain that memory brought, he was filled with relief at seeing her.

"Shortness of breath?" Sarah said, standing by the bed. "You probably didn't see it coming."

"I got to use the bathroom," Domenic's neighbor loudly declared.

Domenic watched him waddle across the room. "Good luck with that scale toilet," he called to him.

The guy laughed like a hyena and tipped his Reading Lines engineer cap. The slam of the closing bathroom door made him flinch. He heard muted laughter from the bathroom, as if the guy had just told himself a joke he'd never heard before.

"You don't look too comfortable," Sarah said, wincing.

"You're not supposed to be comfortable in here," Domenic said, jiggling the tubes connecting him to whatever they had in the two bottles on a bedside tower. Anger and sadness had elbowed his unbidden joy out of the way.

"They can probably adjust how the bed's positioned."

When the bathroom door opened, train man popped out, smiling, and went back to his bed.

"My turn," Domenic said, working his way to a sitting position.

Sarah leaned forward, but he waved her off with a quick traffic cop hand. He stepped into the slippers lying by his bed, wrangling the tubes on his rolling IV stand. He shuffled past Sarah, opened the bathroom door, and slammed it behind him.

He sat on the toilet and shook his head. He waited to hear Sarah's voice, but the SEPTA driver had already launched into a colorful preview of his next surgery. "*Madonna*," Domenic muttered. How long would it be before she commented on the guy's dopey hat? Suddenly, the SEPTA man's voice dropped to nearly a whisper and Domenic had to strain to hear.

"Thought it was just me," the man said.

Domenic flushed the toilet, knowing the noise would fill the room.

"I thought you were his *daughter*."

"*Perfetto*," Domenic murmured. When he opened the door, he saw that Sarah had moved to the head of his bed and drawn the curtain between the beds. Without making eye contact with her, Domenic padded over and climbed back into bed. He propped himself up the best he could. "I'm sick of lying down," Domenic gasped, slipping under the covers. "Why are you here?" he asked, keeping his eyes on his sheets. He immediately regretted his sharpness.

"I'm sick of myself," she said, leaning over the bed but maintaining some distance. "I understand if you want me to leave. Took me time to see straight. Shouldn't have taken it out on you. I've been kicking myself."

"That makes two of us," he said, looking at her. How *stonato* was he? Of course she'd come to see him. Suddenly his anger shifted. *Given a chance, I'd still give that Mike a good kick.*

"You were just trying to help," she said, settling in a chair beside the bed. "Neither of us had a chance that night."

"So, you went back to do your interviews."

"That was going to be Thursday. I was looking for you today."

He shimmied himself up to a more seated position. Instantly, he felt like he was a participant in, not the subject of, the conversation.

She and Mike had written him off that night. He'd done as much to them, but those two were hardly the same.

"If you want, I can raise the pillows for you," she offered.

"No." Domenic readjusted his pillows. "Better," he said. "They're waiting for my numbers to change. Something about the fluid level. I'll only be here a couple more days."

"That's what we need," she said, nodding.

Telling her how stupid he'd felt that night and since then would not help get him or her through this moment. And he wanted no parts of talking about Mike. When Domenic's ancient blunders had bruised Angela, she usually found a way to touch his heart. "I'm just reaching in there," she'd say, tapping his chest. She'd have done that with their children if they'd had any. Given that chance, he hoped he would have found that touch. "You were reaching in there, Sarah," Domenic said. "That night."

"I was loaded for bear," she said, shaking her head. "I don't know what I was thinking."

"There's no guidebook."

"You and your Angela. You must have done that for each other, reaching in?"

"When we could," he said, feeling his face redden.

She managed a slight smile.

"Hey, you'll like this, Miss Teacher," he said. "I got a big test in the next day or two. Stress test. If I pass, they let me out."

"The ones I give are *all* stress tests," she said.

For the first time since he'd been admitted, he believed without a doubt that he'd return home in one piece.

The SEPTA driver cleared his throat loudly.

Domenic rolled his eyes. "I'd rather be eating pizza at Rizzo's," he said.

"Not your usual Monday," Sarah said, shaking her head. "And no novena for you."

"It's all up here," he said, tapping his temple.

"My Jewish friends would have just the right Yiddish expression. They've got one for every occasion."

"Doesn't surprise me," he said. "You grew up Jewish?"

"My mother did. I was one generation removed from all that. Interesting to read about though."

She looked down and her face colored a bit. *Shy?* This was a first.

"My nerd side is showing," she said.

"Your parents must be thrilled with everything you do—you're no nerd," Domenic said. "People pick up all sorts of interests," he went on, scowling at the curtain separating the two beds.

When she left, train man waited all of ten seconds before opening his mouth. "Nice-looking girl."

"One of my hobbies," Domenic said.

When Al and Ginette brought Domenic home on Wednesday, he found his couch in the bedroom and his bed in the living room. The day was cloudy and gray, casting a dull light onto the white sheets. His pillow was smartly propped up, its case carefully smoothed out. *Sarah's doing.* But years of use had faded the once bright blue into an ugly charcoal, and in the dim lighting, it looked sad, dingy, old. His alarm clock, sitting precariously on the edge of the nightstand—the electrical cord almost too short to reach the nearest outlet—blinked in a rapid staccato. *You have to reset it after you plug it back in.*

"The teacher and me did it," Al told him. "Didn't take us an hour."

Domenic unlaced his shoes, breathing heavily with the simple task. He leaned back into the pillow and stretched his legs on the bed.

"Warming up some of my vegetable soup for you," Ginette said, "and I've been to the Conshohocken Italian Bakery."

"*À tantôt*," Al said, then left the room. A few minutes later, he returned with a small television set.

"What's that for?"

"Figure it out," Al said, setting it up on a stand. "We don't need this at home. Help you pass the time."

Ginette swept back into the room with a food tray, setting it on Domenic's lap. Al clicked off the TV.

Domenic eyed the bowl of soup, the small plate of raw carrot and celery sticks, and a hunk of Italian bread.

Ginette returned with two more bowls of soup, and the couple sat in straight chairs at the coffee table across from Domenic, watching him try his first spoonful.

"Hot," Domenic said. "Tastes almost like soup."

"Not supposed to have too much salt now," Ginette offered.

Domenic took another sip. He added more pepper than he had ever put into soup, tried it again. Not quite as bad. The bread tasted like bread, but he knew better than to ask for butter. Like a depressing comedy act—a show for the invalid—Al and Ginette perched on the edge of their seats, awkwardly holding themselves over the too-low coffee table, and brought their spoons to their mouths at the same time. Domenic let out a deep sigh, then immediately faked a smile when their eyes returned to his face. *No one's brought me lunch in ten years. But still.* He ate another bit of soup, told himself it would hasten his recovery and strengthen him. He wanted to be grateful. They were trying to help. But watching Domenic Gallo eat? *This will not become your new evening entertainment.*

"Leftover soup's in the Frigidaire," Ginette said when she and Al were ready to leave. "Bread's in the cupboard."

"Thanks," he said. "Both of you."

"Mind your Ps and Qs until Sarah comes over tomorrow," Ginette said. She patted his hand and followed Al out.

Propped up in bed, Domenic's vantage was limited to the sidewalk and the fronts of the stores on the other side of the avenue. With every light turned out, the paint store might as well have been painted black. A few plant lights in the front display of the florist's enabled him to make out shadows, but he couldn't guess what kind of plants they might be. A beer truck rattled over the Belgian blocks, its engine belching as it came to the intersection. Ten minutes later, a man with a cane shambled up the sidewalk, probably headed for Gilhooley's.

He couldn't remember how many candles he had lit the day before he was rushed to the hospital. *No matter. It all starts with Chico Ruiz.* Domenic ignored the silent television. He said his prayers. Later, afraid he might forget the candle, he slowly crossed the room and blew it out. In bed, he listened to the all-news radio station until his eyes grew heavy with sleep.

In the morning, he remained in bed, except to take his medicines with a piece of bread. He was acting like a first-class patient. The apartment looked cleaner than ever. Sarah was the prime suspect. He had almost drifted back to sleep when he heard the downstairs door open and close. He heard footsteps on the stairway.

"It's only me," Sarah called.

He sat up and made sure that the sheet covered his feet.

"Hope I didn't give you a scare," Sarah said, appearing in the front room with a blue plastic bucket in one hand and a filled shopping bag in the other. "Al gave me a key."

"I really can manage breakfast, you know."

"Just dropping off some cleaning stuff. I'll be by after work."

"This place can't get any cleaner. Are you after some world record?"

She stood at attention. "Dust settles," she intoned.

"God help me."

That afternoon, Al led a barbershop delegation to Domenic's living room. Nick and Clement had never seen the apartment.

"Quite a piece of art," Nick said, looking at the baseball collage. "I wouldn't have pegged you for a baseball guy."

Domenic shrugged.

Clement sat in the chair that had been moved to the other front window. "Place is looking good," he said.

"Sarah's hit it hard," Domenic said. "I'm saying a novena for any surviving germs in here."

"Take it slow," Nick said.

"I'm not going to act crazy," Domenic said. "The Lord will tell me when it's time to do other things."

"You get too rambunctious," Clement said with a smirk, "you're going to have that conversation on his home turf."

Domenic glared at Clement but bit his lip.

"He's right," Nick said. "You'll pay the price."

"That's it," Domenic said. "I got to get me some rest." He pulled his covers up to his chin and looked out at the street.

He heard Al stand up. "We'll come back another time," he said.

Clement shuffled over to the bed and patted Domenic's arm. "Take care, old timer," he said. Domenic kept his eyes trained on the street.

After they left, he clumped his way into the bedroom. Everything missing from the living room had been stowed where his bed had stood. It looked like somebody's attic. He didn't care if they heard his footsteps downstairs. Al had left some salt-free pretzels and a glass of ginger ale on the nightstand, but Domenic ignored them. He had bought some potato chips before going to the hospital and no one was around to stop him. He tramped into the kitchen, making more noise than necessary, and opened the cupboard. The chips were gone! He slammed the door. *Do-gooders.*

Sarah arrived at three thirty in a sweatshirt and old jeans. Tying a bandana around her head, she smiled at Domenic then disappeared into the rear of the apartment, banging and splashing in the other rooms for an hour.

When she finally reappeared, her face looked flushed. "After I run home for a shower, I'm getting us takeout from Rizzo's."

Salt. "Fine," he said, watching her withdraw to the doorway.

When he was sure that she had left, he took a closer look around the rest of the apartment. The white woodwork gleamed. He had to look twice to be sure that the bright yellow bathroom walls had not been freshly painted. Even the furniture now stored in the bedroom sparkled.

Waiting, he drifted off a few times, but soon enough he heard the downstairs door opening, closing, then the slap of footsteps on the stairs.

"Me again," Sarah called.

She set two large white paper bags on the coffee table, but he couldn't identify the smells.

"Caesar salad for me," she said, opening one bag. "Turkey sandwich and a tossed green salad for you. Oil and vinegar on the side. And a couple of birch beers." She spread the contents of both bags on the coffee table then pulled up two chairs.

Moving from the bed to the nearer chair, he noticed another container she had not opened. "What's that?"

"An appetizer. You wouldn't like it."

"Smells good," he said hopefully.

"A small portion of eggplant Parmesan, which will be my lunch tomorrow. I don't want to torment you, but after what you called their lasagna, I thought you might not mind the aroma."

"Don't worry," he sang.

She laughed and dug into her salad. The strips of grilled chicken on it made his mouth water.

"Everything's low-salt," she said, pointing to the bland fare on his plate. "You're allowed a *low*-salt meal once in a while. Right?"

He sank back, watching her slide the clear plastic container of salad toward him.

"Enjoy," she said, handing him a fork and the vinegar and oil.

"A lot of tomatoes," he said, picking through the salad.

"Guess I should have asked for more green," she said. "Tomorrow's St. Patrick's Day."

"Not on my account."

"Oh, I'm not Irish either." She said the words quickly, almost defensively. When Domenic glanced up, she looked away and took another bite of her salad.

He sampled his sandwich. It tasted better than the last one he'd had at Rizzo's.

"I never got into that whole St. Patrick's Day thing," she said slowly. "Even in college when everybody drank green beer. I don't imagine that *he* does either."

Domenic searched her face for a clue as to her feelings.

"I mean," she went on, "I can't picture him in some place with cardboard leprechauns on the wall and green beer. Can you?"

He dressed his salad. "He's Irish?"

"No, he's Samoan!" she laughed. "Flannagan?"

Domenic snickered with her. "Leprechauns and silly songs," he said. *Would that require the guy to smile? Maybe he'd used up his share.*

The smile on her face faded, replaced by a wistful expression. He watched her stir her fork through her salad. "You haven't talked—"

"Heavens, no," he said, bristling.

"Of course not," she said. "Me neither."

"The nineteenth of March," he said. "St. Joseph's Day. That's an Italian holiday. Everybody's got a holiday."

"I celebrate everybody's holidays."

"Except St. Patrick's Day."

"Maybe if they got rid of the green beer," she said with a smile.

He returned to his sandwich. They lapsed into a comfortable silence. He loved her for that. He studied her face. He hoped that she didn't love Mike, didn't go through her days aching over hopes she couldn't reach or banish. He almost asked her if she did, but he knew that if he encouraged her to talk, she wouldn't see that as a one-way street.

Before she left, she told him she planned to return tomorrow with something homemade. He reached out and grabbed her hand in both of his. He squeezed it gently and met her surprised eyes.

Sarah showed up the next night with a baguette, a Tupperware container packed with tuna salad, and a tiny wedge of the eggplant dish that had tantalized him last night. Halfway through his plate, he tasted the eggplant. "What?" he said, catching her dramatic frown.

"Not bad, is it?"

He swallowed then ate the rest of the eggplant. "All right," he said. "I've been severe on the folks at Rizzo's."

"See," she said. "You don't need your damn salt."

"Must have a new cook over there," he said. "But I really like this tuna salad."

Smiling, she put another healthy scoop of the tuna salad on his plate. It was not merely the finished recipe. Neither it nor the cook could have come out better had she grown up at Angela's side in her kitchen. He'd done nothing to earn pride in this young woman, but he drank it in.

"There's no meat here tonight," he said. "How did you know?"

"Dumb luck," she said. "I'll just have to remember that Friday business."

"Only one more Friday in Lent," he said.

"I've been reading a lot lately about Jewish holidays. Going back to my roots, I guess."

"That's great," he said. She brightened.

"Talking with Jewish friends a bit," she said, looking sheepish.

"They do crazy different than we do, but it's all connected," he said. They laughed. "But you know, it's God either way. Nothing for you to feel shy about."

"Watch out," she said. "I might bring you over some gefilte fish."

"That would have been perfect tonight!"

They laughed again. He watched her eat her salad. They finished the bread. Two peaceful dinners in a row. Domenic Gallo, the good patient. Taking his meds. Going to bed when he should. Surprising himself.

Sarah had papers to grade. He was glad she didn't apologize for leaving. It all felt so familiar. Family members in his old neighborhood did this sort of thing. Looked in on old relatives, shared a simple meal, left to resume their regular lives, returned for other meals. He would clear the plates this time.

"*Grazie,*" he said.

On Sunday afternoon, Al and Ginette dropped by with palm fronds they had picked up for him at Mass. They said their son Gerry, the priest in Alabama, had called and asked for Domenic.

"You're on his prayer list," Al said.

That evening, Sarah showed up with a tantalizingly small amount of biscotti. They had tea after he finished the meal that Ginette had made for him. "Happy St. Joseph's Day," she said when she was leaving him that evening.

On Monday, he went downstairs to spend a few hours watching Al cut hair from his barber chair. Al glared at him like a stern old nurse.

"I practiced yesterday," Domenic said. "On the stairs."

"Are you kidding?" Al said. "Got a death wish?"

"Halfway down and back up. Did it again all the way. No tightness in the chest." He thought he heard Al's teeth grinding.

"Don't push it."

Domenic flipped through the outdoors magazine that had arrived in the morning's mail. He caught fragments of the conversation among Al, the customer, Clement, and Nick, but he offered no comment. He, Nick, and Clement exchanged sections of the *Inquirer*.

"Bush's dog had puppies," Clement said. "Dog crap in the White House." He raised his eyebrows, looking at the others.

"Can't be a new thing," Nick said, smiling.

Except for the boys, the waiting area was empty. He sat mum while Al finished cutting a young guy's hair, bid him goodbye, then sat in his barber chair.

"My second point," Domenic declared, "is that I will be responsible for my own dinner tonight. Sarah's been great, bringing dinner over every day, but I can handle this." To his surprise, in five minutes, Al had agreed to his demands. Domenic would do his own cooking. Ginette or Sarah would deliver a weekly grocery order and could prepare a meal only once a week. "I got leftovers to last me a lifetime."

"Let's hope not," Clement said, looking up from the obituaries.

At two, Domenic announced nonchalantly that he did not want

to push it and headed back upstairs. He was wheezing by the time he reached his bed, not as bad as before the hospitalization but enough to make him glad none of them could see him. He took his medicine and settled down in the bed. He closed his eyes, sucking in shaky breaths through his nose and blowing them out through his mouth. At dusk, he glanced at the candles across the room. He should light six of them today, but he was too tired to move. The tightness in his chest was minor but undeniable. *Chico freakin' Ruiz. Steal home and start the whole thing all over again.* The door banged open downstairs. He sat up too quickly.

"Just me," Sarah called out.

He breathed in slowly, a hand on his racing heart, and listened to her quick, light steps on the stairs. In a blink, she was by his side. He felt his heart flipping. If she pressed her ear to his chest, he was sure it would sound like he'd clothespinned a baseball card onto a bicycle spoke and was pumping the pedals furiously down the block. It hadn't felt like this since before he'd gone to the hospital.

"You look beat," she said, touching her hand to his forehead.

"Not great," he said, the words coming out in a gasp. He took a deep breath, let it out. "Went downstairs," he said, putting his index finger to his lips.

"Take your time."

He wanted to say something to sound reassuring, but nothing came out. He closed his eyes. "Bad moment."

"What can I do for you?"

He pointed to the chair by the bed. As she pulled the chair closer, he concentrated on breathing evenly. "It'll pass," he said. "I cheated a bit." He felt her watching him. He didn't try to speak. She said nothing. In time, he felt he could speak again but waited. *Just another minute.* He kept his eyes closed.

"Good," she said.

"Better now."

"Take your time."

After maybe five minutes, his breathing felt under control. He opened his eyes. She hadn't moved. "They said it could happen," he said, shaking his head.

"Are you afraid you won't be able to breathe?"

"Yes."

"Are you afraid that you might die?"

"Let's not pussyfoot around," he said with a laugh, then wiped his eyes. "I thought about that just now."

He closed his eyes again. Same sequence as the day he'd gone to the hospital. Breathing. Then, like in a dream, falling. Watching it. Plummeting. She was being so quiet. He'd spewed bitterness at just about everyone else. Now he was breathing more easily. He opened his eyes again, and there she was. He reached for his water glass and took his medicine.

"Okay?" she said.

"Yeah."

"But it's going to come back." She sat up and looked him in the eye. "And you'll be in it again."

She believed in him, knew that he could handle this. *Those familiar fierce eyes.* He made himself think about nothing but his next breath, then another one. "Some things you can't stop, once they start."

He watched her walk to the front window. She pulled the curtains aside then looked up and down the avenue. "My father's a cancer patient," she said. "*Was,*" she corrected herself. "But he's in New York and I'm here."

"I'm sorry," he said. "I know about cancer."

"I go up on weekends when I can," she said, still looking out the window. Suddenly, she turned around. "What am I doing?" she said. "I didn't come over here to weigh you down."

"I'm already in the basement," he said. "I think about things, crazy things."

"Your wife."

He glanced at Angela's picture. *Go ahead.* "One summer, she got pregnant and finally was able to go for more than a month. She was fifteen years younger than me but still getting kind of old to start having babies." He shook his head, surprised that he was smiling. "Unbelievable. She was watching everything she put into her mouth. Not working too much, not working too little. Starting to show. At least, *I* could tell." He took a breath.

Sarah watched him in tense silence.

It was too late for him to stop. He felt reckless, out of control. "It was right at the beginning of fall, the twenty-first of September."

"The fall equinox."

"She didn't feel right all day. I didn't pay her enough attention. After dinner, she came downstairs. I was listening to the ball game on the radio. The Phillies were good for a change that year, and we even went to a couple of games."

She nodded at him to continue, something like fright showing in her face.

"It had happened upstairs, and I didn't even know. I turned off the radio. Right away, I knew that this was different for her than the other two times. I told her she was young. We could try again." He looked out the window. There was no point in stopping now. "She didn't say a thing. I knew there was no more trying."

"I'm sorry," Sarah said, her eyes bright with unshed emotion.

He glanced across the room again, avoiding her gaze. "Everything changed. She didn't say much, but I knew something besides a baby had died. I lost interest in everything. Didn't listen to another inning of baseball. I couldn't ignore it, though. Customers, you know. Anyway, I kept barbering. I had to."

"And Angela?" Sarah said.

"Ten years ago. The cancer."

Sarah slumped back down in the chair near his bed. She squeezed his hand.

"One long, bad thing," he said.

"And it started that night."

"Damn right," he snapped. His breath came harder. He told himself to relax. Take his time. Talk slowly. That would help. "You think you can have a child because every fool on the planet seems to do it at the drop of a hat."

"She must have suffered a great deal," Sarah said.

"She offered up the pain," he said. "I cursed it." *And cursed her too.* For letting that day change her so much. Change *them* so much. Yes, he had cursed her but never to her face. Or to another soul. Or since she died. Or without the deepest shame he had ever known.

"Domenic?" Sarah said.

"She didn't deserve what she got," he said.

"Neither of you."

"I didn't want to be angry with her," he blurted. "Any more than she wanted to give up."

"On having a baby."

"On everything," he said. "I don't know why I'm doing this." He'd told no one this much, but even good-hearted Sarah would hear no more.

"You're breathing better than when I came."

Domenic shrugged. Had she realized that he'd said too much? She knew when he needed to talk and when he shouldn't talk. "All worn out from doing nothing. I know what that can start."

She bent over, looking down, and let out a long quavering sigh.

"I didn't want to upset you," he said.

"Domenic," she said, shaking her still-bent head. "Domenic."

He resettled in the bed, moving his pillow around, but now even that exhausted him. "It's time I tried to sleep," he said. "You too, probably. Go."

"Yes."

He would sleep in his clothes. Safer. "That switch by the door," he said. "It controls the lights on the pictures. Get that for me?"

"Sure," she said. She walked to the doorway then turned off the track lighting. "I'll turn off the other lights too, except the little one in the bathroom."

"*Mille grazie.*"

She returned, tucked him in under the covers, then gave his forehead a peck.

"Al would get all stirred up if he heard about any of this," he whispered.

"Gotcha," she said.

When he heard her lock the downstairs door, he pushed aside the sheets and reached for the box of kitchen matches on the nightstand. *No.* He turned off the table lamp and rolled over onto his other side.

28

THURSDAY, MARCH 23

After brushing her teeth, Sarah opened the bedroom blinds, flipped on the overhead light, then sat on the side of her bed, still in her pajamas. She ran her finger across the top of her nightstand. Two days and no noticeable dust yet. She had scoured the room after leaving Domenic's apartment three nights ago, unable to sleep. Today her morning class was meeting with a librarian to learn about research methods. She looked at the clock. Running errands would not get her as sweaty as house cleaning, but it would keep her mind busy enough until nine-thirty.

Ignoring the outfit she had laid out on her dresser last night, she rummaged through the closet, finally yanking out a pair of baggy brown slacks that she had not worn in nearly two years. "Comfort over style," she told herself, walking to the dresser. The bottom drawer yielded a beige top that would go well with the old slacks. After packing breakfast and lunch, it was nearly eight twenty, so she hustled down the hallway and out to the car.

The trolley car ahead of her rocked across Cresheim Valley Drive, its wheels screeching as the avenue bent left to begin the slow ascent to Chestnut Hill. It pulled to a stop at Mermaid Lane's large traffic island, where a gaggle of schoolchildren waited. The avenue's Belgian blocks, an array of charcoal shades, shone in the sun's sharp light, and a pigeon fluttered down onto the island and began pecking at the ground.

Two little bent-over Latina women got off the trolley and shuffled past the untended shrubs and scrawny pine trees that framed the island's tall Celtic cross monument. A rusty stand in front of the monument held a drab, aging wreath. As the trolley driver assisted an old woman down to the curb, a squabble started among the kids. One boy chased another around the monument. Sarah cast a quick look past the island to the two-and-a-half-story stone Mermaid Inn, which Mike had told her had served as a stagecoach stop before the Revolution.

They'd gone there once, the Saturday night of Thanksgiving weekend, to hear a band that Mike had heard about from coworkers. More than once, she had suggested that they go out dancing, but he had ruled out any Center City clubs. He compromised on the Mermaid. She remembered parking a half-block away, near enough to hear the ruckus as soon as they opened the car doors.

Inside, Mike gripped her hand and led her through the noisy crowd in the side room to an archway blocked by the backs of several men in their late twenties, cigarettes and glasses of beer in hand. Bobbing their heads to the blaring music, the men peered into the other room. She stood on her tiptoes. The main barroom was smaller than most of her classrooms. People dancing and milling blocked her view of the band. Behind the bar, a broad-shouldered man with shaggy hair filled a beer glass from a tap. She wished she'd brought earplugs. At the near end of the bar, a tall woman with long brown hair took money from a patron then rang up the sale on the cash register.

"I'll get you a drink," Mike shouted.

When he moved, she followed, pressing through the pile-up of people at the doorway. Just as someone at the corner of the bar stepped away, Mike shot into the open space and slapped a twenty on the bar. She squeezed beside him. The woman bartender loudly greeted Mike by name.

"Ro!" Mike yelled back. "Sarah," he added, nodding toward Sarah. He'd told her that he and Ro's older brother had gone to school together.

"What'll it be, doll?" Ro said.

"Diet Coke."

When the band shifted into a New Orleans tune, the dancers sent up a cheer. Ro plunked their drinks on the bar. The guitarist jumped up, pointing his finger at the crowd. "Bro-ther!" he sang.

"Bro-ther!" they roared back at him.

"Brother John is gone!"

Two barstools opened up and Sarah rushed to claim them. Hopping up onto the stool, she finally could see through the crowd. By the soundman's table in the rear, a woman in a Grateful Dead T-shirt kissed a man in a tux. Seated at the soundboard, a young man with shoulder-length auburn hair and wearing headphones smiled beatifically at the couple. When the band took a break, the crowd on the dance floor thinned. If she and Mike didn't get onto the floor before the next tune, they would never find space to dance. When she asked Mike, he scrunched up his face and took a sip of his beer.

The next set began with a James Brown song. Had they turned up the volume on every instrument? In the mirror behind the bar, she watched the floor fill with dancers. She caught Mike's eye in the mirror and raised an eyebrow.

"I don't think so," he mouthed.

The band launched into a slowed down version of Buddy Holly's "Well, All Right," prompting half of the people at the bar to move to the dance floor. She elbowed Mike with more force than necessary—why did they come if they were only going to sit at the bar all night?—but he shook his head. Behind the bar, calling to mind American Gothic, Ro stood beside her equally solemn coworker. They swayed forward and back in time with the bassy groove, one of them going back when the other went forward. In front of the band, a dozen women and one of the guys in tuxedos were boogying. Planting her Coke on the counter, Sarah stepped onto the little dance area and joined in.

When the tune was over, she clapped and smiled at Mike who had turned toward the crowd and was smoking a cigarette. She frowned, gritting her teeth, then turned back toward the band.

"This is for the survivors of the day's nuptials," the singer announced over the PA. Three guys in tuxedos screamed. The band played the Chuck Berry song about a teenage wedding. At midnight, they started a frenzied Caribbean tune. Every time the two singers got to the refrain about being drunk and disorderly, the crowd howled the chorus with them. Only Mike and two other men remained seated.

Three of the six musicians, now playing maracas, a cowbell, and a galvanized Louisiana rubboard, snaked their way through the dancing crowd as the rhythm section held the beat. Even Mike smiled and clapped along. The three musicians led the rapidly forming conga line outside. Sarah put her hands on the shoulders of the woman in the Grateful Dead shirt and felt a pair of massive hands clamp onto the back of her shoulders as the line exited the main door into the cold night air.

Tooting a samba whistle, the leader of the line stepped out onto the Belgian blocks. The dancers meandered across the intersection under the streetlight, stepping in time to the percussion, right, left, right. At the island, the line shimmied past the trees and the Celtic cross. A Chestnut Hill–bound trolley squealed to a stop, several of its passengers gaping out their windows. Its front doors rattled open. An elderly man stepped down, and the leader of the conga line climbed aboard, the other musicians and dancers on his heels. Sarah received a wan smile from the driver as she passed him then capered down the aisle. The rear doors accordioned open as the leader descended the steps. Out they went, dancing toward the bar entrance.

The roar at the end of the song was the loudest of the night. Sarah collapsed onto the stool next to Mike's.

"Great tune!" Mike shouted over the din.

She nodded, plastering a smile on her face. *You missed so much.* When Ro brought her a glass of water, Mike settled the bill. They left before the band finished the set.

The blare of a car's horn behind her pulled her out of the memory. The trolley was halfway up the block. Sarah followed, casting one last look at the now-quiet Mermaid Inn. Clouds, pushed by the breeze, masked the sun's light, sending the building's stone walls and red doors into shadow.

Sarah caught up to the trolley at Willow Grove Avenue. When she passed Caruso's grocery store, she pulled into a metered parking spot. A dime should cover her visit to Kilian Hardware.

The store would just be opening. Unlike the "extraordinary shops of Chestnut Hill," as the announcer on the classical station put it, this place could be on some village Main Street in Iowa or Vermont. She crossed the creaky old wooden floorboards to the rear of the store where they displayed vacuum cleaner supplies. Grabbing two replacement bags off the rack, she headed to the checkout counter.

She still had time to fill before nine thirty. She circled the block, turning back onto the avenue toward Mount Airy. She found Al alone in his shop, sweeping the floor.

"Early," he said, unlocking the door.

"I wanted to catch you before the daily parade."

"Sit," he said, nodding to Domenic's barber chair.

She sat down and leaned back, settling her arms on the padded armrests. "Early bird privileges," she said.

Al swiveled his chair to face her and sat. "Something to do with him?" he asked, pointing toward the ceiling.

"Not exactly," she said. "My father's had health problems for some time."

He nodded gravely.

"He's good, but things could get worse without much warning," she said. "The other thing: there's a chance for a teaching job near them in New York."

"And you're in the running."

"Long process, iffy," she said. "Even if it works out, it wouldn't start until September."

Al turned his chair slightly and stared into the mirror. "You make a difference in his life," he said. "But you can't let that stop you from doing what you need to do." He turned the chair back and looked Sarah in the eye. "You know that."

"If this thing happens, you and Ginette would be here to help him?"

Al nodded. "He doesn't know, right?"

"This is a long shot, so it's too early to say anything to him."

"Keep me posted."

She let out a long breath then heard voices at the doorway. Nick and Clement were peering into the shop.

Al walked to the door and unlocked it. It was a little after nine.

Stepping inside, Clement gave her a puzzled look.

"Just passing through," she said. "I won't be able to stop by this afternoon."

"Good morning," Nick said to her. Holding a brown paper bag, he crossed to his corner spot.

"Fool won't tell me what he's got in the bag." Clement moaned and took his seat, folding his arms on his chest.

"Here I am, bringing in treats," Nick said, "and you make me out to be the bad guy." He pulled a bag of mini Snickers bars out of the brown bag and held it up. "Help yourself, everybody," he crowed.

Al smirked, shaking his head. Nick reached back into the big bag and revealed a bag of miniature donuts. "Who'd like a sweet treat?"

Clement laughed. "He's heartless, Sarah."

"We give something up for Lent," Al said. "It's near the end."

"Sweets?" Sarah asked.

"Or salty, in some cases," Al said, nodding toward Nick.

"If you can't resist temptation this close to Easter, what are you?" Nick asked. He popped a tiny powdered donut into his mouth.

"Ain't no soft pretzels in that bag," Clement said. "Rest assured of that."

"I'll pass on the treats today," Sarah said. She turned and walked to the door. "But if I were coming back this afternoon," she said, "I'd bring a dozen hot, steaming pretzels."

"Yes!" Clement cheered from his corner. "Fresh from Federal Street."

"I'll bring the mustard," Al said, laughing.

Coyly biting into a Snickers bar, Nick waved goodbye to Sarah.

Sarah arrived at her GP's office with five minutes to spare. Dr. Ingram knew all about Sarah's history. Irregular was irregular, but it was time to find out if something else was going on.

"Strong as a bull," Sarah said, answering the doctor's first question. "And I've been fastidious about my birth control."

"Yes, I bet you have been," Dr. Ingram said, allowing a faint smile to crinkle her lips but quickly reverting to her usual quizzical facial expression. "Aside from the obvious stress that comes with not knowing if you're pregnant, are you experiencing any unusual stress or anxiety?"

Sarah laughed. "Does anybody's job not create stress?" she said. "But, yes, this semester has been a nightmare."

"And it's hardly over." Dr. Ingram examined her, then had the phlebotomist draw blood. Results by Friday afternoon. Her office would call.

Sarah walked out of the office, opened the car door, and slumped into the driver's seat. Sighing, she stared at the Plymouth parked in front of her. Its once red paint was chipped and faded to a light salmon, one fender was scuffed and bent. She turned the key. At least the testing part was behind her. She moved a shaky hand to put the car in drive while the other gripped the steering wheel, her veins sticking out in sharp blue contrast to her pale knuckles. Her right hand hovered over the shift control. She felt cold. Placing both hands in her lap, she formed fists, digging her fingernails into her palms to stop the tremors.

She closed her eyes and breathed out, one-two-three. Then in. *What did I assign my writing class?* Her plans were in her satchel in the trunk. Having a plan meant that she didn't have to think, just act. Making a mental list, she ticked off each item. She would teach and clean for the next day and a half, redoing lecture plans and scouring squeaky-clean rooms. The shaking slowed, then stopped. She opened her eyes, released the brake, put the car in drive, then lurched into traffic.

29

THURSDAY, MARCH 23

Domenic flipped through Thursday's paper while Nick vainly tried to persuade Clement that Pete Rozelle had been a great NFL commissioner. Then Nick listened, frowning, to Clement's case that the Phillies had a chance to win it all this season. Domenic swore they'd had the same arguments at this time last year but had taken opposite positions. He passed Nick the metropolitan section.

"This city gets worse every day," Nick said. "The murder rate's enough to scare you off the damn street."

"Who'd bother killing you?" Clement said with a scowl.

"Hundred and eight so far this year," Domenic said.

"Mister Numbers has spoken," Nick said, bowing toward Domenic.

He couldn't remember if he'd read that somewhere recently or if the information had come to him in a dream.

"I guess this means another year that you don't venture into Center City," Clement said.

"You don't go downtown?" Al's customer turned in his chair, his eyes wide.

Al and Clement laughed. "He hasn't been downtown since the war," Al said. "And I don't mean Vietnam."

"It might not exist, for all he knows," Clement said. "Might be nothing but Hollywood storefronts, nothing behind them."

"Everything I need's right here," Nick said. "I'm not afraid to go downtown. But why bother?"

They bantered about the state of Center City and about the changes in the neighborhood. Domenic said nothing about how much stronger he felt, about how close he felt to doing something besides listening to Frick versus Frack. He also didn't mention Sarah, figuring her name was bound to come up. At any rate, she was due to arrive with her tape recorder for her Thursday afternoon session with the boys. At four, when she still hadn't shown, he asked Al what he made of her lateness.

"You missed her," Al said. "She stopped by this morning. Said she had a million errands so she couldn't make it."

"Missed her?" Domenic's question was too loud in the quiet shop. He lowered his voice. "Last week, she was here every time I sneezed. Go figure."

When he left the shop, he took his time climbing the stairs. He was still winded when he reached the top, but it was better. He ate leftover soup and toast for dinner. Lent was officially over that evening, then he'd just have Good Friday and Holy Saturday to get through. By Easter morning, he would let himself eat dessert again, realizing as he made the plan that he had no real appetite for sweets. Abstaining had been difficult when Lent began, but what kind of sacrifice was it if you no longer craved what you'd given up?

In the front room, he lit all nine candles then stood back, gazing at the collage in the warm glow of the candles.

Yes, being two games behind with three more to play left them with grim prospects. Richie Allen's strikeouts were real. Yes, they were losers. And tomorrow he would find Chico Ruiz racing down the third base line to start the whole mess over again. But he could not go through with it tonight. He blew out the candles.

Lying down on his bed, he switched on the table lamp beside him then opened his old missal to the prayers for Holy Thursday.

On Friday, Domenic went down to the shop at eleven with his coat and a five-dollar bill. When Nick took sandwich orders at noon, Domenic walked to the Wawa with him. It was Good Friday, so, like the others, he ordered a tuna hoagie. He handled the half-block trip up the avenue without breathing problems. On the way back, he persuaded Nick to let him carry the lighter bag containing chips, pickles, and napkins. When Al closed the shop at two thirty to get to the three o'clock service at his parish, Domenic took his time climbing the stairs and found he was barely winded from the effort. He'd rested enough days. Tomorrow would be the day. Even if he remained glued to his barber chair all day, he'd put on a clean smock, tidy up his counter. It mattered.

He wouldn't call her. Sarah would come on her own time, even if she didn't see fit to let him know when that would be. He was gaining strength every day. The stairs no longer frightened him. Avoiding him for a couple of days might be her way of pushing him. Well, he could push himself just fine, thank you.

30

FRIDAY, MARCH 24

Sarah had given Dr. Ingram her home phone number so she wouldn't worry about being called at her campus office. She'd driven home right after her last class, set the tuner on her stereo to the classical music station, and sat down in the kitchen with a cup of chamomile tea. On the table, she set the wall calendar, a handful of memos, a notepad, and her appointment book. She scanned the first memo: the literature committee would meet the Thursday after next at two. She made a notation under the appropriate date in her appointment book and again on the calendar beneath April's photo of row upon row of olive trees on a gentle Tuscan slope.

The telephone's ring interrupted a string quartet. A woman's voice explained that Dr. Ingram was running late but would call her within the hour.

"Sure," Sarah said cheerfully.

After hanging up, she penciled in all of her upcoming meetings in her two calendars then began gleaning the weekend section of yesterday's *Inquirer* for details about upcoming cultural activities. When the telephone rang, she dropped the newspaper, jumped to her feet, then grabbed the wall phone before it could ring a second time.

"This is Dr. Ingram, Sarah," the voice said.

"Yes," Sarah said. She switched the phone to her left hand then picked up her pen. She focused on the little blocks of her Italian calendar, as if she were about to record a new appointment, but the newspaper photograph of two ballerinas caught her eye. "Thank you for calling."

"Listen, I'll get straight to it," Dr. Ingram said. "The results are positive."

As her knees buckled, Sarah leaned hard against the table to maintain her balance, but the effort sent her swaying backwards. She shuffled her feet to regain a secure stance.

"Sarah?"

"It's definite?" she said, pressing her knees hard against the edge of the table but still wobbling.

"Nine weeks."

Sarah repeated the words in a daze, sank into her chair, then wrote "9" on the bottom border of the calendar. Her shaking knees refused to settle. She dug her toes into the floor but could not stop the shaking.

"You'll need time to think about all this, Sarah. Not what you expected or intended, I realize. Lots to consider."

Ingram continued speaking, but Sarah couldn't put meaning to the words anymore. She pushed the newspaper with the ballerina photograph off the table. It landed on the floor with a crinkle.

"Sarah, are you still there?" The question came from far away. Had her brain been wrapped in cotton, or only her ears?

"Yes," she said. "All the considerations." *Why did those words come out?*

"If you decide to go ahead with this," Dr. Ingram said.

"Well—"

"We will need to talk about a host of things."

Either way. Sarah pulled the notepad over. She scribbled down words the doctor had said five seconds ago. *What is she saying now?*

Her pen raced across the sheet of note paper. Dietary vitamins. Pre-natal changes. *No.* Or was that right? "Wait," she said. She asked Dr. Ingram to repeat what she had just said.

When had her knees stilled themselves? Her feet felt numb. She dropped her hand to her belly, felt all around. Was it the only part of her body that felt no different? *Impossible.* "My notes are gibberish," she blurted out, instantly regretting that she'd given voice to her thought.

"Sarah, I'll be happy to go through this again."

"No."

"Why don't we stop here. We will talk again, after you've had time. This is so much to absorb."

"Okay."

"I want you to write down a couple of appointment times, all right? And the office will call you to remind you. After we've talked about your plans."

She watched her pen scratch out the times when they'd talk on the phone and a tentative time when they'd meet. *Tentative.* Her pen stopped without her knowing or willing it.

The doctor was talking, but Sarah turned the calendar pages back to January, started counting. Nine weeks. *Positive.* Like the doctor's tone.

31

SATURDAY, MARCH 25

Mike felt no need to rush Robert on his Saturday morning walk. The dog had let him sleep until seven-thirty and Mike was not expected back at the seminary until the afternoon. He would help set up for the Easter service, then he would go in for a few hours following Sunday's festivities. Once he'd fed Robert, he poured himself some cereal and put on the kettle. Easter would be his eighth straight day at the place, another string. *Unholy Week.*

Domenic. A month since he and Sarah had decided that home invasion was a great idea. He'd winced every time something brought either of them to mind since that night. Work, house, and dog routines, plus the whole Delores thing, had made it easier to refocus. Staring at the soggy Rice Chex remaining in his bowl, he caught himself stewing all over again and feeling that overall bruising sadness. He reminded himself that these low moments had become less frequent, as he'd hoped.

After washing out the bowl in the sink, he leaned back in his chair and considered the possibilities for the free Monday ahead of him. With a dog, there was no such thing as a true sleep-in day, but dog walks aside, he anticipated going no further on Monday than up the street to the Acme for a pack of Ball Park Franks or a pound of hamburger, some buns and relish, and a container of potato salad. Perhaps he would tackle the basement, finally.

The ringing of the phone jolted him. He stared at the thing. Letting the caller leave a message meant adding something to his to-do list. He picked it up after the third ring.

"Mike, I'm sorry to bother you so early on a Saturday."

Delores's calm sister sounded far from calm. *Which one of them is this about?* "Go ahead, Lucy."

"Last night, something really bad happened. Brendan ended up in the hospital. We're at their place now."

"*What* happened?"

"He was coming home from the bar. They beat the shit out of him." She started crying.

"Who?"

"Assholes," she said, getting on top of her tears. "He doesn't know."

"Fuck," Mike said.

"This fucking city," she said.

"What did they do to him?"

"He can hardly see. They broke his nose. You'll see."

"Jesus."

"He got released in the middle of the night. Ray picked him up. Robbie and Jessie were going to sleep at our place, so we moved the whole crew to their house. They know about it, but we haven't let them in to see him yet."

"Is he awake?"

"More or less. I just gave him more ice packs. He's got 'em all over himself. He wants you to be with the kids when they go in there."

"He's right. I should be with them," Mike said. "Like now?"

"Sooner the better."

"Does Delores know?"

"We'll deal with that later. The kids are watching cartoons now, pretty subdued. They know it's not good."

"They don't need this," Mike said. It was eight twenty. He hung up, filled Robert's water bowl, then headed to the closet for his jacket. Ten minutes later, he pulled into a parking place four doors down from Brendan's row house.

"Hey," he said, walking into the living room. Jessie, Robbie, and their two cousins turned their heads from the television. Jess and Robbie waved to Mike. They looked worn. He sat between them on the couch and put his arms around their shoulders. Jessie rested her head on Mike's chest. Lucy turned down the TV set and asked her kids to go to the kitchen with her. Some cartoon dog Mike had never seen before was banging his head on a door, trying to get at a dumb-looking cat.

"Thank goodness Dad's home from the hospital," Mike said.

They nodded.

"Sounds like it could have been a lot worse," he said.

"Aunt Lucy says he's already complaining about being stuck in bed," Jessie said.

"That's a good sign," Mike said. "Shows he's on the mend. He's going to get better every day."

"Like *Mom*?" Robbie said, his eyes glued to the dog on the screen.

"You know this is different," Mike said. "I've seen your dad bounce back from injuries before. He's a pretty tough guy."

"He was outnumbered," Robbie said. "It wasn't fair."

"No," Mike said. "Whoever did this wasn't trying to be fair at all."

"They won't let us go in and see him without you," Robbie said.

"We can go see him right now if you want. But you got to help me."

"What do you mean?" Jessie said.

"It's going to be hard to resist making fun of him," he said. "We've been ripping on each other all our lives."

"Let's just go," Robbie said, rising and turning off the television set. *Time to try something other than humor.* Jessie ran to the dining room table, returning with two get-well cards they'd made.

"The only gift I got for him is you guys," Mike said.

He followed them up the stairs and down the hallway to the front bedroom. They waited for him at the closed door. Mike knocked lightly.

"Hey," Brendan called from the bedroom. "Come on in, guys."

Propped up in bed with what might be every pillow in the house, Brendan forced a smile. "I feel better than I look," Brendan said, "as usual." His smile made his puffy, bruised face seem ghoulish. *Stop smiling, Brendan.*

"Hi Dad," Robbie said, approaching the bed. Jessie stood frozen beside Mike. Mike put his arm around her shoulder and squeezed her. Brendan's swollen nose was bandaged. Both eyes were surrounded by purple and black.

"Rocky Raccoon," Brendan said, grinning. No one laughed. One arm was in a sling. Mike wondered how many bandages lay under the covers. *Fuckers.*

Jessie burst into tears and ran to the other side of the bed. Brendan cradled her with his good arm. *My poor reckless brother.* Robbie sat on the edge of the bed by his father's slinged arm, his face a stern mask. Jessie sobbed and clutched the sheets beside Brendan. Mike stood behind her and patted her hair. She shuddered, tears streaming from her closed eyes. *Something. Anything to help them.* Finally, she opened her eyes. "Dad-*dy!*" she cried.

"Bastards," Robbie muttered.

"Hey," Brendan said crossly. "I'm alive."

"He's going to be all right," Mike said, not sure if he believed it.

"That's right," his brother said. He reached out to Jessie, but she pulled away, sobbing again, and ran out of the room.

"That went well." Brendan groaned. Adjusting his position, he grimaced, then flashed that scary smile.

"Lucy's down there," Mike said. "But we should be with Jess."

Robbie raised his eyes tentatively, like a shy dog. "What hurts the most, Dad?"

"Tough question. Ice helps. And I'm on like a million milligrams of Percocet."

"How many guys did this?" Robbie said.

"Three," Brendan said. "I wish I could say they look worse than this."

"It's not fair, Dad." His little hands were balled into fists.

Brendan nodded.

"All this stuff," Mike said, pointing to the bandages, "is going to go before you know it."

"And I'll get some down time out of it," Brendan said, turning to his son. "Be around you guys more. Can you handle it?"

"Yeah."

"If this had happened to you guys or Mom, I'd be fit to be tied, but you'll all nurse me along. I'll be annoying you before you know it."

Robbie tried to smile but it was more of a frown.

"Your sister thinks this is worse than it is," Brendan said. "She's a kid. She's been so strong with Mom. She didn't need this. Neither did you."

Robbie pressed himself against his father.

I can't think of shit to do.

"Maybe you could go check on her," Brendan said.

The boy nodded, gave his father's good hand a light high five, and left the room.

"I better follow up on them," Mike said. "I'll be back."

When Mike got downstairs, they were all sitting around the kitchen table, drinking orange juice. Jessie was sitting on her aunt's lap. Her brother stood beside them.

"I was just telling the kids," Lucy said, "that tomorrow he's going to look better."

"Definitely," Mike said, recalling that when he'd broken his nose playing rough-touch the discoloration actually got worse over the first few days.

"We're all headed up to church to help with the decorations for Easter Vigil Mass," she said. "Ray'll keep an eye on Brendan when he gets back from Home Depot."

They talked about their plans for Easter. They were going to help prepare the church for the evening service, but Lucy and Ray would take them to the Mass in the morning. Lucy gave a preview of everyone's Easter outfit. Mike listened but kept seeing his brother's battered face. Clearly it could have been even worse. He did not want to ask for more details around the kids. At ten, with Ray still on his errand, he suggested that he'd stay with Brendan until Ray returned. When Lucy and the kids piled into Lucy's minivan, Mike climbed the stairs again.

Brendan attempted no smile when Mike returned.

"You need some water or something?" Mike said, crossing the room.

"I'm good," his brother said, pointing to the nearly full glass beside the bedside clock. He grimaced as he shifted in bed.

"What the hell?" Mike said, sitting down in one of the two straight chairs beside the bed.

Brendan sighed. "Beats me," he said. "Ha, ha. No telling who this could have been."

"Didn't recognize them?"

"White guys. Big. They knew what they were doing. Threw me into one of those empty garages on Ridge."

"Did you have a lot of cash on you?"

"They didn't touch my wallet."

"Have you really, really pissed off somebody lately?"

"You want a list?" He reached for the water glass and took a sip. "I had thought I was cool again with the electricians' union. There's people who thought differently about business arrangements than I did." He tried to prop himself up but winced and stopped. "I used to run with some pretty seedy types."

Used to.

Brendan pointed to his chest. "They said nothing's broken inside, but I feel every damn muscle and organ in there. Never been the piñata before."

"Fuckers."

Brendan gave a philosophical shrug. "They didn't touch the kids or Delores," Brendan said, fixing Mike with a knowing look.

"The cops any help?"

Brendan smirked. "I may never know any more than I can guess. Maybe that's good."

"It was dark. You were alone, coming out of a bar. It's so random."

"No. They knew who I was."

Mike strained to comprehend.

"When I thought they'd gotten everything they were going to get out of this piñata, they did this," Brendan said, eyeing his shoulder in the sling. "This is why I won't be working for four to six weeks. Guy wrenched my arm behind me, like a cop would. "How's it feel, *Flannagan!*' the fucker said. I heard the shoulder come out. Nearly passed out. Crawled out of the garage and got to the sidewalk. Some neighbor called 911."

"Jesus."

"That, little brother, is why I keep a deterrent in the nightstand."

"It was a mistake," Mike said, reddening.

"No, but it will be a mistake if whoever it was tries to do something here."

"They wanted me," Mike said.

Confusion swept across Brendan's face.

"I fucked up somebody's shoulder."

"What?"

"You were at my house the night Sarah and the old guy were waiting for me. They must have seen you go outside together."

"Why the fuck?"

"Must have followed her. She hasn't been over since. The guy was about to terrorize her, but he didn't actually see me when I jumped him."

"Who is this guy?"

"Some punk who blames her for getting thrown out of college."

"Some punk who's connected."

"I guess."

"What's he look like?"

"Not big. Wiry and tall. Got a big pompadour."

"These guys were all big, thick. So, he *knows* somebody serious. And they've been setting this up. They must have narrowed it down to the two of us. If they found out anything about the two of us, they went with the percentages."

"It's my fault," Mike said. Part of him had been secretly waiting for a comeuppance like this, but now that it had happened and had been all because of him, it only made him feel worse. "Don't think they're coming back?"

"These people are usually all about proportion. Sounds like they think they squared things for this punk. I'd be dead if that's what they wanted."

"Okay," Mike said, trying to sound more confident than he felt.

"But they could find out they got the wrong guy," Brendan said. "We won't say anything. But you never know. I guess it's best if Sarah doesn't know about this."

Mike nodded. "You're not going to go after these people?"

Brendan laughed. "Not unless I develop a death wish."

Good, he thought.

"But there's no guarantee they won't figure this out," Brendan said. He nodded toward his nightstand. "Second drawer," he said. "Go on."

"Brendan," Mike said.

"Defensive purposes only," Brendan said. "You keep it in your house. Never take it out. You know how to use one of these?"

He nodded. "I don't have a permit."

Brendan laughed. "Neither do I!"

"I don't know," Mike said, standing before the nightstand.

"It's wrapped up, loaded, ready to use if you ever need it. Don't worry, I got another one in the basement."

You keep a loaded gun around these kids?

"You'll need this," Brendan said, reaching under his pillow and pulling out a key on an old Ford key chain. "It's locked."

Mike opened the drawer and pulled out the small metal box. He put the key into his pocket. "I'm probably not the guy who ought to have a fucking loaded weapon around him," Mike said, holding the gray container.

"No, *I'm* that guy."

"How did you?"

"Never mind. I'm not hanging around those people anymore."

As usual, he didn't know whether or not to believe his brother.

"Last night might have been because of you," he said, "but it could have been for any number of things I've done. It could have been worse, and it was only me. Got it?"

"Yeah."

"We need to know who this guy is, Mike. And who he's tied to. Just for defensive purposes."

"All right."

Stopped at a red light on the way home, Mike reached into his pants pocket and felt for the keychain. What the fuck? The gun case was tucked into a box in the trunk that stored a couple of blankets, a flashlight, two bungee cords, a jacket, and a pair of work boots. Taking advice from Brendan? Bringing his gun home? But Brendan was right. Better to be ready. When he pictured his brother's swollen face, he cringed. *What have I done?* Now he had his brother's handgun. And all those Sarah aches had breached his defenses again.

A knifing pain ripped through his gut, bending him toward the steering wheel. Lessening, it left him reeling in a wave of nausea. He'd eaten enough, but his stomach felt raw, ready to erupt. He cracked the window then gently breathed in the cool air, but the grinding in his stomach inched its way around, moving wherever it wanted to go.

When he pictured the gun case in the drawer of his nightstand, the seasick sensation revved up.

A car's honking blare behind him focused him on the green light. The car surged ahead, out of his control, hijacked.

32

SATURDAY, MARCH 25

Entering the shop at ten thirty, Domenic greeted the boys and the balding electrician from Bryan Street then brought his comb disinfectant container to the sink in the middle of the room. He cleaned the combs and the container, sharpened each pair of his scissors.

"Spring cleaning?" Clement asked, interrupting his Phillies update to Nick.

Domenic dried one comb after another while Al remained silent, trimming around the electrician's ears.

Back at his stretch of the counter, Domenic removed the head from his electric clippers then cleaned the unit completely.

"Might be getting ready for a yard sale," Nick opined.

Domenic lined up the scissors beside his talcum brush on the counter. He opened up the linen drawer to find a neat stack of barber cloths. Good. While Al was giving change to the electrician, Domenic grabbed the push broom and began sweeping up cuttings. He looked up. Al appeared on the other side of the sink, the dustpan and brush in his hands, a scowl on his face. Al swept the pile into his dustpan then dumped it into the wastebasket. "Sit down like you're supposed to," he whispered.

The night before, Domenic had fallen asleep confident about his plan to at least give the appearance that he could do the work of his vocation, but he woke up to a bolder conviction. "Just my regular customers," he said. "There's only about six of them, anyway."

"Don't exaggerate," Al said.

Charley Moore walked in and offered a cheery hello to all.

"This would be *your* customer," Domenic whispered to Al.

Red-faced, Al snapped open a barber cloth as Domenic sat in his own chair. When Charlie had paid and left, Al stood before Domenic's chair. "Okay, only your regulars, but if I butt in, you butt out."

Grudgingly, Domenic shook hands with him. He could not remember the last time one of his regulars had been in. He hadn't seen Eddie the painter in ages. Al had clipped Jeff the layabout from Durham Street on Thursday. "Like watching your girlfriend dance with some other guy," Domenic had told Al afterwards. Peter, the lawyer from the public defender office, was the last cut he had given before the trip to the hospital, and he wouldn't be back for a month. By the end of the day, Domenic was convinced that he had been had by his own deal. But he'd been ready.

Upstairs, he lit two candles then ate dinner. When the dishes were done, he blew out the candles and opened his prayer book. He might even consider dressing up and walking to Easter Mass in the morning. He'd felt involved enough, just reading the prayers for Thursday and Friday in his apartment, but it wasn't the same as being there.

Of all the rituals of the week, the end of Holy Thursday service always got him. Smells and bells in slow motion was how Nick put it. Even the most wooden of priests moved with breathless grace that night.

He and Angela couldn't always get to the Good Friday afternoon service, but they never missed Holy Thursday evening. Down the candle-dim aisle Father would walk, slowly bearing the remaining consecrated hosts away from the main altar to be stored for Good

Friday when there was no Mass, no consecration. Holding onto the container, putting one foot carefully after the other, as if dropping the hosts or tripping and stumbling to the ground would send the world spinning off its axis, the priest moved down the aisle to the back of the church then back toward a side altar, while all present sang the mournful "Pange Lingua" unaccompanied. The beginning of the three-day period between Lent and Easter, the name for which he never remembered. Surely, Domenic thought, anyone who'd ever dipped his finger in a holy water font couldn't stand in the midst of all that and not feel something. There was, however, one hardened former Catholic who might bear up pretty well under that kind of sensory assault, but he doubted that the Mike Flannagan he knew would ever find himself in a pew during Holy Week.

Had Mike been their rebellious Catholic son, Angela would have been the one better at handling such conflicts. Even with her gentle touch, he probably would have gone astray but might have kept his mind open as an adult—provided Domenic hadn't made a mess out of it. *Stop now.* He was fooling himself: he had no influence on the guy.

He and Angela had been equally observant, but her approach to faith and religious practice was sweeter and more patient, as it was with all things until her darkness found her. After all that, he'd attended Mass and kept making his novena trips to the Shrine on Chelten Avenue, always feeling her love, sometimes tasting a moment of what it might be like when he found her beside him again. She would have called his baseball candle ritual horrible sacrilege, but if anyone could understand the weight against which scarred souls must push—and that such work was dark indeed—it was his Angela. He would join her. He had to believe that. But he'd been left in the dark, and he would make use of any light he could find. He'd get there. *Angela.* They'd forgive each other.

Easter, now just hours away, was coming early this year. And Holy Saturday fell on March 25, the day the Church celebrated Mary's assent to the angel's news that she would give birth to Jesus. Downstairs, no one had said a word about the coincidence, and, to his surprise, he had not thought of it on his own. People with calendars knew what followed the Annunciation, and, ultimately, the Crucifixion, but Mary hadn't known—and she was there. How alone had she felt that night? Had anyone who loved her tried to help her? Had she let them?

33

MONDAY, MARCH 27

Sitting in the dark, Sarah listened to the hum of the car's engine. She kept the windows up, though outside it was still in the fifties. Her Easter-celebrating friends gladly would have exchanged yesterday's weather for this. Put it on the list of things you couldn't change. With the radio off, she wondered if the faint, raspy noise coming from the engine had always been there. A new list item? "You have a master's in planning, right?" Mike once teased her. Yet, since receiving Friday's news, she had nosed along with no plans at all. She'd tidied up her grading and the apartment while the city's Easter paraders made the most of the messy day. Skipped the normal Sunday call to her parents. Went through the motions in Monday's classes. Only Florence asked what was wrong then advised her to talk to Mike, even if Sarah had no master plan about him, herself, or the new presence within.

Thirty-two days without seeing or hearing from him. Not every one of those days had dragged along, but enough of them had to make it feel like far more than one month. Love leaves hellish history, one of her college roommates had penned in a poem. Nothing in Sarah's life since then had caused her to question the statement. How would she have managed to keep up with the madness at work and Domenic's medical adventures if she'd been absorbed in a relationship with Mike Flannagan? He probably felt well rid of her, but this was not about the relationship, exactly. She revved the engine. The sound jarred her away from thoughts about Mike.

Sometime since Friday, it hit her: she was acting in a film. She didn't know about the other actors, but she'd never gotten the script. Apparently, whoever was directing this nightmare had no intention of ever calling "cut." It was one long, uninterrupted shot that had followed her out to the driver's seat of her idling car, where she sat trembling. She put the car in drive and headed toward Mike Flannagan's house.

Parking in front of Mike's Reliant, she saw that his bedroom was dark. A dim light emanated from the living room. Left on for Robert? Mike could have walked to work and stayed for a long shift, but she had a strong feeling that he was here. Usually she reached a point when a decision or an answer became apparent. Given enough time, clouds went their way, leaving her with a clear view of the problem at hand. So far, she saw only that she needed to talk with Mike. Only once could she remember walking into a situation clueless and rudderless, but here she was again, trusting that she would find her mark on the floor of the next set. Knowing what to say might make this easier, but that didn't matter. Inside her, microscopic cells furiously divided and grew, second by second. He was co-producer, if not co-owner, of the fetus inside her. *Father.* She shuddered. She opened the car door then stepped out into the mild air.

Once she began walking, she felt steadier. Reaching the landing halfway up the cement steps, she heard the theme from *Jeopardy!* emanating from the house to the left of Mike's. Her legs took up her the rest of the steps without any hesitation. When she reached the porch, Robert charged into the foyer and began barking. She knocked. Yes, Mike might catch a glimpse of her from the living room window. Still, she expected that he would at least open the door. She heard him talking to the dog and working at the lock. He swung open the door and looked at her as if she were a page from a rumpled barbershop magazine that he had already read. Whatever faux confidence she had felt climbing the stairs vanished. He looked behind her and scanned up and down the block. *No, I didn't bring Domenic.*

When Robert nuzzled her leg, she bent over and patted his head. "Please?" she said, still looking at the dog.

"Robert," he said, and the dog trotted inside. Mike gestured for her to enter.

She followed him and the dog toward the kitchen, relieved that they were not headed to the living room, site of last month's debacle. *Is he thinking that too?* Except for his nearly empty white mug, the table was clear. Did his cupboard still hold the olive-green ceramic one she had always used when she stayed over?

"There," he said, gesturing toward her regular place at the table.

She pulled the chair out then sat without scooching it back up to the table.

He sat across from her. "That's that color you like," he said, pointing to her earrings.

She reached toward her right ear, finally remembering what she had put on in the morning, azure blue. "Florence's collection of travel souvenirs. Sicily. She just gave them to me."

He nodded.

The empty cup in front of him begged the courtesy question about tea or coffee, but he wordlessly settled into his seat then calmly began cracking his knuckles.

His composure could mean anything, but he hadn't shown her the door yet. Domenic would have some hilarious, snarky way to alert him to his rudeness. *He doesn't know about Domenic's hospitalization.* "Oh God." On their own, the words had slipped out of her mouth.

His eyes narrowed into a look of severe confusion and irritation.

"I knew that you didn't know," she blurted, "but I forgot."

"What?"

"He's better now, but Domenic was hospitalized for a while." She'd lost her place. No film director could help her.

"You came here to tell me this?" Only the irritation remained on his face. "But you just remembered now!"

No! Wait. "Let me start over," she said, barely on top of tears. "His breathing and his heart. They helped him get things straightened out. I probably should have called you." *I've convinced you that I am crazy.* He'd throw her out in a minute.

"Because I needed to know this?"

She felt as if someone had just checkmated her. "He doesn't hate you," she said, pounding her fist on the table.

He closed his eyes. His *I'm being patient* look.

"And I doubt you hate him," she said. "He talks about you. In fact, I think he would like to be connected with you, though he'd never put it into words. It makes sense." When she looked up, his eyes were on hers, a bemused expression on his face. "He might see you almost like a son."

"Jesus Christ," Mike grumbled, shaking his head.

"Makes sense that you two would connect, Mike," she said, waiting until he finally made eye contact.

"Does everything *you've* ever done make sense to you in the cold light of day?" he said.

"Of course not," she said. "But you care about the old guy."

His sour expression made him look like a cranky old man. "I hardly know him, Sarah."

"You know him enough."

"You can say *that* again."

He was staring at her with that blank look again. "He's not as strong as he used to be," she said. "It could get much worse."

"Good thing he's got friends like you," Mike said.

"And Al and Ginette," she said. "Things change, Mike."

"Tell me about it."

"My father's in cancer treatment again. His situation could go either way."

Mike nodded.

"I need to be flexible to deal with all the changes in my life," she said. She pulled her chair closer to the table. "I've interviewed for a job in New York. I'll go for a second interview."

"Your parents will like that."

His facial expression seemed to soften—relief that she might be leaving Philly? Why did this feel like another gut punch? *It's just another cheap shot.* "Thankfully, Domenic has Al and his wife."

"He doesn't want me around," Mike said. "Believe me."

"Every road has bumps, for God's sake," she said. "It's hard to push through that and act, all by yourself."

"Wait," he growled. "If he's so damn important, why are *you* leaving? Oh, right. Family!"

She had neither words nor movement in her, as if she'd lost all knowledge of language and a weight held her down in the kitchen chair, but she could not move her eyes from him.

"You don't want him to think you're walking out on him. Do you?" He leaned toward Sarah, put his hands on the table, and met her glare. "You want me to get you off the hook."

"No," she moaned. She rose from her chair and stood behind it. "He's scared," she said. "Alone." Mike stared down at the tabletop. *Waiting for her to finish and leave?* "Don't you feel anything, any pull?"

"I've let down everyone I've ever known," Mike said, looking up.

"Sins of commission and sins of omission, as he might put it. I'm the last guy in the world anybody should depend on."

"That's not true about everything."

"Trust me. It's true about what matters. But don't trust me about anything else. And you shouldn't be here."

She felt her composure breaking but steeled herself. "You're fooling yourself," she said.

"Tell that to my child. Tell that to his mother. Tell that to all the people I've let down. Big time."

She started to cry, but she clenched her fists and shouted at Mike, "Are you just going to leave him? You're not the horrible guy you think you are!"

"And *you* know what kind of person I am? Only somebody who's been royally fucked over by me can really know what I'm talking about."

"You don't know," she stammered. *So wrong.* She sobbed. Even if she'd come to Mike's with a real plan, she wouldn't be able to access it now, let alone speak the words.

"But I've already *been* a shit to you, so you ought to have some clue."

"Oh God, Flannagan," she moaned. *But there are other words.* She wrapped her hands around the back of her neck. "You need to shut up," she said in a slightly calmer voice. "Shut, shut, shut up."

He pulled back in his chair, crossed his arms, and looked at her. A truck's air brakes squealed out front, and Robert barked. A few moments later, the dog walked into the kitchen and sat by Mike's side. Both of them had their eyes fixed on her.

"Okay," Sarah said. She sat back down. "In senior year of college, I dated this guy. In New York."

The anger had drained from Mike's face.

"That spring and summer, we sort of lived together. In June, I found out I was pregnant. I was young. He was twenty-eight. I didn't tell my parents. Didn't know what to do."

She pushed her chair back again. "It was my decision," she said, looking down at her shoes. "He agreed. Said that all the time, that it was my decision. When I told him that it was just not the right time and that I thought I should do something about it, I saw how relaxed he became." She closed her eyes, trusting somehow that she would continue and he would listen. "We could have a child later, if we wanted to, he said. It was true. I knew that."

She looked up. Mike had gotten up and gone to the sink, his eyes on her. Robert remained beside the table. She looked away again. "I was all set to start graduate school that fall," she went on. "This would have changed everything. Didn't make any sense to me."

When she glanced back, Mike was frowning, his forehead creased, but he was studying her.

"Anyway, I did it by myself," she said. "Went alone. That was important to me. July 7." She let out a long breath. "It was steaming hot and humid." She closed her eyes. "Couldn't breathe."

When she opened her eyes, Mike was extending a glass of water to her. She took the glass and drank half of the water before setting it down on the table.

He took his seat silently. His eyes said, *Go on*. He'd kept that face hidden through the whole conversation. That face that she'd held, that had rushed her heart right out of control more than once. *Do I trust him now?*

"He was good to me," she said. "Before and after."

He nodded.

"After three weeks, I saw my parents. They didn't suspect a thing. I got ready for graduate school. My body felt pretty much like before.

I stayed with him. My nice guy. But by the middle of the fall, we agreed to split. I loved him, but somehow we lost interest in staying together." She felt her face redden but kept going. "I found another life, really. Learning and teaching. In the end, I went my own way." *Alone.* She let out a long sigh.

"You made it through, Sarah," Mike said. "That's something."

She shook her head. "I didn't come here to tell you all that," she said. "I've never told anyone."

"I'm not being very helpful," he admitted.

She was no longer in a movie take. Having put words to what she'd kept to herself all those years sharpened the edges of the story. *New pain.* She winced. But the shock had turned her mind back to what was happening inside her. *Enough.* She planted her hands on the edge of the table then pushed herself back. Eyes on the floor before her, she strode toward the front door. Robert barked twice.

"Sarah?" Mike called out.

She was fumbling at the dead bolt when he caught up to her. "No," she muttered, opening the door. She spun around to face him. "I have to go," she said, pulling away from his tentative reach.

Crossing the porch, she heard him follow then stop. *Home.* She picked her way down the concrete steps. At the curb, she looked both ways then crossed the street. She felt him watching her as she carefully placed her rear on the front seat, leaned back, and pulled her right leg inside then her left. Letting her shoulders sag against the back of the seat, she blew out a long breath, reached for the door, and pulled it shut. She cracked the window.

"Hold on!" Mike yelled. She heard him clopping down the steps then running. She turned on the ignition just as he reached the side of the car, Robert pulling up beside him. *Look up from the steering wheel. Home.*

"Wait!" he pleaded.

She swung her head toward the sound of his voice but was still looking down.

"You're pregnant," Mike said. "Sarah?"

Turning back, she put the car in drive. She rushed the car out of her parking place and up the hill.

"Sarah!"

In her rearview mirror, she saw him and the dog standing in the middle of the street, looking at the car. At the avenue, the traffic light turned amber. She screeched the car left onto the Belgian blocks, swerving off the trolley tracks before getting the car headed straight toward the next light.

34

TUESDAY, MARCH 28

Mike breathed in hard through his nose, startling himself awake, his face pressed against the couch seat cushion. Recoiling from the cushion's musky odor, he rolled onto his back. "Fuck," he groaned, the light from outside jolting his eyes open. Sometime between midnight and now, he must have finally slept. Five minutes? An hour?

Stiff and spent, he turned away from the window's glare, remembering every major problem of his life shared one thing—they all lay in sight but beyond his reach. The realization had hit him at some point during his jumpy night. Or had he merely dreamed it?

He staggered up the stairs to use the bathroom, then took Robert out. Walking past the overgrown bushes in front of the library, he remembered the cannonballs once welded together at the little memorial, long ago pilfered, along with the plaque that explained their origin and history. Also missing was the horse trough near the entrance to the park. As a preteen, he'd been intrigued that the massive cannonballs, once fired by the Turks, had ended up centuries later in his neighborhood. Artifacts of violence. Why had they landed in Mount Airy? Like so much else, they'd disappeared. Why was he here?

Mike's violence had driven Sarah's assailant away from her, as planned, but it also pushed Sarah away from him. Unintended consequences. Back then, his momentary view that he'd killed two birds with one impulsively thrown stone left him with a fatalistic acceptance that her safety had been worth risking an end that probably was inevitable. But dominoes continued falling. He wasn't as disconnected as he'd imagined. Even Domenic had been thrust into his way.

He let Robert lead him down another block to Carpenter Lane. Crossing over to the firehouse, the difference between this hell and New Paltz became clear. No one was dead yet.

Back home, he fed Robert then called out sick. He took a glass of water to the living room and returned to the couch, knowing he needed some of Sarah's organizational strengths. She would use a pad and pen, but he wanted a list that would fit in his consciousness and remain accessible. Though Sarah topped his list, until he heard from her, he would have to compartmentalize. He would push his focus to one of the other names on his mental list.

Delores. He did not have to be with her when they told her about Brendan. That realization brought relief. He could duck her for a few days, but Brendan needed information from him.

Though hardly two peas in a pod, Brendan brought Florence Devereaux to mind. Three days a week, she arrived at the office before Sarah, so he had a sixty percent chance to catch Florence. Sarah had never told him the name of her attacker, probably afraid even then of what Mike might do. He dialed the number.

"Of course I remember you," she said. She didn't sound like she thought he was in the picture, but if Sarah had told her about the pregnancy, she'd be too discreet to say anything.

"Those great earrings you gave Sarah make her think of the Mediterranean," he said. "She loves them."

"I'm glad," she said.

"She's lucky to have you as a friend," he said. "I'm trying to be better at that."

"That's good, Mike. She needs that."

"Ms. Devereaux, I'm worried about that guy who scared Sarah. But I don't want to make things worse for her. She doesn't want to help the police keep tabs on him. You know how she is about getting them involved."

"Right."

"They keep a watch list," he said. "So if a guy messes with another person in the future, they know he's not some innocent lamb."

"But she won't give them the man's name. Right?"

"Her friends are allowed to come forward, but I wanted to ask if you thought it was a good idea."

"They don't actually do anything to the man?"

"Not unless he starts some other trouble. It would be a way to protect her—and others—without worrying her. She sure doesn't need anything else on her plate."

"No."

"And it keeps the guy from being pulled into the legal system."

A minute later, she gave him the student's name.

He thanked her, then called Brendan. "Ed Hearn. You don't need his address?"

"I'm not working with the yellow pages," Brendan said.

"Right."

Brendan sounded better. Mike promised to take the kids out on Saturday and to check on the house.

"I'll call you in a day or two," Brendan said.

Efficacious. That was the word Sarah had used to describe one of her best students. Mike's actions might yield nothing, but doing something made him feel slightly efficacious about one item on his list.

In the afternoon, he hiked to Carpenter's Woods with Robert, giving his sore back and legs a good stretch. As he neared a hilltop, a chocolate lab puppy bounded over the top headed his way. When Mike stopped, Robert dutifully went into a sit-stay. Tail wagging, the little guy advanced jauntily toward Robert. Suddenly, three laughing children crested the hill in hot pursuit of the unleashed pup, followed by a man and a woman. He told the parents that it was fine to let the little dog meet Robert but wished he could avoid conversation. While the dogs sniffed and wagged and the kids patted them, the mom and dad chattered about how they'd just gotten Samson a week ago, how it already had changed their lives. The sight and sound of the blissful family had roped his agony back on stage. Mike nodded, managed a smile, and hoped that they could carry on the conversation without him having to comment. Finally, they put the puppy's leash back on and headed off, telling Mike goodbye. He waved to them then set off, knowing that had he attempted to speak, he would have broken down.

Sarah. Laurie and Michael. He walked behind Robert trying to redirect his thoughts, but the sadness and pain gripped him all the way back home.

When he opened the front door, Robert's paws clattered across an envelope on the foyer floor below the mail slot. On it, he saw his first name scrawled in Sarah's handwriting. Picking it up, he felt something slide around inside. When he ripped it open at the kitchen table, a key and a note fell out.

Mike...

This is for Domenic's apartment. I don't think he would mind. Do with it what you will.

I want you to know that I am going to have the baby. I owe you that much information. I will do this on my own. I will not be a problem for you. I'm sorry I could not tell you. Writing this is hard enough.

– Sarah

He put the key and note back in the envelope and dropped it onto the table. His head spun again. *I may never see this child, but Sarah will be a good mother.* How could she ever be a problem to him? He crossed his arms on the table, leaned forward and rested his forehead on them, panting. "Yes," he gasped. Even if the exhaustion wasn't catching up with him, he couldn't focus on his list anymore. Sarah. Brendan, Ed Hearn, and Delores. Domenic. He could stay awake no longer. He trudged upstairs and collapsed in bed.

When Mike woke, it was light outside. He checked his watch. Still Tuesday afternoon. Call Sarah? Drop off a note like she'd done? She needed time. He thought of the last name on his list.

Domenic was sitting in his barber chair when he entered the shop, so Mike averted his eyes, grabbed a magazine, and sank into a chair beside Clement. Four other men waited, presumably for Al, who was working on a man in a suit. Clement, Nick, and one of the others were arguing about free will and fate. Mike had not spent five minutes in his life reading *Field & Stream*, but he turned to a page and let his eyes rest on an ad for hunting and fishing apparel. When he heard Domenic clear his throat, Mike looked up. Domenic stood beside his barber chair, nodding sternly toward it.

As soon as Mike sat down, the chair dropped twice as Domenic worked the adjustment arm. Domenic clipped a tissue a little too tightly around Mike's neck. Grim-faced, Domenic pulled a fresh barber cloth from a drawer, blinking as he snapped it beside the chair.

Mike closed his eyes. His neck muscles tightened as Domenic raked a comb through his hair, jerking his head to one side.

"Long time between haircuts."

"Pretty shaggy," Mike admitted, his eyes still closed. He felt for Domenic's key in his pocket.

"Not right. Going that long," Domenic said. "In fact, it's a disgrace."

Even the two old guys remained silent. When had so many people in this shop suddenly lost their tongues?

"It's important to look neat."

"You're right," Mike said.

Domenic turned on his electric clippers and began working on the back of Mike's head. "If the person you see in the mirror looks like he doesn't care about looking right, how's he going to act right?"

"It won't happen again," Mike said, opening his eyes. In the mirror, he watched Domenic clip the left side of his head. The old man's severe expression made Mike think of soldiers in Civil War photographs.

"Better." Domenic stepped back then studied the front and top of Mike's hair.

Mike shut his eyes again and bent his head forward, suddenly picturing some poor soul readying to meet his executioner's axe. After a while, he felt Domenic loosening the barber cloth and undoing the tissue wrap around his neck. This awkward dance was no more absurd than anything else he could be doing the day after Sarah's bombshell. He felt warm shaving cream dabbed behind his right ear, the heat startling and soothing him at the same time. Domenic repeated the process behind his other ear.

He listened to the old man stropping the blade, over and over. Domenic said nothing, but the sharpening noise went on. Mike had not felt fearful sadness like this since childhood. He made himself breathe in a steady, calm rhythm. Al's clippers and Domenic's sharpening continued their percussive duet. Still, no one said a word. He sensed Domenic behind him then felt the blade, cool and sharp, pressing its way up his neck to the top of his ear.

Mike kept his eyes closed as Domenic silently did his work. Normally, once a barber quieted after some initial small talk, Mike drifted off for the rest of the haircut, but now he remained on high alert. He heard and felt Domenic step back from the chair then put his razor on the counter.

"You ought to take a look for yourself," Domenic said.

"How's it look to you?"

"Doesn't matter how it looks to me."

"If you think it's done, then I'm good with it."

A pair of open hands clapped sharply against the back of his neck, jolting his eyes open. He smelled witch hazel. Domenic's firm hands smacked his neck again. The old man, still stern-faced, removed the barber cloth and flapped the cuttings onto the floor.

Mike stood up then nodded to the others. He stuck a ten-dollar bill in Domenic's hand. "Fair enough?"

Domenic stuck the money into his pocket without looking at it then turned and began organizing the razors and clippers on his counter.

When Mike returned home from the shop, he reread Sarah's note and walked Robert. Exhausted again, he lay on the couch, watching Robert circle several times before lying down on the carpet, facing him. Mike closed his eyes and smelled a trace of witch hazel.

35

TUESDAY, MARCH 28

Domenic rested on top of the bedspread for the better part of an hour before straggling into the kitchen. He had little interest in dinner but slapped together a sandwich using Easter ham Ginette had sent over with Al. Afterwards, he managed to eat a small bowl of peaches then put the can in the refrigerator beside the containers of Wawa coleslaw and potato salad.

He did the dishes, took his medicine, then put on the new pajamas Al and Ginette had bought him. Under the covers, he lay back, relieved that his day was done.

Noise at the downstairs door startled him. Al again? A sharp tingling shot up his spine. What had kept Sarah away this long? Several heavy treads sounded on the stairs.

"Domenic?" Mike Flannagan called up.

He slumped back into the mattress. Mike fumbled noisily at the top door and clumped down the hall.

"You're not the pizza man," Domenic said.

"No such luck."

"Is there anybody who *doesn't* have a key to this place?"

Mike unzipped his jacket, pulled the bedside chair out a bit, and sat down across from him.

Twice in one day, again. "Does this arrangement work for you?" Mike asked, pointing to the bed.

"Thought I was at death's door up here, did you?"

"No," Mike said. "You were pretty spry downstairs."

"For an invalid on digitalis and Lasix."

He watched Mike's eyes move around the reorganized room, finally locking onto his.

"I could make a weekly run to the store for you," Mike said. "It's no sweat off me."

"The people who shop for me," Domenic said, "I tell them what I want, and that's what they get."

"I'm sure Al's been a regular Boy Scout," Mike said. "And Sarah's done a lot."

"Up to last Monday," Domenic said. "What's going on?"

"She showed up the other night. Short visit."

"She's taking the job in New York," Domenic said. "Is that it?"

"Domenic."

"You're here as the messenger?" Domenic said in a slowly rising voice.

"She's pregnant, Domenic."

"*Madonna!*" he snapped, turning away. *You came here to give me a damn heart attack.* He sat upright in the bed and jabbed his finger at him. "You do this then come here to tell me?" Mike didn't move or speak. "Get out! Now!"

"I *want* to be the father," Mike said quietly.

Domenic grimaced. His heart was racing. "You don't deserve to be the father."

"The baby deserves to have a father," Mike said. "How can I let her go off on her own."

"Is that what she wants to do?"

"She wants to have the baby, doesn't want me around."

"Fair enough." None of this made any sense. If he'd known this when Mike showed up downstairs, he'd have given him a kick to the curb instead of a haircut. He watched Mike stand and walk to the window then slap his hand against the frame.

"Why can't I be there?"

"Because all you've done is make her pregnant."

"You don't have to be a perfect couple to do right by a kid." He turned from the window to Domenic. "I would do this," Mike said. "With her."

"You don't have much in the way of feelings for her," Domenic said coldly.

"Does it have to be that kind of feelings? How could it even *be* that kind of feelings?" Mike sagged back into his seat and stared off into space. "I'd show her," he said, "that I could be a good father."

"Should have thought of that before."

"I could be a good husband too," Mike said. "I'd do what I needed to do, no complaints."

"Don't you think she deserves better than that?"

He watched Mike squirm in the chair. He had never seen him like this before.

"You don't want to see her go to New York," Mike said. "Do you?"

"Not for me to say," Domenic said. "There are lots of reasons for her to make that move. It's her call." He sat up, trying to find a more comfortable position. When he'd settled himself, he realized how spent he felt, as if he had been on his feet cutting hair all day. "Why are you telling me all this?"

"Figuring things out," Mike said. "Trying to."

"Well, keep figuring." Domenic fluffed his pillow, but it still did not feel right. "I've figured out all that I can today," he said.

"My cue," Mike said, rising. "Need your medicine or anything?"

Domenic shook his head. "I don't need any of this," he groaned, rolling so he faced the wall.

"I'll call about groceries," Mike said, then started out.

Domenic's life was not getting any better. Why should it? He looked at the chipped paint on the woodwork and listened to Mike retrace his noisy path, switching off lights, finally locking the door.

Meeting Angela was as close as Domenic was likely to come to experiencing divine grace. He didn't deserve her love any more than Sarah deserved to be tied down with a package like Mike. Of course he'd snapped at him. The shock of the news about Sarah had set him off. Maybe if he believed the guy actually loved her, he'd have held back, but he hadn't seen evidence of that. *My dark anger at Angela.* He cursed himself. Would Mike ever feel such regret? He got out of bed, lit five candles, then stood in front of the newspaper box score caption for the tenth loss: "Curtains."

"But there's a last weekend of baseball left and everything could fall into place," he grumbled. "If you win both games in Cincinnati, and if the Cardinals somehow get swept by the pathetic Mets." *Until the last inning of the season, the chips fall where they need to fall.* "Perfect!"

Domenic blew out the candles in a rage. He climbed back into bed and pulled up the covers. *Loss, loss, loss.* He closed his eyes, waiting for the panting to subside.

The next day the shop was closed, so Domenic let himself sleep as long as he could. Trying to think about anything other than Sarah and Mike, he could focus on nothing other than them. The hell with Mike. He would wait, would not bother Sarah. After a light lunch, he looked out the front window. People were wearing thin jackets instead of parkas. He got his light jacket out of the closet, zipped it up, then carefully descended the stairs. He had not bothered to make a shopping list. He would get what made sense, buy only what he could carry.

He was breathing heavily by Durham Street and wheezing at Mount Pleasant Avenue, where the hill crested. He rested on the low stone wall outside the Protestant church at the corner, grateful that the last block was downhill. Pushing the shopping cart through the Acme, he stopped all along the dairy aisle, if he were reading labels on containers of yogurt or eggs, sticking his head into the cold case to inhale the frosty air, but it provided no relief. Dawdling, however, did the trick. By the time he wheeled up to the register, he had compared prices for every item in his basket and investigated alien territories in the store. He also was breathing normally and feeling confident again. Insisting on bagging the order himself, he balanced the order into two plastic bags that made a reasonable load for each arm.

The groceries did not feel too heavy until he started the return climb up to the church. He leaned against the stone wall, bags at his feet.

"Domenic!" Al's voice jolted his eyes open. "I'll get the car."

Domenic dropped to the pavement, slumping against the wall, his arms around the two bags.

The second day in the hospital, Domenic opened his eyes after his afternoon nap to find Sarah sitting next to the bed.

"April Fools'," she said, patting his hand. "Well, two days early."

"What's the bigger joke," he said, "me landing here again or me seeing you?"

"How did you rate a private room?" she asked.

"It was the only space they had left when Al brought me in. I'm on a real lucky streak. It was Al's day off, but he was coming over anyway."

A nurse entered the room and checked Domenic's chart. When she left, Sarah squeezed his hand. "I haven't been able to come and see you. I'm sorry. I couldn't even call."

"I know."

"Well, there's a lot that you don't know."

"I know too much."

She looked confused and nervous.

"I know what you're going to tell me," he said. He reversed the position of their hands, putting his on top. "Mike came by my place Tuesday. This week, at least, he's like dog dirt, everywhere. Came here last night after finding my apartment empty."

"You should be angry with me," she said. "I wanted to see you, to talk with you. You'd laugh, but I'm trying to figure things out that I thought I already had figured out."

"If there's anything I can do," Domenic said softly.

"That's very kind."

"This must sound like a broken record, but I'm getting out of here. If they get my medications all lined up right, and I follow all their rules, I should be okay."

"Al told me the breathing machine helps."

He nodded. "Have you talked with Mike? Besides the time he told me about?"

"No."

"That one," he muttered.

"History."

He raised his eyebrows again, studying her, then leaned forward. "Could you crank up the bed a little?" he said, pointing toward the control. She hopped up and figured out how to make the thing move. The slight change felt good to his back. She took her place beside him again.

"You never had to stop by the apartment every day," he said. "But you could have called."

"I know," she said. Her eyes started to tear up. "Aren't you going to ask me about the baby?"

His eyes widened. "You've had a baby?"

She let out a laugh then choked up.

Domenic pushed the Kleenex box toward her. "Tell me."

She wiped her eyes and told him she felt great, never better. No, she couldn't feel it move yet, but it wouldn't be long. The doctor said she was in great shape. Once started, she barely stopped to take a breath. Words rolled out of her mouth as if she hadn't had a soul to speak them to, and watching her broad hand gestures and her fiery eyes, Domenic guessed that she hadn't.

"I knew I was going to have this baby before I left Mike's place," she said.

"He said something?"

"No, I did. Hearing myself, I knew." She described what the little one looked like at its present stage of development, what it would look like in another month, what it would be able to do, but Domenic could not get Mike out of his mind. She was occupied. He got that. Upon leaving the hospital, he would get strong warnings against venturing alone down his block for some time, but he figured he was a better bet to visit one of these two before either of them would visit the other. She told him that at this stage the baby was already exercising the muscles he or she would eventually use for breathing and swallowing. *And for talking.*

When she left, he tried to calm himself but realized that the nervous excitement he felt was not bad. It was different but unmistakably familiar, like the face of an old friend he hadn't seen in thirty years.

36

SATURDAY, APRIL 1

Delores had better color than the last time Mike had visited her, despite knowing about Brendan being attacked and everything at home being in an uproar. Wearing sweatpants and a faded Eagles jersey, she looked like he'd caught her between weekend laundry loads. Large, crayoned get-well cards from the kids had been taped to the wall across from her bed. Framed photos of Brendan and both kids ringed the nightstand. She knew that it was Saturday and April 1. "He's under house arrest," she quipped when Mike dragged a small chair next to her larger more comfortable one beside the bed. He told her that as far as he could see Brendan was following his doctor's orders and managing, with a little help from him and her sister, to care for the kids.

"I wanted to kill you," she said calmly, "when I learned what happened to him." Her tone was conversational, as if she were talking about backyard garden plans gone wrong. Food service personnel rattled carts down the hallway, signifying the end of lunchtime. Two of the workers conversed as if they were outdoors and fifty yards away from one another until the closing elevator doors cut them off.

"I didn't want that to happen to him," Mike said. "Believe me."

"Come on," she said. "We've both wanted that to happen. Not that bad, no. Remember when he used to play football? He never felt like he was awake and in the game until somebody clocked him. He's awake." She folded the *Inquirer* weekend section she'd been reading when he walked in and set it on the bed.

"I didn't expect you to be this philosophical," Mike said.

"My philosophy was wanting to kill you when I heard the whole story, dumbass. And he should want to kick your ass."

"Maybe when you get home and his shoulder's healed, he'll come over and axe-murder me."

"You're more surprised than I am."

"I've been around the block a few times with Brendan."

"He's still who he's always been. It's just that his eyes work better now. Well, bad choice of words. The poor raccoon."

"Seems different." He reddened. "Visiting you is a regular surprise fest," he said. When she smiled, he saw that spark in her eyes again, a look that he'd rarely seen when she was with Brendan. "Nothing makes sense," he said. He held up one finger. "You remember stuff about me and my mother that I don't even know about, and," he said, holding up a second finger, "Brendan's on his way to sainthood."

"Not if it requires going to church."

He laughed. "All this change."

She shook her head then reached for the framed photo of Brendan and the kids painting the porch, setting it on her lap and looking longingly at it. "He always knew what he was and was not. The good, the bad, and the ugly."

"But he's a shit."

"Until he takes a good hit."

"Not like his younger brother?"

"Your mom worried more about you than about Brendan, even when you were married."

"She wasn't much in the way of showing motherly concern," Mike said. He hadn't felt hurt and sad until he'd said it. He thought of

Delores with her kids. How could someone who obviously knew all about being a good mother be so wrong about his mother?

"Okay, she despaired."

"Put it another way, she never thought much of me, of what I could do."

"That's not it," she said. "She thought you didn't get it."

"And Brendan got it?"

She looked down at his brother's goofy smile. "'God forbid Laurie ever leaves that Mike,' she said. 'She's about all he's got.'"

"I knew exactly what I had in Laurie," he countered. "And in Michael."

"Of course you did."

He felt the place where he'd worn his wedding band. It still felt odd to not find it there. Holding his palm face up then down, he swore he could make out a pale line around his finger. "Best things that ever came my way."

"Exactly!" she crowed, as if she'd just beaten him in a card game. "She was reading me one of Laurie's letters before the baby came. 'Could never make it by himself.' That's how she put it."

"And how does that set me apart from Brendan?"

"He knows his limits. Knows where he fits in."

"Brendan's wife and kid didn't get killed in a goddamn car accident. That's where he fits in."

She looked out the window, frowning. What was she thinking or feeling? She could have been waiting for a spasm of pain to pass or for a bird to fly into sight. Maybe this was part of the "it" that supposedly he didn't get. "I'm sorry," he said. "You've been through so much crap. You don't need this."

She looked again at the picture in her lap, touched it. "Believe me, I can take it."

He nodded.

"We were always going to be all right, Bren and me," she said. "Two chipped plates from the same set."

Did Brendan have a clue as to how lucky he was? Maybe a little.

When Mike arrived at Brendan and Delores's house the next morning, the kids were already at church with their cousins.

"You look a sight better," Mike said, walking up to Brendan. He still wore the sling, but most of the swelling and discoloration on his face had faded.

"Coffee?" Brendan said, ushering him into the kitchen.

"I'm good," Mike said, taking a seat at the table.

Brendan joined him. "She's coming home tomorrow," he said triumphantly.

"I just saw her yesterday," Mike said. "She didn't mention it."

"She just got the word today, called me."

"Finally," Mike said. "The kids must be thrilled."

"Big time," Brendan said. "They're going to school like a normal day, but when they come home, we'll have a celebration. As long as she knows who the hell we are, and I don't try to flip burgers with my right arm, we'll be golden."

Mike was happy for them all. He already had plans to get someone else home on Monday. He would not intrude on their welcoming party. But he knew that Brendan hadn't called him over just to tell him about his wife's return.

"You're sure you don't want coffee?" Brendan asked.

"Nah."

"I learned some things about your guy. Ed Hearn."

"Who'd you talk to?"

"People you don't know," Brendan said. "And Tommy Coyle."

"Go ahead."

"They call him Hair. Heard of Jack Bonner?"

"Union guy."

"Used to be," he said, frowning. "He's officially clean. Owns a place, Jack's Wild, down off Second Street."

"Don't know it."

"Tommy does, no surprise. This Hair guy's from the neighborhood down there. Kid used to wear his hair like in the fifties, a ducktail or something."

"A pompadour."

"Got thrown out of Catholic school for beating the shit out of some kid that made fun of it. His old man died years ago. Bonner looked out for him. But the kid's a wannabe. Bonner's no saint. And his crew's capable of doing some nasty stuff. Trust me on that."

"Your three friends that night?"

"I'm sure of it. But Bonner's not stupid. What I hear is that he's got Hair on a short leash. Too hot-headed to be trustworthy."

Mike nodded.

"This kid got his retaliation, but he's sort of on probation. Fact is, he's on his way out with these people. His altercation at the college embarrassed Jack, not something he appreciates. Doesn't look like they're going to do anything else."

"So, I can return the .38?"

"I didn't say we've achieved world peace. Hold onto it. Cheap insurance."

"I thought these guys were all about proportion?" Mike said.

"Unless you go down to South Philly and piss on Jack's new shoes, I don't think you've got anything to worry about with the big guys."

"But this Hair?"

"A wild card."

"His healing schedule is ahead of yours."

"I don't think he can talk Bonner into using any more muscle. But if he learns that you're the guy, you never know. Might try to do something on his own."

Mike realized how much his safety depended on Brendan. A word in the wrong place, and he could be in big trouble.

"You're not seeing that teacher?"

"No," Mike said. His brother was going out of his way to help him. It still didn't make sense to Mike, like finding out some schmo he'd stolen beer with when they were in high school had become head of the Peace Corps.

"You're leveling with me," Brendan said. "Right?" He gave him a look that was pure old, scary Brendan.

"We're not together, believe me." But he was not ready to tell Brendan that he was months away from becoming a father. He had things to take care of with Sarah Goins.

37

SUNDAY, APRIL 2

After putting on her tracksuit and lacing up her new running shoes, Sarah made a fruit drink in her juicer. In a few hours, Valley Green's Sunday crowd of runners, riders, and walkers would take over Forbidden Drive, but she was arriving early enough to enjoy the broad tree-topped trail along the creek in relative quiet. She peeked at the newspaper headlines while washing down her vitamins then trotted out to the car. Driving along the avenue, she glanced at the Celtic cross on the traffic island in front of the Mermaid Inn. A tractor trailer crawled through the intersection, forcing her to stop.

Once, in January, when she had finished classes for the day, she had gone back to the Mermaid. The late afternoon light shone through the front windows' stained glass mermaids, casting a warm, varicolored glow on the wood floor. The big man with the wide shoulders puttered behind the bar. A middle-aged couple sat at the far end where the band's keyboardist had been set up, and an old man with a cigar in his mouth perched on the oak bar's middle stool, examining the head on a small glass of beer. She stayed for a ginger ale. The cigar smoker's garbled request for another Bud constituted the only words she heard. The room bore no resemblance to the place Mike had brought her to.

From where she sat in the car, she could not make out the stained glass mermaids. A car's high-pitched beep followed immediately by a deeper honk startled her. She put her foot on the gas and drove through the intersection. Five minutes later, she crossed the old stone bridge over the Wissahickon and into the creek-side parking area.

While she was stretching, a squawking mallard splashed to a stop halfway across the creek, causing uproar among the other ducks. Overhead, she heard the cries of several kinds of birds and wished she'd retained more of what she had heard in an adult evening class two years ago. She had not missed a day of running since hearing the news, and already, she felt looser and more limber. Every day, she noticed runners and walkers wearing headsets attached to radios or cassette players, but she had no inclination to get one for herself. Sure, a world of recorded music was nurturing and soothing, and she had taken to playing Mozart and Debussy on her apartment stereo, but hearing nature's sounds on her morning jaunts in the woods was best. When the developing baby could hear, she wanted the little one to be surrounded by the clopping of horses, the rush of creek water, and, most especially, glorious birdsong. Skirting the edge of the bank, two small girls and their mother tossed bits of old bread and crackers onto the water for the ducks. She pictured herself and her parents at such a place, smiles all around. She wanted never to ask for nor need rescue efforts, but in they would rush to be practical, silly, and loving.

Timing her announcement to them felt like waiting to fete them on a big birthday. She stole another look at the soft-voiced mother and her little ones, not embarrassed by her lingering smile. Sarah rose from the dewy grass, finished her stretching against an old sycamore, then set off at an easy pace along Forbidden Drive toward Harper's Meadow at the Chestnut Hill end of the park.

She took the incline at the first dam with more energy than she had felt the day before, then crested the rise above the falls at her fastest pace. Striding fast toward her came a man and a woman about her age. Even at full gallop, they carried on a conversation, nodding curtly to Sarah as they approached her. Their tops and shorts were of the same lightweight material she remembered track teams wearing when she'd taken Mike to the Penn Relays. She nodded back as they disappeared behind her, still talking. When the covered bridge came into sight, she checked her watch and lowered her speed. At Bells Mill Road, she turned around and began walking. Her next frontier would be Harper's Meadow. In another week, she should be running part of the way back from the trail's end at Northwestern Avenue.

Her father would be proud of her. His streak of good news just might be permanent. She would tell her parents her own news after she sorted out a few more pieces of the puzzle. Single-parenting wouldn't dampen their excitement, but they needed no new worries of any nature. Walking past the covered bridge, she made mental notes about the week's classes. Hearing birds at the creek's next bend, she scanned the trees high above the other shore, finally locating a small but loud wren on a branch. The chattering jogger couple came into sight again, charging from the other direction. Her gains on the trail fueled her desire to follow through on other tasks. She decided to call Mike and calmly suggest that they meet somewhere and talk. She owed him that much. She could handle it.

After stretching, she drove home then took a long shower. Over fruit salad and a piece of toast, she read all that interested her in the Sunday papers. She arrayed before her the books she was using for her literature course and her scribbled notes concerning two possible essay questions on *The Awakening*. Last week she'd determined that her first question gave students more room for analysis, but now she was unsure. The doorbell rang. She walked to the window that overlooked the street. The Reliant was parked behind her car. Even though he still had her key, he was giving her a chance to say no. She drew in a deep breath, let it out slowly, then buzzed him in.

She waited by the open door for the sound of footsteps in the hallway. The refreshed feeling from exercise and the shower had vanished, replaced by a nervousness greater than what she'd felt at the college interview. When Mike reached the doorway, he stopped. In one hand he held a small brown paper bag, in the other a rumpled plastic bag, no key in sight. Gesturing for him to come in, she forced a slight smile. "Saved me a phone call," she said, closing the door. She went ahead of him into the kitchen.

After Sarah piled her school texts to the side, Mike set his bags on the table. Reaching into his pocket, he brought out a folded sheet of loose-leaf paper, opened it, then slipped it under the plastic bag. From the paper bag, he produced two containers of hot coffee.

"Don't worry," he said, looking up. "It's decaf." He removed the lid from one cup and edged it toward her. "Skim milk."

She wrapped her hands around the steaming cup. "Actually, I decided to stop all coffee," she said. "But thanks."

She watched him open his coffee. He brought it up under his nose, smelled it, then set the cup down. When he took a seat, she sat across from him. Different kitchen, but again they sat across from each other at a familiar table. She wondered what was on the note-paper.

"You look healthy," he said. "That's the main thing." He sipped his coffee. "I knew you needed space."

She told him how displaced she'd felt when she first wondered if she might be pregnant. "I busied myself. Hadn't known whom to talk to."

He nodded gravely.

Sure now that her nervousness had lessened just a bit, she went on. It had been a confusing, scary, and lonely time, but she was managing. She'd been able to look ahead.

"If you're halfway around the world, you're still going to let me help you, right?" he said. "Even if you don't want to look at me."

"I never said I didn't want to look at you."

Mike peeked at his sheet of paper then tucked it away again. "I know this looks stupid," he said.

She had seen him angry, excited, tired, silent, but never fidgety.

"You and the baby are going to have a good life," he said, holding her gaze until she nodded. "I want you to make the most out of the situation for yourself and for the baby."

Here it comes. "Your famous plan?" she said, glancing at his paper.

"I'm still a carpenter," he said. He brought out the sheet again and slid it across the table.

He had sketched out a floor plan for his house, covered with penciled-in measurements and calculations.

"This middle bedroom," he said, pointing. "A perfect baby room."

She heard herself emit a sound that was half sigh and half gasp.

"Or I can send half of my earnings to New York," he said quickly. *God, Mike!*

"You've got options. I wanted to make sure you knew which one the father of the child endorses."

Slow. Slower yet. "I'm thinking, Mike," she said. "I'll keep thinking about all this." *Before you destroy what's left of my heart, please leave.*

"You can walk right in there," Mike said. "Today, if you want."

If he exited right now, she could empty herself of the tears she felt welling up. She needed time to let all of this wash over her. Tears, yes. And words that she had abandoned hope of ever hearing from him. *I'll be in touch. Thank you. Say it.* But hearing him and seeing his little sketches made her hope that he would linger at the table. *Hear him out.*

He removed a hardback book from the black plastic bag. "We

had a copy of this in New Paltz," he said, sliding the book across the table.

She looked at the cover: *The First Nine Months of Life.* "Geraldine Lux Flanagan," she said, running her finger across the author's name.

"One N."

She opened the book, standing it at arm's length on the table before her. "Amazing pictures." She turned the page.

"I'm sure the newer books have color photos. Look at the section on the third month."

She found the beginning of the chapter. Pictures of an embryo filled each page.

"That one," Mike said, pointing to Sarah's belly, "is already moving spontaneously. On his own. Or her own. Independent action."

"There's a lot I still need to read about this," she said. She closed the book and looked at Mike.

"You need time."

"This," she said, picking up the sheet of paper and handing it back to him. She shook her head slowly.

He folded it and put it in his pocket. He looked pained.

"I know I didn't give you much in my note," she said. "I was groping."

"It told me where you stood about the pregnancy." He patted her hand and stood up. "I work until four tomorrow. Maybe we could meet afterwards on some neutral ground, like a restaurant."

"Call me after I get home from classes."

He nodded. "You set the pace."

"Okay," she said. She followed him out of the room. When Mike started to open the door, she pushed it shut and kissed him. They hugged by the door. She leaned her head against his chest and began sobbing.

"It's all right," he said. He squeezed her to him. When she stopped crying, he eased his hold and gave her middle a gentle pat. "Whoops."

"It's all right," she said. "You didn't hurt either of us." She wiped her eyes and kissed him hard on the mouth. They hugged, swaying back and forth by the door.

"I love you so much," she said.

He kissed her forehead and hugged her even closer to him.

She grasped him around the shoulders and leaned back, looking him in the face. He looked sad to her. "Mike?"

"Come here," he said, pulling her to him.

She found his mouth and kissed him, and this time he kissed back extravagantly, backing her up a couple of steps. He kept kissing her, but he did not open his mouth like he used to. He kissed her all over her face. He found her lips and kissed her again, hard, but it was the kiss of a stranger, an actor in his first rehearsal. Finally, she pulled back again. When he opened his eyes, he looked stunned.

"You don't," she said, dropping her hands to her sides.

"Sarah, I do. Believe me, I love you. I've thought about it."

"It's not something you have to think about," she said, shaking her head. "It's something you honestly feel."

"I *told* you," he said. "I meant everything I said in there. Everything."

"It's not enough to love the baby, to want to do right by the baby. I respect your wish to help, but that doesn't mean we should act like something we're not."

"But if we both love the child," he said.

When he inched closer, she took a step back.

"You've already said you love me, Sarah. You know that I care about you. Why couldn't that be enough?"

He leaned closer, desperation all over his face. Was he forcing himself to give her space out of respect? How could she not love such tenderness? How could she not feel shattered by his willingness to deceive her, maybe both of them? "I can't help loving you right now, Mike. You can't help not loving me. It doesn't add up to whatever you think it does."

"We'd get closer and closer," he said. "It's not worth trying?"

Touch him. No. "You almost fooled me," she said. "The plans, the book."

"What matters is what you *do*."

The invisible barrier he'd put up now held her back as well. "You were trying, weren't you?" she said. "To show me that you loved me, even though that remains a question for you. Admit it."

"I admit that I'm not smart enough to be sure."

"It's not about intelligence."

"Everybody feels things. *You* have the advantage of knowing what you feel."

"You want to mean it. You wanted to convince me. You knew I wouldn't be with you unless I believed it was true."

"Why can't you just believe me?"

"You don't even believe yourself," she said. He looked like his brain was furiously running through every possible move he could make. "Mike," she said, finally. "I know that in your heart you think you're doing the right thing. But you tried to deceive me here today, and that scares me. The end does not justify the means."

"How can you be so sure it wouldn't work?"

"It's a simple test. The results are pretty clear." He no longer looked as if he were searching for answers. His look of desperation had been replaced by something darker. His fists were balled.

"'Deceive you!'" he snarled. "What I believe and mean one hundred percent is that we should *try*."

"Oh, Mike."

Through it all, he'd moved no closer to her. Now, he stepped back. "Wrong!" he yelled. "Wrong, Teacher!" He spun around and stormed out.

Sarah closed then locked the door, shaking. A loud metallic noise reverberated from the hallway. Had he kicked or slammed a trash bin? Leaning against the door, she placed both hands on her belly. "At least we know where we stand," she said. She didn't know what she would do with her feelings for him, but for the first time she believed that in time she would figure that out. Within her body, two hearts were beating. She was not alone. She owed it to her little one to slow everything, to make herself settle. She walked over to the stereo, slipped her cassette of *The Magic Flute* into the tape player, then pressed the play button.

38

TUESDAY, APRIL 4

When Domenic heard the sound of a key turning in the lock downstairs, his stomach tightened. Since yesterday's closing time, he had prepared himself for the likelihood that the only building noise he'd hear before Al opened downstairs on Thursday would be the delightful Mike Flannagan. As he drummed his fingers on the arms of his chair, he heard the door open then close. The sound of footsteps would tell the story.

"Hey," Mike called up. "A lot of fan mail down here."

Hearing his dour Samaritan clump up the stairs, he sighed, pushed himself to a standing position, then walked across the room.

Mike was at the upper door by the time Domenic reached the dining room. He nodded gruffly to him as Mike dropped a stack of junk mail onto the dining room table.

Domenic started for the kitchen, knowing Mike would head there with his bags of groceries.

"Hamburger meat," Mike said. He put the package into the refrigerator. "Second shelf."

"Right," Domenic said, taking a seat at the table.

"Milk, top shelf."

He looked at the other two plastic bags on the floor beside the kneeling Mike. They contained items from his list that were bought with his money, but he somehow felt humiliated when Mike got them for him.

"Dozen eggs. Under the cheese drawer."

"Great," he said, when Mike put the last item away in the cupboard. "Guess I can stomach another week."

"You're all right with toilet paper? Stuff like that?"

"Maybe next week's list," Domenic said. The dishes from breakfast and lunch still sat in the sink, last night's pots and pans occupied the dry rack. *You'll get no apology from me.* He turned so he didn't have to look at the mess.

"I'll call Monday night," Mike said, lingering in the doorway.

Domenic nodded.

"That shirt's getting a workout," Mike said.

He had meant to change before Mike got there but had forgotten. "So's your mouth."

"Christ, you're more miserable than me," Mike said. "Congratulations. That's gotta be worth some kind of prize."

"Why do you do this?"

Mike sighed.

If he wanted to leave, he'd just hit the bricks. *You're fair game.* "Penance?"

"I don't do the hocus-pocus anymore, remember?"

"Just the blasphemy."

"Did I put some dog shit in your refrigerator?"

Something had stirred his pot before he got to the apartment. Domenic rose and started down the hallway. For once, he was exiting a room before Mike Flannagan did. He felt Mike walking a few steps behind. *Do I have a magnet on me, or what?* "I don't like what you did to her," he said as he entered the living room.

"I'm not wild about it myself," Mike said, now in the living room.

Domenic settled himself on the bed across from the pictures.

Mike stood, facing him, with his arms crossed. "I'm not exactly high on her list either," he said.

"What do you mean 'either'?"

"You can't be happy she's icing you out."

Domenic bristled, rising to his feet. "It's not like that." He jerked the covers on his bed to where they should be and repositioned his pillow.

"She's got bigger fish to fry. It's bound to happen."

"That's a terrible way to talk about the baby," Domenic barked, spinning around. He sat back on the bedspread, eyes on the hallway.

"I mean everything she's dealing with. Try not to take it personally."

"This is the voice of experience?"

"I'm guessing it's not the same."

Domenic's face grew hot. How could anybody anger him with so few words? He turned to Mike. "You think I'm jealous?" he said.

"If you are, you picked the wrong guy to be jealous of," Mike said. His glare was cold, like a shark's.

"I'm not jealous of you."

"I couldn't tell you what the word is," Mike said.

"At least I never did anything to her to make her hate me."

Mike's steely expression held. Predators had that look just before launching themselves at prey.

"Yeah, I've retired that prize," Mike said. "Not the best thing to do when somebody's carrying around your baby. How's that for stupid?"

Domenic studied him. "What is it, Mike? What's got you like this?"

Mike squinted at him. Had he hit him below the belt?

"You," Mike whispered.

"Wait," Domenic said. "You're pissed at me because I've pissed her off so much that she's getting out of Dodge?"

"Fucking ingrate."

"Hard to believe such charm didn't win her over."

Mike spun around toward the hallway and tramped away.

When the door slammed downstairs, Domenic closed his eyes. Sarah dumping Mike was old news. Must be something else. Anger and despair like that scared him. He remembered what it felt like to be flamed to the point that he'd look at his Angela the way Mike had looked at him. Had hoped Mike could unload some of it by directing it toward everybody's favorite sick old man. Another failure.

Domenic could take the abuse. Hell, he owed it to the damn guy. All week, he'd felt detached from everyone he knew, but Mike's nastiness had given him a change of perspective. It was a crazy connection, for sure. But he wasn't done with Mike Flannagan.

39

THURSDAY, APRIL 6

Balance, Sarah thought, as she drove from her apartment to the barbershop en route to Domenic's with a welcome-home food package. Since Mike's roller-coaster visit, she'd noticed that she was able to run harder and longer. All tasks at home or on campus felt less onerous. She felt a lightness in her step. Diet and exercise were working. But she had Mike to thank for the change that mattered most. His deception seemed to have administered the coup de grace to her foolish ideas about them as a couple. Not long after he'd kicked his way down the hallway, that moment of feeling totally alone quickly departed too, as she realized that she carried within her body the other half of the couple that did matter. From the start, she'd been awed that a new person was growing inside, but now she saw that serving as host was making a new person of her. She did have to credit him for giving her the book, her new obsession.

Job interview? Bring it on. Demonstration class for the hiring committee? Get your notebooks ready. Taking steps. She laughed, remembering a house concert she attended with Russell. The funny English folk singer had signed the cover of his LP record with his act's tagline question: "And what steps do you intend to take?" Underneath, he scrawled "FGBO." Years later, she'd stumbled across the album in a box she hadn't been through since the divorce. *FGBO?* As with so much of her marriage, heavy fog had descended on that night. Weeks later, grading papers, it came back to her: Fucking Great Big Ones. *Indeed.*

At the barbershop, Nick eschewed her offer to help him with his Mount Airy Day presentation, promising that next Thursday he would show her what he had prepared. *Out of my control.* "See you then," she said cheerily.

"I need to see him," she said to Al, nodding at the ceiling. He knew that she'd given her key to Mike but had said nothing about it. Al reached into his cash register and fished a key out of one of the little coin compartments. Placing it into her outstretched hand, he closed it around the key, then with both of his hands, gently squeezed hers.

Upstairs, everything she saw indicated that Domenic had followed his medical instructions, though the place could do with some tidying. Propped up in his bed, he told her he hadn't been downstairs at all. "I have to be resigned to my situation," he said. "We all do."

She nodded, standing at the foot of the bed.

"Mike brought groceries again the other night," he told her.

"He came over to see me," she said evenly.

"He didn't want to talk about that," Domenic said. "You don't have to talk about it, either."

"Nothing to talk about," she said, sitting on the bedside chair. "As far as he and I are concerned."

"None of my business, but I didn't think there was much to talk about between you two."

"Ha," she said. "Touché." Was she the only person who hadn't seen how wrong they were as a couple?

Shaking his head, he looked miserable and vulnerable to her.

When he turned back to her, she said, "I'm not going to try to cheer you up, Domenic. You're right about reaching. But reaching goes both ways. People have to reach back too." *Bastard Mike.*

He made a harrumphing noise, his facial expression souring more.

Did he hate this confinement? Did he miss the give-and-take downstairs? "You're not going to stay frozen in your tracks," she said. "When you need to make a move, you'll know what to do."

He made that sound again.

"And you won't worry about what anybody thinks or says."

"You're right about that."

"Even though inside you really don't believe that now. I know it's not easy to be yourself when things give out on you, but it'll be there when you need it."

"What will be?"

"Domenic," she said. "You will be there."

The bitterness on his face had been replaced by a look of genuine curiosity. "Are you talking about me?" he said. "What's got into you?"

My God. He'd put her on the back foot. Sure, some of that could apply to her, but she'd been thinking about him the whole time. "I'm talking about Domenic Gallo, but, yes, I have this drive these days— and I'm convinced you do too."

"Hmm."

"A guy I teach with is a jazz drummer. When he was in grad school and working a full-time job, he wouldn't get back to his apartment until late at night. Banging his drums kept him sane. He'd get home, change clothes, and sit down at his kit, no matter what time it was. 'Hope they like it!' he'd say, and let it rip."

"I don't play the drums."

"Madonna," she muttered. "We're going to kick butt, you and I!"

"Feeling your oats," he said, casting her a dubious look.

"I don't mean it's easy." So far, the week had been anything but easy at the college. Despite her ongoing professional grievances, she hadn't slowed down.

He had a pensive look in his eyes.

"What?" she said.

"I can't think of anything that's easy," he said.

They shared a loud, dark laugh.

"I don't know anyone," she said, "who says things that make me laugh and cry at the same time."

She was glad he seemed to take that as a compliment. It was a good time to leave.

Driving home, she felt a disturbing sense of relief that she'd left when she did. She'd not told Domenic about her mandated meetings with the counselor at the college. In yesterday's session, the woman, a perfectly decent person whom she trusted, had caught her up short. Sarah had told her about the job possibility in New York and about the dramatic turning point with Mike. "Does that make it easier to leave Philadelphia?" she'd asked Sarah. In a way, yes. "Your other connections here, friends, adoptive family members. Hard to leave?" She'd said no. Now she felt the weight of the counselor's question. She felt closer and closer to Domenic and to the crew downstairs. Had she picked the worst possible time to begin new friendships?

At her Monday appointment, Dr. Stafford told her that both she and baby were healthy. So far, her exercise and diet had nearly offset any weight increase from growth of the baby.

"Enjoy that while you can," the doctor kidded her.

Still, she smiled at the small increase in her body weight and the snugness of her clothes. Hardly enough to send her out for maternity clothes, but it was something.

After confirming with Brooklyn College that her teaching

demonstration and final interview would take place on Friday, she consulted her calendar. Her father's treatments and her semester's teaching activities would both conclude by the end of the month. At some point in the past week, she'd realized that her unease about the job-seeking process had disappeared. The imminent prospect of putting herself on the line now felt almost as routine as preparing to teach a new text to her own students. This surprised her, considering her conviction that securing this job would prove key to her future, and to her baby's future. The hiring decision would not be finalized until sometime in May, when she'd be ready to break her other news to her parents.

At the barbershop the day before her interview, she listened to the boys' discussion about whether Mike Schmidt's three home run week should call into question Nick's fears that the star third baseman was washed up. Since the shop was always closed on Wednesdays, they had two days' worth of newspapers to discuss each Thursday. Twice as much gristle for the chatter mill. They duly noted the deaths of Sugar Ray Robinson and Abbie Hoffman amidst the usual skewering of the local sports teams. When the conversation finally reached a lull, she cleared her throat and asked Nick if he wanted to discuss the speech.

"You're going to kill me," he said. "I forgot it."

She smiled wanly and said she would be back the following Thursday.

"Mike's supposed to stop by tonight with some groceries," Al said, gesturing upstairs.

She hadn't mentioned that she planned to go upstairs after her visit to the shop but now realized that she could postpone that stop until next week. The relief that swept over her gave way to a brief pang of guilt, but she said goodbye to the boys, closed the door behind her, and walked briskly toward her car.

Sarah woke up early enough the next day to take a short run and down a yogurt drink before heading for the train station. After purchasing her round trip ticket and a newspaper, she wandered around the 30th Street Station concourse. Like a slot machine's clicking numbers, the electronic board's letters and numbers flipped over and over, the scramble replacing the board's top listing with the Washington-bound train, up from the second line. Her New York train now sat second from the bottom.

She strolled across the floor to the base of the towering statue at the concourse's other end. Smooth and as dark as the statue itself, the lean, vertical base looked more like a part of the sculpture than its support. She circled the base, scanning the engraved names of Pennsylvania Railroad workers who had died in World War II. Near the floor, a soldier's helmet was carved in high relief on the front of the long block. She tilted her head back, taking in the tremendous length of the helmetless dead soldier borne by the angel.

That this statue once had caught her father's eye hardly surprised her. From any vantage point in the great hall, the statue's verticality drew attention, the angel with its lifeless burden appearing to be rising from the floor of the station. The illusion of motion brought footage of rocket launches to mind. All that power at liftoff, in what looked like slow motion.

She felt around in her pocket for her ticket. By itself, the opportunity ahead of her represented a success, the result of all the work she had done since graduate school. If she didn't get this job, different doors would open. This challenge allowed her to play a role in its outcome, just like the baby, she thought, proud of her healthy habits. *But suppose Dad's cancer returns? He could die before I move back to New York.* Such doom and gloom went against all available information, but staring at the board, the surety and emptiness of loss overwhelmed her. The numbers and letters scrambled, leaving her train second from the top. The feeling passed. The board scrambled again, and when it stopped, her train topped the list. The announcement to board echoed in the concourse. She bent to pick up her bag, tucked her newspaper under her arm, and strode off toward her gate.

Before any of the three members of the committee could begin their questioning, she told them she was pregnant and that if they hired her, she wouldn't be able to start teaching until the January term. Sarah was pleased that they were only slightly taken aback by her announcement. By the end of her day on campus, the response from the faculty she'd just met was as warm as the first group's was. They told her the selection process should conclude within a few weeks.

During her short visit, she told her parents how comfortable she'd felt at Brooklyn College. Her father would be in between treatments on Mount Airy Day, so they both planned to visit. Bonus treatments, he called them. Icing on the cake. She left New York nervous, with the same healthy anxiety she felt in senior year of high school when she'd received scholarship offers from five good colleges.

Back in Philadelphia, paper and exam grading forced her to pare down her exercise routine from seven days a week to four. Rest was part of training, she reminded herself. Semesters always ended in a binge of grading, but this one provided valuable diversion. On her next visit to the shop, Nick presented her with an indecipherable loose-leaf sheet of scribbling. "The first half of my speech," he said.

"Great," she said, sighing.

On the day she turned in final grades, Sarah notified her landlady that she would be moving out by the end of June. If the job in New

York didn't pan out and she remained in Philadelphia, she could find another apartment. She wanted a new address for her new life.

Two weeks before Mount Airy Day, she asked Nick about his presentation.

"If I'm not worried," he said, "you shouldn't be."

"I teach speech," she said.

"She don't trust you," Clement said to Nick.

"Look," Nick said. "If Clement here has confidence in me, it must be a done deal."

"A no-brainer," Clement said.

Al hustled out to catch her when she left the shop. Domenic hadn't been doing or saying much, Mike hadn't been visiting. A quick visit from Sarah might work wonders, he said. "Can't do it now," she said, truthfully. She'd see him on Mount Airy Day for sure. She vowed to herself to see him before then but said nothing in case it didn't work out. On campus, she ran into Leona at the copy center, exchanging breezy small talk as if they'd never done anything more than that. She walked away with chilled relief.

Through the week, she rid the apartment of old clothes, two shelves of books, three cardboard containers of magazines, a table lamp she'd never liked, the faux Oriental rug in her bedroom, and the used bicycle in her basement storage unit. The purge of things that just didn't make the cut for her next residence filled her hours while stoking her for the next day's list of activities.

The Thursday before Mount Airy Day, an all-day meeting at the college prevented her from stopping at the shop or visiting Domenic. She heated up some leftovers and began preparing the apartment for her parents' visit. As always, house cleaning invigorated her and gave her a chance to think through the upcoming weekend. The vitamins in the kitchen could be easily explained, but she stashed the pregnancy books in a closet. In two weeks, she would have an ultrasound. Then she would tell her parents.

When she met them at 30th Street Station on Friday, they were each gripping a pair of bags. Before she could say a word, her father announced that the doctors' tests couldn't find any more bad guys in him.

"He wanted to surprise you in person," her mother said. They hugged each other, crying in the middle of the great hall. *They have the whole weekend ahead of them, meeting Domenic and the gang, seeing the community strut its stuff. Wait. Give this good news the attention it deserves.*

"Let's not make a complete spectacle out of ourselves," her father said, wiping his eyes.

She hugged her parents, not sure who was the giddiest. Suddenly, the weekend felt like a present to her.

Wresting a bag from each of them, she led them toward the exit. "I asked someone I know in the art department about that statue," she said, stopping to turn toward it. "It's a memorial."

"World War II," her father said, looking up.

"It's called the 'Angel of the Resurrection.' Took the sculptor five and a half years, 1952."

"I can't imagine," her mother said.

In the car, on the way to South Street Souvlaki, her mother told her that she looked well. "Robust," she said.

"Haven't stopped eating since midterms," Sarah said, patting her middle.

40

SATURDAY, MAY 6

On Saturday morning, before her parents were up, Sarah made herself a yogurt drink. When they were ready, she drove up the avenue as close as parking was allowed. The three of them walked the last block to the edge of the business district. As far as she could see down the avenue, food and craft vendors were bustling at displays and tables in front of the shops. She'd told her parents how much she wanted them to meet Domenic and the guys at the shop. The community day hardly seemed like a Mike Flannagan event, and if he saw her, he'd probably turn right around.

With her first bite of a sticky bun at the Lutheran seminary's table, her mother pronounced Mount Airy Day a success. People had gathered at almost every table, but the middle of the avenue was still easily passable. From previous years, Sarah knew that by early afternoon the two-block trip from one end of the fete to the other could take a good half hour. An empty table stood below the curb at the barbershop, one of the few unmanned spots. They took seats at the Durham Street stage to watch a troupe of young dancers in leotards doing jazz tap. When the dancers had finished their last routine, Sarah and her parents stood with the rest of the audience and applauded. She told her parents that the man she had been interviewing would give his living history presentation here.

After they went to the far end and back, her parents told her that they were going off on their own then disappeared into the crowd. Sarah asked the teenager on a stool behind the information stand for a schedule. Al was very hush-hush about the activity he'd okayed for the front of his shop. Whatever it was, it wasn't getting an early start.

"He's coming down?" she said.

"That's what he told me," Al said. "Said he'll be his helpful self."

Helpful did not describe her these last weeks. Her face flushed in shame. The counselor had been onto something. She'd been dodging him, hoping to avoid unnecessary pain that might be around the corner. Was she making things easier for him? Probably not. *What will I say to him?*

She scanned the sheet. Nick's speech was listed for four o'clock. The sheet's other side listed all of the sponsored activities. "Al's Barbershop," she read aloud. "Bingo."

She strolled the avenue, pausing to admire pottery in front of the dry cleaners' shop. A neighbor from her building tapped her shoulder. "It's sick," the woman tsked. "Flouting such inhumane notions! What a lesson for children."

A crowd blocked Sarah's view of the front of Gilhooley's.

"See for yourself." The woman huffed, stomping away in the opposite direction.

Passing the penny toss fountain and dollar plant display in front of the florist, she saw it. Tommy Coyle, decked out in camouflage gear from head to toe, stood behind a table. A four-by-eight sheet of plywood was propped up behind him, a sign taped across its top: "Your Woods, Your Choice—Vote Here."

"Twenty-five cents a shot!" he barked at the crowd. "All proceeds to charity!"

Three makeshift targets, colorful cardboard pictures right off of an elementary school bulletin board, had been duct-taped to the

plywood. A deer with a full rack of antlers. A hunter in red plaid aiming a rifle at the majestic buck beside him. On the right, protectively
positioned in front of a small doe, a sickly green Gumby-like figure,
staring bug-eyed through oversized spectacles at the crowd. A large
plastic bucket hung below each target.

On the counter in front of the targets lay what Sarah hoped
were merely air rifles. Tommy worked the passing crowd. "Vote the
American way!"

Idiot. She wanted to throw something at him.

One person stood at the table, aiming a rifle. When he pulled
the trigger, a cork struck the picture of the Gumby figure, falling
into the bucket. "Another vote recorded!" Tommy bellowed in his
best barker voice. "Another American heard from! Quarter a shot,
five for a buck!"

"Here you go," a man said, handing a dollar to Tommy.

Fuming, Sarah walked as close to the table as she dared, trying not
to draw the attention of Tommy or his assistant. Two targets looked in
mint condition, but the deer-guarding Gumby showed the effects of
all the corks that had smacked against it. A handful of corks sat in the
other buckets. She glared at the drooping Gumby bucket.

Bang. Another cork plunked against the target then dropped into
the bucket.

"Democracy in action!" Tommy yelled.

When Tommy turned in her direction, she spun around then
walked away from the shooting gallery. A finger prodded her shoulder
from behind.

"Why didn't we come up with something like that?" Nick asked.
He pointed at Tommy's setup.

"A tribute to man's ingenuity," she said, smirking.

"I was first in line," he said. "Two bucks' worth."

"You're so proud," she said. They would have their fun. She realized that steaming over Tommy's nonsense had given her a break from self-flagellation. "Is Domenic around?"

"Haven't seen him yet."

"What's with the bingo?"

"Al and Clement cooked it up. Got donations, borrowed the PA system from St. Vincent's. Al's setting up now. Saw you over here and couldn't resist. Getting out the vote?"

"Oh, stop it," she said and spun away. She made her way through the crowd. When she reached the shop, the door was open and Al was bringing a sign outside. Clement stood by a long table stacked high with bingo cards, pulling brightly colored stuffed animals from one of several large cardboard boxes. Behind him sat two wheels of fortune, one with numbers running the perimeter of its circle and the other with B-I-N-G-O spelled out three times around its circle.

Al leaned the sign against the shop window: All Proceeds Go To Germantown Soup Kitchen. Clement looked up from the box of stuffed animals. "He won't come down," he said, craning his head toward the upstairs apartment.

"Won't even come to the window," Al said.

"Weasel," Nick said. All the chairs from the shop had been brought outside, along with some folding chairs and several long tables Nick had borrowed from Holy Cross. He started setting up chairs around the tables.

"But he'd love this," Sarah said.

"That was the idea," Clement said.

She looked up at the curtained windows above the shop, as angry with him as she was with herself.

"He was supposed to come down and sit behind the table," Nick said, pointing at his regular chair.

"The catbird seat," Clement said. "And call numbers through a microphone. Perfect, huh?"

How could he? Her parents would not get to meet him. *Focus.*

Al moved one of the wheels to the side of the chair behind the table. He made sure it was steady then set up the other one.

"When do you start?" Sarah said.

"A half hour ago," Al said.

"Can I help?" she asked.

They all stopped what they were doing and smiled at her. "Guess who we're counting on to do the first shift in the catbird seat, honey?" Al said.

When Nick gave her a break from running the bingo game, Sarah explored the displays and stands at the east end of the festival. Beneath the nearly cloudless sky, people were dressed for a summer day. Wafting odors of beef and lamb drew her to the karate dojo stand. Deciding that one day's food folly would hurt neither her nor her baby, she ordered a beef roll-up. Nibbling it, she walked to the Durham Street stage, where four Irish musicians were playing a furiously paced tune. She arrived to find a crowd clapping in time with the fiddle, uilleann pipes, tenor banjo, and guitar. She found an empty seat in the back row.

When the tune ended and the hooting and applause died down, the guitarist set his Martin on a stand and picked up another stringed instrument. "I'll play the cittern on this next ballad," he announced. He adjusted the tuning on his strings then started picking a slow, sweet introduction. Sarah scanned the crowd, hoping to glimpse her parents, but people crisscrossing in the street made the task difficult. When she spotted someone up front who looked like her father, she stood. Not him. After a couple in the fourth row rose and left, she recognized the back of Mike Flannagan's head in the row in front of them. She dropped back onto her chair with a deep sigh.

Since his visit, she'd played out a dozen different interactions with him, all of which ended with her feeling vaguely triumphant, no matter what nonsense he offered. Now, her stomach twisted and no clever words came to mind.

The song told of a young maid's lament about her lost love, reminding Sarah of a Scottish ballad she'd heard at the Folk Festival once. The musician sang the maid's pleas to the Belfast Mountains, but neither mountain nor man would ease her pain. Maudlin. Pathetic. Still, she felt the lyric's sting.

Encouraged by the singer, the audience joined in on the chorus, but Sarah silently pondered what Mike might say to her if he saw her. Regret? Anger? Maybe just an evil look.

By the end of the next verse, the maid was defiantly cursing the cur that had broken her heart, wishing him ruin.

Sarah brought her hand up to her forehead to block the blinding sun. Her hot face cooled. The singer closed his eyes. He might sing this song a hundred times a year, but he looked like he felt the full weight of the maid's grief and bitterness.

As the singer and the crowd sang the chorus again, Sarah rose and started back toward the barbershop. Yes. Better to burn with fury and conviction than to wallow in sadness and hurt. Easier said than done. She dumped her crumpled napkin and wrapper in a trash can, avoiding Mike's sight line. Did he see himself as the victim in their story?

Walking into sight of the bingo game, she glimpsed Nick's wild waving. It was her turn. People of all sizes and ages filled the seats. After calling the first game, she realized that before today she had never done anything remotely like this. Wherever she and the baby landed, she hoped they'd be part of something like this. A half hour later, her parents emerged from the barbershop. They moved into a patch of shade near the wall. She glanced up at the second-floor window. Nothing. Apparently, today was not a reaching day for Domenic. The sadness she thought she'd left at the Irish stage rushed through her. "Under the G," she called. "Six."

"Bingo!" a man in the back yelled. Nick walked over to him to check his game card.

A few games later, Clement brought over a young man he knew from church to replace her. When she found her parents, her mother showed her a small plant they had bought for her apartment and told her about the snacks they sampled in their travels up and down the block.

"Over at the deer hunting place," her mother said, "your father became the first person to shoot a hunter."

"Please," Sarah said, laughing.

"A few old hippie types followed suit," he said, pleased.

When her parents moved off toward the Jamaican grill, she noticed Mike standing alone at the back of the bingo crowd. Except for him, everyone watching the bingo game was smiling. She felt no urge to hold him, scold him, or dodge him, but she recalled the counselor's gentle interruption during Sarah's rant about all the noise in her life: "It only feels like that noise is all about us." She walked over and stood beside him until he noticed her. "Can we find a spot where we can talk?" she asked.

"If you want," he said, his blank expression intact.

When she stepped off the sidewalk and waded into the crowd, he followed her. She pointed to Gilhooley's. "They're open," she said, pausing in the crowd to catch his eye. "Why don't I buy you a quick beer."

He looked at her as if she were speaking a foreign language.

"Just one."

"One," he said, then they walked into the bar together for the first time.

Every stool inside was taken, but the two booths at the front were empty, so they sat in the one against the side wall. Tommy Coyle walked up from the men's room and joined a couple of guys at the short end of the bar. He picked up a half-finished mug of beer and looked in their direction. "Hey!"

"Yo, Tommy," Sarah said. "Beer break?"

"Finally," he said, turning to his friends at the bar.

"You know him?" Mike's mouth fell open.

"Yeah," she said. "If I was drinking, we'd get a pitcher. It's lemonade for me. I'll get you a Yuengling, all right?"

When she delivered their drinks from the bar, she urged Mike to try some of the street food when he went back out.

"Doesn't call to me," he said. He sipped his beer.

"This'll be it for me," she said, jiggling the ice in her lemonade. "Have to get to the Durham Street stage for the oral histories." When she explained Nick's presentation, he seemed impressed.

"That's not what I dragged you over here for, though," she said. "Good chance that I'm heading to New York soon, job or not."

Frowning, he nodded. He set his beer on the table.

"I'm hopeful about the job. I should hear back soon."

"Right."

"You'll know about everything," she said. "I'm not going to drop off the face of the Earth."

"I'm sure you don't expect me to be doing cartwheels of joy right now."

"No," she said softly.

"I'm not going to make trouble for you, Sarah," he said, lowering his voice. He leaned forward. "But I have to be in the child's life."

"You will be. I promise you. And we'll be back to Philly." She was not surprised that his expression remained strained but hoped that inside him something had registered, and that he could trust her. "I will get you my address and phone number as soon as I'm settled."

"Please," he said.

"You'll be the first person I tell."

He shifted in his seat, his thumb and index finger turning his beer coaster right then left as if he were working a puzzle. But some of the stress had left his face. "You'll be safe there at least," he said, looking up.

The two of us. "There's something else."

"Hit me," he said.

"Domenic's holed up in his apartment. Won't acknowledge anything going on outside today."

"Domenic," he sighed. He took a long drink of his beer.

"He's in a bad place."

"I know. He hated me for bringing him food. Now he probably hates me for not bringing it."

"Al says he's lost a lot of his fire," she said.

"No offense," he said, gently fixing his eyes on hers. "We both know that we've gone over this ground before. Is something that different?"

"He's not even coming down to the shop," Sarah said, then took a sip from her drink. *You can do this. Find the right words.* "You know how important his routine is for him. He can't go to church or bingo. He won't even look out his window at the bingo game they've cooked up for him today."

Mike nodded.

"He's sad, angry, afraid," she said. "You know about his wife?"

"She died about ten years ago."

"He talked to me about her miscarriage."

"Never said anything about that to me."

"It's like it happened just the other day," she said. "She was upstairs one night. She'd already lost two others. He was listening to a ball game on the radio."

"Phillies," he said.

"I guess. Anyway, he said it was never the same after that. For either of them. Part of their lives ended that night. Somehow, he connected the miscarriage to her getting cancer, even though that didn't happen until many years later. I'm not sure if he's angry at her, at God, or at himself, but a dark cloud hovers over the guy."

"Yep."

"His wife was everything to him," she said, watching a frown form on Mike's face. Had he already decided against reconnecting with Domenic? "I think he faults himself."

Mike's expression was grave. "I *capisce*," he said.

"Twenty-five years."

A puzzled look spread across his face. Leaning back, he looked off, his brow furrowed. "Nineteen sixty-four?" he said.

"Says her spirit died that night," she said. "September twenty-first."

Mike grimaced.

"He remembers every detail about that day, how everything looked. The candles and the lights under those pictures have something to do with that night, but don't ask me what."

Mike stared intently at his glass. "Jesus," he muttered. For a moment, she tried to imagine him at Domenic's age, but all she could see was a man with less erect posture, a bitter old man in a bar.

"I'm just thinking out loud," she said.

He was watching her closely now, undoubtedly waiting for her next move before saying or doing anything. She had seen that look before. "Just wanted to let you know." It was no time to push anything with Mike. At least she'd tried. She felt the eyes of the other patrons on them. She would not make this strange encounter worse for either of them. "Thank you for listening," she said. Smiling for everyone to see, she stood up.

Two steps toward the door, she spun around. "The book you gave me," she said. "It's fantastic. I read it every day." Now her smile was genuine.

"Good," Mike said, rising then catching up to her.

Their entrance into Gilhooley's, probably their one and only, might have given the impression that they were a couple. Throughout their conversation, body language and facial expressions had to have conveyed their awkwardness, but couples had such moments. She'd started out of the place on her own—as if they weren't a couple—then after she remembered to tell him about the book, he joined her and they walked together to the door. What on Earth did people think they were? This afternoon's awkward dance suited their entire history.

When they reached the door, Mike held it open for her. She walked past him into the light and noise of the afternoon.

41

SATURDAY, MAY 6

Outside, competing bands blared from loudspeakers at both ends of the avenue. Mike watched Sarah stop in the middle of the street to look up at Domenic's empty window. Maybe she was determined to wait the old guy out.

A breeze swirled through, a nice cool feeling after the stuffy barroom. Gabbing couples and families picked their way around one another without seeming to miss a beat in their conversations. Their lives couldn't be as simple or normal as they seemed to him. He stepped back so a couple his age could squeeze by. They were all here. Cat people. Dog people. Old neighborhood types. Sarah's kind. Watching them bustle and jabber, he felt empty. The place anchored them. If Mrs. Lamont hadn't shamed him into at least walking by the festivities, he would have stayed home with Robert. Another reason for the old guy to hole up in his apartment.

Finally, Sarah turned and slipped into the flow of people heading toward Durham Street. He watched her until she disappeared. She and their baby. How long would it be until he could spend a day, a night with the child? Like a man behind bars, he'd have to do the time. Another wrong he must live with. He would do it, become the kind of person that their little one would want to call Dad. But that wasn't going to happen overnight.

Head left or right? The beer had made him hungry, and tempting food smells wafted from both directions. Home was to the right. The stage Sarah had talked about would be on his way. Yes, he was a mess—as Sarah would say—but Domenic made him look like Joe Happy. Now it made more sense though. *Nineteen sixty-four.* Domenic had suffered the loss of more than the National League pennant. Mike turned right and moved into the snaking crowd.

Three stores up, a savory whiff of beef drew him toward the grill in front of the karate place. Putting something into his stomach might rid him of his headache and help him think. The building where he stood had been a paint store when he was a kid. Behind the grill, three gaunt, sweaty men in white cotton shirts were grilling meat. *What the hell.*

"Beef," Mike said, absently.

"With rice or like a cheesesteak?" the man said. He held up an Italian roll. "With bean sprouts, special sauce."

"Sandwich," he said.

Mike watched the man scoop the bean sprouts, peppers, and steak onto a long hoagie roll. He wrapped the sandwich in foil, placed it in a bag, and handed it to Mike. He carried his bag toward the Durham Street stage. People already were clustered near the front, leaving empty rows from the middle on back. He chose a seat in the center of the back row. A large banner on the edge of the stage listed the day's activities: Rhythm Steppers at twelve, Sounds of Glorious Praise at one, Poetry Circle at two, Bent Elbow Room at three. He recognized Jimmy Sweeney and Fats Fuller clearing microphone stands and amplifiers from the stage.

Living History Aloud, listed for four o'clock, would be the last event. Two shaggy teenagers set up a podium with a built-in mic at the center of the stage and fashioned a semicircle of chairs facing the audience. A small group, mostly seniors, milled around the side of the stage. Nick walked into view. When he moved again, Mike saw that he was chatting with Clement, Al, and a woman he assumed to be Al's wife. Sarah joined them, sparking a hugfest.

Mike's sandwich was steaming when he opened the bag. Its teasing aroma overpowered him. His first bite into the sauce and juice–soaked roll sold him.

Nick and several others convened on the stage and settled into the chairs. He watched Sarah make her way to a seat in the front row beside a short bald man and a woman whose hair was the same color and thickness as hers. An introduction of sorts, he thought.

Mike finished his sandwich, stuck the foil back into the brown paper bag, then leaned back. A scrawny middle-aged man in wire-rimmed glasses tapped the microphone then began speaking. As the MC rambled on about the neighborhood's unique history, Mike's eyes followed Sarah. She leaned over and whispered something to her parents. The historian from Temple told the audience about early Native American activity and about the area's development as part of the "German Township," which eventually became part of the city. The MC announced that the speakers would proceed in reverse chronological order.

A seven-year-old Black child spoke about recent changes she had seen in the neighborhood. A white kid wearing a Mount Airy Little League baseball shirt covered the period just before that. Before Mike knew it, a middle-aged white man was talking about resistance to blockbusting. A World War II veteran who had driven a truck in France and Germany, one of the few Black people who lived in the area at the time, described what the neighborhood had been like during the war years. An old white woman described the local reaction to Hitler's rise and to Pearl Harbor. Nick was the only remaining speaker. According to the MC, Nick was the oldest neighborhood person willing to speak.

"The thirties," Nick began. "I won't talk about the roaring twenties, because I wasn't doing too much roaring most of that time, as I was a kid.

"I worked in North Philly in different factories in those days. Lived right here on Howard Terrace. Like you've heard other people say today, the shopping area at that time wasn't much like this. It was tidy. You had your movie theater, five barbershops in a two-block area. You had places to eat, bakeries, and a delicatessen. You had clean streets. It's just the way people were."

Nick's poise impressed Mike. As much as he could tell, Sarah seemed pleased. Off to the side of the stage, Clement and the crew all had their eyes glued on their buddy. Nick took the listeners through a typical neighborhood weekday and weekend, even got a huge laugh at one spot. Sarah had told him that the program's closing act was to be its longest. Five minutes into his speech, Nick had the crowd eating out of his hands.

"That's not the way it was for everybody, as you know," Nick said. "But I can't talk about that. I know I'm supposed to do this myself, but that doesn't make sense, so I'm going to have to bend the rules a little. Time to let somebody who would have liked to live here back then talk about what it was like for him. Clement Fuller."

Clement climbed up to the stage. The principals, including Al, seemed confused. Sarah looked up at the podium. Nick and Clement exchanged places.

"I saw some of the things Nick talked about," Clement said. "Lived in West Philly but worked up in Chestnut Hill, so I rode the trolley through this neighborhood many times. There weren't many folks like me around here at the time, but there was one place I knew as well as Nick did. I loved the movies as a young person. Still do. Those days, if you were Black, there weren't many movie houses in the city you could walk into and sit where you wanted. This here theater up the street has been closed down a long time. I didn't know Nick when it was open, and I've known Nick for quite some time. If we had known each other then, we both could have enjoyed the same movies and shows in that that beautiful space. I knew I could go there and not worry. Remember, there were movie houses all up and down the avenue in those days, from Chestnut Hill all the way to Center City.

"After those good times in the theater here, I got the idea that this would be a good place to live. Time came when I did that."

Listeners gazed with rapt attention. If the do-gooders had come up with this, it might have bothered him, but Nick and Clement doing this on their own struck him as just right. When Clement finished, he called Nick over and they stood side by side at the podium, smiling back at the crowd that was on its feet, roaring in approval. Sarah had to be crying. Like Mike and everyone else, she and her parents were standing and applauding. Mike watched the organizers swarm Clement and Nick, giving them hug after hug. When the crowd started to clear, the two friends walked off toward the barbershop with Al and his wife and Sarah's group. Sarah had engineered something good. With New York bidding, this might be her curtain call.

When the crew dissolved into the crowd, Mike started walking home. *New York?* He hated the thought of being that far from the baby, but it wasn't his call. He would focus on what *he* could do. At Mount Pleasant Avenue, he walked past the last of the festival's booths and displays. He continued down the empty stretch of street, still thinking about the barbershop guys. No big fuss, they'd just done the right thing.

Something stirred in him—not the sweet yet painful yearning that accompanied falling in love but close enough to have jostled that memory. He would do something, set a course. Even if what he did heightened the awkward sensation, he would do it.

After taking Robert to the lot up the street, he paused on the front porch and looked down his terraced concrete steps. He counted them and gauged the drop from the porch to the sidewalk. He walked through every room of his house. He stood out on the back shed steps, surveying the driveway. The ground to floor level in the back was far shorter than in the front. Back inside, he stood in the opening between the living room and dining room, examining one room then the other, calculating dimensions.

On Monday, after work, Mike drove to the barbershop. No sign remained of the fair two days earlier. As he opened the door, Al was cutting a tanned construction worker's hair. Nick and Clement lounged in their usual places.

"How you doing?" Mike said, glancing around the room. They nodded.

"Everything else's got a name," Nick said, turning back to Clement. "Saturn, Pluto, even Uranus." He burst into laughter.

As Nick weathered a chorus of groans, Mike sat down in the middle of the row of chairs.

"And I took you serious," Clement said.

"I couldn't resist," Nick said. "But I *am* serious. Every damn planet has its own name. Every tiny star out there in the galaxy's got a name. Why not the moon?"

"It's the moon," the customer in Al's chair said gruffly. "There's only one. The moon's its name. Simple."

"You're as simple as that one," Nick said, cocking his thumb toward Clement. "What about the other planets that have moons?"

"You know their names?" the man in Al's chair said. "Mister Astronomer?"

"No," Nick said, "but I know who would know." He looked up at the ceiling. "I bet that old coot can cite chapter and verse about all your planetary names."

Al gave the customer a hand mirror then turned the chair so the man could see the back of his head. "That'll do," the guy said. "You're a pro, Al."

Mike watched the customer pay Al for the haircut, say goodbye to everybody, then leave.

Al spun the seat around until it faced Mike.

"I came to see Domenic," Mike said.

"You still got the key, don't you?"

"I'm going up directly," Mike said, rising from his chair. "You did a hell of a job on Saturday," he said, turning to Nick then Clement. "Both of you."

"Thanks," they said in unison.

"You didn't ask questions. Just did what needed to be done." He turned and closed the door behind him.

At the top of Domenic's stairs, he took a deep breath then put the key into the lock. "You got company," he called, opening the door. Domenic was sitting up in his bed.

"Well," Domenic said.

"*Como si face si bruto?*"

"How is my face so ugly?" Domenic said.

"I learned it from somebody at work," Mike said. "She's from Naples."

"I saw you out there Saturday," Domenic said, smirking. "The bunch of you. I was in no mood."

"You're breathing good right now."

"It's a good time. Getting stirred up doesn't help."

"When was the last time you were out of here?"

"The hospital," Domenic said. "But I move around enough up here."

Mike looked at his watch. "I checked. Novenas are on the hour," he said. "Get dressed and I'll drive you there and back."

Domenic stared at him for a moment. "We'll be late," he said.

"Not if you change now," Mike said. "The only reason we'll be late is because you're being *stonato*."

When Domenic told him what clothes to get from his chest of drawers, Mike brought them into the front room, then waited in the dining room.

"You're trying to kill me and make it look like it was my idea," Domenic said from the other room.

They made it to the shrine parking lot with eight minutes to spare.

"I can say the whole rosary on the trolley down to Chelten Avenue," Domenic said. "But the way you drive a car? I'm doing some serious praying."

"Let's go," Mike said. He helped Domenic out of the car. When they reached the entrance, Domenic dipped his hand into the holy water font and blessed himself.

"Sit where you usually sit," Mike said. He followed Domenic to an empty pew halfway up the left side aisle. "You get tired, let me know. You don't have to be jumping up and down, kneeling and all that."

"Shh," Domenic said. "You're in church."

Indeed, Mike thought. It was not as large as he remembered it, but the vaulted ceiling, pillars between the pews and the side aisles, and white marble altar with three towering paintings on the walls of the apse behind it made it seem like a small cathedral. It called to mind photos from one of Sarah's coffee-table books. He tried to remember what it had been like to be here as a child, but all he could remember was the stillness when the priest paused and his mother and everyone else privately made their requests to God. He wondered if her pleas had anything to do with his father or with drinking or with other things beyond his seeing and knowing. Did she believe that her prayers were answered? Did she give up? He was nearing the age she would have been when she brought Brendan and him to this church.

"Don't tell me you're staying?" Domenic whispered to him.

"Waiting for the lightning bolts," Mike said. The church was filling up, mostly with elderly people but some younger ones too. He reddened at the thought that someone he knew might see him here. But then, they would have some explaining to do as well.

He had not been inside a church since the funeral in New Paltz. Here, Mary dominated most of the paintings, murals, and statues in the church. It was, after all, a place where people appealed for her intercession with God. Mike studied the three towering paintings behind the altar. A somber figure he took to be Gabriel hovered over Mary in the painting on the left. The one on the right showed Mary and Joseph in that Bethlehem stable, kneeling by baby Jesus in the crib, a cluster of cherubs flitting overhead. Centered between the other two paintings was a triumphant glimpse of Mary rising above the clouds, more plump cherubs fluttering at her feet.

So different from the church where they'd baptized Michael. Mike closed his eyes. The candle smell was the same. He was standing in his bedroom in New Paltz. Baby Michael was snoozing across the room.

Laurie called down the hall to remind him that the baptism was an hour away. He was late for brunch and still had to put on his suit. He watched the baby's chest gently rise and fall and listened to that little rush of breath: the soul of babyhood. Miniature fingers, lips, feet. Fresh, delicate, vital. Everything but wings. No wonder parents called their infants angels.

He heard Laurie's parents and her brother, Michael's godfather-to-be, laughing in the kitchen. What meant nothing to him meant so much to them. Sister Theresa Michael had told his first grade class to always leave a little space at their desks for their guardian angels. Someone to watch over you. That much he would let Laurie pass on to their little boy. Everybody needed such a shadow, somebody in their corner at the right time. He rummaged through the dresser drawer hoping to find a suitable shirt but found only a pair of short-sleeved sports shirts that Laurie had buttoned and folded.

He opened the closet. Two freshly ironed white dress shirts greeted him. Behind them was his wedding suit, with three different matching ties draped across the coat's right shoulder.

Then he was in the New Paltz church, a couple of years later, wearing the same suit he'd worn to the baptism. Michael, more boy than baby now, in his own white shirt. His eyes were closed. People were looking down at him in that little coffin. His brother-in-law, the godfather, was there. All of them were there.

Mike felt an elbow in his ribs, and his eyes flew open. "Praying for a miracle?" Domenic asked, leaning toward him.

Mike was shaking, but not enough to be obvious. He took a breath. "You'd have to help me out there."

Domenic patted him on the knee. "I'll do what I can," he said.

The priest appeared at the altar and the service began. They all sang a hymn Mike was sure he hadn't heard since childhood. The melody came back to him immediately, but not the words, except for the "Ave Marias" in the chorus. A call and response between the priest and the people ensued, the language as stiff and old-fashioned as the raspy soundtrack of an old black-and-white documentary film. *How did these prayers strike me when I was a kid?* When they stopped, Mike knew the silent time had arrived for them to make their petitions. Their God took the time to listen to every single pitch? Up in the pulpit, the priest bowed his head.

In the silence, Mike thought of Sarah. Impossible wishing, he thought, both of them. Just like what these people were doing. At least Mike was doing something. Every day he paid a price for what had happened to Laurie and Michael. Years of digging for strength. Now Sarah and the baby needed that kind of strength, the kind that Delores never seemed to run short of. *Find it.*

He felt Domenic beside him—no doubt, like the rest of them, staking desperate hopes on a prayer. Mike couldn't be more different from the guy in that regard. But he wouldn't be sitting in church if he hadn't recognized the ways they were alike. He rarely let himself consider their common losses and scars, and he suspected that Domenic did the same—because that only brought more pain. He didn't understand why, but he needed to help him. Maybe Domenic thought he was helping Mike right now. Childhood prayer. Mike remembered squeezing his small hands together in dogged concentration. He opened his eyes. Domenic's folded hands looked relaxed, not reddened. No furrowed brow, no clenched eyes. He could be peacefully asleep, except for the hint of a smile around his mouth.

When the service ended, Mike sat in the pew, waiting for Domenic's cue. When most of the crowd had left, Domenic rose. By the time they reached the car, Domenic's breathing had become labored. "I'm all right," Domenic rasped.

"Help doesn't always come in the form of miracles," Mike said. He opened the passenger side door.

"What are you going on about?" Domenic said, climbing into the car.

"Miracles are great," Mike said. "But if something a little less spectacular came along, something that might help you out, you wouldn't ignore it. Right?"

or angry. He couldn't place when he had this feeling before. Then it hit him. The day Al asked him to work for him and offered him the apartment upstairs.

Brendan came in and announced that he was done installing the bench along one of the deck's sides. "See you Memorial Day," he said to Mike. He waved to Domenic then was gone.

"Brendan just showed up whenever I needed a hand," Mike said. "Says it's part of his physical therapy."

"His wife?" Domenic said.

"Her memory's leveled off. Not everything's come back. That's what the doctors say. She swears she can get by."

"And Memorial Day?"

"I have the holiday off."

"Family get-together?"

"I need you to help me christen the deck," Mike said. "Bathroom too. I'll invite the guys at the barbershop and a few neighbors."

So fast, Domenic thought. He walked out to the deck ahead of Mike. "Damnedest thing," he said, taking it in. But Sarah was the one who most needed a picnic. *He will not invite her, and it's not my party or my place.* Like blood sugar, his joy and excitement plummeted. He gripped the deck's railing, steadying himself and keeping signs of pain off his face. Only parents—unfortunate ones—pined over estranged adult children. But how different from their suffering was this private ache? "It's something, all right," he managed, as Mike steered the chair up to him.

"Yep," Mike said, as Domenic sat in the wheelchair. Moving down the ramp, he looked straight ahead, imagining the proud smile on Mike's face.

Perched at his window that afternoon, Domenic saw Ginette

before she reached his front door. He was waiting for her when she reached the second floor.

"Don't be mean to the nice doctor," she warned him. He assured her that the young man had nothing to fear. Riding beside Ginette, Domenic recognized that he was approaching this encounter differently. He'd been going into those appointments with a chip on his shoulder. Today, he expected to stay calm and quiet, even if given sobering news and annoying instructions. Yes, he still wanted to be given a longer leash with a looser hand on it. But even the people they passed on the avenue looked less miserable than usual.

"Use your judgment," the doctor said, after he had finished inspecting every inch of Domenic's body and asking him dozens of questions. "*Good* judgment."

"All right."

"No wisecracks?" the doctor said, raising an eyebrow. "We'd better check your medications."

On their way back to the apartment, Domenic told Ginette, "I've gotten the green light. Actually, it's more of a blinking green."

"Usually," she said, "you get into more trouble with the other two colors."

No Olympic training, he reminded himself, but no refusing to budge from the second-floor window, either. When Ginette pulled up in front of the shop, Domenic saw Al sitting in his chair, reading the neighborhood weekly. "All is well," he announced from the shop doorway. "I'll see you boys in a day or so."

"Learn a new trick," Nick said.

"You old dog," Clement said.

"*Chiacchierones,*" Domenic said, laughing as he shut the door.

Ginette put a casserole in the refrigerator and left a note on the table with heating instructions. When she left, he walked slowly to the front room, sat in the chair beside his bed, and opened the newspaper. After dinner, he methodically put the leftovers into the refrigerator, without any discomfort. Turning off the kitchen light, he heard rattling at the door downstairs, footsteps, then Sarah's voice.

"Just me."

"*Madonna!*" he called back, his breath catching, knees buckling, like when those old elevators in the big buildings suddenly dropped half a flight.

She stopped and stood, hands in the air, at the entrance to his living room. "Nothing," she said, with an exaggerated smile right out of musical theater. "I've agonized over an apology gift for weeks but decided you wouldn't mind if I showed up with nothing."

"Has it been that long?" he said.

"Now, now," she said. "Sarcasm is never anyone's best look." A frown had replaced the smile. "It's too much to explain, but finally I had to see you for myself." She walked over to the chair he'd left by the window, pulled it beside his bed, then, like a guest on Johnny Carson's show, sat in the spot that Mike and every Tom, Dick, and Harry seemed to think was the only possible place to perch when meeting with the sick old man. She put her hand on top of his. "I am sorry, Domenic. Please forgive me."

"I am glad to see you," he said, too weary to organize a more comprehensive response. "You haven't missed much. I've been told I'm not my normal self."

"To be honest," she said, "I've heard mixed reviews."

She looked strained—or was he seeing himself in her?

"How are you really?" she said.

"Better, truth be told." He recounted the whole story about his appointment, including his improved attitude but leaving out any mention of Mike Flannagan's recent reappearance. Was whatever got into Mike catching? But he wasn't going to be the one to bring up Mike's name.

"Great," she said. "That's a relief for you."

She didn't show yet, not to him, but he knew she'd been running. *Running!* "The kid from Kerala with all the diplomas on his wall says my medications are fine for now and that I need to move around, and I didn't even bribe him," Domenic said of his appointment with his young Indian doctor. "Listen to me blab. You're the one all loaded up with doctor appointments."

"Day after tomorrow, I go for an ultrasound. Like taking a picture of the baby inside me." She looked down at her still trim middle and placed her hands on it. "I can find out if it's a boy or a girl."

"Some people can tell by the way you carry."

"I shouldn't find that out, right? Keep it a surprise, even though knowing would make planning easier."

"No planning?" he said, feigning shock.

"For once, I think I'd rather be surprised."

"Not what I expected to hear from you," he said, shaking his head. And she had no idea what her ex was up to. The two people who'd charged into his life this year were full of surprises, but after just a few minutes she'd again convinced him that she could do anything she put her mind to. As great as her challenges were, her future worried him less than that of the guy who was rebuilding his home for him. Mike was bending over backwards, being generous, but he still didn't seem right. Like he might wake up one day and change his mind. Have a little faith in the guy, Angela would tell him. "Guess I'm worried about everybody," he said. "Maybe that's what you do when you're old."

"You're the one who needs to monitor himself," she said.

"You'll have plenty to monitor," he said. "You'll send me pictures, I hope, if you're not here."

"I want to talk to you about that," she said, setting her eyes on his. "So?"

"I accepted the job in New York." She flashed a larger smile.

"News, news, news!" he gushed, smiling back. *Is any part of her smile forced, like all of mine?*

"Wanted you to be the first to know."

"Your parents don't know?"

"They'll hear about it Memorial Day weekend. Plus the other news."

"Two more weeks?" he said. "Your kid could be talking by then."

"In person is best," she said. "They know I'm coming up for the weekend. They don't know that I'm bringing up a first load of things and looking at apartments. I'll tell people at the college, of course. And Mike."

"He's been around again," he said. "Trying to be helpful."

"I'm very glad to hear that," she said. "And you have to learn to accept people's help."

He nodded. No jokes, no qualifications.

She looked relieved. His welfare did matter to her. So many profound realizations came accompanied by awkwardness. For him, their little reunion felt bittersweet, but he'd hold onto the sweet part.

He felt confident that he was radiating understanding and support, at least. Probably not joy. He kept thinking that he might never see her or the baby once she moved to New York. "I'm happy for you," he said.

She nodded, looking content. "So, should I find out the baby's sex?"

"Used to be part of the surprise." He glanced at her belly. If he hadn't been told, he wouldn't have guessed. "I wouldn't," he said. "But that's up to you."

"No," she said, shaking her head. "But I want to hear the heartbeat and see what the baby looks like. That's pretty exciting."

"Amazing."

"I guess I want to know everything else about it."

"Before you know it, all that mystery will be screaming for a dry diaper."

It had been a long time since he had cracked her up. Her joyful laugh put him more at ease. He did not like her going away, but he had no more control over that than he did over his failing heart and lungs. She was young, strong. "It'll go well," he said. "And not to worry, I like that baby already!"

She laughed and clapped her hands. "Good," she said, and stood up. She leaned over and reached her arms around Domenic. He hugged back. He closed his eyes, holding on. Finally, she said, "Thank you." She straightened up and patted his shoulder.

When she turned to leave, he looked from the window at the darkened second floor above the flower shop. Cars clattered down the avenue. A truck's brakes squealed. *Basta,* he thought. Someone shouted at Gilhooley's entrance. He never noticed street sounds when he was talking with someone. Sarah's footsteps clicked down the stairway, each step sounding farther away, like the passing cars on the avenue. He listened to the quick, sure sound of her locking the door behind her. Enough.

43

TUESDAY, MAY 16

As the afternoon waned, Sarah bought a salad in the cafeteria. She left three boxes of trash outside her office door then reviewed the neat stack of books and materials she had readied for next week's trip to New York. Sorting and packing had taken more time than she had expected. A second visit to Domenic in as many days might do them both some good, but she decided to wait until after tomorrow's ultrasound. That would give her enough time today to squeeze in both food shopping and a good run. She reminded herself that before leaving Philly she must return Domenic's extra apartment key to Al.

She bought more items at the Acme than she needed as usual, driving home flush with not only cleaning supplies but also her guilty pleasure, a prepared lasagna dinner from the deli. To avoid a second trip up the stairs with overflowing bags, she set the car doors to lock, grabbed hold of three bags with each hand, bumped the door closed with her backside, and schlepped her load across the street.

At the building's entrance, she realized that she'd never make it to the second floor carrying that load, so she left two bags at the building entrance and climbed the stairs to the second floor. Finally at her door, she dropped the bags, flexed her numb hands, and unlocked the door. She left the apartment door ajar as she lugged the four bags to the kitchen table, figuring the last trip would be far easier. When she turned, she froze. The student from the garage, Edward Hearn, faced her, a grocery bag in each hand. He kicked the door behind him shut.

"Quiet," he said softly, approaching the table.

Her eyes locked on his, and she could hardly breathe. Backing away, she bumped into the refrigerator. Her face felt icy, like she'd been trapped in a meat locker. She realized she had crossed her arms against her chest and balled her fists.

He dropped the bags on the table next to hers.

Scream, she thought. *Scream as loud as you can!* But no sound came from her mouth. Eyes darting about, she spotted nothing to use as a weapon. "Please," she whispered.

"What?" he said. "I get no 'thank you' for helping with the groceries?"

She glanced quickly at the front door, but he laughed.

"As if," he said. He shook his head. "Banging the old guy too?"

"Oh my God," she gasped. Her brain failed to send signals to any other part of her body.

"You got me shit-canned at school," he said. "Not nice." He planted a chair between them, raised one foot onto its seat, and rested his forearm on his bent knee. He leaned toward her. "Kind of humiliating." He leaned toward her like a coach about to give a team a pep talk. "I wasn't going to hit you in the garage. Just trying to send you a little message."

"Leave now," she pleaded, her back pressed against the refrigerator. "I won't tell anyone this ever happened."

"No bitch disrespects me."

"I didn't disrespect you," she said. "But I need you to leave. Right now." She told herself to concentrate so she could raise her voice.

"No one makes me look like an ass!"

"Out!" she screamed. "Now!" Where were the upstairs neighbors?

It was Tuesday, damn it. Shuddering, she willed her mouth to scream, but her diaphragm could muster only a faint wheeze.

Hearn kicked the chair away, lunged at her, and clapped his hand across her mouth, smashing her head against the refrigerator. "No screaming," he hissed, leaning hard against her.

She could not move.

"Don't make me use duct tape."

Her eyes darted to the drawer across the room where she kept the knives. But he still had her arms trapped. When she tried to bite him, he clamped down even harder on her mouth.

"A fighter," he said.

Straining, she worked her arms down until she could thrust them free of his grip, then swept them up and clapped them over each of his ears at the same moment.

"Fuck!" he yelled, raising his hands to his ears as he took a disoriented step back.

She drew her right arm back and whipped it forward, like a softball pitcher, grabbing his crotch and squeezing with all of her might. Hearn screamed before he collapsed, moaning. When she dashed for the knife drawer, he clambered back up and pinned her against the sink then twisted her wrist, forcing her to drop it. She kneed him in the groin and raked her fingernails across his face twice.

"Crazy bitch!" he screamed, stumbling back, bleeding. He regained his balance and lunged forward, grabbing her with one bloody hand, then shoved her with the other, sending her careening toward the stove. She broke the impact with her hands and steadied herself. The drawer was right there, so she pulled out a long carving knife. She watched him, already nearly blinded by the blood, lurch out of the door, his footsteps making a racket in the hallway as they slowly faded away.

She dropped the knife to the floor, then slid down until she sat on the floor next to it, taking deep panting breaths and trying to reconfigure in her mind what had just happened.

When her breathing slowed, her brain finally registered the building's eerie silence. *Where is everyone?* Somehow, her belly had not been hit. She cradled it with both hands. "Oh my God," she moaned, the sound of her voice jarring her. She was sore all over but felt no cuts or bruises. The back of her head stung, but she felt no lump or blood when she reached back. How did he know where she lived? When would he come back?

The door. She pulled herself up then hobbled into the living room and double-locked the apartment door. Leaning against it, she felt her heart racing again. She staggered to her bed and collapsed on it, burying her head in the pillow. "No, no, no, no," she grunted into the pillow. In time, her words became cries, noises that scared her, making her roll over and silence herself.

Thirty minutes later, she heard the people downstairs coming in. Had the old couple next door slept through the whole thing? If she told the police, Mike would learn about it somehow. She just knew. She couldn't take that chance. She could limit the number of days she stayed in the apartment. Start packing and take a load to New York over the weekend. No way could Hearn follow her to New York City.

Settle down. The fucker was gone. One, two, three, she breathed out, then stretched it to four, five. Breathing in, she again counted to five, trying to think of what she should do to get through the rest of this horrible day. Cleaning, packing? Maybe nothing more than what she was doing now.

It was not until a few hours later, trying to set her apartment to rights, that the cramps gripped her.

44

TUESDAY, MAY 16

Sarah did not cry in the car or in the harshly lit entranceway to the ER. She clumped down the hallway, her eyes fixed on the woman standing at the triage station. When she reached the intake desk, the woman asked what she could do for her, but Sarah could not meet her eyes. Sarah looked down at the toweled package clutched in both hands and cleared her throat. "I've had a miscarriage." She saw that the towel was marked where she held it and that her hands were smeared with blood. She started to weep. Knees buckling, she teetered but kept control of the towel.

She was being helped to the triage room where she was told to sit and was asked questions that she answered by blurting out jumbled details about what had just happened to her. Then she was in an adjacent room, still holding the towel. A nurse sat her down on a stretcher while a male doctor pulled the curtain, and the room shrank. They were saying things to her, but she could not hear more than a word here and there over her own sobbing. They asked her about the towel. She closed her eyes. When she felt a hand on her shoulder, she scrunched up her face and pulled the towel tight against her chest. After a while, she felt the hand on her shoulder again. She opened her eyes, released the towel to the doctor. She told them that she might have seen the cord in the toilet bowl. The doctor carried the towel to a counter. When he moved, she saw the towel refolded on the counter, the marks her hands had made like two black eyes in some Post-Impressionist painting.

She told them how long she had been pregnant, who her doctor was, and what had just happened, making no mention of the attack. "And I fell against the refrigerator door earlier today," she added. "Hit the back of my head. My neck. Hard."

The doctor looked at her head and felt her neck. "You hit here?" he said, touching a tender spot on the back of her head.

She winced. "Yes."

"Nowhere else?"

"No." *I should tell them right now. But it won't end with that. Not at all.*

"Didn't fall to the ground?"

"No."

"Lose consciousness?"

She shook her head.

The doctor rested his hand on her shoulder. He explained that they needed to examine her. "Do you feel pain right now?" he asked, pulling on a pair of latex gloves.

"No," she said. *Why do I feel like I'm lying to him?* She was bawling and shaking again, her eyes fixed on the tile floor and the doctor's Adidas running shoes, the model priced ten dollars more than the ones she had bought. Since he'd touched the part of her head that hit the refrigerator, the spot stung and throbbed. "Yes," she said, slowly raising her neck. "Everything hurts. My hands, even my hands."

The doctor nodded.

Grasping that he was ready to do the pelvic exam, she lay down and slid her rear to the bottom of the stretcher. As he began, she closed her eyes and concentrated on breathing evenly, trying to make the same whistling sound each time she exhaled. How long had she held her eyes closed when she'd sat on the toilet at home? When she'd opened them, sobbing and shaking, she knew she would have to look into the toilet bowl. If she'd managed to do that, she could get through this horror too. One blob had stood out in the bowl, larger than the other bits of matter she could make out. She'd dropped to her knees in front of the toilet. Her mouth stretched open as if she were screaming, but only hot breaths sputtered out, one after the other. *Little lumps*. She'd closed her mouth, released one long breath through her nose. But now, unable to restrain herself, she cried out.

"Did that hurt?" the doctor said, pulling her out of her thoughts.

"It's tender," she said.

She remembered reaching into the bowl, slowly bringing her right hand under the largest thing in the bowl of water and blood. Cupping it, she'd lifted it out of the bowl, the pinkish water draining through her fingers and dripping back into the toilet. It was the size of an egg. She heard herself gasp, the details of what she saw registering all at once. Unmistakable. Curled up and still, it seemed to have more head than anything else. She touched it with her left hand and again had no word for the feel of it. Flesh, not rubbery but more like that than anything she remembered ever touching. Cool, like the bloody water in the bowl. Stunted and raw, it was disproportionate yet minutely detailed. She moved it with her finger and found the penis. She counted ten toes. *His* toes. Her baby's toes. She stood up and with her left hand reached for a towel. She placed the tiny body on the middle of it and folded the rest of the white towel over it.

"Oh!" she cried out.

"Is that bad?" the doctor said.

"It's passed."

"The opening to your cervix is closed," he said. "That's good."

Opening her eyes, she looked up at the ceiling. The nurse standing beside her patted her arm.

"Hitting that refrigerator," Sarah said. "It didn't?"

The doctor shook his head. "Unlikely," he said. "We may know more later."

But Mike cannot know. "Oh God," she muttered.

The nurse gently squeezed Sarah's shoulder.

"I was running," she told the nurse. "I've never run before. Never been this healthy."

Then the doctor finished. He stepped beside the nurse. "You could be bleeding a lot," he said. "But you're not, and that's good."

"It's been a perfect pregnancy," she blurted out. "This is impossible. This can't happen like this. Why?"

The doctor frowned. "We may not know tonight exactly what happened," he said.

She moaned.

"I'm going to call your obstetrician before you're discharged," he said.

She nodded then let her head roll to her left, resting the side of her face on the stretcher. She closed her eyes, but the light still cut through painfully.

For a while, she believed that she was listening to the medical staff take care of some very sick or injured person, not her, as if she were lying on her bed at home, too tired to turn off the TV medical drama, her eyes already closed for the night. When the doctor and the nurse were finished, she could not remember all that they had done to her. They had come and gone at different times, getting things, never leaving her alone. She sat in the chair beside the stretcher.

"Who should we call for you?" the nurse asked from across the room. She was blocking Sarah's view of the towel on the counter. The woman, a bit older than she, wore a wedding band.

Sarah shook her head. The nurse turned to write something. Sarah saw the towel again. She knew that they were finishing up. She looked at the clock. Fewer than three hours ago, she had been walking around her apartment, cleaning, planning, regaining her equilibrium after her very bad day.

The woman looked at her. "Whatever you want, dear," the nurse said. "Do you have a way to get home?"

"I drove," she said. "Ten minutes."

"We can get you a cab," the nurse said. "Leave your car here. It'll be okay."

"I don't have to stay overnight?"

"The doctor explained," the woman said. "Remember?"

"How can that be?" she said. "I can go home tonight. It's not even midnight yet."

There were more comings and goings around her. A different nurse showed up and told Sarah that she would help take care of her, that Sarah would not have to stay too much longer. When the doctor reappeared, she looked over at the folded towel on the counter. "What's going to happen?" she asked, nodding toward the towel.

"I was going to discuss that. There's usually some lab work that's done," he said quietly. "Because we may learn something that you and your doctor should know, for the future."

She nodded. "Then?"

The doctor blinked twice. "The hospital takes care of that," he said, rubbing his eyes. "Unless you want to do something else."

The towel looked as if it had been dropped on the counter by someone in a great hurry. Now the smears on it looked like a pair of dark wings. The doctor was staring at her. She shook her head.

At eleven thirty, the new nurse returned to the cubicle. "I think you're ready to go home," she said.

"The other nurse said I could leave my car here tonight." Sarah said. "I have to call a cab."

"It's all taken care of."

The doctor and the first nurse joined them. The woman put her hand on hers. "I'll drive your car," she said, in a voice so soft that she seemed like a different person. "My shift is over. My husband's driven in. Our oldest is watching the younger two. Give me your keys. We'll get you and your car back home."

She fished her keys out of her pocket and handed them to the woman.

The doctor went over her instructions again. Dr. Stafford had been informed of what happened and would call her in the morning.

Sarah nodded and he patted her shoulder.

"That's just about everything," he said. His hand gently pressed her shoulder. In a voice just above a whisper, he said, "Did you want to look before you leave?"

She sat back, pulling away from his hand.

"Only if you want to." He stepped back and folded his hands in front of him.

This is happening. Every last bit of it.

She stood up and walked to the counter. She pulled back the towel. Discolored since she had brought the little body in, he looked smaller than she remembered. Even his perfect nose. She touched one of his tiny feet with her finger then folded the towel back over him.

She turned back to the nurse and heard the doctor say good night. The nurse sat her in a wheelchair then pushed her down the bright, still hallway.

45

TUESDAY, MAY 16

The ER nurse opened the passenger door. When Sarah had seated herself, she fixed the shoulder belt for her. While the nurse walked around to the driver's side, Sarah pulled at her hospital wristband, but it would not rip or come off. "Foggy numbness" was how she'd described her state to the doctor. The description fell short, but even now that fog did not allow her to access a more accurate answer. "Kind of surreal?" he'd asked, but everything that happened during the hot, fast eternity in the kitchen then in the bathroom had felt all too real. "And now?" he'd said. She'd squeezed her eyes shut and said nothing more. Sitting in the nurse's car, she felt the fog thicken, the numbness grow heavier. If she'd not been asked the doctor's question until now, how much muddier would her reply have been? *No more questions.*

The car crossed Chestnut Hill Avenue. The smooth ride abruptly changed as soon as they rolled onto the avenue's first Belgian blocks where the 23 trolley looped at the end of the line. As they rumbled down the avenue, Sarah remembered that the husband would be trailing them. To her right, she caught glimpses of the signs for Kilian Hardware then Caruso's.

"You direct me," the nurse said when they stopped for the red light at Willow Grove Avenue.

Sarah nodded, relieved that the nurse had turned to her, freeing her from having to make words.

The woman switched on the classical station, setting the volume down low.

Sarah shut her eyes, waiting for the light to change. A northbound trolley screeched to a stop on the other side of the intersection. "Jesus," Sarah said, opening her eyes with a start.

"You all right?"

Sarah put her hand over her heart and breathed out. "I didn't expect that."

The light changed, and when the nurse accelerated past the trolley down the hill toward Cresheim Valley Drive, Sarah looked off to her side, away from the Celtic cross at Mermaid Lane. When the sound of the tires deepened in pitch for a moment, she knew that they must be passing under the old railroad bridge and that they were well beyond the Mermaid Inn. Opening her eyes again, she told the nurse to take the next left.

When the car pulled up in front of her building, Sarah asked if the nurse and her husband could walk her to her apartment door.

"Of course," the nurse said. "We were planning on that."

They walked through the entrance where she had left the two bags, now an unholy place. Desecrated, like her kitchen. At her door, they asked if she wanted them to sit with her, but she said no. She thanked the couple, hoping that they grasped how much she appreciated their kindness.

When they left, she found a pair of scissors, cut off the hospital band, then plunged it deep into the contents of the kitchen wastebasket. She took off her clothes by the bed, dropping them onto the floor. No street or building sounds broke the apartment's silence. Had it ever been this still? She walked into the bathroom and turned on the shower, grateful for the familiar sound. Letting the heat and steam build, she returned to the bedroom, picked up the clothing, carried the small pile past the hamper, then dropped all of it into the wastebasket in the corner of her bedroom. She pushed down hard on the pile so that as much space as possible remained for whatever other articles of clothing she would never want to see again.

In the shower stall, she stood in the steaming stream until her legs began to wobble. Stepping onto the thick rug beside the shower, she reached for a towel. It looked identical to the one she'd pulled from the same stack several hours ago. *Four months old.* She groaned, looking at how the scalding water had reddened her torso, arms, and back. *This crying emptiness is grief. A first chapter.*

After over-filling her wastebasket with her sheets and blankets, she made the bed with fresh linens. From the kitchen cabinet drawer, she pulled out a large black trash bag. She shook it open so hard it made the sound of a schooner's sail snapping in a sudden wind. She emptied all of her wastebaskets into it, tied its neck into a double knot, and left it by the front door. Back in the bedroom, she dropped onto the bed without turning off the lights.

The telephone woke her at seven in the morning. "Sarah, this is Jen Stafford."

A first name occasion. The doctor's tone was solicitous, her speech slower than usual. She did not make Sarah feel as if she was making the doctor run into the next person's time.

Yes, it had been a terrible night, the worst of her life.

Stafford already had spoken with the ER doc. She hoped Sarah managed to get some sleep.

Sarah nodded.

"Sarah?"

"Yes, slept."

The woman sounded genuinely saddened. She repeated what Dr. Guerrant had told Sarah about bleeding.

"So far, so good," Sarah said. *What an absurd thing to say.*

Could Sarah get a ride to the office at eleven thirty?

She assured the doctor that she would call a cab. She hung up and sat on the bed, staring at the open bathroom door then at the closed bedroom door. Finally, she crossed to the bathroom. She shed her pajamas and underwear at the door then sat on the toilet. She had not experienced the significant overnight bleeding they warned her about. *Good news?* Not enough to make one inch of her feel the least bit better.

Sarah studied her clean pale face and chest in the bathroom mirror, shaking her head. "No," she said, sickened by the moving lips in the mirror. *Impossible.* Her face contorted. "No!" she wailed, startling herself. Sitting on the toilet again, she closed her eyes and breathed slowly. When she had stopped panting, she rose. She turned on the water in the shower, tested it with her finger, then turned the lever up a notch. The water felt pleasantly warm, nothing like last night's painful cleansing. She backed into the stream, turned her face to the warm flow, and let it soak her hair. When she finished shampooing her hair and soaping and rinsing her body, she turned away from the nozzle and let the gentle water drum against her back. Her legs felt like they would hold her. The warmth enabled her to stretch some of the tightness out of the muscles in the top of her back. Normally, a water massage on her back would relax her entire body, but now it merely lessened her neck and back strain.

Sarah dried herself then stood before the full-length mirror. She turned sideways. Her shape appeared no different from twenty-four hours earlier. Surely she weighed less, yet she couldn't tell the difference looking in the mirror.

The muscles of her neck and back still ached. She was not hungry, but she made a piece of toast and poured a glass of orange juice then sat in the good chair. She pushed aside the notepad and tried the juice, staring at the calendar shot of the villa and the garden in the foreground, all bathed in that morning light. She nibbled at her toast then forced down another sip of juice. Questions for the doctor popped into her head, but she did not write them down. Halfway through the toast, she tore off the notepad's top sheet on which she had written the plan for the day, balled it up, then threw it across the room. She peeked out the window. Another cloudy day. Bright sun would have made her squint, hurt more. *Is this my grief's second chapter?*

She took a cab to the doctor's office. As the driver reprised the route she'd taken last night, she revisited the scared state of that ride when she'd feared she might faint but had steeled herself through the trancelike drive. Entering the doctor's waiting area, she saw with relief that it was empty. The office manager brought her into the examining room she had happily visited two weeks earlier. Dr. Stafford whisked into the room before she had a chance to sit and gave Sarah a long hug.

"I'm so sorry, Sarah," Dr. Stafford said, pulling back enough to look her in the eyes. Stafford let her tell the story all over again before examining her.

"You must have a thousand things racing through your mind, Sarah."

Sarah shook her head. "Why? That's my only question."

"Pathology may be able to tell us something about that," Dr. Stafford said, frowning.

"The bumps I took?"

"Not likely."

She listened to the doctor. It was inevitable. It would have showed up on the ultrasound. She spent half an hour with her, explaining that she fit her in before her regular appointments for the day so they would not be rushed.

"I didn't want to see anybody out there," Sarah said, getting closer to tears than she had been since last night.

"I know," Dr. Stafford said. She handed Sarah a handful of tissues. "I'll need you to do some blood work in about three or four days. Okay?"

Sarah nodded. "I thought I'd be crying all day long, but I haven't been. I don't know."

"There is no way you could have been prepared for this."

"Maybe if I'd known," Sarah said.

"You're one of those who didn't get any indications, any warnings," Stafford said. "You're going to need some time."

"My semester's over," Sarah said. "I don't have to go to work or anything."

The doctor made a consoling face.

"There's no good way to do this," Sarah said. She rubbed her eyes.

"This need not be the end of this chapter in your life," Stafford said. "You don't want to hear this now, but you're young."

"Not anymore."

The doctor gave her that look again. Sarah took it as a sign that there was no more the woman could say to her. She'd already spent more time with Sarah than she had hoped for. After reviewing her patient instructions, Sarah hugged and thanked Dr. Stafford then stepped toward the door.

"One thing," she said, turning back. "When did it happen?"

"It's not easy to pinpoint," Stafford said. "It could have been a couple of days, maybe a bit more. It's hard to know exactly."

Sarah grimaced.

"This may not be the best time or place, but I'll say this and hope that you can hear it. In many situations, Sarah, this is nature's way of preventing something that might not work out later. Do you know what I mean?"

Sarah nodded. "Some of us are not meant for this sort of thing."

"No, Sarah. What I'm saying is that some pregnancies are not viable in the long run. There's no reason to believe that this would happen any other time you conceived."

Sarah reached for the doorknob.

"I'm so sorry, Sarah," Dr. Stafford said. "I'll need to see you again in about a week or two."

"I'm moving. Remember? I know you worked recently in New York. I'd like a referral."

The doctor nodded.

Sarah walked out, closing the examining room door behind her. Without the moment-to-moment grip of the conversation with the doctor, she felt herself in a dazed state, slowing her brain down. *I will not fall to the floor.* She willed her eyes to keep working. The receptionist was speaking on the telephone. A woman perhaps six months pregnant sat in the middle of the seats, a two-year-old boy in her lap. *Wait.* Beside her a man sat, holding a large tote bag with little cartoon ducks on it.

Sarah turned around and went back to the exam room. Dr. Stafford was peering over papers at her desk. She looked up.

"Dr. Stafford, I think we need to talk to the police."

46

TUESDAY, MAY 23

Ahead of schedule, Domenic emptied his kitchen waste bin into a large trash bag, pulled it across the floor to the bathroom, then added the contents of that wastebasket. In the living room, he found the two smaller Acme bags he filled after last night's sorting and dumped them into the larger bag. Taking the collage off the wall had been easy, after all. Last evening, he'd left the frame, glass side leaning against the far wall, and hadn't had a bit of trouble getting to sleep. Now, with the thing sitting on the bedspread, he easily undid the fasteners on its back. Tilting up the frame, he watched game tickets, newspaper clippings, and photographs slide into a heap on the bedspread. When he pulled away the few items still stuck against the glass, they plopped onto the pile. *Relief.* The glass was empty, ready to be cleaned, reattached to the wooden frame, and given to someone who could use it. *Easy.* Soon all of the contents were in the black plastic bag.

The framed photograph of Angela would remain on the wall until the day he moved it to Mike's. He dragged the bag to the table under Angela's picture, then dropped two of the blue candleholders and their nearly new candles into the bag. He let two more tumble onto them. The next pair landed with a crash. He tossed the last three into the bag. *No more.* He tied a twist around the top of the now heavy trash bag then dragged it down the hall to the dining room, where he

"Like what?"

Mike pulled onto the side street then stopped at the Chelten Avenue light. "You take your medicine," he said. "Watch what you eat. That gives you a fighting chance to manage an outing like this." When the light turned green, Mike turned onto Chelten. "And a car ride lets you save your wind for walking when you get there."

"If you're trying to trick me," Domenic said. "After we just went to church."

"No tricks," Mike said. "I'm trying to figure out some things. You'll be the first to know if I do."

When they arrived at the apartment, Domenic's tortured trip up the stairs disturbed Mike. The old man bent over, wheezing in the dining room. Finally moving again, he collapsed on the bed.

"How long before you even out?"

"Can't tell for sure." Domenic gasped. "Maybe ten, fifteen minutes."

Mike pulled a straight chair to the far window. Traffic stalled on the avenue below. Pedestrians came into sight, disappeared. When it was dark and he believed that Domenic had recovered, he stood beside the bed.

"I'm taking some time off from work," Mike said, when Domenic opened his eyes. "I'll be over later this week to look in on you. Next Monday we can go to the novena."

"I got a doctor's appointment," Domenic said. "Ginette's taking me. Four o'clock."

"If you can handle two outings in one day, we'll go earlier."

"They let you take time off whenever you want?" Domenic said.

"Going to take a week off, maybe more," Mike said.

"You're going on vacation?" Domenic said.

"Easier to get it this time of year. I got some projects."

"No trips to Jamaica?"

"Wouldn't know what to do there."

"Even I could help you out with that," Domenic said, smirking.

"So, it's on?"

Domenic hemmed and hawed about the time, finally agreeing that late morning would be fine.

Mike pulled out his keys. "I'll lock both doors."

"Deal."

Domenic punched his pillow, as if each hit might make it more comfortable. "Don't forget to say your bedtime prayers," he admonished Mike.

Mike rolled his eyes.

"You want to know what I'm praying for?" Domenic said.

"Doesn't that ruin it?"

Domenic laughed. "I'm not done with you," he said, pointing his finger at Mike.

He watched Domenic pull up his covers and work his head into the pillow until he seemed to be set. He looked like a kid to Mike, a big, grizzled one.

42

MONDAY, MAY 15

When Domenic stepped outside, he saw a wheelchair on the sidewalk.

"It's not a miracle," Mike said.

"Where's your car?" Domenic said, looking up and down the street. Those fools in the shop would be gawking, even without the damn contraption, but he was not about to give them the satisfaction of looking.

"Too far to walk," Mike said. "Double-parking this time of day is an Olympic event. Climb in. You're saving your strength for the afternoon."

The guy wasn't entirely dumb. If Mike had told him about the chair, Domenic wouldn't have budged out of his bed. When he sat in it, Mike pushed him up the sidewalk, whistling, "O Sole Mio."

Driving down the avenue, Mike pointed his thumb at the wheelchair, stashed on the back seat. "A real steal," he said. "Got it from a neighbor whose aunt had used it."

"Tell me the aunt died."

"The aunt died," Mike said.

"Honesty," Domenic said, shaking his head.

In church, before the service, Domenic closed his eyes and prayed for Sarah. The liturgy kept things moving, minimized his wandering thoughts, but by its end Angela, Al and Ginette, Clement and Nick, and Mike Flannagan had crossed his mind as always. No matter. He had wanted to pray for them anyway. And who needed it more than his maddening driver?

"Beats walking," Mike said, wheeling him back to the car. "Don't it?"

He said nothing until Mike had folded the chair, returned it to the back seat, and gotten into the driver's seat. "I never pictured myself like that," he said.

"Who does?" Mike said.

They returned by the same route, but Mike put his turn signal on as they approached Sedgwick Street. Domenic offered no comment as Mike turned onto his block. Driving slowly past his house, Mike pointed to the sets of steps leading to the porch. "Steep," he said.

"Not in my immediate future," Domenic said. "And nobody's rolling me up there."

At the end of the row, Mike turned into the driveway that led to the back of the houses. Domenic counted down to what he figured was the rear of Mike's house. A deck stood where he had expected to see a shed. They stopped at the base of a four-foot-wide ramp that reached up to the deck.

Mike's brother knelt at one corner of the deck, screwing something into the railing. Tail wagging, Robert paced back and forth across the deck.

"The wheelchair fits," Mike said. "I checked it this morning."

"When did all this happen?" Domenic asked, his eyes widening.

Mike's lip curled ever so slightly into a half-smile. "The shed came down in less than an hour," he said. "The deck's a longer story."

While Mike wrestled the wheelchair out of the car, Domenic gawked at the work.

"My brother, the one-armed carpenter," Mike said, pushing the chair up the first leg of the ramp. On the landing, he pivoted with the chair with room to spare. Mike's brother and the dog waited at the railing above them. Mike put his weight behind the chair, and up they went.

"Excuse the wrong hand," Brendan said, shaking with Domenic. "Not supposed to get carried away for another week or so."

Prompted by Robert nuzzling his leg, Domenic patted him, taking in the deck and the sliding glass doors to the kitchen.

"Just tightening a few screws," Brendan said. "Amazing what the kid can do without his older brother."

"Madonna."

Brendan walked over to the new door. "Won't believe the light it gives you in there," he said, lightly rapping the glass with his knuckles.

When Mike locked the chair's brakes, Domenic pulled himself up and admired Mike's craftsmanship. "Pressure-treated wood," Mike said. "Just have to coat it with water sealant before winter."

"Don't give my brother too much credit," Brendan said. "He's still a moron. You don't want to look at his shithole of a basement."

"That's all part of the plan," Mike said. "Memorial Day, every floor of this place'll look great."

"How's your wife doing?" Domenic asked Brendan.

"Her being home makes a big difference. For everybody." He smiled. "We're making it."

"Going to put up some more wall cabinets to make up for the lost storage," Mike said. He slid open the glass door.

Inside, Domenic stood by the kitchen table, looking out. "He's right. It's like a new room with all this light."

"Come on," Mike said, leading him further into the house.

A spackled length of drywall blocked off the dining room. He walked through the newly created hallway into the living room, where a doorway led into the formerly open dining room. Inside, more drywall framed out a room within the room, containing a toilet, shower stall, and washstand.

"Tommy Coyle puts in a few hours on the plumbing when he can," Mike said. "Ought to be wrapped up for the holiday."

"*Patso*," Domenic said. "Out of your mind."

"Tommy says most new houses have a first-floor powder room."

"Just what you need," Domenic said.

"You do what you need to do," Mike said. "*Capisce?*"

"Your Italian is starting to annoy me," Domenic said.

"You can do everything on this floor," Mike said. "Watch the world go by up front and work on your tan out back."

Ridiculous. Domenic walked back into the living room and stood by the window, looking out at the terraced front yards and the street below. "What's gotten into you, Mike?" Perhaps in five minutes, some of this might make sense, but Domenic wasn't counting on it.

"Always been a lot of house for one guy. Up to you, Domenic. But Al and Ginette can only do so much. You need this."

Somebody else trying to do a good thing. But this went way beyond the rest of them. "I shouldn't say a word right now." He walked back through the new doorway and peeked into the bathroom. Then he went and stood in the middle of the kitchen, almost blinded by the sunlight. He, too, had gotten used to living with more room than he needed. He still had no intention of speaking the words *nursing home* to anyone, but the thought had been hard to banish in these last weeks. It was almost like Mike knew. The guy had just torn this place apart for his sake. So he rarely smiled or laughed. *Who am I to disapprove of that?* Already, Mike's stunt didn't seem entirely crazy. Crazy for Mike maybe. Still, he was reeling, maybe from the shock. The idea of moving in with this guy didn't exactly make him sick set it across from the two boxes of winter clothes he would let Mike take to his place.

He was sweating. He looked across at Angela's face. The same smile she'd flashed when he showed her their little row house for the first time. It was time to behave. He sat down in the living room, pulled out his handkerchief, then wiped his brow. JLP. The monogram belonged to some long-dead lawyer from the Main Line whose house Angela had cleaned for several years. After the widow gave it to Angela for him, he thought only of his wife when he'd run his fingers over the stitched lettering on the handkerchief. As rich as JLP must have been, did he have somebody who'd take him in, a stranger, no less? *Not a thing about this you wouldn't like.*

The telephone ring startled him. Mike liked to do Domenic's shopping near the end of his workday then stop back again after dinner to check on him. He was due in an hour and shouldn't be calling.

"Barbers Anonymous," he answered.

"Domenic?"

Sarah. The soft voice sounded like someone else on the phone. "Did I scare you?" he said.

"Bad time?"

"Not at all," he said, smiling. "Now that more people have my keys than my phone number, I'm not used to answering this thing."

"I can't tell you how good it is to hear your voice."

"Same old me here," he said.

"You just sound good."

Hers was the first voice he'd heard all day. He pressed the phone against his ear so he wouldn't miss a word. "Tell you the truth, I was afraid it was Mike calling to say he couldn't make it until tomorrow. I've got enough trash for the whole block up here."

"It's good that he's around for you."

"He's surprised me," he said.

"Bringing groceries over and all."

He laughed.

"What else?"

"Rebuilding his house so I got a place without stairs."

"His house?"

"Hard to believe."

"He's *what?*"

The sudden loudness in her voice hurt his ears. "Didn't think you heard me," he said, relaxing his grip on the phone. "I think he's a little nuts, but he and Al are right. I can't stay up here."

"You're moving to Sedgwick Street?"

"When he's done with the plumbing and the deck."

He heard a sharp intake of breath. "Deck?"

"Used to build train sets," Domenic said, grinning. "Now he's going off the rails."

"I can't believe you're doing this. I mean, it's great. It's just a surprise."

"Been going on for a while now."

"I don't know who I'm more surprised by, him or you."

"I was convinced the guy was a little short in certain departments," Domenic said. "Know what I mean?"

"Yeah."

"Think I misread him."

"That's good news, Domenic."

He was sure she meant it, but she sounded like she was trying to be nice to a telephone solicitor. "You're doing all right?" he said.

"I've been meaning to call or come see you sooner," she said.

"Well, gab away. I'm all yours."

"I should have come over and talked with you in person, but it's not easy."

"Don't worry about that," Domenic said. He braced himself. From his second-floor perch, her father had looked good, but cancer was cancer.

"I'm going up to see my parents for the holiday weekend. And I'm taking the job, Domenic."

"You kind of went over this last week," Domenic said. "Your dad's all right?"

"They're using the term *cancer-free*."

"Must sound good to you."

"It's great, and they're both relieved I got the job. Didn't wait until the weekend. It's official. I told them I'm taking it."

Despite the good news, she sounded wistful. "I'm happy for you."

"It's the right time, Domenic. I see that now."

"What's wrong?"

He heard her breathing. "The baby, Domenic," she said. "I had a miscarriage last Tuesday."

He felt the air rush out of him, like when the punk in the dark had slammed the back of his head. No, he mouthed. He pulled himself up and looked out the window, as if something out there might help him figure this out. A trolley howled to a stop at the corner. "I'm so sorry," he mumbled. *Useless words.* He fixed his eyes on Gilhooley's sign.

"Domenic?"

"Oh my God," he said.

I'm doing better," she said. "I guess it wasn't to be. That's what they told me."

He wished it didn't sound so familiar. She did not deserve this.

"His tiny fingers," she stammered. "So perfect."

He clamped his hand over the mouthpiece and sobbed. "Jesus," he moaned.

"It was horrible. I know you know that. But I'm going to get through this."

He uncovered the mouthpiece. "You're not all right," he said. "You're not the least bit all right."

"It's over," she said.

He told himself to not correct her. Not his place. And he could be wrong. "You have people, someone, helping you?"

"I'm all right."

"Last week?" he said. "I don't care if I'm a man. You could have called me."

"I'm doing what I need to do," she said.

He heard her fighting back the tears. "Your parents aren't here with you? They must be sick over this."

"They will learn about it this weekend," she said. "None of this makes sense, but it is what it is."

"*Sense?*" he yelled.

"The baby," she said. "It's just not for me. I don't know why. Maybe somebody put the maloiks on my reproductive system."

"For God's sake," he said.

"Gallows humor."

"Nobody put the maloiks on Angela and me," he said. He turned then walked toward Angela's photograph. The telephone cord stopped him five feet short.

"I understand," she said.

"You have to," he said, looking into Angela's smiling, canny eyes. "That's the one thing you must understand." He heard her whimpering but waited. "Sarah?" he said, finally.

"My Italian calendar," she said. "Seems like I've been looking at this villa and garden forever. I just realized there are no people in the photographs. Never noticed that before."

"I am sick for you."

She squealed something between a laugh and a cry. "I don't believe it, Domenic. Twelve shots of Italy and not an Italian to be seen? Impossible. Isn't it?"

"Who exactly knows about you and the baby?"

"Now you do," she said. "Besides the medical people and so on."

"How do you expect other people to learn about this?"

"You mean Mike?"

"*Madonna.*"

"I need you to help me."

"Help?" he cried.

"When I'm gone this weekend, tell him I called you. Tell him what happened. That I'm okay. That I am sorry for him too. Truly. That I'm managing the best I can."

If Angela were here, they'd figure out what to do, what to say. It wouldn't feel impossible. His heart was racing. He retreated to the couch, sat, then leaned forward. "I'm sorry, Sarah," he said, looking down at his soft-soled barber shoes. "I am sorry to do this for you."

"Will you?"

"Tell him that?" he said. "Just that?"

"Yes," she said. "But after Friday. It's better that way."

"You expect that he'll want to leave it at that?"

"This is hard enough."

He heard goodbye in her voice. There was no reason to push her. "Then that'll be that," he said quietly.

"Thank you, Domenic."

"*Buona sera*, my dear child," he said, then hung up.

47

TUESDAY, MAY 23

Domenic took his post by the window as soon as he heard Mike fiddling at the downstairs lock. Across the avenue, a couple of mailmen opened the door to Gilhooley's then walked in, the first of the daily communicants. The door looked like it could use a coat of paint, but soon he wouldn't have to look at, except on trips to the barbershop. Mike's heavy footsteps on the stairs sent a charge up Domenic's spine, ending his efforts at distraction.

"Hey," Mike called as he opened the upper door.

"Hey."

He listened to Mike rooting around in the kitchen.

"You're not keeping a cat in here, are you?" Mike called to him.

"Cat?"

"You're going through milk like there's no tomorrow."

"Spoiled on me," Domenic said. "I threw it out."

"Time to buy smaller containers," Mike said with a laugh.

Laugh while you can.

"Lotta action today?" Mike said, entering the room.

Domenic closed his eyes.

"You could probably blackmail half of this neighborhood with what you see," Mike said. "Won't be so interesting from your new lookout."

Domenic turned to him. "Last chance to back out. Spare yourself a lot of old man noises and smells."

"I knew you'd start to chicken out when it was time for the first load to move out of here," Mike said. "I saw all the stuff in the dining room. All that goes?"

"Boxes go to your place. Big trash bags go to the curb."

"I got stuff to do up at the seminary before I call it a day. I'll load the boxes in the car and take the trash out." Finally he noticed the collage was missing. "What the hell?"

"Packing and pruning," Domenic said.

Shaking his head, Mike started down the hallway. "I got you hamburger for tonight," he called back. "On sale. And broccoli. Don't make a face."

He listened to Mike opening the top door, hoisting the boxes.

"Back in a minute to play trashman," Mike shouted.

From his window, Domenic watched Mike tote the two boxes across the street then disappear into the parking lot behind the florist shop and Gilhooley's. He remembered when he was strong enough to lug such weighty cargo. But young strength like that was useless in the face of the kind of burden Mike would have to bear come the weekend. Mike came into sight again, trotting across the Belgian blocks toward Domenic's downstairs entrance.

Domenic pulled himself up and reached the dining room by the time Mike opened the upstairs door.

"Can't stay put?" Mike said.

He couldn't remember the last time he'd seen Mike smile like this.

"You better know your limits," Mike said.

Mike lifted the trash bag then swung it to the base of the door. It landed with a thump and the sound of breaking glass. "No wonder this is so damn heavy," Mike grumbled. "Throw out all your dishes and glasses?" A shard of blue glass stuck through the middle of the bag.

"Careful," Domenic said.

"Should some of this stuff go into the recycling?" Mike asked.

"Too late," Domenic said. "Don't cut yourself."

Mike touched the side of his leg and raised a bloody finger. "Jesus," he said, wiping blood off on his jeans. He rolled up his pant leg. "Just scratched it," he said.

"Leave it," Domenic said. "I have to sit down." He pulled out a dining room chair. "Mike," he said, pointing to the chair on his side of the table.

"I'm kind of on the clock," Mike said, touching the top of the chair.

The glass sticking out of the bag looked bigger, more menacing that he'd thought. "Hold it far away from you when you go downstairs," he said, watching Mike take a seat. "Somebody's going to shoot me."

"It's not a big deal," Mike said.

"Not that," Domenic said. "Somebody's definitely going to shoot me."

"Why would I want to shoot you?"

He thought of Sarah alone in her apartment, surrounded by nothing but her own boxes and bags of trash.

"Domenic," Mike said. "What's wrong?"

He met Mike's eyes then looked down. "You'll both want to kill me," he said.

"Sarah," Mike murmured.

Domenic's face flushed. He looked back at Mike. "She's going up on Friday. I'm not the only one who's packing boxes. She'll make another trip later, I guess."

"You're not telling me anything I didn't expect," Mike said softly.

"That's not it," he said, shaking his head. "She ordered me not to tell you until after she left."

"Tell me what?"

Domenic looked him in the eye. "She lost the baby."

"Lost?" Mike looked as if he couldn't quite make out the words Domenic was saying.

"Last week. She called me this afternoon."

"At four months?" he said, the same look of puzzlement on his face. "No," he barked, pushing his chair backwards. He shook his head furiously.

"She says she's okay," Domenic said.

"The hell!" Mike snapped. He slammed his fist on the table.

"She's trying to march forward," Domenic said. "But alone."

"And she expected you to tell me?" Mike said. "*After* she left? Jesus, Domenic."

Domenic watched Mike's expression break, like he was about to sob. Mike clapped his palms against his face, shuddering. "I'm sorry you had to do this," Mike said. "She's too smart for her own good." He wiped his face then rose awkwardly from his chair, gripping the top of it, his eyes darting about like a boxer getting his bearings after a punishing hit.

"I didn't know what to do," Domenic pleaded. "I'm sick for both of you."

Mike nodded, still holding onto the chair and not looking at Domenic.

"She's sorry for you," he said. "She told me that."

"Got to go now," Mike said. He turned, lumbered downstairs, then closed the door.

Shutting the upstairs door, Domenic leaned his weight against it. He closed his eyes, saw Sarah's face looking at him with a sadness for which he had no cure. He blinked his eyes open and looked about the room, finally resting on the bag Mike left behind, the glass shard poking out. He closed his eyes again, sobbing.

48

TUESDAY, MAY 23

Clutching his keys, Mike stepped off the curb but stopped, blocked by the creeping line of cars. He might reach her apartment sooner if he simply ran the five blocks. No, he would do this right. She might want to be driven somewhere. Valley Green. The arboretum. Some café where nobody knew either of them. Finally, the long column halted. Mike shot through the gap between a mail truck and a Toyota, sure that Domenic was watching him. Chances were that she was scouring a sink or filling up boxes for her move. Reaching the nearly filled lot, Mike scanned the row of cars in it. Out of habit, he'd parked near the rear, passing on open spaces near the front.

Thirty minutes ago, all he could think about was the building project and how much progress Domenic had made. Tipped off his bearing by one sentence, he kept stumbling forward, expecting to regain the balance he'd felt these last few weeks. He knew that comforting her would help him do that, but it was Sarah who concerned him. How many times had she met him more than halfway? He'd been miserable to her, even when she tried so hard to help him. The night she'd created the most amazing meal he'd ever had. Instead of telling her that it was the anniversary of the car crash, he was miserable all night. He owed her for that night and for so many others.

Hustling past a painter's van, he glimpsed his car, parked on the other side of an old red MG. Breaking into a trot, he felt for his car key. "Shit," he said finding Domenic's apartment key. He hadn't dealt with the trash bags. His exit would have to wait.

Hearing an approaching car behind him, he stepped between two cars to let it pass. The dented door to the car parked beside him swung open, making a screeching metal on metal sound.

"Coming or going?" Tommy Coyle boomed, climbing out of the Taurus.

"Going," Mike says. "Can't talk."

Tommy's face turned serious. "Your teacher friend," he said.

"Yeah?" Mike said, frozen in place. *Is nothing going to make sense this afternoon?*

"I'm sorry," Tommy said. He offered Mike his hand.

"What the fuck?"

"I called Brendan as soon as I heard about it."

"Brendan?" Mike shouted. "How did you know?"

Tommy gave him a funny look. "He called you, right?"

"Never mind!" Mike growled. "How the hell did you know about her?"

"I still have my contacts."

"With doctors?"

"Cops," he said, confidentially.

"Cops?"

"And people in South Philly."

"What?" Mike felt like he was struggling to keep up with a foreign language.

"The *asshole* is from South Philly. Hair. He must have followed her. Roughed her up some."

"Wait, wait, wait." Pompadour? He held up a hand.

"It's good that she told the cops."

"Slow the fuck down," Mike yelled. "And tell me you're not shitting me. When was this?"

"Last Tuesday."

"Fuck."

"I just heard that he got out on bail. Two days ago. His mother. I was going to call tonight."

Nobody wants me to know about this. Had Domenic deliberately kept this part of the story from him, or did Sarah not tell him everything? He could think of no good answers.

"They're throwing the book at this guy, doing that to a pregnant woman," he said, shaking his head. "That crowd down at Bonner's bar won't let him walk into the place."

"Do *what* to her, Tommy?"

"I don't know if they can get him for attempted rape or some sort of assault. That I don't know."

Mike slammed the rear door of Tommy's car.

"Fucked up," Tommy said.

Mike stepped back, turned, and looked toward the other side of the street. "Then she lost the baby?"

Tommy nodded. "Didn't tell the cops until the next morning. Must have freaked the shit out of her."

He grabbed Tommy by the collar, slammed him against the side of his car. "Are you *drunk*?" An inch from Tommy's face, he pressed harder on Tommy's collarbone.

"No!" Tommy screamed. "I'm for real!" Tommy's legs buckled. He flopped, spread-eagled against the side of the car. "I ain't shitting you!"

Mike let him go, dropping him to the ground.

Tommy crawled away a few feet then got himself back to his feet. He straightened himself up, fixed his shirt. "I'm sorry, Mike."

Burning, Mike turned, started toward his car. In New Paltz, the news froze him in place. Not this time. For all his rage, he saw the night ahead of him clearly.

Behind him, Tommy yelled, but Mike heard only Sarah's screams. She probably was suffering. Domenic's news was her whispering to him: *I need a friend*, but all he heard now was her screaming. All he could see was that bastard hurting her. Brushing past a Honda, he slammed his fist down on the trunk. Somebody behind him shouted. The Reliant sat four cars away. The guy yelled again, louder. Mike jerked open the door to his car. The late spring sun had roasted the interior, so he rolled down the windows. A hellish breeze wafted through the windows. He backed out, screeching the brakes. A loud thwacking sound on the top of his trunk stopped him.

"I'm talking to *you*, asshole!" a guy screamed from behind the car.

Mike floored the gas, racing around the tight turn at the back of the lot, the squeal of his tires blocking out most of the screaming.

49

WEDNESDAY, MAY 24

Stalking him the first time, Mike worked with the disadvantage of not knowing Edward Hearn's name. Last night, he'd walked around South Philly, getting to know the neighborhood near Jack's Wild. Tonight, he nursed a couple of beers and listened to the chatter at the bar. In less than two hours, he learned that Hair lived up the street and was having a hard time finding a new local watering hole, news that sparked hearty laughs from two thick-necked regulars at Jack's.

Back home, he walked then fed Robert. Robert did not follow Mike through the first floor but settled into his bed, as if he were adjusting to being ignored. Five messages blinked away on the answering machine. One or more of the calls must be from work. The others likewise were of no concern to Mike. Dishes filled the sink. His bed was unmade. The mess remained in the basement.

The next night, he parked a block from Jack's. When Edward Hearn, still sporting his trademark hairstyle, walked out of a row house halfway between Mike's Reliant and the bar, Mike scurried after him on foot. He crossed to the narrow street's other sidewalk, where he kept his distance, following Hair east toward the river. Blocks later, just before the elevated stretch of I-95, Hair crossed to Mike's side of the street then opened the door to a small corner bar.

Though the evening rush hour had passed, traffic noise from the expressway overhead remained steady. Mike walked past the shabby-looking bar, crossing the street to the cavernous de facto parking area beneath the elevated roadway. Cars occupied maybe half of the unofficial parking spaces in the dank, unlit lot. "Abandoned" stickers decorated numerous windshields. Above him, vehicles roared north and south, parallel to the nearby Delaware River, but he saw no sign of life below the roadway.

Keeping an eye on the bar, Mike explored the side of the lot nearer the river. A long, rusty chain-link fence ran the length of the block, separating the rear of several old warehouses from the area locals used for parking. Mike walked back to a row of abandoned cars facing the bar. He crouched between two vehicles with no tires. Half of the Christmas lights in the bar's dingy window remained unlit; the rest blinked intermittently. Boards covered the windows of the block's four other old brick buildings.

Mike looked inside the cars. The one on his right contained neither doors nor seats. The other car lacked a door and front seats. He climbed into the rear seat. The car's inside reeked of cat piss, but after a while he hardly noticed it. He stretched out his feet, peering through the cracked windshield at the entrance to Dooley's Bar.

Was Hair a shot and a beer then bolt kind of guy? But why walk all this way only to leave before getting a decent load on? Doing things right took time. Patience paid off, for assholes and everyone else.

He was back in New Paltz, leaving for good in the morning. He'd given Laurie's family all of her clothes and cleared the house of everything that wouldn't fit into his truck. In Philly, he'd buy cheap used furniture filled with strangers' memories. The boxes and bags destined for Philadelphia sat neatly in the family room beside the sleeping bag he'd been using since taking the bedroom set to Goodwill. At the morning walk-through, the buyers paused by his gathered possessions and told him they wouldn't be moving in for a week and that he could stay in the house that night.

The place was more warehouse than home now. Sitting on a rolled-up rug, he ate a ham sandwich and paged through the last issue of the New Paltz weekly paper he would ever have delivered. He found a photo of the kid's parents. The Wells family had started a foundation to support people who lost a family member to suicide. Lights of Hope. He felt himself broiling on the inside. They were using the funds they'd reserved for the kid's college expenses, and a hefty sum besides that. Friends of young Jerry were encouraged to contribute. The article concluded with the contact information. Had this kid killed a different mother and child, Laurie might have already sent a check. But Wells did not leave her that option.

When he heard knocking on the front door, he put the newspaper down and got to his feet. Roger from across the street frowned through the door's glass. Mike opened the door then told him that Monica probably was looking for him. "I don't think so," he said, sounding perfectly confident.

"You shouldn't be over here," Mike told him. "Crossing the road and all."

"I don't get out much."

"No," Mike said.

"Always taking care of him. Not much excitement any more. But that's okay, at least he's still alive, you know?"

"Who?"

"The man across the street."

Mike nodded.

"Do you know about the people who aren't here anymore?" Roger said, a mournful look on his face.

"I know all about them."

Roger scratched his chin, as if in deep thought. "They're to be pitied," he said.

"No, they're not."

"She was wonderful," Roger said. "The child was adorable. And the man used to be such a decent person. We don't want him to cut the grass anymore though. Too bitter. They're to be pitied."

"Roger, you ought to contribute to the suicide fund."

"Would they like that?"

Mike nodded.

"Where do we go for that?"

Mike looked the old man up and down. He was wearing the same shirt he'd worn the last time Mike cut the grass. "You can help," Mike said.

"I guess," he said.

Together, they carried the partly caned rockers to Mike's truck. "And that," he said, pointing to the gasoline can that held the last of the lawn mower's gas. He grabbed a large plastic bag filled with old rags he'd planned to use in his furniture restoration work. "Squeeze this in there."

Roger did a masterful job of packing.

"Climb in," Mike said, holding the door for the old man.

He drove into the cemetery then meandered through winding drives, peering through the dark until he found the kid's grave. He and Roger got out of the truck. Above them in the dark sky, a thousand stars were shining. "Lights of hope," Mike said, pointing above. Standing on the middle of the grave, Mike balled up every section of the weekly paper, littering the gravelly dirt. On top of the papers, he placed the chair he had started working on. The evening breeze blew some of the paper away, so Mike wedged paper into the nooks and crannies made by the stacked furniture. When Roger carried the other chair over to him, Mike laid it beside the first one. Mike soaked the rags with gas and tied them around the chair parts then emptied the gas can on the pile.

He told Roger to watch the stars then drove the truck halfway down the hill and parked. Walking back, he found Roger looking into the night sky, his hand resting on an upside-down rocker runner.

He led Roger back to the oak tree up on the cemetery's fence line. "Wait here." Mike walked back down to the grave, lit a match, then tossed it under one of the chairs. He did the same on the other side of the pile. Wind rushed through the pile, sending a towering, crackling flame to the stone at the other end. Mike ran back up to Roger and turned around. The fire roared and jumped above the pile. Strips of cane sizzled and sparked. A cloth in flames flew off, swirling above neighboring graves. It dropped to the ground and burned out. The flame above the grave reached six feet high. The chairs crackled. The headstones next to the fire shone in a rich glow.

"Lights of hope," Roger said, his eyes wide as a child's.

Somehow, no one had driven past the cemetery yet. Holding Roger's elbow, he guided him down past the fire toward the empty truck.

When the bar's door opened, Mike snapped to. A laughing guy exited. Mike strained his eyes. A woman followed, carrying a six-pack. The couple stepped down to the sidewalk. Mike leaned back, watching the pair round the corner, headed toward the rest of their evening. Ten minutes later, the door opened again. Hair. Mike slipped out of the car then worked his way behind the line of cars. Hair lit a cigarette on the bottom step. Mike reached the end of the line of cars. He scanned the sidewalk. Nothing. "Yo, Hair!" he called from the other side of an old Dodge.

Hair dropped his match, looking right then left, like a raccoon on high alert.

"It's me."

"Who is it?" Hair said, still searching.

Mike moved out into the open and took one step into the street. "From high school," he said.

Hair squinted at him. "Who?"

Who? "Jerry Wells," Mike said, and strode toward him. "Jerry!"

"Wells?" he said.

Beaming, Mike offered his hand as he stepped onto the sidewalk.

When Hair extended his hand, Mike shook it firmly then snapped it around behind him and clamped his hand against Hair's mouth. He spun him across the little street, then trotted him past rows of cars to the back area near the fence line.

When they reached the fence, he rammed him into it.

Hair turned to face him. "You're the fucking guy in the garage!"

Mike belted him in the mouth then pummeled his middle. Hair doubled over, groaning. Mike pulled the .38 from his pants. He cracked him over the back of the head.

Hair collapsed, his head resting against the sagging chain-link fence.

Panting, Mike sat on the ground three feet away from him.

This was not for Sarah or for the baby. Not for Laurie or Michael. Not for Mike. It needed to be done. None of them would approve. He knew that. It didn't matter.

Hair stirred, moaning. Mike reached over and smacked his cheek with the side of the gun. "Hair!"

"Fuck," Hair sobbed. He was bleeding from the mouth. "I only meant to scare her," he said. He pressed his back against the chain-link fence and grabbed hold of it with his right hand.

"Yeah?" Mike said. "How's this working for you? Feeling scared yet?"

"Oh Jesus," he said. "No, please. I'm going to jail."

Above them, a tractor trailer shook the roadway as it barreled toward Center City, the noise masking everything else.

"That's right," Mike said. "Justice."

"I'm sorry," Hair said, edging himself a few inches away along the fence line.

"A few years, you think?"

"I don't know," Hair said. "Yeah, a long time." Not taking his eyes off Mike, he inched his butt closer to the street, reaching for a new hold higher on the fence. "Please?"

"Did she ask you to stop?"

When Hair slowly brought his knee up under him, Mike scrabbled to his feet, clamped his left hand onto Hair's shoulder, then shoved him back to the ground. "Stop," Mike said. He aimed the gun at Hair's nose. Hair cringed. Mike squeezed the trigger. The blast echoed under the roadway, shaking him. Hair's head hung back against the fence, his face a red mess. His body slumped to the ground. Grimacing, Mike wiped blood off his own face. "Fuck," he muttered, feeling the warm wetness on his arms. He wiped his hands on his jeans, but his hands remained sticky.

"Son of a bitch!" he screamed, standing up. Traffic roared above him, but surely someone must have heard the gunshot. Hair's body lay crumpled like a rag doll. Mike felt nothing but disgust for him. Looking at the bloody hole where his nose used to be, he felt more anger, more drive to do something else to the bastard. He rolled the body over. The exit wound had erased most of the back of his head, the only part of him that he might have recognized. That piece of shit terrorized Sarah and killed their baby. He stood over the body. Blood had pooled around Hair's head. The guy wasn't about to pick himself up and go terrorize Sarah or anyone else again. Mike had done what needed to be done. This whole chapter was over, but standing over Hair's body, he wanted more.

He was not worried about the police or neighbors who might come upon him at any moment. He closed his eyes. Since running into Tommy in the parking lot, he had not imagined what this moment might feel like, only that he had to get to this moment. He felt Laurie's eyes bore into him. Little Michael's eyes too. He had not held back. Some people needed to be killed. There was a list. It took a lifetime of false starts for him to realize that. But feeling those eyes on him, he knew that he had put himself on the list.

Laurie would have him give himself up, confess to God and to the authorities and accept the punishment for his crime. He had leaped, alone, toward a different kind of justice. He was nothing like her. If he ever deserved her, he had fallen far from being that person. He couldn't imagine it, but somehow if she had lost her bearings and done something this final, he would have urged her to run away, to put it behind her and live in the light that he could bring her. But she could not live in that kind of light. He had never made the life he needed to make. He had just rid the world of one rotten monster, but with him standing there the world was no better off.

Sirens wailed in the distance. Closer. Two days ago, before he crossed the avenue to Gilhooley's parking lot, he had been closer to the people that mattered to him. Now the distance between him and them could never be bridged. Laurie and little Michael. The baby. Sarah. Even Domenic. He had been closer than he realized. He could have turned left on the avenue and gone to Sarah, but instead he flew home to find that box holding the gun, like some avenging angel.

He slid down the sagging chain-link fence to the ground then tightened his grip on the gun. He had ruined so much for so many. He had not eased their way. He had ruined himself. No ride away to New Paltz or escape from there to Philadelphia. No letters of transit. He hated what he knew about himself. There remained only stopping that feeling, nothing more.

50

MONDAY, MAY 28, 1990

They arrived at the shrine just as the one o'clock novena crowd began to stream out to the parking lot. Sarah wheeled Domenic to the elevator. A year had passed since that horrible weekend.

Once upstairs inside the main building of the church, Domenic got out of his chair. Sarah rolled it to the corner at the rear. People moved about, some individually but most in couples or small groups. Clusters of worshippers kneeled at the church's side altars and devotional spots. She followed him as he slowly made his way up the aisle to the same pew he had used for the past year, just ahead of the middle. They took their seats near the aisle. The service wouldn't start for several minutes. She watched him close his eyes. She closed hers.

In a way, living upstairs from Domenic had converted her. Saturday, she had stood with the minyan, saying the mourner's kaddish for the last time. Her parents still didn't quite believe it but promised they wouldn't disown her for reclaiming at least parts of her mother's discarded religious past. By the high holidays, the boys at the shop were teasing her about being the Jewish equivalent of a cafeteria Catholic, but now they said nothing but nice things about her explorations. Domenic insisted that she read him the kaddish, even after her explanation that it was something one did in the minyan, not alone. "Can you and I be your minyan?"

"We're a little short on numbers, but I'll read it to you anyway," she said. When she finished reading the translation to him, he smiled.

"What?" she said.

"The prayer doesn't mention him or death."

"Right."

"Why could I see him sitting in my barber's chair?"

The priest's voice broke the silence. She watched Domenic open his eyes and face the pulpit. Along with the priest and congregation, he said the words of the novena prayers.

In the car, driving up Chelten Avenue, neither of them spoke. Stopped for the light at Germantown and Washington Lane, she asked if he felt okay after yesterday's little episode.

"Usual symptoms, another narrow escape," he said.

"Just a reminder to be careful," she said.

"I never expected to outlive him."

The light turned, then she pulled out. It had been months since Mike was the subject of every day's conversation.

At the house, she watched Domenic inspect the long picnic table, grill, and lawn chair on the deck. "Where'd this all come from?" he said.

"Abington," she said. "Place Delores told me about."

"No Olympic-size swimming pool?"

"Better be glad we don't have one," she said. "Your physical therapist might make you do laps every day."

"I get all the water I need in the shower."

"There's some dip in the refrigerator and potato chips on the kitchen table that need to come out. You up to it?"

She watched him walk into the kitchen. By the time she set up the grill, he returned with a basket filled with chips and a container of sour cream and chive dip.

"Down here," she said, pointing to one of the new chairs. When he sat, she swooped into the house, headed straight to the hallway closet. Returning with a large straw hat, she placed it on Domenic's head and handed him the newspaper. "If it gets any hotter, just yell and I'll bring you inside."

He pulled the hat off, gave it a scornful look, then returned it to his head. At four o'clock, the Lamonts walked over from next door with a fruit platter, then Florence arrived with what she called "Perfect Potato Salad," made from a recipe she'd learned in Nantucket. Sarah had invited the Jennings on the other side of the house, but they were attending a family get-together in Lansdale.

The sound of a car approaching along the back drive drew everyone's attention. Brendan, Delores, and the kids. For the first time today, she felt tightness in her chest. The two kids took the steps at full speed, their parents following with an enormous bowl of green salad and a cooler. After mobbing Domenic, they ran to her and hugged her. The tightness gave way to a feeling of sadness, but that, too, passed quickly. Domenic had proven right about healing. Pain didn't live with you every minute of every day. It visited. You became familiar with the visitor's habits. Pain didn't leave forever, but you *could* bid goodbye to the false hope that it would. She could not imagine doing that alone.

Her adjunct teaching job might turn into a full-time position. Her new colleagues had helped, as had her friends at the synagogue, and her understanding parents, and this patchwork family she had gained. And Domenic most of all.

Soon he, wearing a watermelon apron—a gift from Al and Ginette—was aloft, towering over the smoking grill.

"Behold," Nick intoned, climbing to the deck. "The king of suburbia."

Domenic turned a skewer of zucchini and yellow squash without looking at his friend. "That shows how much you know. You haven't left the city."

"Still in Holy Cross," Clement said, taking a seat beside Al and Ginette.

Sarah had read in the morning paper that it had been a year since Mike Schmidt retired so unexpectedly—something else from last Memorial Day. Over beers and sodas, they talked about the Phillies, but none of the baseball fans mentioned Schmidt or anything else from that weekend. *A whole year.* And that was how much time the doctor estimated the failing Domenic had left. They all knew this. She might never take care of another person in her life, but she would not regret this time.

Sarah joined Domenic at the grill, squeezing in beside him. The kids had been promised that they could each pick another item from the trains packed away in the basement, so they ran down to choose.

Robbie returned with a box kit for a passenger station. Jessie brought a B&O observation car. They placed them beside their plates, but Brendan centered them on the table, like a set of candles.

Smoke whirled above the grill, making Sarah choke. Domenic stood there as if nothing had happened. Fighting the smoke, Sarah pulled one of the small pieces of chicken off the grill and put it on a plate. "Done." Finally, the smoke calmed down.

"Get that one off the grill," Domenic ordered, pointing to a chicken leg.

She moved it to the plate.

"Look at the two of them," Nick called from the table. "America's great cooking team, The Maloiks."

The chef in the straw hat and apron ordered everyone to the table. Sarah turned one of the chicken legs.

"You're going to burn that chicken," Domenic whined. "I don't like chicken all charred."

"It's not charred."

"I don't trust you on this thing."

"Take them off if you think they're done," she said, standing back from the grill.

Domenic probed a piece of chicken with his fork. "Let's serve the hungry masses," he said.

They were all looking at the two of them with great expectation. Robert wandered out and settled under the table at the kids' feet. Sarah scanned the table laden with more food than they could possibly eat. Another cloud of smoke wafted up from the grill. Sarah stepped away to be clear of it. Domenic stood behind the grill, fork in one hand, serving plate in the other, the smoke blowing everywhere but in his face, as if he had complete power over it.

When she held out her serving plate to him, Domenic set the last burger on it. With his free hand, he closed the grill lid.

"*So 'rivat*," he said, looking at the array of food on the matching yellow Tuscan platters the two of them held.

Nodding, she took a step back. Domenic glided past her to the table.

"*Perfetto*," Sarah said.

READING GUIDE
FOR *MORTAL THINGS*

PUBLISHER'S NOTE

We recommend that you avoid looking through this guide
until after you've finished the story, as some of this content
does contain spoilers! We hope you enjoy these additional materials, which include a conversation with the author,
book club discussion questions, and a playlist put together
by the author to enhance your reading experience. Follow
Tree of Life on social media for more updates on author
events and book promotions.

"WE STILL CAN HAVE EACH OTHER"

A CONVERSATION WITH AUTHOR NED BACHUS

What inspired you to write this story?

NB: During my MFA program, Mike and Sarah elbowed their way onto my computer screen both separately and as a couple. The original story that began the *Mortal Things* journey included a version of the dinner party evening. You might say they were not meant for each other from the beginning. Or were they? Through revisions of that story, which I called "The Cat Test," that question remained. My short story collection, *City of Brotherly Love*, includes "Home," a story about Sarah's first week in Philadelphia as a community college teacher, sort of a Sarah Goins origins story. Mike is an offstage character in "The Wig," in which his sister-in-law Delores cares for Mike's dying mother. Likewise, his brother, Brendan, is an offstage character in the story. So, both of those stories are set before the time of *Mortal Things*. As to particular triggering moments, no one big thing but a hundred different moments at the computer screen or standing in line at the supermarket sparked "What If" thoughts. And then I let the characters sort things out.

Do you have a favorite character in this story, or a character you most closely relate to? Or were any of the characters based on real people?

NB: Madame Goins, *c'est moi*. But then I can say the same thing about Mike and Domenic. All three protagonists carry parts of me, I'm sure. Harder for me to rank-order them as to which personality I most resemble. Maybe close friends who read the book will have an opinion, but I long ago let Sarah, Mike, and Domenic be who they are and haven't thought much about common proclivities or mannerisms. It doesn't matter to me whether or not I relate to a character. I want to know them as fully as possible. And to be hands-off enough that they surprise me by what they say and do. To the best of my knowledge, none of them is based on any particular person.

The setting of Mount Airy is vibrant and an important backdrop to the characters' lives in this novel. Can you talk about your own relationship with Philadelphia and why it felt important to showcase this neighborhood so prevalently in the story?

NB: Sarah, Mike, and Domenic were all in Philadelphia when they first made their presence known to me. I, too, happened to be there, but it wouldn't have mattered if I'd been halfway around the world. When I first glimpsed them, they walked on Philly streets, ate food in Philadelphia neighborhoods, went to work in Philadelphia locales. The city's neighborhoods, especially Mount Airy, were part of who they were. I had no agenda in setting the story in Philadelphia; I felt like I had no choice in the matter.

Living in a place as long as I did guarantees that dozens of landmarks are not just familiar but also conjure up memories that might otherwise be completely lost. Walking down a block in Mount Airy sparks a whole series of stories and people. An observer might see a man taking a leisurely stroll, but I'm on an emotional roller-coaster ride. You could call that neighborhood your own, no matter who you were or what you looked like. I believe there are more neighborhoods like that now, in Philly and elsewhere, but I was blessed to live in such a place from childhood through adulthood.

This book covers heavy themes and topics, but it ends on a hopeful, lighter note. What message do you hope readers take away from this story and from your other writing?

NB: Come tragedy, come loss and grief—in the end, we still can have each other. And we are so different because of the other people we let into our lives. Give free rein to fear and anger, and you push those people away. For fictional characters (as for people), this is true whether they wake up in urban or rural America or halfway around the world, chase their dreams and demons today, hundreds of years ago, or in a vision of tomorrow.

What is your writing process like? What's most interesting or important to you when it comes to storytelling?

NB: Discovering a story idea is a gift. But it doesn't come alive until you've got a flesh and blood character who keeps you up at night and pushes you to the computer in the morning. Taking a manuscript from igniting idea to completion involves a great deal of writerly work. At each stage, progress hinges on my ability to know the character's voice or soul. Without that, I get nowhere. As a teenager, I discovered that I could mimic different accents or do impersonations of teachers, Hollywood actors, political figures, and so on. I was very shy, but when my close friends prodded me to do a particular accent, I automatically did it as a characterization. Without thinking, I was off on a comic riff. I didn't realize it at the time, but with each prompt I was creating or discovering a character. To write fiction, I think you need to have that kind of ear. But while making progress in a manuscript requires time and patience on the part of the writer, once you turn those characters loose to get their hands dirty, they immediately start doing their thing as only they can do. They show you the way.

BOOK CLUB
DISCUSSION QUESTIONS

1. What is each character's relationship to faith—is it important or not? Does it change during the course of the novel? If you have experienced a faith journey in your life, what factors have impacted your experience? Do you see any parallels with what the characters experience?

2. This novel is set in 1989 and includes topics such as abortion, single parenthood, race, class, sexual abuse by Catholic priests, miscarriage, violence against women, and disability. These are all issues that continue to be relevant—and sometimes controversial—today. Select a few to discuss. How have society's views on these issues changed or not changed since the time in which this novel is set? Religious affiliation in America has declined significantly throughout the last few decades; how do you think this has impacted cultural and social influences over time? What do you think would be different about this story if it were set today? What would remain the same?

3. Discuss the dinner scene at the start of the novel, when Mike and Sarah visit Sarah's colleagues. Why is Mike so uncomfortable at the dinner? Is Sarah aware of his discomfort? Why and how does this outing change the trajectory of Mike and Sarah's relationship?

4. Sarah's close circle of friends at the beginning of the novel is very different from the one she has at the end of the novel. Discuss the differences between them. Which community is a better fit for Sarah, and why do you think so?

5. Chosen family is a big theme throughout the novel. What are some of the different bonds among the characters in the novel, and what are some of the various ways in which characters take care of and care for each other? Who is part of your chosen family? Do you see parallels in your life with the family Sarah has gathered by the novel's end?

6. Throughout the novel, we hear about Mike's life in New Paltz and why he returned to Philadelphia. In what ways does he attempt to assuage his guilt over what happened to Laurie and little Michael? How well does he succeed?

7. Sarah, Mike, and Domenic each make a telling choice at the end of the novel. What factors impact each character's choice? Faced with similar circumstances, what might you have done in each situation?

8. In the novel, all three of the main characters are touched by loss around parenthood. Explore this. Do the characters ever find themselves playing a parental role? If so, describe why that might have happened and what such behavior might tell us about the three characters.

9. Each of the book's main characters handles their emotions and crises in a different way. How does each character's approach to handling emotion and crisis impact those they love and their relationships with them? With which character do you relate most, and why?

10. Nick and Clement, the two old friends who spend their days socializing at Al's Barbershop, have their moment in the spotlight during Mount Airy Day. What did you think of Sarah's interest in Nick and Clement's storytelling about the neighborhood's history? What are your thoughts about how Nick altered his presentation to include Clement?

11. Mount Airy, a neighborhood of Philadelphia, Pennsylvania, is an important setting in the novel. What are your thoughts about the neighborhood? Have you ever been to it, or a neighborhood like it? What is your neighborhood like? What is your ideal neighborhood like, and what leads neighborhoods to change over time?

12. The novel is titled *Mortal Things*. What do you think this title refers to?

A PLAYLIST FOR MORTAL THINGS

Music plays an important part throughout this novel. Below are songs and music mentioned throughout the novel.

The Goldmans play an album titled *Cold Blow and the Rainy Night* by the Irish band Planxty at the dinner party Sarah and Mike attend. Among its songs you'll find a track of reels: "The Old Torn Petticoat / The Dublin Reel / The Wind that Shakes the Barley."

While at the ill-fated dinner party, Mike recommends playing the Clancy Brothers, but his recommendation is nixed. A few of their songs to check out include "The Wild Rover," "Finnegan's Wake," and "The Moonshiner." A particular anthem for Mike, given its mournful theme, is "The Wild Colonial Boy." Give its lyrics a listen and you'll see why.

And a final selection for that party is, of course, "Rescue Me" by Fontella Bass, which plays in Mike's head as he tries to acclimate to the atmosphere and conversation with Sarah's colleagues.

After leaving the party and dropping Sarah off, Mike runs into Tommy Coyle at Gilhooley's. The two discuss the Mummers Parade, a longtime Philadelphia tradition. If you look up the song "I'm Looking Over a Four Leaf Clover" by The Uptown String Band, you'll have some idea of what kinds of songs the String Band Brigades perform in this famous New Year's Day parade. It's worth looking up videos of the parade to see the costumes and routines, as it's quite a sight.

On their movie and pizza date, Mike and Sarah watch *The Big Easy*. The soundtrack is full of Cajun music and includes the Mardi Gras song "Tipitina" by Professor Longhair. Try to sit still while you listen to this one.

Before they watch the movie, Sarah plays an album by Stan Rogers called *Between the Breaks ... Live!* Mike tries to turn off the stereo just as her favorite song, "The Mary Ellen Carter," comes on, and she asks him to listen to it with her. The song is about a crew's heroic efforts to raise and relaunch their sunken ship—a bit of musical foreshadowing for Sarah and Mike?

When Domenic starts to feel unwell, Al at the barbershop becomes concerned and checks on him. Domenic wants to be sure the boys at the barbershop know he's up and about, so he stomps around his apartment singing "Come Back to Sorrento," certain he can hear booing from the first floor. Check out the version by Luciano Pavarotti and see what you think. It's called "Torna a Surriento" in Italian. Dean Martin also sings a great version.

As Sarah drives away from the college on a February afternoon thinking about the job application she's submitted to a school in New York, she listens to the song "Matador" on the local jazz station, played by Grant Green with McCoy Tyner on the piano.

Mike takes his niece and nephew to watch a movie at the Bala Theater and take their minds off their mother's recovery. During intermission, the theater manager plays a game of musical chairs using "Zorba the Greek," a song composed by Mikis Theodorakis for the film of the same title. The song's gradually building tempo makes it pretty perfect for the increasing chaos of the game.

When Sarah and Domenic go to Mike's house and await his

return on his porch, Sarah realizes Domenic is humming a popular tune: "Don't Worry, Be Happy" by Bobby McFerrin.

In the happier days of Sarah and Mike's relationship, they went on a date to the iconic Mermaid Inn, where they saw a band play. Two of the songs they played that night are James Brown's "Papa's Got a Brand New Bag" and Buddy Holly's "Well All Right." Check out covers of each song by the band The Sacred Cowboys, a band featuring none other than author Ned Bachus. (https://thesacredcowboys.bandcamp.com)

When Domenic thinks about attending service on Good Friday, he recalls how the congregation sings an unaccompanied chant, "Pange Lingua." For an idea of what this sounds like, listen to the rendition by the Cistercian Monks of Stift Heligenkreuz.

After her big fight with Mike, Sarah tries to settle down and calm herself for the sake of her baby. She puts on a tape of Mozart's opera *The Magic Flute* to help. The rendition by the Boston Philharmonic Orchestra is particularly enjoyable.

The ballad played by the Irish musicians at Mount Airy Day that Sarah stops to listen to is "The Belfast Mountains." Check out Craobh Rua's performance of this song for a lovely rendition.

ACKNOWLEDGMENTS

Marian Lorenz, Rich Piluk, Al Puntel, and Bep and Jackie Donadeo all shared their valuable knowledge, for which I am grateful. At key points in the writing process, manuscript readers blessed me with their insight, and I thank these teachers, editors, and writers—Alyssa Miller, Victoria Lynn, Vincent Allen, Dianne Benedict, Sena Jeter Naslund, Susan Dodd, Vince Castronuovo, James P. Brady, and, last but not least, editor extraordinaire Raquel Beatriz Pidal. She and her visionary Tree of Life teammates—Joy Stocke, Tim Ogline, Vincent Allen, and Ava Mancing—expertly nailed the many tasks, large and small, that turned my manuscript into a Tree of Life book. *Merci mille fois!* Thank you also to the wise and indefatigable publicist Lissa Warren. Finally, without the daily support and love that I receive from my wife and best friend, I couldn't do much of anything. Thank you, Kathleen, for sustaining me through this whole endeavor.

Ned Bachus

ABOUT THE AUTHOR

Ned Bachus's collection of short stories, *City of Brotherly Love*, was awarded the 2013 Independent Publisher Award (IPPY) Gold Medal for Literary Fiction. About the book, Sena Jeter Naslund, author of *Ahab's Wife*, said, "[My] life is variously enriched by reading Ned Bachus's superb stories." The recipient of two fellowships from the Pennsylvania Council on the Arts and two artist residencies at Ireland's Cill Rialaig Retreat, Ned's 2017 memoir *Open Admissions: What Teaching at Community College Taught Me About Learning* was the product of his nearly four-decade career at Community College of Philadelphia, where he won multiple teaching awards. Author and UConn professor Gina Barreca called his memoir "brilliant, engaging, and instructive … a must read."

Ned holds a BA from Temple University, an MA from Gallaudet University, and an MFA from Vermont College of Fine Arts. Born in Quebec, Ned was raised in Philadelphia, where as a longtime resident he rode every bus, subway, train, and trolley line, and shopped, worked, and explored in most of its neighborhoods. He now lives in Camden, Maine. Find Ned online at his website, NedBachus.com, where you can also find links to his social media and upcoming events.

CPSIA information can be obtained
at www.ICGtesting.com
Printed in the USA
BVHW051648061022
648847BV00004B/25

9 781734 956382